TWELVE-GAUGE GUARDIAN
BY
BJ DANIELS

AND

SHOTGUN SHERIFF
BY
DELORES FOSSEN

MILLS & BOON

TWELVE-GAUGE GUARDIAN

BY

MILLS & BOON

TWELVE-GAUGE GUARDIAN

BY
BJ DANIELS

All the characters in this book have no existence outside the imagination of
the author, and have no relation whatsoever to anyone bearing the same name
or names. They are not even distantly inspired by any individual known or
unknown to the author, and all the incidents are pure invention.

First published in Great Britain 2011
by Mills & Boon, an imprint of Harlequin (UK) Limited,
Eton House, 18-24 Paradise Road, Richmond, Surrey TW9 1SR

© Barbara Heinlein 2010

ISBN: 978 0 263 88536 1

46-0711

Harlequin (UK) policy is to use papers that are natural, renewable and
recyclable products and made from wood grown in sustainable forests. The
logging and manufacturing processes conform to the legal environmental
regulations of the country of origin.

Printed and bound in Spain
by Blackprint CPI, Barcelona

BJ Daniels wrote her first book after a career as an award-winning newspaper journalist and author of thirty-seven published short stories. Since then she has won numerous awards, including a career achievement award for romantic suspense and many nominations and awards for best book.

Daniels lives in Montana with her husband, Parker, and two springer spaniels, Spot and Jem. When she isn't writing, she snowboards, camps, boats and plays tennis. Daniels is a member of Mystery Writers of America, Sisters in Crime, International Thriller Writers, Kiss of Death and Romance Writers of America.

To contact her, write to BJ Daniels, PO Box 1173, Malta, MT 59538, USA or e-mail her at bjdaniels@mtintouch. net. Check out her webpage at www.bjdaniels.com.

This book is dedicated to mothers.
Please warn your children not only about strangers
but what to do if they are approached by them. We need
to keep our little ones safe.

Chapter One

Cordell Winchester almost missed the Whitehorse Hotel. The old four-story brick building sat in a grove of cottonwoods on the far edge of town, the morning sun glinting off the worn structure.

More than a hundred years old, the place looked deserted. He took note of the vacant surroundings as he parked and went inside. The first thing that struck him was the aging smell, reminding him unpleasantly of his grandmother's lodge. It wasn't a reminder he needed this morning.

He'd been seven the last time he'd seen the Winchester Ranch—twenty-seven years ago—but he recalled the rambling old place only too well. He had always thought nothing could get him back to Whitehorse—let alone to the ranch.

The hotel lobby was done in overstuffed couches and chairs, the upholstery fabrics as dated as the furniture. At the unoccupied registration desk, he rang the bell, then turned to look toward the small parking area outside. No sign of his brother's black pickup.

Where was Cyrus? Not at Winchester Ranch. Cordell

had called out there and their grandmother hadn't seen or heard from him. So where the hell was he?

Cordell took off his Stetson and raked a hand through his thick dark hair as he studied the small Western town in the distance. At a sound, he spun around to find an ancient man had appeared behind the counter as if out of nowhere.

"May I help you?" asked the stooped, gray-headed old man.

"My brother Cyrus Winchester is staying with you," he said, settling the Stetson back on his head.

The man nodded, showing no sign of surprise at seeing Cyrus's identical twin. Clearly this man hadn't checked in his brother last night. The clerk thumbed through a file with gnarled fingers. "412. Shall I ring him for you?" He'd already picked up the phone and dialed the room.

Just as Cordell had expected, Cyrus didn't answer. He'd been trying his brother's cell since late last night and gotten no answer and Cyrus's truck was missing. A sure sign Cyrus wasn't here.

Cordell wished now that he'd insisted his brother wait and they ride together, but Cyrus wanted to leave a few days earlier and stop to see friends in Wyoming. Cordell had been tied up with a case and couldn't leave until yesterday. He'd flown into Billings, spent the night and had driven the rest of the way this morning.

He and Cyrus had planned to go out for breakfast when he arrived, where Cordell had planned to make one last attempt to try to talk his brother out of this visit to their grandmother.

"I'm afraid there is no answer in his room."

"Did you happen to see him leave?" Cordell asked even though he figured that was doubtful. The parking area, he'd noticed when he'd driven in, was at the back of the hotel. The clerk couldn't see it from the front desk.

The old man's head wobbled back and forth. "I just came on duty."

"I'm worried about him." He couldn't put his finger on what had him so worried, but it was more than just being unable to reach his brother by phone since yesterday afternoon. "I'd like to check his room."

The elderly clerk hesitated.

Cordell took out his wallet, flashed his driver's license ID and Colorado private investigator license, explaining he was Cyrus's twin brother. He also laid a twenty on the counter. "I wouldn't ask except my brother hasn't been himself lately." Unfortunately true. Cyrus had been acting strangely since getting the letter from their grandmother's attorney inviting them back to the ranch.

The letter implied that their grandmother, Pepper Winchester, who'd spent the past twenty-seven years as a recluse, was dying and anyone who didn't come to the ranch would be exempt from a share of the legendary Winchester fortune.

Neither of them believed the fortune existed. And if it did, they weren't about to let their grandmother manipulate them with it. They'd seen the way their grandmother had used it to control their father and his brothers and sister.

But Cyrus had been insistent about wanting to go back to the ranch one last time. "Remember Enid and Alfred? I wonder if they're still alive. Come on, Cordell, haven't you ever wanted to see the ranch again?"

"No."

"Maybe I just want to see if that rambling old lodge is as scary as I remember it or the ranch is as vast as I recall."

Cordell didn't get it and said as much.

"You just don't want to go because Grandmother liked me best," his twin joked, a joke because their grandmother hadn't given a damn about any of her grandchildren even before she'd holed up at the ranch.

"I suppose it would be all right if you had a look in his room," the hotel clerk said now as he pocketed the twenty. He reached behind him and removed a key attached to an orange piece of plastic with the number 412 engraved on it and laid the key on the counter.

Cordell noticed that the other key to 412 was missing.

Rather than take the antiquated elevator, he ran up the stairs. He'd never liked small spaces. They reminded him of a room on the ranch that had been used as punishment when his father was a boy. The room had given him the creeps.

Just the thought made his stomach knot. What the hell was he doing here? Whitehorse, Montana, was the last place on earth he wanted to be. He had no desire to see his grandmother. Nor did he have any desire to return to the ranch and dredge up even some of the happier memories because, in his mind, the ranch was—if not haunted—then definitely cursed.

From the get-go, Cordell had had a bad feeling. That was why he hadn't been about to let Cyrus go out there alone. Cyrus and trouble just seemed to find each other.

And that was what had Cordell worried now. He should have heard from his twin by now.

At room 412, he knocked lightly as he studied the worn carpet under his boots. A warm breeze blew in through a window at the end of the hallway near the old-fashioned metal fire escape exit. The place smelled of decay and cleaner. It was just like Cyrus to pick a hotel like this to stay in, what his brother would have called "authentic."

He knocked again, a little louder this time just in case his brother had hung one on last night at the four bars in town and walked the half mile back from town, leaving his pickup wherever it had been parked.

"Cyrus," he called as he used the key and opened the door.

"He's not in there," said a female voice from down the hall.

Cordell turned to see an older woman with a cleaning cart.

"From the looks of his room, he didn't sleep here last night," she said and pursed her lips scornfully.

Cordell didn't like the sound of that and felt his anxiety multiply. He'd always "felt" his identical twin, sensed him on some cell-deep level even when they were miles apart.

He couldn't feel his brother. It was as if Cyrus was… The thought that his twin might be dead sent a gut-wrenching terror through him.

Pushing open the door to the room, he saw Cyrus's bag next to the undisturbed bed. The housekeeper was right. It didn't appear Cyrus had spent any time in the room other than to drop off his bag.

Moving through the small hotel room, he saw that his brother hadn't even dirtied a glass or broken the paper band on the toilet seat and his fear intensified.

Cordell pulled out his cell, saw that he hadn't received any calls from his twin, and started to call the ranch again when he spied Cyrus's cell phone on the table by the window.

Cyrus didn't go anywhere without his cell phone.

Heart pounding, he walked over and started to pick it up when he saw his brother's room key lying on the floor next to the wall where it must have fallen. Next to it was a paper convenience-mart cup on its side on the carpet in the middle of a dark stain that looked like spilled coffee.

Cordell fought to remain calm as he surveyed the scene, noticing that the curtain was pulled back, the window opened a few inches as if his brother had heard something and looked out and seen…what?

The room was located at the back of the hotel. A strip

of pavement made up the parking area. Beyond it was a stand of huge old cottonwoods that grew along what could have once been a ditch or creek.

Past that were piles of old lumber and scrap iron, and in the distance, Cordell could make out a weathered old run-down farmhouse. Several old cars were up on blocks and the yard was littered with toys. A bunch of sorry-looking kids were outside. They seemed to be hunting for something. He heard them calling for someone.

A large woman stood on the front steps of the farmhouse, her hands on her hefty hips. She appeared to be giving the children orders in a strident voice.

Cordell turned his attention back to the parking lot below the window. He could see the glitter of glass on the patched pavement under the only light post. When his brother had arrived last night, it would have already been dark—especially in the parking lot without a light.

What could he have seen?

There were two cars parked between the faded painted lines, an old brown sedan with local plates and a blue VW bug with California plates. The VW had a flat tire on the left rear.

He stared at the flat tire unable to shake the bad feeling that had settled over him. Cyrus must have seen something down there last night. Something that had made him drop everything and run down to help?

He picked up his brother's cell phone and checked

to see if he'd gotten any messages other than Cordell's this morning, then checked Cyrus's outgoing calls.

Fear settled like a boulder in his belly when he saw that the last number his twin had called was 911.

Chapter Two

As Cordell started to look for a phone book to call the sheriff's department, he saw his brother's pickup coming up the road. Relief flooded him and yet at the same time he wanted to throttle his twin for scaring him like this.

He watched the pickup come in from a back way and wondered why he couldn't feel that connection that had always been there between the two of them.

It unsettled him and made him more anxious as he glanced at his watch. Cyrus was more than three hours late. Not only that, he'd also apparently spent the night elsewhere. It wasn't like his brother to have met a woman and been tom-cattin' around all night.

Cordell couldn't throw off the feeling that something had happened.

As the pickup pulled into the back lot and parked, he watched anxiously, just needing to see that his brother was all right.

The door of the pickup opened and with a start Cordell watched as a woman wearing a baseball cap over her short bluntly cut black hair climbed out. She was dressed in jeans, a jean jacket over a T-shirt and sneakers. Not really Cyrus's type, he thought.

Then she did something that sent a jolt through him.

She glanced nervously around the parking lot before her gaze shot up to the window where he stood. Cordell stepped back at the same instant and watched from behind the edge of the curtain as she opened the VW, took out something and seemed to stuff it under her jacket before heading for the back door of the hotel.

He quickly pocketed his brother's cell phone and room key and stepped into the closet, leaving the door open just enough that he could see most of the room.

It wasn't long before he heard voices out in the hall-way, both female. He knew without hearing all the conversation that the young woman driving his brother's truck had conned the maid into opening Cyrus's room for her.

He heard the door open, then close and lock. For a moment, she stood perfectly still as if listening, as well. Then she quickly moved to Cyrus's overnight bag on the end of the bed.

Cordell had a good view of her backside from where he was hidden. The woman appeared to be five-six or seven, slim with an athletic build and enough curves to fill out her jeans nicely. Had this woman been in trouble, Cyrus would have jumped to her defense without a second thought.

She unzipped the bag and hurriedly rummaged through it. He wondered what she was looking for. She definitely hadn't come to get something for his brother. So what was she doing with his pickup?

That was when he got a glimpse of the pistol stuck into the back waistband of her jeans. It peeked out from the hem of her jean jacket as she bent over the bag. Was that what she'd gotten out of the car?

Cordell moved swiftly, knowing the minute she heard the closet door roll back, she'd reach for the weapon.

She was fast, faster than he'd anticipated. Just not as fast as he was. He came out of the closet, diving for her and the weapon. At the sound behind her, she spun around, her hand going for the gun and coming out with it in her left hand.

As she swung toward him, leading with the weapon, he grabbed her wrist, driving her back and onto the bed. He wrenched the gun from her hand, tossing it across the room. It skittered to a stop near the door.

The woman got in a kick that only missed his groin by a couple of inches. Her right hook, though, caught him squarely in the jaw, surprising him by the force of her punch, before he could grab both her wrists and pin them and her to the bed.

Her eyes widened in alarm. *"You?!"* she cried, looking at him as if she'd seen a ghost and confirming that she'd at least seen his twin before she took his pickup.

"Where is my brother?" he demanded, holding her down on the bed.

"Your *brother?*" She stared at him as if dumbfounded.

"You're driving his pickup. You're in his room going through this stuff. Where is my brother?"

"I thought you—"

"I asked you a question." He knew what she thought. Few people could tell him and Cyrus apart.

Cordell pulled her arms up over her head, secured both wrists with one hand and reached for his cell phone. "You want to tell me or the sheriff? Your choice."

"Could you get off me? I can't breathe."

He studied her face. She was pretty but she hid it well with too much eye makeup along with a small silver nose ring and dyed black hair cut in a sleek bob that made her pale porcelain skin even paler.

"Come on. You're hurting me. Let me up and I'll tell you everything."

"I don't think so," he said, seeing something in her blue eyes that warned him this woman couldn't be trusted. "Let me say this again. My brother, where is he?"

As he started to dial 911, she said, "The last time I saw him, he was being taken to the hospital."

"The *hospital?* What happened to him?"

"I'm not sure. I think he was struck by a vehicle in the parking lot last night," she said, motioning with the snap of her head toward the back of the hotel.

The open drapes, the spilled coffee, Cyrus's cell phone on the table and the 911 call to the sheriff's department. Cordell felt his heart drop. "Is he all right?"

"I don't know."

Cordell shook his head in confusion. "Why did he go

down there unless… You! You didn't just witness this. You were involved somehow. How else did you get his pickup?" He could only assume his brother had rushed downstairs to save her. But from what?

She seemed to relent. "I was crossing the parking lot. I stopped, surprised to see that I had a flat tire on my car. Just then I heard an engine rev and this van came roaring out of the darkness."

"My brother saved you." It was the only thing that made sense. Cyrus must have seen the van and realized it was waiting for her.

"He shoved me out of the way. I fell. When I came to, a man who looks a lot like you was lying nearby." Her gaze skidded away. "I heard sirens. I didn't know what had happened. I was afraid the van would come back. I saw your brother's keys lying next to him and took his pickup."

"The sirens—"

"It was an ambulance," she said.

"Did you happen to notice while you were taking his keys if he was still alive?" Cordell asked with sarcasm that she seemed to ignore.

"He was still breathing from what I could tell."

Cordell couldn't hide his relief. "Nice of you to stick around and make sure he was all right."

She glared at him. "I'd had a scare. I didn't know your brother from Adam. For all I knew he was with the guys in the van."

He studied her. This whole mess sounded just like Cyrus. Maybe he'd even seen the driver of the van flatten her tire. The moment the man went back to his van to wait for her to come out of the hotel, Cyrus would have started to call 911. How, though, had the man in the van known she would come back out again last night?

"You'd just returned to the hotel? Wasn't it late?" he asked her. She looked surprised he'd figured that out. "So why leave again so soon?"

"I came back to check out. I'd changed motels."

"Why?"

"Isn't it obvious? I didn't like the feel of this place, too far from town and it's old and crumby."

Maybe she was telling the truth, though he had his doubts. He was still shaken by the news that his brother had been taken to the hospital after possibly being hit by a van to save this ungrateful woman's neck.

Fortunately Cyrus was tough. He would be all right. He had to. And yet that foreboding feeling was still with Cordell.

"So my brother saves you, first you take off and just leave him lying there and then you come back here to go through his belongings?"

"I'm not a thief," she snapped, her blue eyes darkening.

"What's your name?"

Again her gaze shifted away. "Raine Chandler."

"I'd like to see some identification."

She shot him a disbelieving look that said she'd couldn't show him anything with him on top of her.

He eased off and she reached as if to get something out of her hip pocket. The blow took him completely by surprise, knocking him back. As her fist connected with his nose, the pain radiating up through his skull, she wriggled out from under him. His vision blurred as his eyes filled. Blood poured from his nose as he reached for her.

But she was too fast. Through the film of tears, he saw her vault over the bed to the spot where he'd tossed her pistol by the door. She came up with the gun.

For a split second he thought she'd turn it on him. But then she was out the door.

He didn't try to stop her. A few moments later he heard her rev his brother's pickup engine and tear off, tires spitting gravel. No reason to give her chase. He was more concerned right now with getting to the hospital and seeing his brother.

Cyrus could deal with retrieving his pickup, Cordell thought as he went into the bathroom to clean himself up. He couldn't wait to hear his brother's side of the story. Downstairs, the hotel clerk gave him directions to the hospital.

"They're in the process of moving from the old hospital to the new one," the clerk told him.

It wasn't hard to find since the entire town of Whitehorse was only about ten blocks square. The new hospital was on the far east side of town in the opposite direction from the hotel where Cyrus had gotten a room he hadn't used.

When Cordell walked into the small reception area, the nurse behind the desk looked at him as if she'd seen a ghost. He'd gotten used to being an identical twin and often forgot about the effect it had on other people. They always did a double take when he and Cyrus were together.

When they were younger they played tricks on their teachers and even their girlfriends. The tricks often backfired, landing them in hot water.

Now as private investigators in Denver, he and Cyrus used being identical to their benefit. It was almost as if they could be in two places at one time.

Their grandmother had never been able to tell them apart, he remembered, then chastised himself for letting her creep into her thoughts. He knew he was just trying not to worry about Cyrus.

"I'm Cyrus Winchester's brother. Twin brother," he said to the nurse now as if that wasn't obvious.

"Oh," she said, both hands going over her heart. "You did give me a start when I saw you standing there." She patted herself as if trying to still that heart. "I thought, 'It's a miracle.'"

His stomach dipped. "A miracle?"

She seemed to realize what she'd said. "I'm sorry. Hasn't anyone told you? Of course not. Until you walked in here we didn't know the patient's name so we haven't been able to notify his next of kin. Your brother is in a coma and has been since he was brought in last night."

SOMEONE HAD BEEN in her room.

Raine realized it the moment she opened the motel-room door and saw the tiny piece of cardboard from the coffee cup she'd stuck in the jamb lying on the floor.

She froze, her gaze taking in the cheap motel room. She'd put the Do Not Disturb sign on the door and it was clear that the maid hadn't been in.

The bed was rumpled from the few hours of sleep she'd managed to get the night before and her towels were on the bathroom floor where she'd dropped them after a quick shower this morning.

She glanced behind the door, then at the open closet. She didn't like surprises and almost laughed out loud at the thought as she stepped cautiously in, pulling the pistol and closing the door and locking it silently behind her.

The room was small. Lumpy double bed, bathroom, closet. Not a lot of places for a person to hide. She checked under the bed, in the closet and behind the bathtub shower curtain. Empty.

Tucking the pistol back into the waist of her jeans, she checked her overnight bag. Someone had gone through it. What had they been looking for? Evidence, she thought. Or identification? She'd left neither in the bag.

Walking over to the window, she saw how they'd gotten in. The latch was broken on the sill. She'd planned to go to another motel tonight anyway. The window looked out on the alley, a stand of trees and an old house that had once been painted white.

Raine felt her pulse thrum in her veins and her heart began to pound at the sight of the aging house. She could almost smell the rank mustiness. She hated old houses.

Closing the curtain on both the window and the past, she quickly packed up the few belongings that she hadn't put in storage when she'd left home, then placed a call to a local car repair shop and made arrangements to have her flat tire fixed and her car brought into town, saying she would pick it up later.

She knew it was just a matter of time before that cowboy came looking for her. She was still shaken by her run-in with him at the hotel. He'd looked so much like the man she'd seen lying in the parking lot last night that it had taken her completely off guard.

Glancing around the room, she made sure she hadn't left anything, then walked to the door with her overnight bag in hand. She opened it a crack to look out. The hallway was empty.

She pulled the gun from her waistband and, unzipping her overnight bag, laid it on top, making the weapon more accessible should she need it.

As she pushed open the outside door, she scanned the parking lot. The lot was empty except for the pickup she was driving and a large, luxury car with Texas plates parked at the opposite end.

Trying not to hurry, she walked to the pickup, tossed in her bag and climbed in after it. For a moment, with the doors locked and the gun handy, she just sat, not sure what to do next.

Run. Just drive in any direction and get the hell out of here. She could dump the pickup somewhere down the road. Early this morning, she'd dug in the pickup's glove box looking for information on the man who'd shoved her out of the way of the van last night and had pulled up short when she'd seen who the truck was registered to. Cyrus Winchester of Winchester Investigations of Denver, Colorado.

What were the chances that the man who'd come to her rescue just happened to be a private eye?

She started the pickup but still didn't hit the road. She was kidding herself if she thought she could leave. Even if she had her car and had left this pickup where Cyrus's twin brother could find it, she couldn't run. She'd hate herself the rest of her life if she didn't follow through with this. Wasn't it time she learned the truth—not to mention got the justice she deserved?

Last night the parking area behind the old hotel had been too dark to see the person driving the van. But Raine figured he had to be the same one who'd slashed her tire. He'd been waiting for her.

You were set up, girl.

It certainly looked that way. But why had someone gone to the trouble of luring her to Whitehorse? Surely not just to run her down in the hotel parking lot. They could have killed her in L.A. since at least one of them obviously knew where to find her—and where to send the messages that had gotten her here in the first place.

Why, after all these years, try to kill her? It made no sense. They had no reason to believe anyone was after them. But now the sheriff's department would be looking for the dark-colored van because the driver had put Cyrus Winchester in the hospital.

And his brother would be looking for Raine. Finding her in a town the size of Whitehorse would be child's play—for both the cowboy *and* the attempted killer.

Any woman in her right mind would hightail it out of town and not look back.

But Raine Chandler wasn't just any woman, she thought with a curse.

Chapter Three

Cyrus looked pale, his head bandaged and a series of tubes and cords running from his lifeless body.

Cordell took his brother's limp hand in both of his and sat down hard on the chair next to the hospital bed. No wonder he'd felt the connection broken between them.

"Cy, I'm here," he said, his voice breaking. "I'm going to find out who did this to you and take care of it. In the meantime…" He glanced away from his brother's face, trying to compose himself. He didn't want his brother to hear the fear in his voice. "I just want you to rest so you can wake up soon."

He heard the scuff of a shoe sole behind him and turned to see the doctor standing in the doorway. He squeezed his brother's hand and, reluctantly letting go, rose.

"Tell me about my brother's condition," he said, motioning for the doctor to come out into the hallway with him. He didn't want to talk about it in front of Cyrus. He'd heard that comatose patients could hear what was being said to them and around them, and from the doctor's grave expression the diagnosis wasn't good.

"I'm Dr. Hanson," the elderly man said, searching Cordell's face. "Identical twins. You certainly gave my nurse a start." He grew more sober. "As she told you, your brother is in a coma. He was already comatose when he was brought in so we were unable to get any information from him."

"What caused the coma?"

"Blunt force trauma to the back of his head. There was also some bruising around the hip and left leg as if he'd been struck."

"Like being struck by a vehicle?" Cordell asked. "Apparently he pushed a woman out of the way of a speeding van. She didn't see what happened to Cyrus, but found him lying on the pavement."

The doctor nodded. "That would be consistent with his injuries."

Cordell had thought he would get the whole story from his brother once he reached the hospital. Now he saw that if he wanted to know any more about the accident he'd have to ask the woman. But first he had to make sure Cyrus was going to be all right.

"What can we do for him?" he asked the doctor.

"There appears to be no bleeding or swelling of the brain that requires surgery, but we will continue to monitor your brother closely. Right now he is stable, his vital signs strong. A coma rarely lasts more than two to four weeks."

Others last for years, Cordell thought. "I know my

brother. He's a fighter. He'll come out of this." Soon, he prayed.

The doctor gave him a sympathetic smile. "We certainly hope so. Some patients recover full awareness. Others require some therapy." His look said some were never the same. "We won't know the full extent of your brother's injury until he regains consciousness."

If he ever does. Cordell kept hearing the words the doctor *didn't* say. He felt helpless. But there was one thing he could do while he waited for his twin to come back and that was to get the bastard who'd done this to him.

That meant finding Raine Chandler, and getting the truth out of her.

As Raine drove through a residential neighborhood in Whitehorse, she pulled out her cell phone and hit a speed dial number, realizing she was calling in late.

"I was just about to call out the cavalry," Marias drawled.

"Sorry, I've been a little busy."

"Uh-huh." Her friend had been against her coming to Whitehorse from the get-go. "What happened?" Marias knew her too well.

"I ran into a little trouble last night, but I'm fine."

"They know you're there *already?*" Marias let out an unladylike oath. But then there was nothing ladylike about the biker-turned-cop-turned-P.I.

"Not a huge surprise under the circumstances. I'm not sure where I'm going to be staying so I might not be able to get Internet or cell phone coverage. Seriously," she said when Marias snorted in disbelief. "Whitehorse is in the middle of nowhere and once you get outside the city limits, all bets are off when it comes to high-tech devices."

"You're leaving?" Just like Marias to latch on to that.

"No, just maybe staying outside town if I can find a place." Up the block, Raine spotted a tan sedan like the one she'd seen behind the hotel this morning. The car was parked in front of the new hospital. Of course he would go see how his brother was doing and his brother would tell him everything.

He would find out she'd been telling the truth. She hoped that would be the last she'd see of the cowboy.

Unless, of course, he and his P.I. brother were some-how involved. What if the plan last night hadn't been to kill her but to save her? She would have been in-debted to Cyrus Winchester. Maybe something had gone wrong and instead of saving her, he'd ended up in the hospital.

And now his identical twin was putting the strong arm on her.

A little paranoid, are you?

No, just covering all her bases, Raine thought. "I promise to try to stay in touch." She hung up before Marias could argue that this trip was nothing more than a suicide mission. If she only knew how complicated this had become.

Raine pulled over under a large tree next to a house

just down the block from the hospital. This might be the perfect opportunity to check out the car—and the man driving it.

She was about to get out of the pickup when she saw the twin come out and climb into the tan mid-size sedan. It had rental car written all over it. At least she'd been right about the car being the same one she'd seen parked behind the hotel this morning.

Sliding down in her seat, she peered through the steering wheel as he pulled out and headed toward downtown. Where was he going? She decided to follow at a safe distance and find out.

She was surprised though when the trail led to the sheriff's department. If last night's attack had been a ploy, then this cowboy wouldn't be going to the sheriff about it. He would want to keep all this as quiet as possible—and handle it himself.

She pulled over again and dialed information for Winchester Investigations in Denver, Colorado. The phone rang three times before a woman picked up and from the brisk way she answered, Raine guessed it was an answering service.

"I'm calling for Cyrus Winchester."

"I'm sorry, he's not available. Both Cyrus and Cordell Winchester are out of the office. If you'd like to leave a message—"

Raine hung up. *Both* Winchesters were private detectives? No way would a P.I. go to the cops unless he was on the up-and-up.

So what *were* they doing in Whitehorse?

THE WHITEHORSE COUNTY Sheriff's Department was located along the main drag in an old brick building. As Cordell climbed out of the rental car, he scanned the street.

In the diagonal parking spaces were a half-dozen trucks in front of the various businesses from a couple of bars and a café to a clothing store, beauty parlor, hardware and a knitting shop. None of the pickups were his brother's, though.

Inside the sheriff's department, Cordell spoke first to the dispatcher.

"I'll see if the sheriff is busy," she said.

He watched the street while he waited, feeling anxious. His fear was that the woman who'd called herself Raine Chandler would flee town. Her VW had California plates on it. What was she doing in Whitehorse? Apparently not just passing through. He'd had the good sense to take down the car's license plate, assuming it wasn't stolen. He wouldn't put anything past the woman given that she was toting a gun and clearly involved in something more than a near hit-and-run.

"Yes?"

He turned at the sound of a female voice to find an attractive dark-haired woman in a sheriff's uniform. Her head was cocked to one side as she perused him, her lips turning up into an amused smile.

"Which one are you?" she asked.

"I beg your pardon?"

"I'm sorry. I'm McCall Winchester, acting sheriff. I

recognized you from some photographs my grandmother showed me of you as a boy."

He caught her name and couldn't help frowning.

"Trace Winchester's daughter," she said.

He felt his eyes widen.

She let out a laugh. "Yes, I did turn out to be his daughter no matter what my grandmother said at the time. I'm the true black sheep of the family."

Cordell smiled at that. "It's a family of black sheep."

"Why don't we step back to my office?"

He followed her down the hallway, surprised that his cousin was the acting sheriff. She took a chair behind her desk and he settled into one of the others facing her. "My brother and I are up here because of our grandmother's letter."

McCall nodded. She didn't look happy about it.

"I'm guessing she isn't dying and wants something from us."

"That would be my guess," McCall agreed.

Cordell hadn't come here to talk about his grandmother and didn't give a damn what she was up to. He was too worried about Cyrus.

"Do you know about my brother's accident?" He saw that she didn't, probably because Cyrus hadn't had any identification on him. Which meant either the woman took Cyrus's wallet—or the van driver had stopped long enough to take it.

"Cyrus was attacked last night behind the Whitehorse Hotel. He's in a coma at the hospital."

"I'm so sorry. I'd heard a man had been injured and taken to the hospital but I had no idea it was your brother. The deputy on duty last night talked to the clerk who'd apparently called for an ambulance, but he said the only vehicle in the lot belonged to a woman."

Cordell nodded, thinking of the woman he'd tangled with earlier at the hotel. "The woman took my brother's pickup. She told me a crazy story about almost being run down by a person driving a dark-colored van. Her tire was flat on her VW, she said she was scared and saw Cyrus's keys on the ground and took off."

"So you talked to her?"

He looked away embarrassed that he'd let her go. "I was about to check her identification when she got away."

McCall raised an eyebrow at that. "I suppose that explains the blood on your shirt. It's yours?"

He looked down, not realizing some had dripped onto his sleeve. "She said her name was Raine Chandler, but I really doubt—"

"The VW bug with the flat behind the hotel is registered to a Raine Chandler of Los Angeles, California."

So she had been telling the truth—at least about that.

"Do you have some reason to doubt her story?" the sheriff asked.

Did he? Just a gut feeling that she was leaving out a whole lot of it. "I'm not sure. But with Cyrus in a coma, she is the only one who knows what really happened last night."

McCall frowned. "I heard that you and your brother are private investigators, but I hope you're not planning to take this matter into your own hands again. I'll put out an APB on her and your brother's pickup since she apparently didn't have permission to take his truck and she left the scene of an accident and possible crime last night."

"When you pick her up, I want to talk to her."

His cousin seemed to consider that. "I think we can work something out. I take it you haven't seen Grandmother yet."

"No."

"I'll let her bring you up to speed on everything that's been going on out there." His cousin shook her head as if whatever it was wasn't good.

Cordell rose from the chair, not bothering to tell her he had no intention of seeing Pepper Winchester. He had to find out who had injured his twin. He knew it was his way of dealing with Cyrus's coma. He told himself that by the time he found the bad guys and at least saw that they were behind bars, Cyrus would be all right again.

"It was nice meeting you." He reached into his wallet and took out his card. "My cell phone number is on there, but I'll check back with you."

RAINE CALLED MARIAS AGAIN. "I need your computer expertise. Can you check on a couple of private investigators out of Denver? The name is Winchester, Cordell and Cyrus Winchester of Winchester Investigations. See what you can find out."

"Anything special you're looking for?"

"Why they're in Whitehorse, Montana, would be helpful."

"I see. If you want to hang on… Do you happen to have a license plate number?" Marias asked.

"I can do better than that. I have Cyrus's pickup registration."

"I don't want to know, right?"

"Right." Raine reached over and opened the glove box. "Hold on, he's about to move again."

"He?"

"Cordell Winchester." From down the street, he had just come out of the sheriff's department. Raine leaned over out of view as she dug through the glove box, found the registration, then peered out cautiously as he climbed into his car.

Where to now? she wondered as she watched him start his car and pull away from the curb.

"What information would you like?" she asked her friend, then read what Marias asked for from the registration form as she waited for two cars to go by, then followed Cordell Winchester.

"Two brothers apparently," Marias said into the phone. "Same birth dates?"

"Identical twins."

"Really? Handsome?"

"As sin."

"This is a professional request, right?"

"Strictly business," Raine said and winced as she remembered the way her fist had connected with his nose. "No love lost between us."

"Oh, so that means you've 'met,'" her friend said with a laugh. "I hope it was romantic."

"If romance is him holding me down in the middle of a queen-size bed."

"Sounds good to me," Marias quipped. "Hell, sounds damned good now that I think about it. Hmm, that's interesting."

"Are you going to tell *me?*" Raine asked as she tried to keep Cordell's rental car in sight.

"I just did a little familial search. Father's name Brand. Mother a Karla Rose French. Divorced. Grandfather Call Winchester, deceased. Grandmother Pepper Winchester, still living. Got to be a nickname, wouldn't you think?"

"That's what you thought was interesting?"

"No, it's the part where Pepper Winchester's address is Whitehorse, Montana."

Cyrus and Cordell Winchester's grandmother lived here? Pepper Winchester. "Why does that name sound so familiar?" Raine said more to herself than Marias. Up the street, Cordell Winchester made a quick turn at the corner two blocks ahead of her. He'd tagged her. "Gotta go."

CORDELL COULDN'T BELIEVE it. He'd glanced in his rearview mirror and seen his brother's pickup a dozen car lengths behind him. The woman was following *him?!*

He made a quick turn, then another down an alley. Unfortunately, he met a delivery truck coming in and had to back up and take another street.

Around the next corner…

No sign of the pickup.

Cursing under his breath, he searched each side street. She couldn't have gotten away that quickly. No way.

Then he got lucky. Down a side street he spotted his brother's truck go past a few blocks away. She was headed out of town!

Unfortunately, he had a stop sign, then several cars pulled out that he had to wait for. But the second he'd gotten the chance, he'd gone after her, not surprised to see the pickup hightailing it out on one of the secondary roads south.

He had to floor the rental car to keep the pickup in sight. Cyrus would have had a heart attack if he saw the way this woman was driving his truck. The thought brought a stab of pain.

The pavement ran out. Dust boiled up behind the truck. She took a curve, throwing up gravel from the tires. Cordell backed off a little after getting the wind-shield of the rental car pelted, several bits of gravel pitting the glass.

He fished out his cell phone to call the sheriff's department, but found there was no cell phone service. It was just as well. At least now he could say he'd tried to call. The truth was he wanted to talk to Raine Chandler alone. He didn't want her pleading the Fifth and getting locked away behind bars where he couldn't get the truth out of her.

The narrow dirt road wound south over the rolling prairie, a roller coaster ride at this speed. He just prayed they didn't meet another vehicle coming up the road. There was barely enough room for one car. Going this fast, Raine would never be able to get far enough over to let another car pass.

At first he was convinced he would come up over a hill and find Cyrus's pickup wrecked at the bottom. But this apparently wasn't her first time driving on roads like these. He wondered what part of California she was from that she'd learned to drive on narrow dirt roads rutted with washboard.

He gave her a little space, confident that with all the dust she was throwing up, she wouldn't be able to lose him.

They left Whitehorse long behind them. As the country began to get more rugged, he realized they must be nearing the Missouri Breaks. He'd driven through the Breaks on the way to Whitehorse, crossing the Missouri River as it cut a deep gorge through this desolate, isolated country.

The country was familiar, too familiar, since he'd spent his first seven years living out here in the middle of nowhere on the Winchester Ranch. Unless he was mistaken, they weren't that far from the ranch.

Cordell was beginning to worry he'd never be able to catch her if she cut across to Highway 191. But then he saw the pickup fly over a cattle guard and come down hard, the right rear wheel hitting loose gravel on the edge of the road. He got on his brakes to keep from going airborne off the cattle guard, as well, and saw the rear of the truck fishtailing.

He could see her fighting to regain control. She almost pulled it off. Then she hit a stretch of deep washboard. The pickup tires lost traction and the next thing Cordell knew the truck was headed for the ditch adjacent to the road.

Fortunately, the ditch wasn't deep, but it was filled with water and mud which streamed up and over the truck before the vehicle finally came to a stop bogged down in the gumbo. Raine Chandler wasn't going anywhere.

Cordell was already out of his car and running toward the pickup before the driver's-side door swung open. He grabbed her and dragged her out, this time not giving her chance to go for her weapon.

Taking the gun from her jacket pocket, he stuck her pistol barrel against her temple, forcing her to her knees in the dirt next to the ditch as he held both wrists behind her. "Who put my brother in the hospital?"

"I told you—"

"I swear I will drown you in that ditch if you don't start telling me the truth."

He heard her take a deep breath and let it out slowly. She was shaking, no doubt from the adrenaline of the chase—certainly not from fear of him. There was a determination in her eyes that he'd misjudged before. He wouldn't make that mistake again.

"If you let me up, I'll tell you everything."

He let out a bark of a laugh. "You think I'm going to fall for that again?"

"I already told you. I was crossing the parking lot behind the hotel when someone tried to run me down. Your brother shoved me out of the way, I fell and that's all I remember. I must have blacked out for a moment because when I came to, your brother was lying there on the ground and I could hear sirens."

He pushed her down harder, pressing the gun barrel into her temple. "Why didn't you stay and tell the sheriff's deputy what had happened?"

She shook her head, making him want to throttle her. "I told you. I was scared. I panicked."

"Bull. You didn't want to be involved. Why?"

"I was scared."

He couldn't imagine anything scaring this woman. He also didn't believe she'd come back to the hotel this morning to find out Cyrus's name. So what had she been looking for?

"Do you have a permit to carry this gun?"

She hesitated a little too long. "Not in Montana."

"Why are you carrying a gun anyway?" he demanded.

"I live in L.A. You'd carry a gun, too."

Cordell didn't know what to think. Was it possible Cyrus had just been in the wrong place at the wrong time? Or was this woman lying through her teeth?

"Why would someone want to run you down?"

"How would I know? Maybe they mistook me for someone else. Or maybe it was an accident. Now would you please let me up?"

"Like your tire on your car just happened to be slashed?"

He sighed. He was getting nowhere with her. He let go of her hands, standing back in case she came up fighting, which he half expected. To his surprise, she got slowly to her feet.

"How is your brother?" she asked quietly.

"He's in a coma." Cordell had to look away. Just saying the words made it all too real.

"I'm sorry." She sounded surprised and sympathetic.

"Good," he said. "Because you're going to help me find the person who did this to him."

"I told you I don't know who was behind the wheel of that van."

That, he thought, might actually be the truth. But he suspected she knew damned well why the person had cut her tire and then tried to run her down. Cyrus couldn't have gotten downstairs from the fourth floor fast enough, unless he'd seen the man knife her tire and then go wait for her in the van with the motor running.

Cordell stepped to the open door of the pickup and took out her purse, an overnight bag with a small laptop computer tucked in the side and a large leather satchel. Laying each in the grass, he began to go through them, keeping the gun within reach should he need it.

"Please, that's my personal—"

"Stay right where you are," he warned her.

She stopped moving toward him, looking resigned as he opened her purse and quickly searched it. A little over two hundred in cash, most in crisp new twenties probably straight from the ATM machine. A California driver's license. He glanced at the information on it. Twenty-six.

Nothing unusual in her overnight bag.

He was beginning to wonder if she might really be telling the truth when he opened the large leather satchel. *"What the hell?"*

Chapter Four

Raine was still reeling from what he'd told her. His brother was in a coma? She felt sick to her stomach even before Cordell opened her satchel.

"I asked you what the hell this is," he demanded, taking a step toward her, shock and disbelief contorting his handsome face.

"I'm a journalist." The lie didn't come easily even though it was the one she'd been using for her cover. She hated lying to him. She'd inadvertently gotten his brother into this. She felt guilty enough. Lying didn't make it any easier. But she still couldn't be sure she could trust this man....

"A *journalist?*" Cordell grimaced as he glanced again at the photographs in the satchel. "This is about some *article?*"

"Are you going to question everything I say to you?" she demanded, going on the offensive.

"I am until I hear something I can believe."

She tried a little truth on him. "I'm working on an old missing person's case, a child who was abducted sixteen years ago from Whitehorse. Her name was Emily Frank."

Cordell studied her openly before pulling out the stack of photographs from the abductions. As many times as she had looked at the photos, she never failed to be moved to tears by the piles of charred bones, the rusted fifty-five-gallon barrels where the remains were found or the faces of the children still missing—and presumed dead.

Cordell shoved back his Stetson, looking shaken and uncertain, as he pulled out all the research material she'd gathered. "All *this* is related to the article you're working on?" he asked in disbelief.

She nodded.

"This child, Emily Frank… Tell me you aren't here looking for her remains."

"No. I'm interviewing the people who knew her."

He was watching her closely as if he knew she was leaving out some key piece of information—and wondering why. "So how many people have you interviewed?"

She knew where he was headed with this. He was trying to decide if her article research was connected to his brother's accident.

"None. I only got to the town yesterday," she said. "I haven't had a chance to talk to anyone yet."

He frowned. "Someone knows you're in town."

He was right about that, she thought and added truthfully, "I have no idea how they might have found out."

Cordell sighed. "What newspaper or magazine do you work for?"

She tried not to glance away from his black bottomless gaze. "I'm freelancing this one."

"How about a home address, a former newspaper or magazine, someone who can verify your story."

She felt her eyes narrow as she met his gaze. "My mother took off when I was a baby. I never knew my father. I've been on my own since I was eighteen. I put all my things into storage before I left California. I wasn't sure how long I'd be gone. So, no, I don't have a home address or anyone who can verify what I'm working on."

"*Someone* knows," he snapped and pulled off his Stetson to rake his fingers through his hair. "Chucking it all for a story, that's some dedication to your work. Why Montana? I'm sure there are missing children in California. There must be hundreds of stories you could have done there, if not thousands. Why this particular case?"

She was forced to look away. "I saw a picture of her. There was just something in her eyes…" She swallowed back the lump in her throat.

"I'm going to have to go through all of your notes, everything you have on this case."

She balked, just as she was sure he'd known she would.

"I should mention," he said, his words like thrown stones, "I went to the sheriff this morning. She just happens to be my cousin. I told her you stole my brother's pickup and might have been involved in the attack on him. She's already put an APB out on you because you left the scene. Unless you want to go to jail, I suggest you reconsider."

"I've told you what *I'm* doing here," she said, shaken to hear that his cousin was sheriff. "Why don't you tell me what brings two private investigators to Whitehorse, Montana?"

His eyebrows shot up. He hadn't expected her to find out who he was. Along with surprise though, there was grudging admiration in his gaze. "Not that it's any of your business but my brother and I came here to see our grandmother, Pepper Winchester. She's…dying."

She flinched as a shaft of guilt pierced her conscience. She believed him. Just as she believed his shocked reaction to the photographs in her satchel. This man wasn't working for a sexual child predator. At least she hoped not.

"Come on, we need to go somewhere so I can go through all of this," he said. "Or are you going to lie to me and tell me that all of this doesn't have something to do with you and the article you're writing?"

She wasn't.

He nodded, seeming relieved for once she wasn't going to argue the point. "Since my brother's pickup isn't going anywhere until a wrecker pulls it out, you're riding with me."

"I'd like to speak to the nurse at the hospital first," she said.

He turned back to look at her.

"I just want to verify what you've told me about your brother."

"I've heard that journalists don't take anyone's word on anything without at least a backup source, but do you really think I'd lie about my brother being in a coma?" Even under the shade of his cowboy hat, she could see the piercing black of his gaze. He was angry and she really couldn't blame him.

He shook his head in obvious disgust. "Fine. When we get to a place where my phone works, you're welcome to call the hospital." He swore under his breath. "Are you always this paranoid?"

"Only when people really are after me."

He sighed and pulled out his cell phone. "No coverage. Or do you want to check yourself?"

"I'll take your word for it until cell phone service is available."

He shook his head. "That's real damned big of you. Let me make something clear, I'm not sure what happened last night but I have a pretty good idea. You and your article got my brother into this. If guilt or the threat of jail doesn't work, then I'll use whatever methods I have to, but you *will* help me find the people who did this to him, one way or another."

CORDELL COULDN'T believe this mess. Cyrus in a coma and him saddled with this journalist and her paranoia.

Now what the hell was he going to do with her? he asked himself as he studied Raine Chandler. The cool breeze stirred the hair at the nape of his neck and he turned to see a dark bank of clouds on the horizon to the west. Great, just what he needed. A thunderstorm and him miles from a paved road.

He remembered as a kid how the roads would be impassable until after a storm when the wind and sun dried things out.

He considered making a run for town, but he could tell by the way the clouds were moving in that he would never make it before the storm hit. The rental car would be worthless and his brother's pickup was buried in the mud and not going anywhere. He swore under his breath again.

There was only one place to go.

As much as he hated it, he knew it was the best plan given the storm and the fact that he needed to take Raine somewhere so he could go through all of her research materials. His brother might have stumbled onto trouble last night, but Raine Chandler was up to her neck in it.

All he had to do was find the people after her.

That meant going to a private spot where she didn't try to get away from him until he found out what he needed. Cordell groaned at the thought though. "Come on."

"Where are we going?"

"To my grandmother's ranch. It's closer than town." He saw something flicker in her eyes. "Or would you rather go to jail?"

"Maybe I'd be safer there."

He stopped to give her his full attention. "If you think

your virtue might be at risk coming with me, then let me set you straight. You aren't my type and I have much more important things on my mind than sex. That blunt enough for you?"

"Quite. Did I mention that I believe Emily Frank was taken by someone in one of Whitehorse's more prominent seemingly upstanding families?"

Cordell let out a hoot of laughter. "Like the *Winchesters?* Think again. We've never been upstanding. Not even seemingly."

"You might be surprised how money and power tip the scales toward upstanding."

"No, actually I wouldn't be surprised." He eyed her, realizing she'd researched his family. Before or after Cyrus had crossed her path? "Winchester is just a name to me. I haven't been back here in twenty-seven years and if there were any money or power, my father and brother and I have never been a part of it."

She cocked a brow at him. "What about your grandmother?"

"Not that it is any of your business, but until recently my grandmother was a recluse who hadn't left the ranch in all those years. None of the rest of us had seen her in all that time or lived anywhere near here. Even if she hadn't been locked away for twenty-seven years, I can assure you she wouldn't abduct a child."

"If you haven't seen her, then you have no way of knowing—"

"My grandmother," he interrupted, "is so fond of children she doesn't even know how many grandchildren she has. She had to pay her lawyer to try to track us all down. I won't even go into how she treated her own children, even her favorite son."

"And this is where you're taking me? To see this grandmother?" She sounded incredulous.

"It wouldn't be my first choice, but you've left us no other option." Thunder rumbled in the distance. "You know anything about storms up in this country? Unless we get moving and damned soon, that storm is going to catch us and we are going to be stuck, literally, out here until someone comes along and that could be a damned long time. Once it starts raining, this road will become gumbo. We'd never be able to get back to town before the storm hits so we're going to wait out the storm at the Winchester Ranch. And believe me, I'm much unhappier about that prospect than you could ever be."

What in her research was she trying so desperately to keep from him? he wondered. Well, he'd soon find out. Once they reached the ranch, he'd go through everything in that satchel. She was his only possible connection to the men who'd put his brother in a coma. She was going to help him even if he had to wring her pretty little neck.

It would make it easier if she trusted him though, but he didn't take it personally. If he'd learned anything from his first marriage and subsequent divorce, it was that trust is a fragile thing that once broken badly is impossible to get back again.

He wondered, though, who had broken Raine Chandler's trust. Whoever it was had done a bang-up job.

RAINE REALIZED SHE had little choice but to go with him to the Winchester Ranch. Fighting Cordell would be futile since right now he held all the cards.

Also she wanted the man who'd hurt his brother just as badly as he did. If it was true and Cyrus Winchester was now fighting for his life, she owed him for his chivalry in saving her last night.

Cordell Winchester was another story. He didn't have a chivalrous bone in his body and she balked at being forced into anything, especially by him.

But she also realized it couldn't hurt having an obviously high-priced private investigator now helping her find the person who'd been driving that van last night—the same person she'd come to Whitehorse to find.

As she started to gather up her things he'd dumped in the grass, Cordell stopped her. "I'll take care of this."

"I'd prefer to carry my own things."

He smiled. "I'd prefer you not bloody my nose or kick me in the groin or pull a gun on me."

"That's right, you have my gun. I'd like that back."

"I'm sure you would. But you don't need to worry. From now until we're finished with this, I will keep you safe."

She lifted a brow questioning whether he thought he really could handle that job. Fortunately she'd learned to take care of herself. "I'm not sure you won't need my help."

He gave her a look that said she was pushing her luck. She heard him swear under his breath as he walked away. She watched him, trying to gauge what kind of man he really was. One thing was for sure—he had no idea who the woman he'd just taken captive really was.

As she watched him, for the first time, she took a good look at Cordell Winchester. She was suddenly aware of the man on some primitive level. He looked like an ad for Montana, a cowboy who was just as comfortable in the wild outdoors as in a large city or a boardroom.

She must have been blind not to have noticed before this how his jeans hugged his tight behind, the legs long, the hips slim. His shoulders seemed broad enough to block out the sun.

Raine felt desire warm her blood. It had been a long time since she'd been even remotely aware of a man. She'd been too busy with her career. She'd apparently forgotten what it felt like to want a man so much it made her ache. Or maybe she'd just never known a man like Cordell Winchester, a man who could unleash that kind of primal need even when she couldn't stand the sight of him.

This was a man who had to be used to getting what he wanted from women. She was glad she wasn't that type of woman. But the thought also came with a little regret that she wouldn't be finding out if Cordell was as sexy as he looked.

As he started to the car with her things, he saw her eyeing him. "Something wrong?"

She scoffed at that. Everything was wrong. She couldn't wait to see the last of this Winchester and, judging by the expression on Cordell's face, he felt the same way.

CORDELL HATED THE IDEA of dragging this woman out to the ranch with him as much as he hated going there in the first place. He knew he had no business taking her prisoner and the last person he wanted to see was his grandmother.

But the storm had given him no other option other than being trapped in the small rental car with her. That, he thought, could definitely be worse than the ranch. At least at his grandmother's they should be able to get something to eat and drink and, if they were stuck there overnight, a place to sleep.

He didn't trust Raine Chandler as far as he could toss her and needed this time to find out everything he could about her—and this article she was writing.

As it was, he'd have to watch her 24/7. At least at the ranch, she was far enough from Whitehorse that taking off would require she hoof it forty miles. Or take a horse. He couldn't see that happening.

"This is just temporary," he said as they climbed into the car. Once he found the person who hurt his brother, Raine Chandler was free to do whatever the hell she wanted.

"So," he said and started the car, "why don't you tell me about this article you're working on."

She sighed. "Her name, as I already told you, was

Emily Frank. She was ten when she was taken as she walked home from school. She was never found. Neither were her abductors."

He shot her a surprised look. "You said abductors? Are you saying there was more than one person who took her?"

"A man and a woman."

"How do you know that?"

She seemed to hesitate. "I have something of the girl's."

He felt a chill trot the length of his spine. "It's just hard to imagine a woman—"

"Sometimes a woman in these situations is more dangerous than the man. She often goes along with it to make him happy but resents it—and is hateful to the child because she is jealous. In a few cases, it is her idea."

Cordell gripped the steering wheel tighter as he drove, sickened by the things she was telling him. "These people are monsters."

"A common misconception is that they are recognizable psychos," she said, as if warming to her subject. "Look at the famous cases. The neighbors always say, 'They seemed like such a normal family.' They hide behind the facade of being upstanding citizens. Often they are very involved in their community, do a lot of good deeds and are high profile. Money and power masquerading as the wholesome family next door. They're people you could pass on the street and never suspect. These people appear so normal that the good people of Whitehorse have no idea that these child abductors live right among them."

CORDELL LOOKED SHOCKED and sick to his stomach. She saw him grip the steering wheel tighter.

"You said Emily was taken sixteen years ago," he said after a long moment.

She knew what he was asking. "Who knows how many more children they have taken since that time."

"Come on, residents would become suspicious if a bunch of kids went missing from a small Montana town."

Raine shook her head. "These people are serial child abductors. They don't stop. They don't have to. They're bulletproof because they're so deeply rooted in the community and the children they take are on the remote edge of society."

He frowned over at her.

"Children from families with few resources or connections to the town. Foster children."

"These children are still going to be reported missing."

"Missing and presumed runaways. Because of that the foster parents often don't alert the authorities right away. Even when they do and the child isn't found, the victim is considered a runaway until her body is found."

Cordell didn't say anything for a long time. "Isn't that going to make the abductors nearly impossible to find?"

"That's why they haven't been caught. These people

will do anything to keep their twisted secret." She felt his gaze on her.

"Including making another run at you?"

Cordell Winchester was smart. She liked how quickly he'd understood the situation.

She started to argue that the hit-and-run last night had nothing to do with her—or her reason for being in Whitehorse. She saved her breath. "They'll send someone after me again," she said simply.

If they haven't already, she thought, studying the cowboy sitting next to her. "That is, if they can find me at some isolated ranch in the middle of nowhere."

He chuckled as the car sped down the narrow dirt road. "We're just sitting out the storm at my grandmother's. Don't worry, I'll make sure you can use yourself as bait if that's your plan."

"What a relief." Raine stared out at the rolling prairie. He'd also been right about the storm. It moved in quickly, the first drops of rain splattering against the windshield. Ahead the land seemed to break up into badlands and she knew they must be nearing the Missouri Breaks. On her way to Whitehorse, she'd dropped down into the Breaks to cross the winding river as it made its way through Montana.

She'd never seen such wild, isolated country. Now she realized just how far they were from civilization. Normally, she felt she could hold her own. But Cordell Winchester outweighed her and was obviously much stronger. He also had her gun. And now a storm had blown in, one that he swore could strand them out here.

So why wasn't she terrified? She glanced over at him, studying his expression and seeing nothing but pain. She could see that he was worried sick about his brother. And he'd been visibly shaken by the photographs of the abducted children.

Was it possible he was in town just to see his grandmother, and his brother had just been in the wrong place at the wrong time last night? It was beginning to seem that way.

She studied him, realizing he was much harder to read than most people. He must make a damned good private investigator. And like her, she suspected he didn't let most people in.

There was something about him that made her also suspect he'd been hurt by someone. She felt that, rather than saw it, a built-in empathy for others you recognize because they've gone through something akin to what you have. A sixth sense. Who had hurt him? she wondered.

Raine heard Cordell swear as rain pinged off the hood, falling harder and faster. The car swerved several times in the mud forming on the surface of the road. Ahead she spotted a huge log arch over a narrow, weed-choked road. The sign on the arch read, Winchester Ranch, and Cordell seemed to relax as he slowed the car to make the turn.

She felt her heart beat a little faster as he drove down the road, the weeds between the ruts scraping loudly along the undercarriage to the beat of the pouring rain. She could feel the tires spinning out as the ranch lodge came into view.

Out of the corner of her eye, she saw that Cordell's expression was one of dread. "So you really haven't been here in twenty-seven years?"

"Not since I was seven. This is the first time I've been invited back."

"You must have been a pretty awful kid."

Through the rain and the sweep of the wipers, she stared at the ranch buildings nestled against the hillside. The place looked very Western and rustic. A sprawling log structure, it ran out in at least a couple of wings and climbed to three stories on one of what appeared to be an older wing.

"About my grandmother... She's..." He seemed at a loss for words. He let out a sigh. "You'll see soon enough."

Raine sat up straighter as they dropped down the slippery slope to the massive ranch lodge, not surprised that she was anxious to meet Cordell's grandmother.

"How do you plan to explain me?" she asked.

He gave a devastating smile that made the interior of the car seem too intimate and definitely too close. "I'm going to tell her you're a car thief."

"That should impress her," she said as he brought the car to a stop in front of the log mammoth. A curtain moved on the second floor. An old blue heeler hobbled out into the rain to growl next to the car. Other than that, nothing moved.

"Didn't I hear something about a couple of murders on this ranch a month or so ago?" Raine asked as it suddenly hit her why the name Pepper Winchester had sounded so familiar.

Chapter Five

"I'm sure it won't be the last murder out here, either,"
Cordell said as he stared at the ranch lodge. If it hadn't
been for the rain, he would have turned around and left.
But the roads had already begun to turn to gumbo.

Now he would have to see his grandmother when he
hadn't been the one who'd wanted to come here in the
first place. Cyrus had been the one determined to see
this place and now— Just the thought of his brother
brought a wave of pain. The twin connection that had
comforted him since they were born was still gone. He
felt as if a part of him had been ripped out.

He'd left his number with the hospital along with instructions that they were to call if there was any change
at all in his twin's condition. Unfortunately, there was
no cell phone service out here. He checked his phone
anyway. No messages. He didn't know whether to feel
relieved or more concerned. He just had to believe that
Cyrus would come out of this.

"Looks like we'll have to make a run for it," he said,
noting that the rain didn't look as if it planned to let up.

As he got out of the car, Cordell realized it had probably

been a mistake to bring Raine here. Next thing he knew she'd be doing an investigative piece on the Winchesters and who knew how many more secrets were hidden in these old walls?

The front door opened as he and Raine ran toward the lodge. He was taken aback to realize the small, broomstick-thin elderly woman in the doorway was Enid Hoagland. His brother Cyrus would have gotten a kick out of the fact that the mean old woman was still alive.

"Which one are you?" Enid demanded as she stepped back to let them into the small foyer.

Before he could answer, his grandmother appeared. "He's Cordell," Pepper Winchester said. "Enid, why don't you make something hot to drink for our guests? They're soaked to the skin."

Enid didn't look the least bit happy about being sent away. For a moment, Cordell thought she would refuse to go. But with a huff, she turned and disappeared into the dim interior.

He was shocked that his grandmother had recognized him. She hadn't been able to tell him and Cyrus apart when they were younger. Why now? Unless maybe she'd heard about Cyrus's accident.

"This must be your wife," Pepper said, turning her gaze on Raine.

Cordell flushed, realizing of course his grandmother hadn't heard about his divorce. He'd just assumed everyone for thousands of miles around would have heard since it had been such an ugly one.

"No, this is Raine Chandler," he said. "My wife and I are divorced."

His grandmother raised a brow. "So like my attorney to get it wrong. I'd fire him if he was still in my employ." She smiled as she shook Raine's hand, her old eyes seeming to bore into the younger woman.

"Raine is an investigative reporter," he said.

Pepper winced.

"Don't worry, she isn't investigating the Winchesters." He took a breath and let it out slowly. "At least not yet," he said under his breath. "So you've heard. Cyrus was attacked last night outside his hotel room in Whitehorse and is in the hospital in a coma."

Pepper's hands went to her chest. "I hadn't heard. Is he…"

His grandmother's concern surprised him. That and the fact that she really had been able to distinguish him from his brother apparently. Had she always been and just hadn't bothered?

"It's too early to know his prognosis," Cordell said. "The doctor is hopeful he will regain consciousness soon. We all are."

"Yes," his grandmother agreed. "I'm sorry." She glanced out at the rental car. "You'll have to bring in your own bags. Alfred…"

"Yes, I heard. But we won't be staying," Cordell said.

"Why ever not?" his grandmother demanded.

"We're just here to wait out the storm," he said.

She raised a brow. "You were just in the area and

decided to drop by? Enid has already made up two rooms anyway."

Cordell started to argue, but realized this might be for the best. He and Raine would have the privacy they needed if they had rooms away from his grandmother and Enid. And if the storm let up…

"So this investigative piece you're writing…" Pepper said, turning to Raine now that the lodging was settled.

"It's about child abductions, one in particular. You might remember it. A ten-year-old girl named Emily Frank. She was abducted on her way home from school sixteen years ago in Whitehorse."

Pepper frowned. "I'm sorry, I *don't* remember." But clearly she also didn't want to hear any more about it. "I'll make sure Enid has your rooms ready while Cordell gets your bags." With that she turned and left them.

THE PHONE RANG AS Pepper Winchester started down the hall. She picked up one of the extensions before Enid could. "Hello."

The news about Cordell's twin had shaken her. But given the information, she wasn't surprised to hear the voice on the other end of the line.

"Mother?" She hadn't heard her son Brand Winchester's voice in twenty-seven years. It surprised her that it could fill her with such a landslide of emotions. "Have you heard about Cyrus?"

"Yes, just now when Cordell arrived. He's out bringing in his bags."

"He's staying there?" He sounded both surprised and disapproving.

"Don't worry, there hasn't been a murder here in weeks," Pepper said, unable to contain her annoyance.

"I heard about that. I'm going to be coming out."

Her daughter, Virginia, had said it would take a gun to Brand's head to get him to ever come back to the ranch even for a visit. Pepper couldn't wait to tell Virginia how wrong she'd been. It had taken his son's accident to get Brand back here.

"I hope you'll stay here at the ranch." She didn't mention that his old-maid sister Virginia was also here. She didn't think Virginia's presence at the ranch would be a draw for her brother, but just the opposite.

Brand hesitated so long Pepper found herself getting irritated and had to squelch saying something she would regret.

"All right," he finally agreed and Pepper heard the telltale sound of Enid replacing the extension in the kitchen. "I'll be there tomorrow after I see Cyrus at the hospital."

"Plan on having supper with us," Pepper said. "The roads should be dry enough by then." She hung up and stood for moment thinking that her plan had worked in ways she hadn't expected.

After twenty-seven years, they were all wandering back to the ranch. She found little satisfaction in it, though, as she walked down the hall and shoved open the kitchen door. She'd thought that letting them believe she was dying would do the trick—that and greed. Surprisingly only one had fallen for that—Virginia.

Pepper shoved her annoyance with her only daughter away and considered that things might work out after all. With luck she would discover which of her spawn was a traitor and a murderer.

"My GRANDMOTHER WASN'T being insensitive about the story you're working on. Although she *can* be insensitive without much effort," Cordell said, seeing Raine's expression when he returned with the bags from the car.

He shook off the rain from his jacket as he set down the bags in the entryway. She hadn't packed much for a possible extended stay in Montana. He wondered how long she'd planned to stay.

"As I told you, my grandmother's been a recluse for the past twenty-seven years," he continued when she didn't say anything. "I'm sure she didn't hear about anything that's happened during that time."

"What made her become a recluse?" Raine asked, looking into the dim interior of the house beyond the entryway.

"Her youngest son had disappeared, believed to have run off," he said, keeping his voice down. "Apparently it was more than she could bear." Cordell hesitated as a thought struck him. "Funny, but she seems to be taking his murder better than his disappearance. Odd, huh."

"He was *murdered?*"

Cordell nodded. "Twenty-seven years ago. So what do you think she did? She invited the rest of her family back to Winchester Ranch, a family she hadn't seen in all those years."

"Maybe she wants to try to make up for it before she dies."

He shook his head. "She's up to something, something no good."

"But you still came back."

"I only came back because of my brother Cyrus. You and I are here only because of the storm and I needed someplace where I can keep an eye on you."

"You're not very trusting, are you?"

He didn't bother to answer. "You couldn't get me within five hundred miles of this place and that old woman in there if I had any other choice." He saw Raine's reaction. "Do you believe in evil?"

She seemed startled by the question.

"I don't know if it is this place or what this place does to people."

"Places aren't evil. People are," she said with conviction.

"Are you going to spend the rest of the day out there talking or let me show you to your rooms?" Enid demanded as she suddenly appeared, startling them both.

"Speaking of evil," Cordell said under his breath.

RAINE LOOKED AROUND the ranch lodge, wondering about the Winchesters, especially Cordell Winchester, as she followed Enid up the stairs.

Divorced. She should have known. That could explain

the coldness she'd felt in him. His ex had broken his heart, she'd bet money on it. He had all the classic symptoms of a man who had been betrayed by the woman he'd loved.

She dragged her gaze away from him and considered his weird family and this place where they lived that he thought evil. The Winchester Ranch lodge looked as if it had been dropped from an old Western movie set. The log walls, a rich patina, were covered with Native American rugs, dead animal heads and Western art that looked old and expensive.

Enid was faster than she looked and Raine had to hurry to catch her, Cordell coming slowly up the stairs behind them.

Enid opened a door into a large room with a sitting room and huge bed and private bath. "This is your room," she said as if she thought Raine planned to sneak off and find Cordell's as soon as the lights went out. "Cordell's room is across the hall." Enid glanced down the stairs as if to make it known that anyone on the lower floor would be able to see her if she left her room for any reason.

"Thank you," Raine said, wishing she was in some nondescript motel room. She'd never liked staying with strangers and the Winchester family and the hired help seemed about as strange as anyone could get.

As she glanced at Cordell, she was reminded of his brother. She could see the worry on his face and felt overwhelmed with guilt at the knowledge that the twin brother who'd saved her life was now fighting for his. She had no choice but to help Cordell.

"Your room is across the hall," Enid said to Cordell.

"Thank you," he said. "That will be all."

The elderly housekeeper gave him a withering look, spun on her heel and disappeared down the staircase.

Cordell stepped through the open door to his equally large suitelike room and set down Raine's overnight bag, purse and satchel on the table. He glanced at the fire going in the fireplace, then at the open-curtained French doors that led out onto the small balcony.

"I'm not going to try to escape," Raine said, entering his room. "I'd like my things in my room."

He nodded toward her overnight bag and purse. "They're all yours. I still need to go through the satchel."

Her gaze went to the double bed on the ornate iron frame. It was identical to the one in her room and would take a footstool to climb into it. Several homemade quilts were piled onto the end of the bed, making her wonder how cold it got out here at night.

Enid had made a point of letting them know she thought they were already sleeping together and that being forced to get two rooms ready only made more work for her. The old woman wasn't as sharp as she thought she was, Raine thought. But the grandmother... well, Raine thought everyone probably underestimated her.

Cordell dumped the contents of her leather satchel

onto the table by the window and Raine closed the bedroom door behind her. She didn't want him going through everything without her here. Nor did she want everyone in the household to know what they would be discussing. Cordell didn't seem to notice she hadn't left.

She liked the sound of the rain as she stepped to the French doors, opening them a crack. She felt as if she needed the fresh air. She'd never liked being closed in. She looked out over the ranch, feeling antsy and wondering how long they would have to stay here. There was something about the place that made her uneasy. Or was she just anxious about what was going to happen next?

"Hopefully the rain will stop soon and it will dry up enough that we will be able to leave later tonight," Cordell said behind her.

Raine watched the pouring rain thinking his grandmother was probably right. They were stranded here at least for the night.

She closed the door and stepped back into the room. Cordell had sat down at the table and was gingerly looking through the photographs and other information she'd gathered. She took a chair across from him.

"If you're just writing about Emily Frank, why do you have all these other photographs of missing children?" he asked.

She could tell the faces of all those missing children were taking their toll on him. It was impossible to look into all that innocence and know horrible things had been done to those children before their bodies had been dumped or buried or, in the case of the people Raine was looking for, burned like trash when they were finished with them.

"Because this isn't just about Emily," she said. "There are serial child abductors out there. Some keep the children a short period of time and kill them. Others keep them until the child is too old, then they get rid of that one and get another one the right age."

Cordell swore under his breath. "These statistics can't be right. About eight hundred thousand children are reported missing every year or two thousand a day?"

"Over fifty thousand of those are victims of abductions by strangers. The others are taken by family members or people they know."

"I had no idea," he said, clearly upset.

"Few people do unless it hits closer to home for them. Almost all of the ones abducted by strangers are taken by men."

"I don't understand how this can happen."

"In eighty percent of the abductions by strangers, the first contact occurs within a quarter mile of the child's home. In many cases, so does the abduction. Most strangers grab their victims on the street or try to lure them into their vehicles. About seventy-four percent of the victims are girls."

Patiently, she stood and picked up a map. Opening it, she spread the map of Montana out on the table and saw his eyes widen when he noticed the dozens of colored stars.

"Don't tell me that is where children have gone missing," he said.

"The blues ones are believed to be runaways. The yellow ones are considered solved cases based either on a suspect's confession or the discovery of remains. The red ones are unsolved missing children cases."

He stared down at the map, a look of horror on his face. "And the green stars?"

"Those are only the cases a man named Orville Cline confessed to in this state. In only one study, child molesters averaged over a hundred child victims per molester."

Cordell pushed back his chair and walked over to the fireplace. She watched him grab the mantel and lower his head. "This Orville Cline, where is he now?"

"Serving time at Montana State Prison in Deer Lodge. He confessed to taking Emily Frank and killing her."

Cordell spun around in surprise. "Wait, if—"

"He lied. I have evidence that he couldn't possibly have taken Emily Frank." She picked up the folder on Orville Cline and handed it to Cordell, who read it standing up. She watched him read the confessions Orville had made during the trial. Raine had read this so many times, she could have recited the man's confession to Emily Frank's abduction and murder verbatim.

Cordell snapped the folder shut and looked up in surprise. "Why would he confess in horrific detail about an abduction and murder he'd didn't commit? Maybe he confused her with another little girl."

Raine shook her head. "They don't forget or mix up

their victims. That's part of the high they get out of it, remembering. He knew he didn't take Emily Frank."

"Then why confess?"

She rose and walked over to the French doors again. The rain had stopped and now a cool breeze swept across the balcony smelling sweet and summery. "I think he made some kind of deal with the couple who really abducted Emily."

"But you don't know that for a fact."

"No, but I do know that he lied about it," she said, turning back to him. "Open the small manila envelope." She opened the door wider. The breeze felt soothing against her cheek as she listened to him sort through the items on the desk. She heard him open it, heard his sharp intake of breath, then the silence that followed broken only by the rustle of the sixteen-year-old spiral notebook pages.

"My God," Cordell said behind her. "Emily wrote this?"

"She kept a diary of the days she was imprisoned after her abduction. Her handwritten notes contradict what Orville Cline said happened. He lied."

Cordell frowned. "Where did you get these?"

"They were sent to me recently."

That surprised him.

"I don't know from whom or what their motive is, but I believe they want me to find out the truth about Emily Frank's abduction."

"Orville Cline?"

"Doubtful. I think it was one of the people who abducted Emily."

"Why would… Are you telling me you think one of them wants the truth to come out?"

She shrugged. "That's what I thought until someone tried to run me down last night."

"Exactly. It looks more like they just tricked you into coming up here. If you're telling the truth, someone tried to kill you last night. That was no accident behind the hotel." He was frowning again. "But why? If Orville Cline confessed to Emily Frank's killing, they are in the clear. So…why contact *you?*"

"Journalists are often targets," she hedged. "Especially ones who might have some new information on the case."

"Can you prove this Orville Cline couldn't have taken Emily?"

"Not yet," she admitted. "But that diary Emily kept proves he lied about the details."

Cordell looked down at the pages with the heartbreaking words neatly printed on them. Like her, he had to be awed by the girl's courage, her hope and faith in a world that hadn't been kind to her, her perseverance in such a horrible situation. Emily believed she would be rescued.

"The person who sent you these has to be involved," he said quietly as if the full weight was just now making an impact on him. "If you're right and Emily wasn't the only child they abducted and there is even a chance that this person wants the abductions to stop…"

"Now do you understand why I'm here, why I'm willing to risk my life?"

ENID HAD A SCOWL ON her face when Pepper walked into the kitchen. Nothing new there. She studied her housekeeper, considering giving her hell for eavesdropping on her private conversation. But Enid had been eavesdropping for years. It was one reason she was still employed here. She'd overheard too much.

"Brand is coming," Pepper said. "Please make a room for him. I told him to plan on having supper with us."

Enid grunted unhappily and Pepper had to wonder why the woman stayed. Then grimaced at her own foolishness. Enid was here only for one thing: the Winchester fortune. She planned to get her share. One way or another.

An uneasy truce had hung between them since the latest secrets had been uncovered at the ranch. Though no bargain was made, it was assumed that Enid would stay on at the ranch as housekeeper and cook. But she would be rewarded for her loyalty.

The elderly Enid never spoke of her husband's murder nor did she seem to grieve for his loss. If anything, Alfred appeared quickly forgotten by his wife.

Pepper understood such behavior, though she secretly believed she'd been grieving for her own lost husband for years.

"Did you see what your latest grandson dragged in here?" Enid said, raising her eyes to the ceiling where she'd made up rooms for Cordell and the young reporter. "We'll be lucky not to be murdered in our sleep."

Pepper laughed at that. She'd put money on herself and Enid being much more dangerous than that young woman upstairs. She watched Enid make a vegetable beef soup for their lunch. It had been days since the elderly cook had attempted to drug her.

For months after her son Trace's disappearance, Pepper had welcomed the drugs Enid surreptitiously slipped her. She had welcomed the oblivion. She hadn't even considered why Enid was doing it.

But once Trace's murder had come to light, everything had changed. Pepper now wanted her wits about her. She was in search of the truth about her son's murder and suspected there had been an accomplice—right in this house.

It was why she'd gotten her family back here. Also why she dumped most cups of tea her housekeeper brought her down the drain.

Enid was no fool. She had to know. Which made her wonder what Enid would do next.

One thing Pepper knew for certain. It was just a matter of time before the aging housekeeper would demand payment for keeping Pepper's secrets.

"I'm going to find Cordell," Pepper said, gripping her cane.

Enid shot her a disapproving look. "I hope you're not planning to ask another one to stay on the ranch."

"With Alfred gone, we need Jack here," she said of her grandson Jack Winchester. Jack had promised to come back. He and his new bride, Josey, were on an extended honeymoon, but Pepper was hoping when he returned that he would take her up on his offer to turn Winchester Ranch into a working ranch again.

"That new bride of his isn't going to want to come back here," Enid said.

"It can be lonely and sometimes the wind…" She shook her head, remembering how the sound of the wind had nearly driven her crazy when her husband had brought her here after their honeymoon. "It can be a harsh, unforgiving place."

Enid huffed at that. "Life is what you make it." Her gaze met Pepper's. "But I guess I don't have to tell you that. You've managed fine, haven't you?"

She heard the insinuation in Enid's words. Keeping secrets was a dangerous proposition, Pepper wanted to tell her. Enid thought she had her right where she wanted her. But Pepper had a plan.

Actually, she felt it was her duty not to leave this world without first making sure this mean, old bitch was sent straight to hell ahead of her.

Chapter Six

Cordell started at the knock and quickly put all of the documents back into Raine's satchel.

At the door he found the housekeeper. "Your grandmother wants a word with you down in the parlor," Enid said. "Also dinner will be served tonight at six sharp. Don't be late."

Cordell had been waiting for the other shoe to drop since receiving the letter from his grandmother's lawyer. He glanced back at Raine, hating to leave her alone.

"Do I have time to take a bath?" she asked, getting to her feet. When she reached to take the satchel with her to her room, he stopped her, saying, "Leave that. I'd like to look at it again. I need to go see what my grandmother wants."

She nodded and scooped up her computer. He didn't say anything, pretty sure she couldn't get Internet service out here and what difference would it make if she could?

"We'll leave as soon as we can. Believe me, I'm more anxious to get out of here than you are."

Cordell waited until Raine disappeared into her room

across the hall before he stepped out, closed and locked his own room. Enid saw him pocket the old skeleton key. He knew he'd only managed to increase her curiosity.

Pepper was waiting for him, standing at the window leaning on her cane in what Enid had called the parlor. It was a nice-size room with leather furniture, a stone fireplace and a single large window that opened to the front of the house. Even though it was June, a blaze burned in the fireplace, but did little to do away with the chill in this house.

When she heard him enter the room, Pepper turned and took one of the chairs. He sat across from her in a matching leather chair. It creaked under his weight and he realized this was the same furniture they'd had when he was a kid living here. In fact, little about the lodge had changed over the past twenty-seven years. Everything was more worn, but the memories were still fresh.

"I had hoped you would have answered my letter to let me know when you would be arriving," his grand-mother said reproachfully.

"The letter wasn't from you, but your attorney, and I didn't see any reason to answer it. Truthfully, I'd hoped I could change Cyrus's mind about coming out to the ranch. I don't have a lot of good memories of this place."

"You don't like me."

"No."

She smiled. "You and your brother look so much like your father."

His jaw ached from clenching it. "I don't really think you want to talk about that, do you?"

"Brand called. He'll be here tomorrow and will be staying on the ranch."

Cordell couldn't help being surprised. He'd called his father after he'd received the letter from his grandmother, figuring Brand had gotten one, as well. He had. He'd been adamant about not coming back except for his mother's funeral and, even then, he wasn't sure about that.

Cordell's father never talked about the ranch or his childhood here. He'd thrown himself into raising his boys after their mother had taken off when they were babies. Brand never said it, but he blamed Pepper. She couldn't stand any of the women her sons brought home and made their lives hell until they couldn't take it anymore and bailed.

After the twins left home, Brand threw himself into work. To Cordell it seemed his father had spent his life running away from the past.

"I know everyone blames me for their unhappiness. Do you think it is fair though, blaming me for what your grandfather did?" There was an edge to his grandmother's voice, a blade of both anger and pain.

"You were the *mother*. Mothers are supposed to protect their children."

He was instantly reminded of photographs of the children who'd been abducted from this area. "You didn't protect my father."

"No, I didn't. I let Call discipline them."

"Until Trace came along. What was it about him that made you protect him and not the others?"

She actually looked uncomfortable. "I was older. I felt as if I'd lost the others a long time ago. I guess you could say I drew a line in the sand."

Cordell laughed. "Is that what you call it? I'd always heard that my grandfather rode off one day and just never returned. Apparently that wasn't the case, huh. And, no, I don't believe for a moment that Alfred Hoagland killed my grandfather."

"His wife, Enid, swears that is the case."

He shook his head. "Why don't we cut to the chase? What do you want? You didn't invite me and Cyrus back here out of the goodness of your heart. Or because you're dying. You don't have a sentimental bone in your body."

She lifted her chin, body erect, and he saw a steely gleam in her dark eyes. She was still a beautiful woman, graceful and elegant, but cold and unfeeling, no matter what she said. "You might be surprised. Jack has already told me that you boys were in the third-floor room the day Trace was murdered," she said, her voice strong. "I need to know what you saw."

He wasn't sure what he'd expected her to ask him. Not this. That awful room was where his father and aunt and uncles had been sent as punishment. He and his brother had been forbidden to go to the room so of course they'd sneaked up there. *"Saw?"*

"Jack told me that you and your brother had a pair of small binoculars that you were arguing over."

Jack, the nanny's son? "Why would you believe anything Jack—"

"He's my grandson." She smiled wryly. "Those rumors about the nanny and my son Angus? They were true."

Cordell shook his head. "What a family."

"Yes, isn't it?" She lifted her cane and pointed toward the window. "See that ridge over there? That's where Trace was murdered."

His eyes widened. He'd had no idea his uncle had been killed within sight of the ranch. No wonder she was asking about this. From the third-floor room with a pair of binoculars was it possible one of them could have witnessed the murder? Apparently his grandmother thought so.

"I didn't see anything."

She nodded solemnly. "What about your brother?"

He shrugged. "You're going to have to ask him." He felt that awful pain and fought the thought that if Cyrus had seen something, they might never know. Cyrus might never regain consciousness. "What is it you think he might have seen? I thought Uncle Trace's killer was caught."

"Yes, but died after suggesting there was a co-conspirator."

That took him by surprise. "If Cyrus had seen a murder, he would have said something."

His grandmother didn't look convinced. "Not if he'd seen someone from this family on that ridge that day."

"If you think my father—"

"I didn't say it was Brand. Cyrus might have been so shocked that it was a family member he might not have dared tell. I know there were more children in that third-floor room than just you and Cyrus and Jack. Who else was up there?"

Cordell shook his head. "I just remember the three of us." He could feel his grandmother's gaze boring into him. She knew he was lying. He wasn't sure why after all these years he was still keeping the secret.

Because he'd promised. It was that simple.

The question was, how had his grandmother found out? Had Jack told that there had been two girls, one a year younger than him and her kid sister? They had ridden their horses over from the ranch down the road and he and Cyrus had sneaked them up into the room.

His grandmother would have gone ballistic had she known they were in the house. Pepper had never liked any of the neighboring ranchers—not that any of them were close by. But she'd especially disliked the McCormicks.

When she didn't come out and ask about the girls, he realized Jack hadn't told.

That made Cordell feel better about his "cousin" Jack.

"I called the hospital," his grandmother said. "There is no change in Cyrus's condition."

Cordell said nothing. He'd checked his cell phone on the way downstairs. There'd been no messages. That meant no news.

"Is that all?" he asked, getting to his feet.

His grandmother nodded, though she didn't look pleased.

Now at least he knew why she'd invited them all back to the ranch. She was looking for a traitor in the Winchester family.

Cordell smiled to himself at that as he headed back upstairs. Didn't she know that you couldn't throw a rock around here without hitting someone with traitorous motives?

RAINE TURNED ON THE tub water and poured in a shot of bubble bath, waiting until she was sure Cordell and the old housekeeper had gone downstairs before she pulled out her cell phone. No service. Tossing it back into her purse, she opened her small laptop. It only took a moment to get online via satellite.

Just as she suspected there would be, there was an e-mail from Marias.

"Get in touch."

She replied through instant messaging. "No cell service. What's up?"

A few moments later. "Winchesters squeaky clean, good rep, tough and damned good-looking from their photos on their Web site."

Raine shook her head, smiling as she got up to turn off the water in the tub. It was just like Marias to check them out to see just how handsome they were.

"So nothing to worry about, right?" she typed when she returned to her computer.

"Doesn't look that way."

They'd apparently taken time off from work to come visit their grandma. Except Cordell hadn't wanted to and couldn't wait to get out of here. She wondered how things were going downstairs with the two of them.

No reason to be suspicious of the Winchester brothers apparently.

"But you did get another package from Montana."

Raine jumped, startled by the tap on her door.

"Raine?"

Cordell.

She typed, "I assume you opened it."

Marias typed a smiley face.

"What's in it?"

"A crude map. Almost looks like a kid drew it. I think it might be a map to the house."

Raine felt her heart clutch in her chest. "Can you e-mail it to me?"

"Could take a few minutes."

Cordell tapped again, then she heard the creak of the hardwood floor as he went across the hall. She listened to the sound of a key in the lock, his door opening and closing, then silence.

In the bathroom, she tested the water. Still hot. The room was steamy. She closed the door and stripped off her clothing before gingerly stepping into the tub and sinking down in the scented bubbles.

She felt confused and unsure. Trust came hard for her. But in her job she'd become good at reading people. Did she still believe Cordell and his brother had been hired by someone to set her up?

She sank down deeper in the tub. She was starting to trust him and that scared her more than she wanted to admit. What if she was wrong?

That answer was simple. She would never leave Whitehorse, Montana.

In the other room, she heard the sound of another e-mail alert.

The map? With a chill she sank deeper in the water, terrified of what might be waiting for her at some remote house used by the child abductors.

SHERIFF MCCALL WINCHESTER wasn't surprised when Cordell called to say he'd found Raine Chandler and gotten his brother's pickup back. She was surprised, though, to see he was calling from a landline—at the Winchester Ranch.

"I still want to question her about your brother's assault," she told him, suspecting that her private investigator cousin had already done that.

"It sounds like it was an accident. Cyrus was just at the wrong place at the wrong time," he said.

"Uh-huh. Still… Do you know where I can reach her?" She heard him hesitate.

"We're waiting for the roads to dry out," he said finally.

"Oh?" McCall said. So there was more to this story, just as she'd suspected.

"After what happened last night, Raine was upset. I thought coming out here would get her mind off it."

Raine, huh? "Did Ms. Chandler say what she's doing in Whitehorse?"

"She's a journalist. Doing a story up this way."

"Know what about?"

"Didn't really get into that much."

McCall bit her tongue. "Could you ask her to stop by my office when you get back to town? Or better yet, let me ask her."

"She's in the bathtub across the hall in her room," he said, making McCall smile at how careful he was to make it clear she had her own room.

"Well, then why don't you have her stop by my office," McCall said. "I heard your father is coming to the ranch tomorrow. Grandmother invited me out for dinner. I hope you'll be there. I assume Aunt Virginia is still there?"

"Haven't seen her."

"Dinner should be interesting."

"More like pure hell. I wouldn't count on me being there. Is there anything new on the dark-colored van and the man driving it?"

"We found the van. It had been stolen from Havre. Forensics will be coming in tomorrow to see what they can find. I'll let you know if they come up with anything." McCall hung up, irritated with her cousin but sympathetic.

Earlier she'd stopped by the hospital. Cyrus was still in a coma. She picked up the report the deputy had given her on the altercation in the parking lot behind the hotel, anxious to talk to Raine Chandler.

Something was definitely wrong. McCall hoped her cousin knew what he was doing taking Raine to the ranch. She feared he didn't have a clue who the woman was—or what she was capable of, for that matter.

After all, he believed she was a journalist up here on a story.

IMPATIENT AFTER HIS CALL to the sheriff, Cordell turned on the television but he couldn't find a channel that could hold his attention so he just left it on the news and turned down the volume.

He began to go through the information again that Raine had collected on missing children. It was shocking and he suspected it was only the tip of the iceberg.

He found an article from a psychologist who dealt with the children who were recovered from child molesters. "Trust is devastated. Often the victim is made to feel responsible for what happened. They feel powerless, trapped. That sense of learned helplessness can last a lifetime." He skimmed the rest, words jumping out at him. *Humiliation. Alienation. Trauma. Vulnerability. Psychological shock. Postvictimization.*

He got to his feet. He couldn't read anymore. He had so many questions he wanted to ask Raine. What was taking her so long? She hadn't seemed like the kind of woman who would lounge around in the bath this long.

Picking up the Emily Frank file, he saw that she'd been a foster child. He realized he knew nothing about foster care. Sitting down, he began to read.

A line jumped out at him. "Children in foster care live in an uncertain world. They lack the stability and permanence that other children take for granted and are often moved at a moment's notice, all of their belongings fitting into no more than a plastic grocery bag."

He could relate to that. He and his twin had moved constantly from the time they were seven until they were able to go away to college. His father, Brand Winchester, was a quiet, taciturn man who worked as a ranch manager, moving like the wind from one job to the next. He'd never remarried after the twins' mother had left them when the boys were babies.

Brand never blamed his mother for the failure of his marriage or his life, but it was unspoken.

Cordell and Cyrus had been old enough to remember the day their grandmother had kicked them all off the ranch where they'd lived since they were born. He and Cyrus had learned at an early age to give their grandmother a wide berth, spending their days outside as much as possible with the horses or playing in the barn or outbuildings.

The family had scattered like fall leaves after that, none of his father's siblings keeping in touch except once in a long while. At least he and Cyrus had each other and had never been abandoned by their father.

Looking back though, Cordell realized how they could have ended up in foster care if things hadn't worked out for his father once they'd left the ranch and the only life his father had known.

His gaze settled again on the words in front of him.

"Foster children's lives are about leaving behind things and friends and places they know, their lives haunted by neglect and child abuse. In foster care they often lose their sense of identity."

He picked up a grainy newspaper photograph of Emily Frank. The girl was wearing a dress that was too big for her. She looked gangly and a little too thin, but she wore a beatific smile.

He saw something he hadn't noticed before. A tiny silver horse pin. Even in the photograph he could see that it was in an odd place because of a small tear in the fabric that not even the pin could hide.

His heart ached for the little girl. According to the foster home paperwork, Emily had been kicked around from one foster home to another since she was two and had only been at the new foster home in Whitehorse one night. Before that she'd run away from her last foster home.

He could see how the foster parents might have thought she'd run away this time, too. They wouldn't have acted right away, a huge mistake.

He wondered how she'd ended up in foster care to begin with. Maybe Raine would know. He glanced toward his door, wondering how long before she finished her bath. He was anxious to find these monsters and hoped to hell Raine had a plan other than using herself as bait.

The tap at his door startled him. He quickly put everything back in the satchel and went to answer the door.

Raine stood out in the hall, her hair damp, her face

glowing from her bath. She hadn't taken the time to put on that awful white makeup or the dark eyeliner. He marveled at how young and clean and fresh she looked without it. Like a different woman.

It struck him that she used the makeup almost like a mask—or a disguise. Was it possible Raine had known this girl Emily Frank? He felt his pulse quicken. Was it possible she'd been a foster child at the Amberson house when Emily was taken?

That, he realized in a flash, would explain why she wrote about these abducted children, why she knew so much about foster children, why she'd come all this way to do a story on Emily Frank.

"Is everything all right with your grandmother?" she asked, and he realized he must have been frowning as he wondered about her. "Is she upset about me staying here?"

"No, she is more interested in the past than the present. I don't want to talk about her, if you don't mind." He sighed and motioned for her to come in, reminding himself that it didn't matter if Raine had a connection to Emily Frank or not.

All that mattered was finding the bastard who'd put his brother in a coma.

The moment the door closed behind her, he demanded, "How do we find these people?"

RAINE HAD SEEN THE WAY he was looking at her and regretted that she hadn't taken the time to put on her makeup.

But she wrote off his behavior as impatience the moment he spoke. He just wanted to find the man who'd hurt his brother. On that they could agree.

"Emily had just come to Whitehorse the night before so only a limited number of people knew about her," she said. "From her diary, I think it is clear that her abductors knew she was a new foster child. They might even have been tipped off by the foster parents or possibly the social worker."

"You can't really believe they were in on this?"

Did she? "Everyone is a suspect and they knew Emily had run away from her last two foster homes. Emily Frank had unknowingly made herself the perfect abduction victim."

"Last *two* foster homes? I only read about one that she ran away from."

Raine sighed. He'd been studying the material while she was gone and was just looking for discrepancies. "The other foster family kept it quiet. It reflects poorly on the foster family if the children run away, but you'll find it in the social worker's report." She stepped to the table and pulled it out of the stack of papers to hand it to him.

He looked chastised. "How did she end up in foster care anyway?"

"The way a lot of them do. Single mom. Dad never in the picture. Mom deemed unfit. The state takes the girl in the middle of the night and puts her in foster care with complete strangers."

"Why was the mother deemed unfit?"

"All it said on the report I was able to get was child endangerment. Could have been anything." She glanced from him to the television and froze.

"I have to admit I knew nothing about foster children until I started reading the material you'd gathered…" His voice trailed off as he finally noticed that she was no longer listening. "Raine?"

She groped blindly for the remote, unable to take her eyes off the newscaster and the words streaming across the bottom of the television screen.

CORDELL SAW HER REACHING for the television remote and turned to look at the television screen. A woman newscaster was standing in the Whitehorse Hotel parking lot. He thought it must be a story about last night's hit-and-run—until he caught the words running along the bottom of the screen and felt as if he'd been punched in the stomach.

Raine turned up the volume an instant later, the news commentator's voice filling the room.

"The girl disappeared from her home last night."

Out of the corner of his eye, Cordell saw Raine drop onto the edge of the bed with a sound like a wounded animal.

"Lara English had been playing hide-and-seek with her foster siblings at the time of her disappearance behind the Whitehorse Hotel. One of the children reported seeing a dark-colored van leaving the area shortly before hearing sirens."

"What the hell?" Cordell said under his breath. It couldn't be a coincidence that a child had been abducted from behind the hotel—the same area where Raine had nearly been run down and his brother struck by someone driving a dark-colored van.

"The foster mother, believing the child was hiding or had run away, didn't call the sheriff's department until late today."

An angry-looking woman came on the screen. "You don't know this kid. I do. So of course I thought she was just hiding from the other kids and refusing to come out or that she'd run. What was I supposed to think? You have no idea what some of these foster kids are like. No idea."

Lara English's photo flashed on the television screen.

"Hell," Cordell said on a shocked breath. He stared at the photograph that came up on the screen. The girl was blonde, blue-eyed and grinning into the camera. He felt his heart drop like a stone. The girl looked enough like Emily Frank to be her sister.

The news report ended with the usual. "If anyone sees this nine-year-old girl, please call the sheriff's department." The number flashed on the screen.

His cousin McCall came on in uniform and encouraged anyone with information to contact her immediately.

As the news changed to the construction of a new bridge in Great Falls, he took the remote from Raine's trembling fingers and turned off the television.

"Okay, no more lies. What the hell is going on?" he demanded even though he could see she was in as much shock as he was. "And don't tell me it doesn't have something to do with you."

RAINE STARED AT THE blank television, her heart racing as if she'd just had to run for her life. She tried to breathe but couldn't seem to catch her breath.

She could still see the little girl's face that had only moments before been on the television screen. Emily Frank. No, she thought with a mental shake, only a child who looked enough like Emily to—

"Raine? *Raine!*"

She blinked and dragged her gaze away from the now blank television screen.

Cordell handed her a paper cup half full of cold water. "Here, drink some of this." She took a sip, hating how weak and afraid she felt, how helpless. He motioned for her to finish it.

She did and he took the empty cup from her trembling hand. Her mind seemed scattered as she watched him ball up the cup and throw it into the trash. He came back to kneel in front of her.

"These are the same people who took Emily Frank, aren't they?" he said, taking both of her hands in his.

She was aware of the warmth of his hands and how her cold ones seemed to disappear in his. She looked up into his dark eyes and wondered how she'd ever thought them cold and unfeeling. There was heartbreak in them.

Raine wanted to pull back from the pain she saw there. It too closely mirrored her own.

"Talk to me," he said quietly. Of course he'd seen the resemblance between Lara English and Emily Frank. He knew it had been no coincidence they looked so much alike.

Raine felt sick to her stomach. Cordell knew, just as she did, that this was about *her.* It had been from the moment she'd received the lined pages torn from Emily's school notebook. "They took that girl because of me."

"Why would they do that?" Cordell asked. "It can't be because of some magazine article. You were a foster child, weren't you?"

With her gaze locked to his, she knew she didn't have to answer. He'd seen the answer.

"You knew Emily Frank?"

Raine shivered and dragged her gaze away to look toward the French door she'd left partially cracked open earlier. A cool breeze blew in. She watched it stir the row of tall old cottonwoods flanking the massive log lodge. Beyond them was a huge red barn and horses in a summer-green pasture.

Not even that picturesque scene, though, could lift the horrible weight resting on her chest. How was it she could feel for these lost children, but she couldn't appreciate beauty or feel love? Because something had died in her sixteen years ago the day Emily Frank was taken.

She turned back to Cordell, surprised at the tears that

brimmed in her eyes and the sobbing ache that hitched in her chest. "I am Emily Frank. That's why they took that girl. Because of me."

Chapter Seven

Cordell stared at her in disbelief. "That can't be. Emily Frank is dead."

"That's what a lot of people believed especially after Orville Cline confessed to her abduction and murder," she said, slipping her hands from his as she rose to go to the window.

Cordell shuddered as he recalled the graphic description in Orville's confession as to how he killed her and what he did with her body.

"Emily escaped," she said, her back to him. "They never found her. Then a week ago I got the pages from Emily's notebook."

He rose to his feet, unsure what to do or say. He couldn't help noticing the way she was talking about Emily as if she was a separate person from her. He suspected that was the way she thought of her. But now, at least, he knew the connection.

Outside, a fierce warm wind howled across the eaves. In this part of the country, the weather changed in an instant, often with huge ranges in temperature, as well.

The roads would be drying out. For once, luck was

with them, he thought, since this latest news had changed everything.

"Emily was one of those foster kids bounced from home to home from the age of two," Raine said. "She never knew her father. She could barely remember her mother, a teenager who dumped her at strange people's houses so she could go out partying with her friends. From such a young age, it makes a kid resilient."

"Still—"

"It's amazing the way we're able to accept what happens to us," she said. "We don't know any differently. It isn't as if we have that much contact with kids from normal families."

Cordell couldn't believe that. She would have seen other children at school or in the neighborhood who had a father and mother, families, secure lives that didn't change in an instant.

He frowned as it all began to sink in. "You're not a journalist on a story."

She shook her head, her gaze settling on his. "I'm a private investigator in L.A."

"A *private investigator?*" Small world. But that explained a lot, including the gun she carried and how she'd managed to get away from him at the hotel this morning.

"If you don't believe me you can call my partner, Marias Alvarez."

"I believe you." He realized he did. Just as he'd believed her confession about being Emily Frank. "How did Emily get away?"

She stood silhouetted against the afternoon light, her back to him. Earlier she'd looked defeated, but now there was a new strength to her, a new determination as she turned suddenly to face him.

He wondered how many times this woman had been forced to find that strength. Cordell couldn't bear the thought of what she'd been through.

"When Emily was found more than two hundred miles from Whitehorse, she was near death. No one knows how she got there. She didn't speak for two months and when she did, she had no memory of what had happened to her."

"My God," Cordell said and hoped with all his heart that she would never have any memory of what had happened to her. "We have to go to the sheriff."

"If we do, he'll kill Lara right away. You have to trust me on this. If you go to the sheriff, it will cost Lara her life and I fear it will be the last I hear from the person sending me the information."

Cordell didn't doubt she knew what she was talking about. But what if she was wrong? "What are you saying? The person who sent you those pages just got you back here to kill you."

She shook her head. "Why would they do that? Orville Cline had already confessed to Emily's murder."

"Maybe they're worried that your memory has come back and are afraid you can identify them."

RAINE HESITATED, then said, "I still believe that one of them wants this to stop and is helping me to bring the child abductor down." She told him that her friend and partner Marias Alvarez called the person CBA or Crazy Bastard Abductor. "I think Crazy Bitch Abductor might be closer to the truth. I believe it's the wife sending me the information and that she got me back here because she knows she can't stop him without help."

"That's some theory. I hope it doesn't get you killed."

"What choice do I have? There's a little girl out there missing. I have to find her before it is too late," she said, her voice breaking. The news about the latest little girl had chilled her to her very bones. She knew exactly what Lara English was going through.

But she couldn't give in to her emotions. She had to be strong. "I have to put all my energy into finding Lara."

"And you believe this CBA will help you do that," he said, sounding more than a little skeptical.

"Now that he's taken Lara, I have to believe it," she said.

Cordell studied her for a long moment and she could see he was considering her argument. "You do realize that he knows someone leaked you the information. That's how he knew where you'd be last night when he took Lara."

She nodded solemnly. "That means the woman could be in as much trouble as Lara. Another reason we have to find them and Lara before it's too late."

"How do you suggest we do that?"

"The Crazy Bitch Abductor sent us a map."

"I HOPE THIS MAP MAKES more sense to you than it does to me," Cordell said as Raine stared at her computer on the way to Whitehorse.

The wind dried the top of the road bed. As long as he avoided the mud puddles, the rental car got enough traction to keep them out of the ditch.

Before they'd left the ranch, he'd called to have a wrecker pull out his brother's pickup. He planned to pick it up in town. For these Montana roads, a truck worked much better. He'd also called the hospital. There was no change in Cyrus's condition.

"I would assume it's a map to the house where my abductors took me sixteen years ago," Raine said.

The map was crude at best, hand-drawn as if by a child. He felt a chill the first time she'd showed it to him back at the ranch. He'd had to agree with her when he'd seen it. Maybe someone was trying to help her. Or not.

"I still think we should go the sheriff," he'd argued when he'd seen the map. "McCall needs to know what's going on."

"Your cousin is already searching for Lara. She's a cop. Don't you think she's already considered that Lara might have been abducted? Especially after what went down behind the Whitehorse Hotel last night?"

He'd agreed that she was right and he didn't want to take a chance with Raine's life any more than he did Lara's. The problem was he didn't trust whoever was sending her this information.

Raine was the only one they knew of who'd gotten

away from her abductors in this area. Orville Cline had confessed to her murder. Raine was living proof of his lie—and knew that he hadn't taken her.

Wasn't that more than enough motive to get her back to where it had all happened to tie up the loose end in the cruelest of all ways? By making her relive her abduction through Lara English?

His heart broke for the child Raine had been just as it did for Lara. He swore he would see that these people paid—or he'd die trying.

"You don't think this house is where he took Lara, do you?" Cordell asked.

"No. The CBA would be too afraid to give that up—if she even knows. No, I think there is something at the house on the map that she wants me to find, though."

He glanced over at her, hearing the fear in her voice she was trying hard to hide. "You never told me what happened after you were found miles from Whitehorse," he said, not comfortable with his own thoughts right now.

But he needed to know everything about Emily Frank if he planned to help Raine. When she didn't answer, he glanced over at her. "I'm sorry, if you'd rather not tell me—"

"No. I want to tell you. If I had come forward before this, maybe Lara English wouldn't have been abducted."

"You can't remember what your abductors look like," he pointed out. "And as you said, these people are chameleons, blending in with society. All you would have done was put yourself in the line of fire earlier."

RAINE COULDN'T ARGUE THAT, but the truth was she hadn't been ready to face this. She wasn't sure she was now.

But she knew she had to be honest with Cordell if they hoped to find Lara before it was too late. Together they might stand a chance, a slim one, but at least a chance. And she knew he had a lot of questions. Anyone would.

"I told you Emily didn't remember anything. That wasn't true."

"Raine, you don't have to—"

"I don't remember what they looked like. Either I didn't see their faces or I didn't want to remember them. That night while the thunder and lightning boomed around me, I wrote the pages in my notebook to keep myself calm. I guess that's when the idea came to me how I could escape."

"You didn't try before that?"

She shook her head and smiled over at him.

"I can't imagine having the presence of mind to do that. Not at age ten. I would have cried and screamed myself hoarse."

"You never know what you would do in a situation like that," she said. "I was a foster child. I'd been thrown into so many uncomfortable situations, I don't think I was as terrified as a child who'd never known adversity.

Also I was used to being alone and pretty much taking care of myself."

"What happened after you escaped?"

"I found my way to the highway, followed it until I came to a farmhouse. It was early in the morning. I hid in the back of a pickup that was running in the yard. After the truck pulled out of the yard, I fell asleep curled under an old tarp and when I woke up I was in a town I had never seen before.

"As it turned out, I was in Williston, North Dakota, not even in Montana any longer, hundreds of miles away from Whitehorse. When the driver went inside a store, I climbed out of the back of the truck. I must have been a real mess when a nice woman found me. I was running a fever, sick and weak. They were afraid I wouldn't survive."

"They didn't know you and how strong you are," he said, his voice filled with admiration.

Raine felt her face heat from it and hurried on with her story. "The Chandlers took me in. It was Mrs. Chandler who'd found me and got me medical attention. They say I didn't speak for months and by then I was smart enough to make up a story so I never had to go back to that foster home in Whitehorse. I think I knew I would be abducted again or sent away to possibly somewhere worse."

"The Chandlers were nice to you?"

"Tom and Minnie Chandler were in their forties. Their only son was away at college. I think they were thankful to have a child under their roof. They adopted me after a time. They let me chose my own name. Raine seemed appropriate since the storm was what had saved me."

Cordell shook his head, awed by her story. "They never put it together that you were Emily Frank, this girl missing from a town just across the hi-line a few hundred miles?"

"Emily was believed to have run away. There wasn't much of a network for missing children sixteen years ago. That was before Amber Alert. And as I've said, from my experience, foster children often run away or fall through the cracks. I'd only been with the Ambersons in Whitehorse one night. They didn't know anything about me except that I'd run away from the last two homes I'd been in."

"You're saying they weren't invested in looking for you." He couldn't believe what he was hearing. "So there wasn't much of a search for you. Still you would think that someone in Williston would have heard about the missing girl. The Chandlers had to wonder why no one was looking for you."

She smiled. "When Minnie found me, I was wearing a hand-me-down worn dress that was too big for me and no shoes. I think she realized when no one came looking for me that I was better off with her and that's why she didn't try to find out where I came from."

Cordell's thought exactly. "I'm glad they were good to you. They must have been relieved when Orville Cline confessed to abducting and killing Emily Frank. They probably thought you were safe."

"We all did," Raine said. "I was at college when I read about Orville Cline's arrest and his confessions. I wanted to believe he was the one. It was easier than believing that the people were still out there, still taking little girls. I thought he lied about killing…" her voice caught "…Emily because he didn't want anyone looking for me. It never dawned on me that he could have made a deal with my abductors."

Cordell heard the pain in her voice, the guilt. "You can't blame yourself. After what you'd been through, you had to know that if you did anything, they could find you."

"But they still found me, didn't they?"

"How? That's what I don't understand," he said.

"I've been asking myself that. I assume someone put two and two together in Williston."

"Is it possible the truck driver saw you when you got out of the back of his pickup?"

"Maybe. I jumped out and ran and hid. But wouldn't you think he would have told someone?"

"Maybe he did. Maybe he told your foster parents back in Whitehorse, but since it appeared you'd merely run away…"

Raine nodded. "I've known all along I would have to talk to them eventually. But first I have to see where this map leads me."

Cordell could hear how anxious she was as he looked down the road they'd just turned down and wondered where they were being led—and, more to the point, by whom?

He saw Raine glance at her watch. She'd told him that if Lara could be found within seventy-two hours, she stood the best chance of being found alive.

They'd already lost precious hours. He could almost hear the clock ticking.

Chapter Eight

Cordell looked out at the growing darkness, his anxiety growing.

"According to the map, it's just a little farther," Raine said in the pickup cab next to him. "He wouldn't want the house to be too far from town and yet far enough away and remote enough that he knew no one would accidentally stumble across it."

Cordell had insisted they stop in Whitehorse long enough to trade the rental car for the pickup. The moment he'd realized the roads would be passable that they could leave the ranch, he'd called a towing service in town.

The wrecker had gotten to the pickup in the ditch, just minutes before they did. They'd followed the tow truck driver into town and made the switch, losing only a little daylight.

From Highway 2 they'd turned off a dirt road, then another, each road getting smaller and less used until now they were in a creek bottom of narrow ravines, rocky bluffs and twisting juniper-choked coulees.

"The next turn should be up here on the right," Raine said.

"I don't see a road," he said, squinting through the twilight. Deep shadows hunkered in the underbrush along the creek.

"There it is." Just then a whitetail deer bolted from the brush and ran directly in front of the pickup, startling them both. He hit the brakes. Raine let out a breath as the deer swept past unhurt.

Cordell didn't like the closed-in feel of this river bottom. Nor did he trust that whoever had sent Raine the map was interested in confessing and ending this. Ending this, maybe. But with someone dying and he feared that someone the informant had in mind was Raine Chandler, aka Emily Frank.

The road dropped down into a thicket of stunted aspen trees along the creek bottom. A perfect place for an ambush, he thought as he pulled a pistol from under his brother's seat, checked the clip and rested the weapon next to him as he turned down the road.

He noticed that Raine had apparently thought the same thing as she already had her gun resting in her hand, no doubt loaded and ready to fire. It made him feel a little better to realize that she wasn't putting all of her trust in this CBA.

She'd tucked away the computer and lowered her window. The air smelled of summer, the grasses tall and green. A wisp of cloud floated along on the breeze against the pale twilight.

It was one of those perfect Montana summer evenings.

He wanted to breathe it all in, to stop by the creek and watch stars come out in the awe-inspiring big sky. He wanted more than anything to not go around the next bend.

Instead, they were on the hunt for monsters, the worst kind, the kind who hurt children. Just knowing the man and woman who'd hurt Raine were so close by made him homicidal. He feared if he didn't get them first, they would get Raine.

As he drove around the bend in the road, he saw the house. Raine saw it, too. She let out a heartbreaking sound. This, he knew, was where her abductors had brought her sixteen years ago.

RAINE THOUGHT SHE WAS prepared. For so long the abduction had been buried deep enough that she really hadn't been able to remember anything. Parts of it had come back over the years.

But there were still holes in her memory, holes she wasn't so sure she shouldn't leave empty and dark.

Unfortunately, her instincts told her that the only way she'd be able to find Lara was if she remembered everything.

As the pickup's headlights swept over the abandoned old farmhouse, the past washed over her, taking her breath away, sending her heart hammering as she smelled the dank darkness, felt the aching cold, heard the sound of the door opening. And closing. She knew this house.

"Stop!"

Cordell hit the brakes as she threw open her door.

She heard him call to her to wait, but the house pulled her to it, metal to magnet. It was as if she no longer could hold back the nightmare. Sixteen years ago she'd believed she would die in this house.

Behind her, she heard Cordell running after her.

As she neared the house, she thought she tasted blood.

The cut lip. She'd forgotten about that, but not about the woman who'd smacked her and told her she'd better do everything the man told her if she knew what was good for her.

The door to the old place was partially open, a sliver of darkness gaping behind it.

Cordell caught up with her, shoved a flashlight into her hand. She looked over at him, grateful. He wasn't going to try to stop her. He knew nothing could, not even him.

He played the light over the front step with his flashlight, then into the dank musty interior. She turned hers on and moved up the creaking steps. Her fingers ached as she touched the door. It swung open with a creak that sent a blade of ice into her heart. A blast of cold, putrid air rushed out at her.

"Let me go in first," he whispered as he stepped past her.

The door yawned all the way open. The smell triggered thoughts and feelings and fears that made her pulse pound in her ears and legs weak beneath her. She clutched her gun in one hand, the flashlight in the other and told herself she could do this. She was the little girl who'd survived. She was Emily Frank.

She'd put off facing this all these years. Now she had no choice. The clue to where they'd find Lara English was here. Why else lead her here?

To kill you?

No, she thought as she followed Cordell inside the house. Taunt her, maybe. Terrify her, absolutely. But ultimately, the answer was here.

The house seemed full of whispers and skittering sounds, creaks and groans. One dark room after another appeared in the beam of their flashlights until she reached the stairs that dropped down into the partial basement.

"Hell, no," Cordell said beside her.

PEPPER WINCHESTER STOOD in the third-floor room in the dark. She didn't want to turn on the lights. This evening she wasn't up to reading what her children had scratched in the walls.

She'd been coming up here for weeks now. As some form of punishment for her sins? Or just because she had nowhere else to go?

In this room was where she'd let her husband, Call, send their children. It was small and always made her feel closed in. There was a window that faced out toward the ridge where her youngest son had been murdered.

She looked out it now, barely able to make out the ridge in the growing darkness. It came to her why, after so many years, she'd begun to frequent this horrible

reminder of her failure as a mother. It was also a reminder that one of her children had betrayed her in the
worst possible way.

One of her children had helped with the murder of
his—or her—youngest sibling. And to make matters
worse, she feared one of her own grandchildren had
witnessed it from this very room—and kept quiet all
these years.

A rustling sound startled her. Her hand went to her
throat before she realized it was only the party hats that
had ended up huddled in the far corner. There must be
a breeze coming up from the elevator shaft.

It was the party hats that had clued her into the fact
that her grandchildren had been in this room the day of
Trace's murder. Trace, her youngest, her most precious,
her favorite. He had died on that far ridge the day of his
birthday.

Pepper blamed herself, this house, this life, her long-
dead husband, Call. Trace's alleged killer was dead. But
in her heart she believed that her son's true killer remained free and unknown. At least for the time being.

At the sound of a car engine, she turned to see lights
coming up the narrow ranch road. Brand. She hadn't
seen her son for twenty-seven years, had yet to speak to
him since the day she'd sent him away and all the others
when Trace hadn't shown for his birthday party.

She knew her children had reason to hate her. She'd
taken away their birthright: Winchester Ranch.

But that was the least of what she'd deprived them of
over their lives.

In the last of the day's light, she fumbled for the elevator button. The door opened, she shoved aside the gate and stepped into an even smaller space. Heart pounding and her breath coming in gasps, she descended to the ground floor and hurriedly got out, her cane tapping on the wood floor.

She knew the kind of reception she would get from her son Brand. Like his son Cordell, he hated her, blamed her, wanted nothing to do with her.

Pepper had only one hope as she hurried to greet him. Out of her five children, she hoped Brand wasn't the one who'd betrayed his brother.

"I HAVE TO GO DOWN THERE," Raine said as she took a step down the stairs.

Cordell heard both pleading and determination in her tone. The message was clear: *Please don't try to stop me.* He doubted he could even if he tried.

He shone his flashlight into the cold damp darkness below the house and cringed. He wouldn't have kept a dog down there, let alone a child.

He'd done his best not to imagine where Lara English was being held. But seeing this partial basement, which in truth was nothing more than a crawl space, he could imagine the horrible place that little girl was in right now. Alone? Or were they with her?

He shuddered at the thought and followed on Raine's heels into the pit below.

She stopped suddenly, the beam of her flashlight flickering over a pile of old lumber. Raine played the light over the boards, then the wooden slats of the wall behind it. Cordell kept his flashlight pointed at his feet, trying to stay out of her way. He didn't doubt that this was something she needed to do. He couldn't imagine what thoughts and emotions were going through her head right now.

Suddenly she seemed to sway on her feet. He reached for her and saw in the ambient glow of their flashlights that her eyes were as vacant as this old house.

"Raine?" He couldn't help the fear that gripped him. *"Raine?"*

She didn't answer, but blinked and her face contorted in a mask of pain. Dear God, she was reliving what had happened to her down here.

"Raine!" He grabbed her arm and shook her. Her eyes fluttered and he watched as she fought her way to the surface, gasping for breath, a high keening sound coming from her lips.

He could see the memories trying to pull her back under, a riptide wanting to take her, drown her.

He dragged her into his arms, holding her, saying her name over and over. "Raine. Raine." But he feared she was Emily Frank again and there was no bringing her back.

A few moments later she surfaced and seemed surprised to find herself in his arms. "What happened?"

Cordell shook his head. He didn't have a clue.

She closed her eyes and for a moment, he thought he'd lost her again.

"I remember," she said in a hoarse whisper. "I wasn't

molested. Only because I fought back. Only because I would have preferred to die than let that man touch me again." Her eyes opened and he'd never been so relieved to see that sea of clear blue. "I bit him. Cordell, are you listening to me? I bit the man who abducted me. I bit his left hand so hard there is no way I didn't leave a scar."

He was too busy thinking how relieved he was that she was her old self again.

The realization of what she was saying finally sank in. A scar. It might be a way to identify the man. If they ever got that close to him.

Raine stepped toward the wall behind the small pile of old lumber. Her flashlight beam scoured the boards, then froze on a spot.

He stepped closer.

It had been sixteen years so the letters scratched in the wall were almost too faint to read. When he did make them out, he wished he hadn't. His insides seemed to liquefy and he knew he would remember those words until the day he died.

There carved in the wood was, *Emily Frank died here.*

Chapter Nine

Emily Frank's former foster family was just finishing dinner. The night breeze carried the scent of boiled chicken and root vegetables.

Cordell noticed that Raine seemed to hang back as they neared the large rambling farmhouse even though he doubted the couple would recognize her—not after sixteen years. Also she'd changed her appearance from the blonde little girl they would remember, having dyed her hair dark.

The only thing about her that was recognizable from the girl she'd been was her eyes. They were that incredible sky-blue, so clear they seemed infinite. He'd gotten lost in them enough to know just how unforgettable they were.

He could tell she was nervous about seeing her former foster parents again even though she'd spent only one night there. He knew she feared they might have been in on the abduction.

"The abduction was planned. It wasn't spur-of-the-moment," she'd told him on the way to town. "The couple who took me knew who I was. That means they'd known the Ambersons were getting a foster child."

"And not just any foster child," Cordell had said. "One who'd run away from the past two homes she'd been placed in."

Raine had looked over at him as if impressed that he was beginning to understand how this had gone down. Either that or she was wondering why it had taken him so long to figure things out.

"You all right?" he asked now. They'd parked down the road from the house, deciding to walk up the narrow lane that ended at the front door. Cordell had thought it would be easier on Raine.

The question seemed to jerk her out of her thoughts, her gaze going to the house's second story where a pink curtain billowed out the open window on the breeze.

"I was just wondering what makes people become foster parents," she said.

A love for children would have been his first guess— at least before he'd met Raine. A more cynical answer would be the money, though he couldn't imagine that foster parents were paid enough per child to make it worthwhile taking on children who often had problems—and were a problem.

"I would imagine there are some who are wonderful and feel they are called to do this," he said.

She nodded and gave him a wry smile. "I'd just like to know who called the Ambersons," she said under her breath.

As they neared, the screen door swung open and

a man stepped out onto the large porch. He smiled in greeting, squinting a little as he studied first Cordell and then Raine as if he thought he should know them. That was the thing about Whitehorse. Most everyone did know each other.

His eyes seemed to narrow before his gaze returned to Cordell.

"Good evening. Can I help you?" he asked. He had a deep, rich voice. His hands were large and callused and he looked strong and solid. A man who did physical labor, Cordell guessed.

"Abel Amberson?" The serious man was in his late fifties, graying at the temples, lines around his eyes and mouth more from being out in the sun than from laughing, Cordell thought.

Abel gave a slight nod, looking instantly wary.

"I'm Cordell Winchester. This is Raine Chandler. We're here about one of your former foster children."

The man arched a brow. "You aren't with Social Services."

"No. We're looking into the disappearance of Emily Frank," Cordell said.

"Emily?" he repeated, clearly taken aback.

"We hoped we could ask you some questions. I'm sure the local sheriff will be speaking with you as well about the latest abduction."

"Latest abduction?" asked a woman coming through the screen door. Grace Amberson was a small woman with a kind face and eyes. "Why would you be questioning *us*? She's not our foster child."

"No, but Emily Frank was," Raine said.

The woman's gaze swung to Raine and held there long enough Cordell thought she might have recognized her. "Emily wasn't abducted," Grace said. "She ran away."

"A child molester now serving time in prison confessed to taking Emily Frank," Cordell said.

Grace Amberson clasped both hands as she cried, "Emily wasn't taken by a child molester. What are these people talking about, Abel?" Her voice broke and tears welled in her eyes.

"The man's name is Orville Cline," Raine said. "Maybe you've heard of him."

Cordell knew she was watching for a reaction. She must have been disappointed.

"Who?" Abel asked. His wife showed no sign of recognition, either.

"Orville *Cline*. He confessed to abducting and killing Emily Frank."

"No, that's not possible," Grace cried, her voice filled with horror.

"Why don't you let me take care of this, Grace," her husband said quietly. Behind them a half-dozen children from about five to thirteen peered out from the screen. "Take the children in and give them some ice cream. I'll be in shortly."

"I'm sorry if we upset you," Raine said to Grace and smiled through the screen at the children. "Would you mind if I used your bathroom?"

Cordell could see that the woman wanted to say no but it wasn't in her nature.

"Of course." Grace held the door open behind her as Raine entered.

"I think you'd better show me some identification," Abel said the moment the women were gone. "You've upset my wife."

Cordell took his driver's license and P.I. license from his wallet and handed it to the man. "We're investigating the Emily Frank case for a client. Ms. Chandler and I are both private investigators."

Abel Amberson's eyes widened in surprise as he handed back the licenses. "This comes as a terrible shock. We were told she ran away."

"Who told you that?"

"Social Services and the sheriff at the time. She'd run away from two other foster homes. Was she really taken by this man?"

"According to him. His confession is very...detailed," Cordell said, putting his ID away and pocketing his wallet.

"Is that what they think happened to this other girl, Lara English?" Abel looked stricken. He glanced back toward his house as if worried about his family inside it. "Why hasn't someone warned us?"

Cordell shook his head. Probably because the local news media hadn't picked up on it. Emily Frank's abduction was one of a dozen crimes Orville had admitted to committing. Cordell wondered how many more the man had lied about.

The screen opened and Raine came out. She looked pale. "Ready?"

He nodded. "Well, thank you, Mr. Amberson, for your time." He held out his hand and Abel shook it. "If you think of anything that might help." Cordell handed him his business card. "My cell phone number is on the back."

As he and Raine walked down the narrow road to where they'd parked the pickup, Cordell could feel the tension coming off her like a live wire.

"Abel Amberson didn't have a scar on his left hand," he said once they were out of earshot.

"No, but I found something in the house," she said. "I was admiring the children's drawings tacked on the refrigerator when I saw an invitation to the Whitehorse Summer Gala. Apparently it is invitation only. That means only the cream of Whitehorse crop will be there tomorrow night."

Raine looked over at him as they reached the truck. "And care to guess who the guests of honor are this year? Abel and Ruth Amberson for their years of foster care. Do you think your grandmother can get us an invitation?"

FROM THE WINDOW, Pepper saw not just one son, but two climb from the car in front of the lodge. Both men were tall and handsome like their father.

Brand glanced toward the window where she stood and she braced herself. From his expression this was the last place on earth he wanted to be.

She shifted her gaze to her older son Worth, or Worthless, as Call had called him. It surprised her how old he looked. Both of her sons were in their fifties.

That was hard for her to accept, that, like her, they had aged. She remembered them as being strong and determined, wild as this land. She could see them riding across the ranch, young and free.

Guilt wedged itself into her heart as sharp and painful as a knife blade. What had she done to them? Turned them out, took away what they thought was their legacy: the Winchester Ranch.

Pepper straightened, setting her expression as she headed for the front door leaning more heavily than usual on her cane. Facing her sons would be harder than anything she'd ever done, she realized.

If only she was the cold, uncaring bitch they thought she was. It would make this so much easier.

As she reached the top of the stairs, she saw Virginia go to the door. She could tell by the set of her daughter's shoulders that she thought Brand and Worth were only here for the money, money she felt was owed to her.

Her old maid daughter, her oldest child and only girl, wore her bitterness like a shroud. That, too, Pepper thought, was her fault. Was it fear that made Virginia so greedy? Or did she really not care for anyone but herself?

Maybe she thought that with the Winchester fortune she wouldn't feel so alone. Of course, she was wrong. Her mother could attest to that.

At the door, Virginia gave her brothers awkward

hugs, then the three of them turned and looked up the stairs as if they'd sensed their mother watching them.

Pepper put steel in her back as she slowly descended the stairs. She could feel their gazes riveted on her, each of them wondering just how frail and close to death she was.

She kept her chin up. She wouldn't let them see the mountain of regret that lay on her chest, making it nearly impossible to draw a breath.

"Mother," Brand said.

"Brand," she said with a nod. "Worth." Her oldest son didn't meet her gaze. Up close he looked even older and in poor health. It broke her heart.

"Any news on Cyrus?" Pepper asked of her grandson.

"The same," Brand said, the pain evident in his expression. He glanced around the lodge. "The place hasn't changed." His gaze settled on her again. "Neither have you." He didn't make that sound like a good thing.

Enid appeared, giving them all a start and making Brand smile to himself.

"I suppose you want me to show them to their rooms," Enid said.

"I can do it." Virginia took hold of Brand's arm. "But maybe Enid could get them something to drink before dinner."

Enid shot Pepper a look that said she didn't take orders from Virginia especially with Virginia talking as if she wasn't even in the room.

"I think that is a wonderful idea, Virginia. I'll help

Enid and meet you all back down here in the parlor before dinner."

Enid turned on her heel and with a huff took off for the kitchen.

"She *really* hasn't changed," Brand said, sounding amused.

Virginia snorted. "I don't know why you haven't fired her a long time ago, Mother."

Pepper watched the housekeeper disappear down the hall. "Oh, I suspect Enid will die here."

Virginia led her brothers up the stairs and Pepper listened to the three of them whispering among themselves, joining ranks against the enemy. And she knew only too well who the enemy was.

CORDELL DIDN'T HAVE TO CALL his grandmother about tickets to the gala.

When Raine checked her cell phone as they left the Ambersons, there was a message from Marias that her CBA had sent her something.

Raine felt her stomach drop. "What now?"

"The message I got was that there will be two tickets for you at the door with your name on them for the Whitehorse Summer Gala. You've been invited to some exclusive party."

"What is it?" Cordell whispered, no doubt seeing Raine's expression.

"Apparently we're going to the dance," she said. "My benefactor left us tickets at the door. Anything else?" she asked Marias.

"Not that you want to hear," her friend and partner said. "I just keep wondering who's pulling your chain and why."

"Yeah. Me, too. Maybe they just want to see if I can dance."

Marias laughed. "Aren't they in for a thrill."

Raine hung up and looked over at Cordell. "What?" she asked, seeing his frown.

"At least if they're at the dance, then Lara is safe," he said.

She certainly hoped so. It felt as if time was running out. The last thing she wanted to be doing was going to some socialite dance in this wide spot in the road of a town while knowing Lara English was out there somewhere, scared and alone.

But she had to hold fast to her theory that the CBA wanted the truth to come out. As hard as it was for her to believe it was the same woman who'd kicked her over to the side of the floorboard as she'd gotten into the car sixteen years ago. The same woman who'd helped her husband abduct that terrified ten-year-old.

Suddenly a set of headlights flashed on. The next moment Raine heard the roar of an engine as what appeared to be a large truck ran right at them.

She saw Cordell swerve, the truck missing them by only inches as it sped past, and they crashed into the bushes at the edge of the road, breaking through and dropping down a small hill to come to an abrupt stop just feet from a narrow creek and in a stand of cottonwoods.

"Are you all right?" Cordell cried.

All she could do was nod. She was shaking all over after almost being run down for the second time in two days.

He turned to look back. She did the same, but she could see nothing but darkness. She could only think that she'd almost died on the road that she'd been abducted from so many years before. Was that how this was supposed to end? She was to die here sixteen years ago and had cheated the grim reaper—but only until now.

"That was no accident," Cordell said. "That means the driver of that truck knows that we went by the Ambersons. They must have tipped him off. Or whoever they called about Emily tipped the driver off. The Ambersons were upset. Of course they would call someone to see if it was true about her abduction by Orville Cline and tell the person that we'd been by."

Raine felt his gaze on her.

"Are you sure you're all right?"

She was trembling, still shaken by the near accident and that horrible feeling that this was where she was meant to die.

Cordell unhooked his seat belt, then reached over, unhooked hers and pulled her to him. The night was dark as a cloak around them. "It's going to be okay," he whispered against her hair.

Raine drew back and looked up at him. "You are such a terrible liar."

He smiled, eyes crinkling in the faint glow of the

dash lights, and suddenly it was as if they were the only two people left in the world. She leaned into him, wanting desperately to believe him. The night and the cottonwoods closed around the warm cab of the pickup like a cocoon.

She looked into his dark eyes and willed him to kiss her. She wanted to forget everything for just a while, to lose herself in this man's strong arms.

As if in answer, he lowered his mouth to hers. She snuggled against him, relishing the heat of his mouth, his body. He pulled her closer. Her body melded into his as he deepened the kiss. His tongue brushed over her lips, the corner of her mouth.

Her nipples hardened against the thin sheer fabric of her bra. She swore she could hear the quickened beat of his heart in sync with her own.

She encircled his neck as he trailed kisses along her jawbone and down the column of her throat. A shiver of naked desire moved through her. Raine could feel her pulse throb under his touch, a primitive beat like drums in her ears.

A moan escaped her lips as she felt his fingers unbutton her shirt. His mouth dipped to the tops of her breasts. She arched against him, felt his thumb flick over her aching-hard nipple. She bit her lip to keep from crying out as his mouth rooted out her naked breast from the sheer fabric of her bra.

The windows steamed over even on the warm summer night. Raine lost herself to the sound of their combined frenzied breathing, the rocking of the pickup, the feel of Cordell's body as he cradled her to him.

Her release came with a cry of pleasure that echoed through the cab, followed shortly by Cordell's own. They clung to each other, naked, breathing still ragged.

"I didn't mean for that to happen," Cordell said after a few minutes. "At least not in the pickup."

Raine kissed him. "I did," she said as she reached for strewn clothing.

Her cell phone rang as she was pulling on her jeans. "Hello," she said, still sounding winded.

"You all right?" Marias asked. "You sound funny."

"I'm fine." She glanced over at Cordell. "More than fine. What's up?"

A beat of silence that sent her heart off again, then Marias asking, "Then you haven't seen the news?"

"Have they found Lara English?" Raine asked, hope filling her.

"Orville Cline," Marias said. "He walked away from a work release prison program yesterday morning in Deer Lodge and hasn't been seen since."

Chapter Ten

Pepper Winchester studied each of her adult children as Enid served supper.

None of the three looked in the least bit happy to be here. So why were they here?

She could understand Brand coming. His son was in the hospital in a coma. But then if he was so miserable here at the ranch, then why not stay in a motel in town?

He could have easily come to Whitehorse without seeing her—or setting foot on the ranch.

"So has it changed that much from when you were last here?" she asked into the weighty silence.

All three seemed to be startled out of their thoughts.

"What?" Worth said. He was large like his father but without the extraordinary good looks that the other Winchester men had inherited.

"The ranch," she explained. "I was wondering if you'd missed it."

She saw Brand's jaw tense. He looked back down at

the food on his plate, his fork suspended over a piece of dried-out roast beef.

Pepper felt oddly sad to see that he had missed the ranch. The sting of being sent away all those years ago was still there in his expression.

They'd all been so vocal about getting away from the ranch and her, but they'd never left. She'd assumed they'd been waiting for their share of the infamous Winchester fortune.

Now she saw, in at least one case, she'd been wrong.

"You missed the ranch?" The question was directed at Brand.

He put down his fork, clearly refusing to look at her. His anger when he finally spoke was edged with disappointment.

"What do you expect, Mother? That we wouldn't miss this place?"

Not her, but the ranch.

She glanced at Virginia, who merely looked confused by the conversation, then shifted her gaze to Worth.

"What does this ranch mean to you?"

Virginia frowned. Worth opened his mouth, then closed it before looking across the table at his brother.

"We *were* the ranch," Brand said through gritted teeth. "It was us. We lived and breathed this place from the time we could sit a horse."

Pepper remembered all of them, Brand, Worth, Angus and even Virginia, working the ranch—and complaining about it. Back in those days even Enid and Alfred saddled up to help with branding and moving cattle.

"Don't you remember the cattle drives?" Brand asked, finally looking at her. "I thought you actually enjoyed them."

She had. She felt tears well in her eyes and turned her attention to her plate as she reminded herself that one of these people at this table—or even all three—might have been in on their youngest brother's murder.

ACTING SHERIFF MCCALL Winchester had her hands full. Everyone was out looking for Lara English. Fortunately it was June and the warm weather was holding. If Lara was just hiding somewhere, she should be fine.

And if she wasn't… That was what had McCall worried, especially after she'd been advised that Orville Cline had escaped. The child molester had confessed to abducting and killing a ten-year-old girl just outside of Whitehorse sixteen years before.

McCall would have been about the same age as Emily when the girl was taken. So why hadn't she heard about it?

She made copies of Orville Cline's mug shot and called in the deputies and leaders of the volunteers on the search parties.

"Pass this around," she'd told her deputies when she'd given them photos of Orville Cline. "Make sure everyone is on the lookout for him."

The girl's disappearance had made her cancel dinner at her grandmother's as well as her talk with Raine

Chandler. It bothered her that Raine had apparently let both McCall's cousin and grandmother believe she was a reporter.

What that might have to do with Cyrus's attack she had no idea. Maybe nothing. Maybe it had been as cut-and-dried as Cordell believed. Or not.

Suspicion came with the job, McCall thought as she nodded for the deputy to send in another of the children. She'd commandeered a room in the large farmhouse where the children lived with their foster mother. The foster father was a long-haul truck driver and on the road.

McCall had wanted to talk to each of the children. She had a feeling that one of them might know more than they told their foster mother.

A moment later, a skinny boy who looked to be about twelve came in. The first thing she noticed was how nervous he appeared. According to her list, his name was Clarence.

"So what is it you'd like to tell me, Clarence?" she said, smiling.

He started to say something, but she stopped him.

"I know you saw something. Don't worry, it's just between you and me and you'll feel better if you tell me. You liked Lara, didn't you?"

He nodded and swallowed, before choking out the words, "It was the bogeyman. He took her."

McCall leaned back. "The bogeyman?"

He nodded excitedly. "I saw him when we were play-ing hide-and-seek."

"What did he look like?" she asked casually.

"He was really big. I'd seen him in the trees before."

"You say he was big? Fat or tall?"

"Tall and big and strong."

"What color was his hair?"

Clarence shook his head. "He always had his hood up."

"Did you see his eyes? Were they dark or light?"

He shook his head. "I didn't get that close because he saw me. If he finds out I told—"

"He won't. I promise. Did you happen to see what he was driving?"

The boy looked confused. "He wasn't drivin' nothin'. He was hiding in the trees."

"He must have had a vehicle, though, right? Maybe parked over behind the hotel."

Clarence frowned and looked down. When he raised his gaze, she saw that he'd thought of something. "I guess that old brown van could have been his."

McCall felt her heart beat a little faster. "Did you see it last night when you and Lara and the other kids were playing hide-and-seek?"

"I was the only one who saw it when it hit that guy." The moment he'd let the words out, she could tell he wanted to snatch them and stuff them back into his mouth. "I wasn't supposed to say anything about that."

"Who told you not to say anything?" McCall asked, though she could guess.

He looked toward the door.

"I'm sure your mother had a reason for telling you to keep it to yourself," she added.

"She didn't want no one knowin' we were outside playing that time of the night," Clarence said.

Understandable. So he'd seen the van being driven by the bogeyman hit Cyrus Winchester.

"And you didn't see Lara after that?" she asked.

He shook his head. "She probably ran away after seeing the bogeyman hit that guy."

McCall figured that was exactly what his mother had thought, as well.

She showed the boy Orville Cline's mug shot, but he only shook his head. Even though he couldn't identify Cline as the bogeyman, she had a bad feeling Orville was already in town.

"THERE ISN'T ANYTHING ELSE we can do tonight," Cordell said as he shifted the pickup into four-wheel drive and drove down the creek to a spot where he could get back on the road above them.

Raine knew he was right. She was sure that the person who'd just run them off the road was more concerned with them than Lara. If Lara survived tonight she should be safe until after the Whitehorse Summer Gala tomorrow night.

Unless, of course, you added Orville Cline into the mix.

She told herself that something was going on between him and the couple who'd abducted her sixteen years ago.

Raine could only hope it was a falling out and not some kind of deal.

But as Cordell said, there was nothing she could do about it tonight. Who knew where Lara might be hidden. With all the old abandoned farmhouses and sheds around she could be anywhere.

All Raine could do was pray that Lara was still all right. She had to believe that whoever had gotten here would finally make contact tomorrow night at the dance.

They drove over to the hospital to visit his brother. Cyrus's condition hadn't changed. Raine could see the toll this was taking on Cordell and wished there was something she could do. Finding the person who'd done this was the only thing she could do. Tomorrow night at the dance, she promised herself. Someone would contact her. She had to believe that.

"Are you all right?" she asked Cordell as they left the hospital.

"Every hour, every day, that he doesn't wake up…" He took off his Stetson and raked a hand through his hair. "I keep telling myself that Cyrus is strong and no one has more determination. If anyone can come back from this it's him."

Raine took his hand as they walked out to his brother's pickup.

"Let's get something to eat. No way am I going

back out to the ranch. Want to take our chances at a motel?"

She nodded and squeezed his hand. They needed each other. She didn't kid herself that their lovemaking earlier had been anything more than that. But they had made love, tenderly and sweetly, and just the thought of being in his arms again warded off the chill of their circumstances for a while.

Cordell pulled into the drive-thru at the Dairy Queen and ordered them dinner, then drove to a motel on Highway 2. They ate sitting in the middle of the bed, eating and talking about anything but what was going on right now.

He told her about growing up on ranches, moving from one ranch to another as the jobs changed with his father and brother. Raine told him about growing up in North Dakota, fishing with her adopted father.

They watched the late news. Nothing new about Lara. Also no sign of Orville Cline, but law enforcement officers across the state were looking for him.

They showered together, then made love, lying afterward spent in each other's arms, and fell asleep comforting each other.

CORDELL WOKE TO FIND the bed beside him empty. He sat up with a start. Raine stood silhouetted against the open curtains of the window. Star and moonlight glittered around her.

He could see that she was hugging herself, staring

out at the night. He could well imagine her thoughts. Lara was never far from his.

Rising from the bed, he stepped up behind her to wrap his arms around her and look out into the night. She leaned back into him with a sigh and he felt the intimacy of this moment more strongly than even their lovemaking.

She turned in his arms to look up at him. "I don't know what I would have done without you and if it hadn't been for your brother…"

He kissed her gently.

"Do you believe in fate?"

Cordell smiled at that. She sounded like his brother. Even under the circumstances, Cyrus would have believed this was meant to happen. Cordell couldn't accept that. "I don't know why this has happened but I'm glad that you're safe."

She smiled and closed the curtains, letting him lead her back to bed. They lay side by side, both staring up at the ceiling.

"Who was she, the woman who hurt you?" Raine asked, turning to lean on an elbow to study him in the dim light of the motel room.

"Who said…" His voice trailed off as he met her gaze. "My ex-wife."

Raine nodded. "She broke your heart."

He smiled at that. "Let's just say she made me gun-shy when it comes to trusting women."

"I've noticed." She pushed a lock of his hair back from his forehead. "How long has it been?"

"Four years."

She let out a low whistle. "She really must have done a number on you."

He nodded and dragged his gaze away. "She wasn't who I thought she was."

Raine lay back again to look up at the ceiling. "Neither am I."

"You're Raine Chandler," he said, pushing himself up on an elbow to gaze into her wonderful face. "One of the strongest, most determined women I've ever met."

She smiled at that. "I don't feel very strong right now."

"You came back here even though you had to have suspected it was a trap," he said.

"As corny as it sounds, I wanted closure. I thought if I could get justice, as well, then…" She shook her head. "Now I couldn't quit if I wanted to."

No, and neither could he.

"What will you do when we find the person who hit your brother?" she asked, looking concerned.

Cordell shook his head. "If you're asking me if I will want to kill him, hell, yes. Will I? No."

"It will be enough for you to just turn him over to the sheriff?" she asked, surprised.

"It will have to be. I don't take the law into my own hands."

She said nothing.

"Raine? Is there something you're planning to do that I should know about?"

She met his gaze. "What if I was planning to kill the person responsible for Emily Frank's abduction?"

"I wouldn't blame you if you wanted to."

"But you wouldn't try to stop me."

He studied her for a long while before he said, "No."

She looped her arms around his neck and pulled him down to her. The kiss was filled with passion and heat. He felt the fire catch flame inside him. This time their lovemaking was fierce.

They weren't so different, the two of them, Cordell thought later as they lay spent in each other's arms. Both of them were afraid to trust, especially when it came to the opposite sex. And both of them wanted justice but could easily take vengeance.

He feared that after tomorrow night there would be no going back for either of them.

Chapter Eleven

The next evening Cordell looked up and saw Raine standing at the top of the stairs at the ranch lodge. His breath rushed out of him. She was beautiful. The gown his grandmother had given her fit like a glove, running over her curves like flowing water.

She hesitated, looking shy. But as their eyes met, she smiled and came down the stairs to take his outstretched hand.

"Wow," he said as he closed her hand in his. Something was changing between them. He could feel himself falling for this woman and it scared the hell out of him. With a start, he noticed she was wearing a tiny silver horse pin—the same one she'd been wearing the day she was abducted.

"You look beautiful," his grandmother said to Raine. She looked older and Cordell had picked up on the tension on the ranch with his father and aunt and uncle under the same roof.

"And you look very handsome," she said to him and reached out to touch his cheek. It was the most loving she'd ever been to him and it surprised him. "You look lovely together."

Raine looked away as if embarrassed. Or maybe, like him, for a moment she'd forgotten why they were dressed like this.

Cordell hoped her embarrassment wasn't because they weren't really together, not a couple, no matter how much Enid and his grandmother suspected they were. This was about catching monsters. He didn't doubt that Raine would hightail it back to California once it was over.

They didn't say much on the ride into town. For Cordell, the gravity of this evening had set in. Raine seemed lost in her own thoughts.

The moon came up, a huge golden orb that climbed up over the horizon into a vast sky studded with glittering stars. A warm breeze sighed among the leaves of the trees along the street as they parked outside the large old school where the dance was being held.

"You're sure about this?" he asked her as he cut the engine. Silence fell over them, the warm summer night making the inside of the pickup cab intimate. Cordell wanted to hang on to this moment, sitting here with Raine. It felt like a high-school date, both of them nervous and expectant. And for a moment he could pretend that was all this was.

DINNER COULD HAVE been much worse, Pepper Winchester thought halfway through the meal, although she couldn't imagine how.

The food was Enid's usual tasteless fare, Virginia hit the wine hard right away and her sons were more morose than ever.

She was counting down the minutes, hoping to put this meal and this night behind her when Brand tossed down his napkin before dessert was served and demanded, "What is it you want from us, Mother?"

"I don't want any—"

"She thinks one of us is responsible for Trace's death," Virginia spat out, sloshing her glass of wine as she put it down. "And she thinks one of her grandchildren saw the whole thing from the third-floor room."

That definitely answered the question of whether or not Virginia had done some eavesdropping of her own, Pepper thought.

"Well?" Brand demanded. "Is that true?"

There seemed no reason to deny it.

"You think one of us *killed* our own brother?" Brand was on his feet now, his face twisted in anger. "Have you lost your mind?"

Enid appeared then in her usual fashion—sneaking up on them. "Does this mean you won't be having dessert?"

"I'll have dessert," Virginia said, refilling her wineglass.

Pepper waved Enid back into the kitchen. "I have reason to believe that someone in this household conspired with the killer to have Trace murdered within sight of the lodge, yes."

"Someone in this household?" Worth asked.

"Don't you mean someone in the family?" Brand snapped.

"I suspect it was a member of this family because if I'm right, one of my grandchildren saw the murder—and covered for that person."

Brand was shaking his head. "So that's what this invitation back to the ranch was about." His rueful smile broke her heart. "I should have known. But for a moment there, I thought maybe, just maybe, you had changed. That you regretted what you did all those years ago. That you wanted to make amends. Or at least bring your family together to say goodbye."

His gaze bored into her and she felt his disappointment in her like a knife to the heart.

"Brand—"

"Don't, Mother. You want to know who killed your beloved son? You did. If one of us conspired with a killer to get rid of Trace, then you have only yourself to blame for pitting us against him." With that he stormed out of the dining room.

In the silence that dropped like a wet blanket over them, Enid appeared with a chocolate cake. She set it down in front of Virginia, along with a knife. Before Enid could turn to leave, Virginia picked up the knife and looked at the only other brother left at the table.

"Worth, are you going to have some cake with me?" Virginia asked. "It has to be better than dinner was."

"Sure," Worth said, his gaze going to his mother's.

Pepper felt a chill snake up her spine at the look in her son's eyes. As Virginia cut the cake, she watched her, realizing that either of these two could have been behind Trace's death.

But then they weren't the only ones at the table who were capable of murder, she thought as Virginia handed her a piece of cake.

"Who says you can't have your cake and eat it, too?" Virginia said with a laugh. "Isn't that right, Mother?"

THIS WAS IT, RAINE THOUGHT as Cordell parked the pickup. She could feel it. "They'll be here tonight," she said as she watched a group of laughing couples enter the building for the Whitehorse Summer Gala.

Music escaped as the front door of the school opened and died just as quickly as the huge doors closed.

She hoped this wasn't a mistake. All those people inside the school, all the noise... How would they find her? Or her find them.

But in her heart, she believed she would recognize the couple when she saw them. And if all else failed, recognize their voices. Some things she remembered only too well.

Still she felt torn, feeling they should be out looking for Lara instead, even though she knew their chances were next to impossible of finding the girl without help.

She met Cordell's dark gaze. What a gorgeous man both inside and out. She'd come to trust him, trust him with her life—and her secrets. That said more for his character than his good looks.

At his gentle, caring expression, she felt her heart kick up a beat.

"Raine, I just want to say—"

"I know," she said quickly, afraid of what he was going to say. They'd grown close too quickly. She didn't trust the feelings she had for him and certainly wouldn't trust his for her right now. This was too emotional for both of them. Maybe when this was over...

Raine refused to let her thoughts go there. "Let's do this."

He nodded, though looking disappointed she hadn't let him say what was on his mind, and reached for his door handle.

Outside the pickup, the warm summer breeze caressed her skin. She looked up at the stars in the midnight-blue canopy overhead and breathed it in, memorizing all of it. The feel of the breeze, the smell of summer, the awareness of the man beside her, knowing this could be the last time.

Cordell took her hand and squeezed it as they started up the steps and Raine took one more look at the summer night—a night made for lovers—before he opened the door and they slipped inside.

As they walked in, Raine felt as if everyone turned to look at them. Cordell pulled her closer, his hand warm on her waist, as they worked slowly through the crowd gathered around the dance floor.

She took strength in his touch and tried to relax. The couple who'd abducted her were in this room. She could feel it more strongly than ever.

Groups of people stood around talking, drinking and eating the food that had been laid out along several tables. The school gymnasium was decorated as if for a prom with glittering lights and a dark blue backdrop.

The voices, laughter and music blended together in a din. How would she ever be able to distinguish any one voice?

Fear seized her. This had been a fool's errand. She and Cordell should be out looking for Lara—not here at a dance.

As if seeing her panic, Cordell whispered next to her ear, "If they're here, they aren't with Lara."

She nodded. Lara was safe. At least until the dance was over.

They worked their way around the large room, picking up bits of conversations, looking for one couple, listening for a voice she recognized. After they'd made the loop twice, Cordell asked with a slight bow, "May I have this dance?"

Raine took his hand and let him lead her onto the dance floor. The band was playing a slow song. She laid her head on his shoulder and pretended they were merely a man and a woman dancing on a warm summer night.

But being in Cordell's arms sent her senses soaring. She loved the smell of him, the feel of him, and when he danced them into a dim corner, the taste of him as he kissed her.

He pulled back to look in her face. His gaze caressed her face, then settled on her lips an instant before he lowered his mouth to hers again. She melted into his embrace, into the kiss, and then he was dancing her back into the crowd, holding her closer as if they really were lovers.

Raine closed her eyes, wishing they had grown up in this town, been high-school sweethearts who'd settled on the ranch and went every year to the Whitehorse Summer Gala dance.

But instead she'd been abducted on the edge of this town and Cordell had been exiled from the ranch and his brother Cyrus now lay in a coma because of what had happened all those years before.

Earlier, she'd heard Cordell on the phone with the hospital. His twin's condition hadn't changed. She reminded herself that he was only helping her to get the people who'd injured his brother and find Lara and save her from these monsters.

But it was good to remind herself what they were doing here tonight and not let desire or emotion make this more than it was.

"Are you all right?" he asked, looking worried. "If you're right, the person will contact you."

She smiled and nodded. The song ended. "I'm going to find the ladies' room." She started to step away, but he grabbed her hand.

"Hurry back."

Her smile broadened as she saw the concern in his expression. She nodded and he released her, but she could feel his gaze on her as she wound through the crowd and away from him.

She studied the faces she passed. How different her life would have been if she'd known these people all her life. If she and Cordell really had been high-school sweethearts and there wasn't a child molester about to kill a little girl if they didn't find her.

Suddenly she was blinded by regret and rage, disappointment and determination. Life had not been kind to her and yet she'd survived it all. She'd never thought about being happy. She'd just been glad to be alive, not to be hungry, to have a roof over her head and a job.

She'd asked little of life.

But tonight she yearned for more. She wanted Cordell. She wanted happily ever after. And yet she feared that wasn't the destiny that awaited her and hadn't from the moment that car pulled up beside her sixteen years ago.

The music drifted on the air, growing fainter as she finally found a ladies' restroom deep in the building without a line. This one was empty. Her heels echoed on the tile as she rushed to the sink.

Turning on the cold water, she cupped it in her hands and splashed it on her face to wash away the hot angry tears that flowed down her cheeks.

Her heart ached at the memory of being in Cordell's arms on the dance floor, the way he'd looked at her when she'd come out in the dress, that amazing kiss and the look in his eyes just moments ago—

She grabbed one of the cloth towels and began to dry her face. Her makeup was ruined, her eyes red and swollen, and she could practically hear the clock with Lara's name on it, ticking down the minutes.

She knew what had her so upset and felt guilty for it. All her thoughts should be with Lara. But she was falling for Cordell Winchester. Last night in the pickup and again in the motel, it had been about lust and comfort and the need not to be alone with their thoughts and fears.

Tonight, though, in his arms on the dance floor… She couldn't bear the feelings he'd evoked in her. And she'd seen something in his gaze—

At the sound of the bathroom door swinging open she hurriedly rushed to the end stall.

The voices of two women melded together as they came through the restroom door. Faint music swept in with them, then the door closed and everything grew quiet.

Raine leaned against the stall wall, her face feeling hot. She was tired, completely drained, both emotionally and mentally. She knew she couldn't trust her emotions and had to pull herself together.

She'd hoped by now that one of them would have made contact. She had to believe that her theory was right—even though by all appearances the person had only gotten her back here to kill her.

No, she told herself. It was the man who'd taken Lara and tried to run Raine down. Just like tonight with that huge truck that had run them off the road. It was the man. The woman had to be the one who Marias called

CBA and she would contact her. Why else leave tickets for the dance at the door for her and Cordell?

But as she stood, her back against the stall wall, she felt as if this was hopeless. She would go back out there and mill until it was over and pray that she spotted the couple. After that…

She didn't have a clue what to do after that. A stall door down the line creaked open, then closed and locked.

"I can't believe what Nancy Harper is wearing," the woman in a far stall said.

"Ghastly," the other woman said from somewhere over by the long row of sinks. She sounded as if she was standing at the mirrors no doubt checking her makeup.

The woman flushed the toilet, the door unlocking and opening. Raine heard the woman's heels on the tile floor as she joined the other woman.

Neither seemed to realize Raine was in the last stall at the end of the long line. She thought about flushing the toilet and letting them know they'd been caught gossiping and might have, if the woman at the mirror hadn't spoken again.

"Do you think you can talk Frank into coming over for a drink after the dance?"

Raine froze at the sound of the woman's voice.

"It's going to be awfully late."

"I know but I picked up a bottle of wine I think you and Frank will like."

"Honey, is everything all right with you and Bill?"

"Of course." She laughed, a laugh that sent a blade of ice up Raine's spine. "It's just that he'll be tired and I'll be all wound up and not wanting the night to end."

"Well, I can ask Frank…" Their voices started to trail off.

Raine could barely hear the other woman's reply her heart was pounding so hard. The woman's voice, the one who'd stayed by the sinks. That was her! That was the voice of the woman who'd helped abduct her sixteen years ago.

CORDELL HAD WATCHED RAINE head for a ladies' restroom in the far recesses of the building. Now he felt anxious as he waited for her to reappear. The crowd kept obstructing his view of the hallway just enough to set his nerves on edge.

For a while with Raine in his arms on the dance floor, he'd forgotten that someone had made certain that she was here tonight by seeing that they got an invitation. But he hadn't noticed anyone taking any particular interest in either of them.

Oh, there were always a few men who couldn't help but notice Raine. But he hadn't seen anyone watching them and no one had made contact.

He was beginning to wonder if all of this wasn't just a way to torment Raine. The dance was almost over. If this woman, the one Raine's friend Marias called CBA, had gone to all this trouble to get Raine to Whitehorse and to this dance, then what was she waiting for? Had the woman lost her nerve?

As his cell phone vibrated in his pocket, Cordell began to move in the direction Raine had gone. He pulled out his phone and checked caller ID.

He was jostled by the crowd and forced to step outside one of the open doors. Standing on a small landing in the darkness, he snapped open his phone.

"How did you get this number?" he asked, still watching the hallway Raine had disappeared down.

A woman's chuckle. "Didn't Raine tell you? I'm amazing." Marias quickly turned serious. "I've left a dozen messages on her cell. This couldn't wait."

Cordell felt his blood run cold as he listened. "What did you just say?"

RAINE QUICKLY BENT DOWN and looked under the stalls. She saw two pairs of women's high heels. A pair of bright red strappy sandals and a pair of classic black high heels.

She didn't know which ones belonged to CBA. As the outer door closed, Raine quickly stepped from the stall and hurried after them.

Several more women were coming in as she reached the door and she had to wait as they passed before she could exit. By then, the two women had dissolved into the crowd.

She looked around frantically for Cordell, then at the array of shoes on the dance floor. She'd never find the woman before the dance ended and all she had was a name: Bill. There must be dozens of Bills in this town.

Raine moved along the edge of the crowd as quickly

as she could, searching for Cordell and the woman with the strappy red heels. There were too many black heels on the floor. She'd never find that woman.

As she passed an open door, she felt the cool summer night air beyond the darkness and wondered if Cordell had stepped out for some fresh air.

"Raine."

At the sound of her name, she turned back to step out into the dark. She blinked, trying to get her eyes to adjust, and saw no one. Had she just imagined someone calling her name?

She turned to look back into the huge glittering room. That was when she saw Cordell across the dance floor. He'd just stepped in from outside. He appeared to be searching for her, his cell phone to his ear. But it was his expression that turned her blood to ice.

There was a sound like the scrape of a shoe sole on the concrete behind her as she started to go back inside hoping she could reach Cordell before she lost him again in the crowd.

She was grabbed from behind. The cloth clamped over her mouth brought it all back. She was ten again on a dirt road in a strange place and terrified of what was about to happen to her. Only this time, she knew.

CORDELL DIDN'T THINK he'd heard Marias correctly over the music and the din.

"Orville Cline was sighted yesterday—just miles from Whitehorse. Do I have to tell you where he's headed?"

Cordell stepped back into the gym and began to push his way through the crowd in the direction Raine had gone. "You think he's the one who got Raine up here."

"Don't you?"

"He couldn't have done it alone. The van that tried to run her over, the tickets for this dance, the map. Raine is positive it's the woman—"

"Don't you get it? Raine needs to believe that. I'm catching the next plane out of here—"

"No, she needs you there in case she gets any more messages and there is nothing you can do here," Cordell said as he hurried down the hallway, the restroom door in sight. "I'll have Raine call you."

He reached the door, slammed it open. Several women at the sinks jumped, startled by his abrupt entrance—and the fact that a man had just burst into the women's restroom.

"Raine?" No answer. *"Raine?"* He bent to check under the stalls. Only one pair of heels, the wrong ones.

He turned and rushed out, his gaze frantically searching the crowd. No Raine. Cordell told himself not to panic. She was here somewhere. The dance had begun to thin out as the band wound down for the last song.

Raine, where the hell are you?

He bumped into a man, registering the man's conversation as he did.

"Don't be ridiculous, Adele," the man was saying.

Cordell's gaze went to the woman as he mumbled, "Excuse me," to the man. The man had backed her into a corner. She had tears in her eyes, her lipstick was smudged as if he'd just kissed her hard on the mouth.

The crowd didn't move and for a moment Cordell was unable to move, either. Next to him the man took the drink the woman was holding. "Are you trying to get me drunk, Adele?" He tilted his face toward her, moving in closer, dropping his voice as he gripped her jaw in his large hand. "Do you really think that will keep me home tonight?"

Cordell heard the anger in the man's words and saw fear in the woman's face—or was that open defiance? The crowd moved but Cordell stood rooted to the floor. What had stopped him cold was the hand gripping the woman's jaw—and the scar on the man's hand.

The bite mark was a perfect child-size half moon.

Chapter Twelve

"When was the last time you saw her?" Sheriff McCall Winchester asked.

Cordell rubbed a hand over his face. "No more than thirty minutes ago. I called you as soon as I found her pin out on the steps by one of the open doors."

They were sitting across from the school and had been watching everyone who came out of the building. No sign of Raine.

McCall picked up the tiny silver plated horse pin. "You think she dropped this on purpose?"

He nodded. "I knew the moment I saw it on the outside step glittering in the moonlight."

The sheriff eyed him. "Sorry, what is the significance of the pin?"

"She was wearing it when she was abducted here sixteen years ago."

"*Abducted?*" McCall sighed. "I think you'd better start at the beginning." She listened, taking notes only when necessary, as he told her about Emily Frank.

It was only after he'd finished that she demanded to

know why he hadn't come to her the moment he'd heard about Lara English being abducted.

"Raine said he would kill Lara if we did."

"Raine?" So that was the way it was, McCall thought, hearing the way he said the woman's name revealed just how involved his cousin was with her.

"But you called me now."

He gave her a tortured look. "I didn't know what else to do, especially since Orville Cline has escaped."

McCall nodded. "So we don't know who has Lara or Raine."

"But I do know who took Raine sixteen years ago." He told her about the bite scar. "I followed him to his car and got his license plate number." He handed her the gala napkin he'd written it down on. "I would have followed him and his wife home but I had to find Raine."

"And when you didn't, you found the pin and called me." She looked at the local license plate number. It wouldn't take long to run it. "You realize a scar on the man's hand isn't enough proof to arrest him."

"No, you need Raine to identify him. That's why we have to be careful. If Raine is right and his wife is the one who got her here…"

"What are you suggesting?"

"If this man took Lara English, then he will lead us to her."

"Us?" McCall said.

"I know you don't have the law enforcement officers to watch his house 24/7."

It was true.

"But I'm going to be watching him. I'll let you know the moment he makes a move."

McCall chewed on her cheek for a moment. "If you saw the man with the bite scar after Raine vanished…"

"He could have hidden her somewhere and returned to the dance. Or Orville might have her."

McCall didn't like the sound of that. "But why take Raine?"

"She was the only one who got away," Cordell said.

"I suppose it could be that simple." She ran the plate number and felt her pulse take off like a wild stallion.

The name Bill and Adele Beaumont came up on the screen.

"Do you know them?" Cordell asked, glancing over at the screen.

"Yeah," McCall said. "They own half the town."

"Raine said they would be above suspicion."

"So far the only thing you have against them is that they were at the dance tonight, they are prominent citizens and Bill has a scar which could be from a human bite—but may not be," McCall said.

"I also know that he's rough with his wife," Cordell said. "What about matching the bite scar with Raine's teeth prints? I realize she isn't ten anymore but I thought bite marks were like fingerprints, no two exactly alike?"

"Even if the crime lab could match Raine's bite with that of the marks on Bill Beaumont's scar, that doesn't prove that he abducted her. It would be hard to even prove that Raine is Emily Frank."

Cordell groaned. Clearly, he hadn't thought of that. "There has to be something we can do. Raine said the man who took Lara will keep her alive until tonight. If he thinks the sheriff is suspicious of him…"

McCall had to agree. Moving on Bill Beaumont if he was guilty would only cause him to get rid of the girl and Raine—if he had them both and if he hadn't already killed them.

"Okay, I'll put you on surveillance on the Beaumonts," McCall said, realizing she had little choice. She couldn't trust that if she used one of her deputies, it might get leaked to the Beaumonts. No one in this town would believe Bill was a child molester. Everyone would be ready to protect the local family against some weird-dressed California private investigator here stirring up things—and even more so against a Winchester.

"But the minute anyone makes a move, you call me. Don't you go playing Lone Ranger on me, cuz," she said.

"You got it." He reached for the door handle. "Raine's tough. She's gotten through a lot."

McCall nodded but knew he was just trying to convince himself because the fool had fallen in love with the woman and he couldn't bear the thought of her being with some sick monster. McCall couldn't, either.

If Cordell was right and Bill Beaumont had abducted Raine again, then he couldn't have taken her far. After she left her cousin, she began to search the area around the school, looking for an old house or shed, somewhere he could stash her.

If whoever grabbed her had seen that she got tickets to the gala, then he would have made prior arrangements.

AS McCALL DROVE AROUND the area behind the school, she called her mother. "What do you know about Bill and Adele Beaumont?"

Most people when asked something like that would respond, "Why do you ask?"

Not Ruby. Her trade was gossip, she served it up with every order she delivered at the diner. It made up for the bad tips days.

She heard her mother take a long drag on her cigarette, turn down the television as she exhaled and ask, "Beaumont? Are they squabblin' again? I'm not surprised."

"Why do you say that?" McCall asked.

"You ever meet Bill, talk to him for two seconds, and you can see what a chauvinist he is. He's a jackass or worse."

"Worse?"

Ruby sighed. "Look how he treats Adele."

McCall pictured the slight petite woman. Every time she'd seen her, Adele was dressed to the T and made up as if she lived in a metropolitan area instead of White-horse, Montana.

"He doesn't seem to treat her too badly from what

I've seen," McCall said, thinking of the big new SUV Adele was driving.

"He has his thumb firmly on that woman. He says jump. She says, 'How high?'"

"Are you saying she's abused?"

"Depends on what you call abused. She lives in the nicest house in these parts, wears the best clothes money can buy, drives the nicest car, everyone in town treats her like she's royalty."

"And this is bad how?"

"I'll bet you this week's paycheck that once the two of them are alone inside that big house of theirs things are a whole lot different."

"What are you getting at?" McCall asked.

"Just a feeling I have," her mother said, usually not this noncommittal. "Let me tell you this. There are a handful of men who run this town. They all have coffee in the diner mornings, sit at the same table, even sit in the same chairs. Sometimes another man or two will join them. No one ever sits in Bill Beaumont's chair."

"Bill and Adele never had any kids," McCall remarked. "He would seem like a man who would want to leave his genes behind."

"They couldn't have any," Ruby said. "Her fault," she added before McCall could ask. "I heard he almost left her over it."

McCall shuddered. If Cordell was right, this could explain in some warped sick way why Adele went along with Bill's horrible "hobby."

"They could have adopted," McCall said.

"Bill? Are you serious? Why are you so curious about the Beaumonts?"

"I thought I saw them squabblin' outside the dance tonight." It wasn't exactly a lie. Cordell had seen them, even overheard them.

"He'll never leave her and he'll never let her leave him," Ruby said with authority. "He'd have to give her half his money. But I'll bet he makes her pay dearly for what she gets out of this marriage."

CORDELL SAT PARKED down the street under a large weeping willow tree and watched Bill Beaumont's house.

He and his wife, Adele, hadn't come home alone. Another couple had followed them from the dance and were now inside.

He could see the lights through the sheer drapes, catch glimpses of people moving around inside the house. He glanced at his watch anxiously.

Raine had been gone now for almost two hours. He wouldn't let himself think about what could have happened to her in that length of time.

She was smart and capable and stronger than any woman he'd ever met. He had to believe that she was all right and would survive this, just as she'd survived being a foster child and her abduction at ten.

His cell phone rang, startling him out of his thoughts. He checked the caller ID. Marias.

"I told you I would call you when I heard something," he said into the phone.

"Another message just came through from the CBA." Marias took a breath and let it out. In that breath he heard her anger—and her fear. "This one, though, is for you. It says, 'Unless you want to end up like your brother and your girlfriend, back off. This has nothing to do with you.'"

"Like hell," Cordell said under his breath and hung up.

Just after 2:00 a.m., the couple who'd been visiting the Beaumont house walked out to their car. They appeared to be arguing, their voices carrying on the cool night air.

Cordell whirred down his window.

"I'm telling you she didn't want to be left alone with him," the woman said.

"It's two in the damned morning, Theresa. You want to go back in there and babysit her, fine, but I'm going home and going to bed."

The woman looked toward the house, clearly conflicted. "She's afraid of him."

The man scoffed as he opened his car door. "Yeah, Bill's a real scary guy," he said sarcastically.

The woman seemed to make up her mind. She opened her car door, glanced back at the house once more, then joined her husband, closing the door behind her.

Brake lights flashed, the engine turned over. Inside the house someone moved behind the sheer drapes as the couple drove away down the street.

Cordell glanced at his watch again twenty minutes later. The dial glowed. He could feel the minutes ticking by. What if he was wrong? What if the real monster was with Raine right now?

There were two vehicles parked in front of the Beaumont home. A pickup and a large SUV. When the porch light snapped off, Cordell felt his heart drop. Was it possible Bill Beaumont wasn't going anywhere tonight?

He couldn't bear the thought of Raine in some horrible place any longer. He started to open his door, not sure what he planned to do, but he was going up to that house and if he had to, he would beat the truth out of Bill Beaumont.

Through a crack in the drapes he could see movement. Someone was pacing back and forth and appeared to be having a heated argument.

He eased his door open and climbed out. Working his way through the shadowed darkness of the trees, he neared the house. He could hear muted voices, the man's more strident, the woman's meek.

Along the side of the house, he found an open window and eased it open wider. He could hear snatches of the argument.

Bill was worked up, yelling at his wife, who seemed to be trying to console him.

Cordell was about to go in the window when he realized everything had gone silent.

At the sound of the front door opening and slamming shut, he rushed to the edge of the house. Bill was climbing into his pickup truck. An instant later, the engine turned over and Bill threw the truck into Reverse and roared out of the yard, the tires spitting gravel.

Cordell waited a moment to make sure he wasn't seen before sprinting to his brother's pickup and following.

For the first time all night, he felt hope that he might actually find Raine before it was too late.

Out of the corner of his eye, he saw the drapes part on the front window of the Beaumont house. He had only an impression of a woman watching him as he drove off.

"SEE IF YOU CAN FIND any connection between Bill Beaumont and Orville Cline," McCall said into the phone.

"The child molester in Montana State Prison?"

"There have to be phone records or even visits." Would Beaumont be so stupid as to visit Orville Cline in prison?

McCall hung up and glanced at the clock. She hadn't heard from Cordell and could only assume that Bill hadn't left his house.

She'd known Bill since she was a kid. He was one of those do-gooders, as her mother Ruby called him.

"A terrible tipper though," her mother had always been quick to point out. "He and his cronies come in to the café, drink gallons of coffee for hours and leave a measly tip for one cup of coffee. His wife is worse. You'd think they were headed for the poor farm the way they pinch pennies. That's the rich for you."

Ruby Bates Winchester measured everyone in town by how generous they were with her at the diner. McCall wondered if it didn't have more to do with the service they got from her mother than how tight they were with their money.

For a moment, she thought about her mother and how much she'd changed since she started dating Red Harper. McCall had never seen her mother truly happy before and now that she was, it was a beautiful thing. She hoped it lasted.

Her mother had taken the news about her husband Trace Winchester's murder twenty-seven years ago in her stride. At least on the surface.

But McCall had happened to see her mother at the cemetery one evening just before dark. Ruby was sitting beside the huge ornate tombstone Trace's mother, Pepper, had insisted on. But Ruby had won the battle about where her husband and the father of her daughter would be buried.

"I want him in town so I can visit him," she'd told Pepper on one of the few occasions the two women actually spoke to each other.

Pepper had wanted Trace buried in the family plot on the ranch. It was one of the few times her grandmother have given in.

McCall had been touched by Pepper's generosity in letting Ruby have this small victory, especially since Pepper had tried so hard when Trace was alive to split them up.

McCall told herself that was all water under the bridge. Her father was dead and buried. Any doubts she had about who had killed him, she'd tried to bury with her father.

That evening, though, when she'd seen her mother sitting on Trace's grave in the cemetery, McCall had stopped and watched Ruby gently touching the gravestone, talking to the husband she'd lost when she was pregnant with McCall.

Maybe they would all find peace, she'd thought that night. Someday.

It was one reason she'd agreed to have her wedding with Luke at Winchester Ranch. Even with the animosity between her mother and grandmother. She hoped the two could call a truce—at least until the wedding and reception were over.

McCall had reluctantly accepted her grandmother's generous offer to host the wedding at Winchester Ranch on Christmas. She knew Ruby was excited about finally setting foot on the ranch after all these years.

McCall just hoped the wedding went off without any bloodshed. With the Winchesters, you just never knew.

Her phone rang. She picked it up thinking it would be Cordell with an update on what was or wasn't happening at the Beaumont house. She feared letting him run surveillance might be a mistake.

But the call was from one of her deputies letting her know that they hadn't found Lara English and were calling it a night. They'd begin again in the morning.

"Thanks, Nick. Please thank the volunteers and make sure everyone gets home safely." McCall had spent hours earlier as part of the search party and knew how emotionally draining it could be when you might be looking for a body instead of a little girl.

Unable to wait any longer, McCall called Cordell's cell. The phone rang four times before going to voice mail.

She frowned and hung up, her anxiety growing. She waited a few minutes and tried the number again. Still no answer.

Grabbing her hat and keys, she headed for her patrol SUV.

Chapter Thirteen

McCall drove by the Beaumont house and didn't see Cordell's pickup anywhere on the street—nor any sign of him. Didn't mean that he wasn't still watching the house, she told herself.

Before driving over here, she'd gone out to her cabin on the Milk River and changed into dark jeans, boots, a dark long-sleeved T-shirt. She'd left the patrol SUV and took her pickup instead.

Now she parked and walked down the deserted street watching for any sign of her cousin. As she neared the Beaumont house she caught a glimpse of Adele through the sheer drapes at the front window.

Like McCall, she'd changed her clothing since the dance and now wore jeans and a shirt. She seemed to be pacing. McCall slowed at the edge of the yard and stepped into the shadows of the trees that lined the property as Adele suddenly froze, then hurriedly picked up her cell phone. She glanced at caller ID, then took the call.

McCall moved closer, never taking her eyes off the

woman. Adele looked upset and Bill's pickup wasn't in the driveway. Could be in the garage.

Peeking in the garage, McCall found it empty. No Bill. No Cordell. She didn't even have to venture a guess where Cordell had gone. Wherever Bill had headed. She silently cursed him for not following her orders.

As she moved away from the garage, she saw that Adele was still on the phone. But if the woman had been upset before the call, now she seemed to be in a panic. She moved one way then another, appearing frantic as if looking for something.

McCall saw her snatch up her purse from where she must have dropped it earlier and, snapping the phone shut, headed for the door.

Ducking back into the shrubbery and trees, the sheriff stayed hidden as Adele, wearing a black jean jacket, got into her car and backed out. The headlights flashed over McCall, then darkness closed in again.

As she hurried to her truck, McCall wondered where Adele was headed this time of night and what had her so upset. Who had been on the phone? Bill? And if so, where was Cordell?

CORDELL HAD KNOWN that tailing anyone in a town this small was tough. At this time of the night with no traffic at all, and Bill Beaumont looking for a tail, it was nearly impossible.

His heart was racing at the thought that the man driving the truck in front of him was about to take him straight to Lara English and Raine.

But where was Orville Cline? He and Beaumont had to be in this together.

He thought about the fight he'd overheard between the Beaumonts. By her tone, Cordell knew Adele had been pleading with her husband, but Cordell hadn't been close enough to hear what she was saying. But earlier Bill had accused her of trying to keep him home tonight.

Apparently Adele Beaumont had lost the argument since her husband had left the house.

Cordell drove up a few blocks and pulled over, cutting his lights as Beaumont continued down the main drag, then turned right through the underpass. From where he'd pulled over, Cordell could see the street on the other side of the underpass. Beaumont turned left.

Cordell went after him, through the underpass and up onto Highway 2. He saw no sign of taillights. He should have been able to see him, Beaumont didn't have that much of a lead. Cordell swore. Maybe he'd taken a right on Highway 191 and was headed for Canada.

But as he pulled out, he saw Beaumont's pickup parked in an empty dirt lot at the turnoff. He appeared to be on his cell phone.

Cordell drove past and pulled into the open-all-night Westside gas station. He got out, and watching Beaumont across the road, paid with his credit card and filled up his tank. Beaumont got off the phone. A few minutes after 3:00 a.m., a car came up the highway. The driver slowed, glancing over at Beaumont. As the car headed north, Beaumont fell in behind it.

Heart in his throat, Cordell climbed back into the pickup. His hands were shaking. He'd only gotten a glimpse of the man in the car—but it had been more than enough to know that the driver was Orville Cline.

Orville was now leading Bill Beaumont north out of Whitehorse.

McCALL GOT THE FIRST CALL just after she turned off the road. Keeping Adele Beaumont's SUV taillights in her view, she slowed and picked up. "Winchester."

"I'm following Beaumont north," Cordell said without preamble. "He just picked up Orville Cline."

McCall didn't waste her breath giving him hell for not calling her sooner. "Stay on them, but don't make a move against them. I mean it, Cordell. You call it in when they stop. Got that?"

She waited for a reply but realized she'd already lost him. She cursed under her breath. Adele wasn't headed north but south out of town. McCall had hoped that Raine and Lara were being held together. Now that didn't look as if it was the case.

Ahead Adele was turning off onto a side road. McCall followed slowly, not about to use her headlights or brakes and cause Adele to know she was being followed. The moon was bright enough that she could see the road well.

McCall knew this area south of town. There was an old farmhouse down in a hollow, the same hollow Adele's big SUV had just dropped into. She drove only a little farther up the road and pulled off far enough that her pickup couldn't be seen from the road.

When her cell vibrated again, she jumped and realized how tense she was. Everything about this had her on edge. Three civilians lives were at risk. Her first thought was to call in the troops, but she immediately changed her mind. She couldn't be sure who was waiting in that farmhouse and what they would do if backed into a corner.

She was on her own, she thought as she took the call.

"I got the warden up at the prison out of bed," Deputy Shane Corbett said. "He said to tell you that you are on his mud list for getting him up at this hour."

"I can live with that. What did you find out?"

"He had the information handy since every law enforcement officer in the northwest is looking for Orville Cline right now. He'd already checked on Cline's visitors, especially recent ones. Bill Beaumont wasn't one of them."

McCall had been hoping for a connection. Right now she had nothing against the Beaumonts except a scar and a suspicion—both flimsy at best.

"But Cline did have another visitor two days before he escaped," Shane was saying. "The two got into an argument and the visitor was asked to leave."

The sheriff couldn't hide her shock as Shane told her the name of the prisoner's visitor.

"Adele Beaumont visited Cline?"

"She was supposedly there to deliver some books as part of an inmate reading program Cline was involved in."

A cover. Her heart was beating so hard she could barely make out Shane's next words.

"Orville Cline was worked up good after that. The warden said he didn't think too much about it when he was told about the encounter. Now though…"

"Yeah," McCall said as she continued to follow the faint glow of taillights into no-man's-land. "I might need some backup. I'm going after Adele Beaumont right now. We're about fifteen miles south of town on Alkali Creek Road."

She heard Shane let out a breath.

"The Beaumonts may be involved in the abduction of Lara English," she told the deputy. "It's a long story, but one of their alleged victims got away sixteen years ago. She's back in town but has disappeared. Better call Luke and bring in the rest of the deputies. My cousin Cordell was watching the Beaumont house earlier tonight and is now following Bill Beaumont and Orville Cline. They are headed north out of town."

Shane swore under his breath. "Is there anyone who's not missing?"

"Don't do anything until I call," she said, afraid that if they all went in like gangbusters, it would jeopardize both Lara's and Raine's lives. "Just be ready."

"You got it," Shane said.

McCall checked her gun, grabbed another clip and

her shotgun, before stepping out into the summer night to begin walking across country toward the old Terringer place.

CORDELL SAW THE TWO VEHICLES in the distance turn off the highway onto a side dirt road that led back toward the Milk River.

He noted the way they slowed and knew they were waiting to see if the car they'd spotted behind them slowed, as well. He kept going, driving past, keeping his speed up. He could see them waiting and had to drive another five miles up the highway before the road turned and his taillights disappeared from view.

Hitting the brakes, he pulled over. For the past five miles, he'd been looking for other side roads that headed down to the river. There was one about two miles back. It wasn't ideal. He couldn't be sure it would take him in the direction he needed to go, but he could be sure that Cline and Beaumont would be watching the road they'd taken.

Turning out his headlights, he flipped a U-turn in the road and headed back to where he'd seen the other road. In the distance, he couldn't see any lights from the two vehicles and assumed they'd driven down into the river bottom. There must be some kind of old building down there. They sure as heck weren't going fishing at this time of the morning.

He had to believe that the two would lead him to Raine and Lara.

Taking the side road, he drove down until the dirt

track ended at the river and he saw that it was nothing more than a fishing access. He parked and checked his gun, then got another clip out of the glove box, before he sprinted south along a game trail that ran parallel to the river in the direction Cline and Beaumont had gone. Even in the moonlight it was hard to run along the uneven path.

But Cordell could feel the minutes slipping away. He had to get there in time.

LARA PULLED THE OLD blanket around her not sure what had awakened her. When she'd heard the door open, her only thought had been food. But she was also cold. Maybe the woman was bringing her dress back after washing it for her.

She reminded herself to thank the woman and not make her angry. But she was so tired and cold and hungry that it was hard to concentrate. She just hoped whoever was coming would bring her food and something to drink.

Too late Lara had realized she shouldn't have eaten all the food they brought the last time or drunk all the water. It had been hours now that her stomach had ached for something to eat.

Lara felt a gush of cold air as someone entered the room she was in. She shivered and sank deeper into the blanket wrapped around her.

As badly as she wanted food and water, she was filled with dread at seeing the people who had taken her again. She'd tried not to think about why they were keeping her here or what they wanted. But after all this time, she couldn't help but worry.

She caught the scent of perfume and the single beam of a flashlight, her dread deepening as she realized the woman had come alone. The woman set something down. A moment later the room was filled with light.

The lock scratched open and the door of the box swung out. Lara closed her eyes against the glare of the light, huddling in the blanket, shivering from more than the cold as she sensed the woman standing over her simply staring down at her.

"Little girl," the woman finally snapped. "Your new mommy is here."

Lara swallowed the lump in her throat and parted the blanket to peer up at her. Her new mommy?

The blanket was suddenly jerked away. Lara cowered, afraid the woman was going to hit her. Instead, all she did was stare at her for a long time before she said, "Stand up."

Lara did as she was told even though her legs threatened to fold on her. Weak and cold, she stood shivering, hugging herself.

"Put your arms down," the woman snapped.

She did. Then the woman did something that surprised her. She reached out and brushed a lock of her hair back from Lara's face.

Lara looked up at her expectantly. Maybe the woman wasn't going to hurt her. But she didn't seem to have brought her anything, either, no food, no water, nothing to wear, and she'd thrown the blanket in the corner of the rotting floor of the old house as if she no longer needed it.

For just an instant, there was something almost kind in the woman's eyes. Or was it regret?

"I'm hungry," Lara said and instantly wished she hadn't. She felt her heart begin to pound under her skinny chest as she saw the woman's expression change.

"You're just like all the others, aren't you? No matter what we do for you, it's just never quite enough."

"I'm not hungry," Lara said quickly. "I'm not."

The woman shook her head as she reached into the pocket of her jacket and drew out a knife.

"You're a bad girl. A very bad girl. Mommy is going to have to punish you."

Chapter Fourteen

"She's still alive?" The voice if not the words sent a cold blade of terror through Raine. It was the man who'd abducted her sixteen years before. She would never forget that voice.

"I'm not trying to do your dirty work for you again. The deal was I get her for you and you get me what I want. What you do with her is your business. I've done my part."

"You're sure it's her?" asked the man whose voice she recognized.

"I got her to town for you. If you don't believe it's her, have a look for yourself. But don't be questioning if I know what I'm doing, all right?"

"Sorry, Orville."

Raine froze as the beam of a flashlight flickered over the box she was in. She'd gotten the tape off but now left a piece loosely wrapped over her bare ankles. She hoped it would appear she was still bound, but she couldn't see her ankles well enough to know if it worked or not. She put her hands behind her and wrapped the tape as best she could on her wrists.

Raine had no plan, just a determination to survive. She thought of Cordell as she heard what sounded like a bolt being slid back on the top of the box. Earlier tonight Cordell had tried to tell her how he felt about her but she'd stopped him. She silently cursed herself for doing that. Now she might never hear those words.

The door swung open with a loud groan. She blinked as the light fell over her. Two men stood in the glow of the ambient light from the flashlight. One was tall, thin, his face angular and narrow giving her the impression of a fox. Orville Cline. She recognized him from his mug shot.

The other was handsome, square-shouldered, blue-eyed with a head of thick black hair. It was no wonder he'd gotten away with this for so long. Who would ever suspect a man who looked like that?

Sheer terror filled her. She'd told herself all these years that she didn't remember what either of her abductors had looked like. Their faces had been lost in the other memories, the ones she'd refused to let surface.

But the memory came back in a rush. It felt as if she'd been kicked in the stomach. She remembered him.

"Emily?" He stepped closer.

It took every ounce of her self-control to remain still as he knelt down beside her and, holding the flashlight in one hand, grabbed her jaw between his fingers to force her to look into his eyes.

She cringed, remembering his hands on her. Her mind went numb. She lay there unable to move, hardly able to breathe.

His eyes searched hers and then he laughed and let go of her. "Oh, yeah, you're Emily. My sweet Emily."

Anger stirred in her. Raine felt her heart begin to pound wildly as rage raced through her veins hot as lava. He was still kneeling in front of her, this horrible man. Last time he'd touched her, she'd been only a child, defenseless. But she would no longer be his victim. She felt her hands fist behind her. The past seemed to shed from her like snakeskin.

He rose as if seeing something in her gaze that warned him.

But he didn't know she was no longer bound. All she had to do was kick out at his ankles. She could be on her feet in an instant. She'd spent years studying martial arts for just this moment.

"Come on," Orville Cline said behind him. "I gave you what you wanted. Now you give me mine, Billy Boy. Take me to mine and then you can come back to your sweet Emily," Orville Cline said mockingly.

"I'm not going to tell you again that my name is Bill."

"Whatever you say, Billy Boy," Orville said, amusement in his voice.

Raine realized with a jolt what Bill-Billy-Boy had done. He'd made a deal with Orville and that deal was Lara English. She'd been wrong. She'd thought for sure it was the woman who'd gotten her here. Now she saw her error.

But where was the woman?

Realization came with a flash.

The woman was with Lara.

Raine knew that if she attacked the man now, she would be jeopardizing Lara's life. As furious as she was, she knew she could take him and would stand a decent chance of taking Orville Cline, as well.

But what if the woman was waiting for a call from Billy Boy?

Common sense won out over her fury. She lay perfectly still as he slammed the lid on the box and turned to leave.

He'd forgotten to slide the bolt!

Raine held her breath, praying he wouldn't remember as the beam of his flashlight headed for the stairs, Cline following him. She listened to their heavy tread on the stairs, then start across the floor upstairs.

She couldn't stand it a moment longer. As quietly as possible, she lifted the lid of the box and, stripping off the ripped tape from her wrists and ankles, she got to her feet in the pitch blackness. She felt dizzy and her legs were weak from being in such a cramped position for so long.

She realized it would have been folly to have tried to attack him. A mistake that would have gotten her killed—if she was lucky. She hated to think what he had planned for her.

Carefully she stepped out of the box into the pitch blackness. She recalled where the door to the room was and moved cautiously toward it. Beyond that was the bottom of the stairs. She was halfway up the stairs when she heard the sound of footsteps coming back across the floor toward the top of the stairs.

One of them was coming back.

LARA WONDERED WHAT THE woman was going to do with the knife. She stared at the shiny blade in the glow of the flashlight beam, hypnotized.

A whisper of a sound behind her new mommy with the knife made her look toward the darkness. She caught movement and for just a moment she thought it was the man.

All hope that he'd brought her food and something to drink evaporated as she saw that it was another woman and the only thing she had in her hand was a gun. The second woman put her finger to her lips for Lara to be quiet.

Lara was always quiet. She brought her focus back to the knife. Her new mommy had a grip on her wrist, her nails biting into her flesh, but Lara didn't cry out. She bit back on the pain the same way she did the fear.

Her stomach growled and her throat was so dry she could barely swallow. She felt dizzy and weak and just standing took all her energy.

Lara saw that the other woman was dressed in a uniform. The woman again touched her fingers to her lips and Lara nodded and felt tears fill her eyes. She wondered if she should tell her new mommy.

As if sensing something wrong, her new mommy looked up at her. "Don't you dare start blubbering."

Lara hurriedly shook her head and made a swipe at her tears with her dirty hand.

But the tears wouldn't stop. It was as if a dam had broken. Her body began to tremble, then shudder with the sobs.

"I told you—"

The slap came as no surprise to Lara. It rang out in the empty house like a gunshot as she tried desperately to quit crying, knowing that what was coming next would be much worse.

CORDELL SAW THE FLICKER of light through one of the glassless windows of the old house ahead. He slowed to catch his breath and scope out the scene.

There was a car and a pickup parked outside. As far as he could tell that meant that only Bill Beaumont and Orville Cline were inside the house.

Beside the car, he caught a small flash of light, then something glowed for a moment in the darkness. The smell of cigarette smoke drifted on the night breeze. Orville Cline leaned against the side of the car waiting.

Cordell moved cautiously around the other side of the house, the side by the river. No light now shone in the house. Had Bill come back out? Nearing the corner of the building, he peered around it.

Orville was still smoking over by his car. No one else was in sight. That had to mean Bill was still inside the house. With Raine and Lara?

Cordell backtracked to the first large glassless window opening and hoisted himself up onto the sill.

He knew he would be a perfect target against the moon-lit night and quickly lowered himself to the floor as soundlessly as possible.

The worn floorboards creaked under his weight as he took a step, then another as his eyes adjusted to the darkness inside the old abandoned house. As he moved deeper into the house, he saw light coming up from a stairway that led down to what must have been a partial basement.

That was where Raine and Lara had to be. The thought sent a shaft of fear through him as there was no sound coming from down there except for the heavy tread on the stairs.

Weapon ready, he moved toward the stair opening.

The board under his boot heel creaked loudly and he froze as a male voice yelled up from below, "I told you to wait. I just need to take care of something and then we'll go."

A sound outside, then the flicker of a flashlight beam as it headed this way. Cordell had a split second to make the decision whether to fire, kill Orville and then take care of Bill Beaumont in the basement.

He couldn't risk what Beaumont would do to Lara and Raine before he could get to them. He ducked around the corner into a small room as Orville Cline entered the house.

IN THE GLOW OF LANTERN LIGHT, McCall edged up behind Adele Beaumont. She was so filled with disgust that her heart was pounding. Lara huddled in the corner of the dirt floor, a filthy hand covering the red cheek that Adele had slapped.

Adele seemed to be alone. McCall made sure before she stepped closer. That was when she noticed the knife in the other woman's hand.

The girl had seen her and burst into tears no doubt with relief.

Just the sight of the girl huddled there naked, shivering from cold and fear, broke McCall's heart. She'd known Adele and Bill Beaumont, not well, but had seen them around for years. How could they do something like this?

She had never felt such fury. It was all she could do not to rush at the woman. She wanted to hurt her like she'd hurt Lara.

Timing it, McCall shoved the barrel of the pistol into Adele's back and knocked the knife out of the woman's hand.

"You touch that child again and I will blow your brains out," McCall said through gritted teeth.

She felt Adele freeze, then begin to cry. "I was trying to save her. I—"

McCall started to call in her location when Adele made a lunge for the knife.

She swung the gun, catching Adele across the side of the face. She howled as she fell over onto the dirt.

"Are you crazy?" Adele screamed. "I was trying to rescue—"

"Get up and take off your jacket."

"What?" Anger flared in Adele's gaze.

"Take off your jacket and give it to the girl. Now!"

Adele shoved herself up into a sitting position, glaring angrily. "I will sue the sheriff's department for everything it's worth. You have no idea what you've done. Your career is over. I will destroy you."

"Shut up." McCall snatched the jacket from Adele's fingers and tossed it to Lara. "Put that on, sweetie. Everything is going to be all right now."

"Where are this child's clothes?" she demanded of Adele, the weapon aimed at her heart.

"You're making a huge mistake, Sheriff," Adele said with venom. "You will live to regret this."

McCall looked down at her and felt her finger caress the trigger of the pistol. Why waste taxpayers' money with a trial or letting this woman live for years in prison or a mental hospital? What if Adele pulled strings, hired the best lawyer money could buy and got out one day to do this again?

She glanced over at Lara, who'd pulled on the jacket. "It's going to be all right." McCall smiled over at the girl, keeping an eye on Adele, the gun pointed at the woman's heart.

Lara took a shuddering breath and nodded, not looking all that sure.

McCall eased her finger off the trigger. It was the hardest thing she'd ever had to do. And she again started to make the call for backup.

Adele came flying at her with a piece of broken chair leg McCall now remembered seeing nearby. The blow knocked the gun from McCall's hand. It skittered across the dirt floor out of her reach.

Adele hit her again, knocking her to the floor. McCall got an arm up to ward off the next blow, but Adele was relentless. As McCall lunged for her gun, she saw Adele scoop up the knife from the floor.

McCall snatched up her weapon and swung around but too late. Adele had Lara and was holding the knife to her throat.

"Drop the gun, *Sheriff,* or you know what I'll do to this precious little girl, don't you?"

IN THE DARKNESS, Raine backed down the stairs as quickly as possible as a flashlight beam played on the steps above her. She'd just reached the bottom when she heard Bill stop, turn back and yell at Orville.

Like Bill, she'd heard the other set of footfalls on the wooden floor overhead. She'd hoped that it was Orville being impatient enough that Bill wouldn't come back down. Why was he anyway?

"What the hell is wrong with you?" It was Orville. She heard him come storming into the house.

Her mind raced. The other footfalls couldn't have been him then.

Bill had stopped at the top of the stairs. "I told you to wait out by the car."

"What do you think I was doing? Then I hear you yelling…"

Raine backed up, stumbled into something that teetered and threatened to topple over. She spun around and grabbed for a small wooden crate that someone had stood on end. She could barely make it out in what little light spilled down from the stairs from Bill's flashlight.

But as her hand closed on it and she heard the footsteps lumbering the rest of the way down the stairs, she hefted it up and pressed her back to the wall. There wasn't time to close the lid on the box, which meant that within just a few seconds Bill would shine his flashlight beam into the box and realize she was gone.

Not gone. Since there was no way she'd had time to leave this room. Which meant—

The flashlight beam flicked over the box.

"What the hell?!" Bill cried.

Behind him, Orville said, "What is it?"

Raine stepped around the edge of the wall and swung the crate with all her strength.

The sound of the wood splintering as it connected with her abductor's face couldn't drown out his scream. It surprised her that she took no pleasure in the sound.

His flashlight fell to the floor, the light cutting a swath through the empty room toward the far wall. As he reached for her, Raine kicked out at him, catching him in the knee.

He slammed into the wall next to him as the knee gave way.

But before she could strike again, she saw the gun and heard the click as he snapped off the safety and aimed the barrel at her heart.

"I should have killed you sixteen years ago."

CORDELL MOVED FAST. He had no idea what was happening down in the basement, but something was definitely happening.

He came up behind Orville Cline swiftly and jammed the gun into his back. "Downstairs," he ordered, forcing Orville ahead of him.

The basement was a partial one just as Cordell had thought. The ceiling was low, the air dank, the space dark and claustrophobic. He'd feared that the moment they reached the basement, Bill Beaumont would see them.

But Cordell couldn't take the chance that Beaumont would hurt Raine and Lara if he waited. He kept the gun in Orville Cline's back as he quickly assessed the situation.

No Lara. And Beaumont was holding a gun on Raine.

"Got a problem here," Orville said.

"Well, I'm about to end this problem," Beaumont said.

"I wouldn't do that," Cordell said.

Beaumont swung around in surprise, leading with the barrel of his gun. He got off a shot before Raine attacked him. That shot caught Orville Cline in the chest. He let out a grunt and started to fall forward.

Cordell shoved him out of the way, Orville crashed through an open doorway and into a coffinlike box, as Cordell scrambled to get to Raine. Raine and Beaumont were on the floor, fighting over Beaumont's gun.

Just as Cordell grabbed for the gun, Beaumont pulled

the trigger. Fire shot through Cordell's arm. Then he was knocked back, his gun wrested from him, and Beaumont had an arm locked around Raine's throat and the gun pointed at Cordell's head.

"Emily and I are leaving," Beaumont said, sounding winded. "If you follow us, I will kill her."

Cordell looked into Raine's eyes. One of them had started to swell where Beaumont must have hit her.

"Do as he says," Raine said. "I'll be all right." She was looking at his bleeding arm with concern.

"Listen to her. Emily was always the smart one," Beaumont said. "The only one who got away."

Cordell watched him drag Raine up the stairs, the gun to her temple. He didn't dare try to stop Beaumont.

Just as Beaumont reached the top, he swung the gun barrel away from Raine's temple and fired back down the stairs. Cordell dove, but not fast enough.

BILL MADE RAINE DRIVE, all the time holding the gun on her. She'd known when he hadn't killed her the moment they stepped out of the old house that he was taking her to where he'd hidden Lara.

She thought she would die at just the thought of Cordell lying, bleeding in that basement. She'd called his name as she was being dragged out of the house, the gun again to her head, but Cordell hadn't answered.

He's not dead. She would know if he was, she would feel it.

Of course, he hadn't answered when she'd called

his name because Bill might have gone back to finish him off.

Think of Lara. Once Lara was safe…

As she drove down to the highway and, following his instructions, turned onto it, Bill pulled out his cell phone. She could hear the phone ringing. Once, twice, three times before it was finally answered.

"I need you to meet me. You know where." He swore. "You're what?" He swore again and barked into the phone, "Damn it, Adele. Don't do anything until I get there. We're on our way." He snapped the phone shut and glared over at her. "This is all your fault."

Did he really believe that? Apparently so. She wanted to argue the fact, but she feared he'd lose his temper and kill her beside the road. He'd already gotten in a few punches. She could feel her left eye threatening to swell shut and her ribs hurt where he'd gotten her with an elbow.

Bill looked worse than she did, she thought. His face was scratched and bleeding when the slats of the crate had connected with it. His nose looked broken. He kept wiping it with his sleeve, glaring at her since it must have hurt.

Raine drove down the deserted highway, trying to focus only on saving Lara and getting back to that house by the river. *Hang in, Cordell.* It was the wee hours of the morning and there didn't seem to be another soul alive in the entire world.

As she drove, though, Raine memorized the way so she could return as soon as Lara was safe.

But Bill's phone call troubled her. The woman he'd called Adele was obviously with Lara—just as Raine had suspected. So why had Bill been surprised by that?

Because if Cordell hadn't shown up when he did, Bill would be taking Orville Cline to Lara now. Adele wasn't supposed to be there. Was it possible she had gone there to free the girl?

"So is Adele your wife?" she asked.

He didn't answer for a moment and she was thinking of asking another question when he said, "Thirty-six years of marital bliss."

Raine shot him a look to see if he was serious. She must have looked surprise to find that he seemed to be because he demanded, "What?"

"I just thought you must not be happy in your marriage if you have to steal little girls and—"

"I don't molest them," he snapped. "What do you think I am?"

She thought he really didn't want to go there. She checked her words. "Then I guess I don't understand why you—"

"No, you don't understand. I love children. I only take the ones who need me." He swore, seeing that she still wasn't getting it. "I wanted children but Adele couldn't have any. I didn't want someone else's child so adoption was out of the question."

"So you pick up children to satisfy your temporary need for a child." Raine couldn't believe what a sick bastard he was.

"You make it sound dirty," he snapped. "But it's not.

I'm good to them. I show them probably the only love they get. It's not my fault that it is only for a short time. They become demanding after a while. They no longer appreciate what I've done for them. They want to go home." His tone had turned nasty.

Raine stole a look and saw that he'd become angry. She didn't dare open her mouth for fear of what she might say.

He glanced behind them as he had several times since they'd hit the highway and mumbled that he should have made sure that bastard was dead or at least disabled the car Orville Cline had stolen.

Raine hadn't dared look back. But from Bill's satisfied expression she knew there were no headlights behind them. That, however, didn't mean that Cordell wasn't alive and following them at this very moment with his headlights turned off.

She prayed that was the case because she needed it to be so. She needed to believe that Cordell was all right— because once they reached wherever Lara English was being kept, Raine knew she was going to need all the help she could get.

Chapter Fifteen

From the floor, the sheriff stared for a moment at the woman holding the knife to Lara English's throat. There was a wild, inhuman look in Adele's eyes that glowed in the lantern light.

McCall slowly dropped her gun.

Adele smiled. "Now don't get up. Just kick the gun over here."

She did as she was ordered and kicked the gun over to Adele. McCall had left her shotgun outside against the door. She hadn't wanted to scare Lara. She looked at the little girl. She seemed calm again. Earlier she'd cried when it looked as if she might be saved. Now she seemed to know better.

"Lara, sweetheart," Adele said as the pistol came to a stop at her feet. "I'm going to put you down. I want you to hand the gun to Mommy. But be really careful."

"Yes, Mommy," Lara said in a robotic voice that tore out McCall's heart—the same thing she wanted to do to Adele Beaumont.

Lara knelt down slowly, the blade pressing against

her small throat, and picked up the pistol. "Here, Mommy."

"Thank you, sweetheart. You are such a good girl," Adele said, as she took the gun in her left hand. She made the exchange from the knife to the gun too quickly for McCall to do anything more than watch. The gun was now pointed at the back of Lara's head.

Lara gave a small brave smile.

"Now," Adele said, holding Lara's arm and the gun to the child's head, "the first thing we are going to do is walk over and take the sheriff's pretty handcuffs. Don't move, Sheriff. You don't want this poor child to die, do you?"

McCall pulled out her handcuffs and handed them to Lara.

"Snap one on the sheriff's wrist. That a girl. Now let me." Adele grabbed the handcuffs, letting go of Lara just long enough to snap the other end of the cuffs to a pipe protruding from the wall.

"Now we're going to walk out to the car and Mommy is going to take you someplace nice for dinner. Are you hungry?"

Lara nodded enthusiastically.

"That's my girl."

The exchange turned McCall's stomach. She couldn't stand the thought of Adele leaving with that child. "Adele, don't do this."

Lara looked concerned again. The prospect of food was too much for her and McCall wondered how long it had been since she'd eaten.

"Do what? Sheriff, I'm a hero. I found Lara and now I'm taking her back to town for a hero's welcome. I tried to tell you that's what I was doing, but you wouldn't listen."

McCall felt sick to her stomach. But as long as Lara was safe.

Adele's smile could have ripped flesh. "In fact, I think I might tell everyone that I caught you here with the little girl. You were about to do something horrible to her. If I hadn't stopped you…"

"No one will believe that."

"Of course they will. I'm Adele Beaumont. Do I look like a woman who would hurt a defenseless child?" She backed toward the front door, still holding the gun to Lara's head. "And by the time I get this child back to town, I know Lara will back up my story. Won't you, Lara. Didn't Mommy come to save you?" The girl nodded obediently. "The poor child has been through so much. She seems to think I'm her mommy. Isn't that sweet?"

"TURN HERE."

Raine slowed and turned down the narrow dirt lane. Ahead she could make out a house sitting in a stand of old cottonwoods. The house looked even more run-down than the one that she'd been held in but a light glowed inside.

There was a large newer model SUV parked on the back side, Raine saw as she pulled in front of the house and stopped. Bill shut off the engine and took the keys.

He glanced back over his shoulder. Still no sign of anyone behind them.

He turned back around just in time to see what Raine saw: a woman coming out of the house with a little girl. Raine barely recognized the child as Lara English. Her hair was matted, her face smudged with dirt and she was wearing a jean jacket that swam on her and apparently little else.

In the light that spilled from the open door of the house, Raine looked from Lara to the woman holding the girl's hand and felt her heart drop. *You can call me Mommy.* Her earlier fear seized her at the sight of the horrible woman who'd been part of her abduction sixteen years ago.

Beside her, Bill swore. "Damn that woman. She's going to mess everything up." He threw open his door, then seemed to remember Raine. "Get out," he ordered, brandishing the gun.

Raine climbed out and when she did she saw something that made her heart soar. A glint of light from the moon reflecting off what had to have been a vehicle. It disappeared over a rise in the road Raine had just driven up. She listened for a moment but didn't hear the sound of a car engine. Could she have just imagined—

Bill grabbed her arm and shoved her toward the house. "Get back inside, Adele. Now!"

Adele had stopped beside her car. The door was open and she'd apparently just dragged out a jacket from the back. As she slipped into it, she watched her husband thoughtfully. Raine could tell the woman was thinking about trying to make a run for it with the girl. Would her husband of thirty-six years shoot her?

"Adele." The warning in his tone seemed to force Adele's decision. She grabbed Lara more roughly and pushed her toward the house.

Lara entered with Adele behind her. Raine followed, Bill with his gun on her.

He seemed to notice the sheriff handcuffed to a pipe about the same time as Raine. "What the hell, Adele?" he demanded. "What is the sheriff doing here?"

Raine watched Adele seem to shrink under Bill's anger. "She must have followed me from town," she said in a small, childlike voice.

"You think?" He turned on her and Adele shrank away from him. "You just never learn, do you, Adele? Now I'm going to have to clean up the mess you made. Just like I always have to do."

CORDELL HAD BANDAGED his side as best he could but it was bleeding again as he got out of the car. He'd searched Orville Cline's body for the keys the moment he'd heard Beaumont's truck engine turn over.

Now he followed a small gully toward the house where he'd seen Beaumont's truck stop. He had to stop once to adjust the makeshift bandage he'd constructed out of an old sweatshirt he'd found in the car. The sweatshirt said Montana State University across the front. Now it was wet with blood.

He moved through the trees that once sheltered the house in time to see a woman and child go inside, followed by Raine with Beaumont close behind holding a gun on her.

As he neared the edge of the house, he saw something by the door glint in the moonlight. Stepping closer, he saw that it was a shotgun.

Inside the house, he heard Beaumont's raised voice. He seemed to be hollering at his wife.

Cordell plucked up the shotgun and moved quickly back from the open doorway to check to make sure it was loaded.

It was.

Then he moved toward the door again. The last thing he'd heard Bill Beaumont say was something about cleaning up his wife's messes. Life, Cordell thought, was all about timing.

He knew he would have the advantage of surprise, but he would also have only an instant to assess the situation and act. He would be jeopardizing Raine's and Lara's lives. Unfortunately there was no one else here to rectify things and he was losing blood and wasn't sure how much longer he'd be standing.

He prayed for perfect timing as he rounded the doorway, leading with the shotgun.

RAINE WAS NEVER SO HAPPY to see anyone come through that doorway. She felt such a well of emotion to see that Cordell was alive. If she'd ever doubted it, she knew now. She loved this man.

Bill had taken his eyes off her just moments before to go over and berate his wife. Raine had taken advantage of his inattention and pulled Lara over to her. The girl came willing enough. She seemed dazed, lost, and Raine recognized that look and felt sick inside that this child had had to go through what she'd experienced.

And suddenly Cordell appeared in the doorway with the shotgun. Adele saw him and let out a cry to warn Bill.

Raine acted on instinct, shoving Lara in the direction of the sheriff as Bill spun around. McCall grabbed the girl and covered her head as the sound of the shotgun blast boomed.

The boom reverberated through the old house. Bill made a gurgling sound, stumbling backward. Cordell suddenly seemed to be having trouble standing and Raine realized he'd been shot earlier just as she'd feared.

He took a step toward her, then dropped to one knee. A wadded-up piece of clothing fell from inside his jacket. Raine's heart dropped at the sight of the blood-soaked material.

As she started to rush to Cordell, she saw Adele trying to get the gun from her jacket pocket.

"Cordell, watch out!" she cried as she dove for Adele, slamming her back against the wall.

Adele had managed to get the gun from her pocket. Raine grabbed the gun, trying to wrench it from the woman's hands, but Adele was much stronger than she looked.

MCCALL HELD THE GIRL to her as she worked with her foot to get the pistol that Bill Beaumont had dropped when he was shot. She finally got a boot toe around it and dragged it back toward her.

She could see Raine trying to wrest the gun from Adele, but she knew only too well how strong Adele was. That strength came from that inhuman part of her, McCall thought, as she dragged the gun to her.

Letting go of Lara, she grabbed up the gun with her free hand and fired two quick shots. Neither seemed to have any effect on Adele for a few moments.

McCall prepared to fire again when she saw Adele's fingers slip from the gun she was fighting to keep from Raine. The woman glanced over at her, a horrible hateful look in her eyes, before she looked down at where the bullets had torn through her jacket. The cloth blossomed red as Adele Beaumont slowly slid to the floor.

Leaning back, McCall laid the gun next to her and pulled Lara close again. Past Lara, Raine rushed to Cordell to press the wet cloth to his side.

Lara sat up as if sensing it was over. "I'm hungry," she said.

McCall started to tell Raine to go down the road to her patrol SUV to call for backup but before she could two deputies burst in followed by one very good-looking game warden.

"Adele has the key to the cuffs in her pocket," McCall said as Luke Crawford started to rush to her.

He went to the fallen woman and came back with the key. As he unlocked the cuffs, he sat down next to McCall on the floor and pulled her to him.

"How did you—?"

"Shane told me where you were when you called in the last time," Luke said. "I remembered this old farmhouse. I know we were supposed to wait for your call, but when we didn't hear from you…"

She smiled up at him, then pulled him down for a kiss. What would she ever do without this man?

Across the room, one of the deputies was seeing to Cordell as they waited for the ambulance to arrive. Another deputy had given Lara a stick of gum, promising her a candy bar once they reached his patrol car.

McCall leaned into Luke, absorbing his warmth. "I should have followed my first instinct and shot her right away. I sure wanted to."

Luke pulled her closer. "But you didn't."

No, she thought as she looked across the room to where Adele Beaumont lay, all the crazy wild gone from her blank eyes. "But I'm not sorry she's dead. I'm not sorry they're both dead. How is Cordell though?"

Luke shook his head. "He's apparently lost a lot of blood, but the ambulance is on the way."

Chapter Sixteen

Raine stepped into Cordell's hospital room. It was right down the hall from his brother Cyrus's. Her relief and joy at hearing that Cordell was going to pull through was tempered with the news that Cyrus's condition hadn't changed.

As she neared his bed, Cordell opened those wonderful dark eyes of his and smiled. His face, though pale, seemed to light up and she felt weightless and silly and ecstatic. Tears welled in her eyes as he reached for her hand and pulled her closer.

She leaned her face against his and tried not to cry.

"Hey," he said. "I'm okay."

She nodded through her tears.

"You were amazing."

Raine didn't feel amazing. She'd endangered all of their lives.

"How's Lara?" he asked.

"Good." Drying her eyes and pulling herself together, she told him about the deputies taking her out for breakfast at the Great Northern. "She put down pancakes, eggs and bacon without blinking an eye. It turns out that the girl's grandmother saw the story on the news. Apparently, she'd lost contact with her daughter and granddaughter. McCall is helping her get custody. Lara is very excited since she has happy memories of staying with her grandmother when she was younger."

"That is good news," Cordell said.

She heard the change in his voice. "Cyrus is still stable."

He nodded. "I know. I'd hoped that by the time this was over, he would be back with us."

"I'm so sorry," Raine said, her voice breaking. "This is all my fault."

"Baby, this is the Beaumonts' fault and Orville Cline's. But they are all gone now, may they never rest in hell." He stroked her hair. "If it hadn't been for you, Lara would have been another casualty of those monsters."

Raine laid her head on his chest and listened to the steady beat of his heart.

"I need to tell you how I feel about you, Raine."

She lifted her head, afraid of what he was going to say, afraid he didn't feel the way she did.

"No, I won't let you stop me this time," he said before she could speak. "I love you. I know this is sudden and you probably don't feel the same way but—"

Raine smiled through fresh tears as she touched a finger to his lips. "I feel the same way."

He laughed, then grimaced at the pain. "You do?"

"I do."

He grinned. "Those are words I'd like to hear you say one of these days real soon."

Epilogue

McCall was amazed how quickly life had gone back to normal. Her first calls had been the usual White-horse crimes: complaints about barking dogs and loud teenagers, requests to make checks on the elderly and giving rides home from the bars to those who weren't able to drive.

She'd come down from the shock of the events of the past few weeks. Cousin Cyrus was still in a coma, but he was stable and they were all holding out hope he would regain consciousness at any time.

Fortunately her cousin Cordell had recovered nicely, Lara had been placed with her grandmother until a per-manent custody could be arranged and even the gossip had died down somewhat about the Beaumonts.

Other than that, life seemed to be getting back to normal, well, as normal as it could in Whitehorse, Montana.

Then her cell phone rang and she saw that it was her grandmother.

"Good morning, Grandmother," McCall said. It still seemed strange to call Pepper Winchester Grandmother.

She'd gone all twenty-seven years of her life with Pepper denying her existence.

But all that was behind them and even McCall's mother, Ruby, was starting to come around. Ruby was actually looking forward to her daughter's Christmas wedding at Winchester Ranch.

"I just talked to the local florist," her grandmother was saying. "She said you hadn't been over to look at flowers for the wedding. Tell me you've at least ordered your dress. You do realize the wedding isn't that far away?"

"It's June and the wedding isn't until Christmas."

"Exactly. You can't keep putting this off. Tomorrow I could have Enid drive me in—"

"That's not necessary," McCall said.

"I know, but I'd like to help you. That is, if it's all right with your mother."

She heard the plea in her grandmother's voice. "I would love it if you'd come with me to pick out the flowers."

There was a lightness to her grandmother's voice that McCall hadn't heard before. "When's a good time?"

"We could meet at Jan's Floral at noon," McCall suggested. "Would that work for you?"

"That would be perfect. Maybe we could have lunch afterward. That is if you don't have to get back to work right away."

McCall smiled, listening to how formal they sounded. "That would be nice."

"Thank you. Would Luke like to join us?"

"To pick out flowers?" Her game warden fiancé would have no interest in picking out flowers for the wedding. Luke had been great, though, about having the wedding at the ranch.

"You deserve to have your wedding there," he'd said. "You're a Winchester and it's high time everyone accepted it. Also I suspect it's your grandmother's way to trying to make amends."

McCall hoped that was the case and that her grandmother wasn't using the wedding as part of one of her hidden agendas.

"Luke's working down in the Missouri Breaks," she told her grandmother now. "It's fishing season, you know. Lots of licenses to check."

"All right then. I will see you tomorrow." Pepper sounded as if she wanted to say more but McCall got another call and had to let her go. Whatever it was, McCall figured she'd find out soon enough. Hopefully *before* the wedding.

CORDELL SAT DOWN NEXT to his brother's bed and took Cyrus's hand in his. That twin connection that had always been there was still gone and he felt such a weight on his chest that sometimes he couldn't breathe.

"We got the bad guys," he said quietly. "Just as I promised. I sure could have used your help though. Now it's time for you to come back."

The only sound in the room was the beep of the monitor.

Cyrus was still alive. That meant there was hope.

Cordell latched on to that slim thread and held on for dear life.

"I can't wait to tell you about Raine. You're going to love her. The two of you met already." He swallowed, feeling the burn of tears and fought them back. "She's a lot like you. Brave to a fault and she's a private investigator. Can you beat that?"

Cordell realized how foolish he'd been to think that once he caught the people responsible that Cyrus would wake up.

It had been crazy. Cyrus's condition hadn't changed since the accident. It might never change.

He shoved that thought away and stood as the doctor came into the room. Cordell knew he had to make a decision. He followed the doctor out into the hall.

"You have to face the possibility that your brother might never recover from his injury," the doctor said again.

Cordell nodded, though he doubted he could ever accept that.

"I would suggest moving him to a long-term care facility that specializes in these kinds of cases."

"I want to take him back to Colorado. Is there a problem with transporting him in his condition?"

"He is breathing on his own, his vitals are strong, I see no problem with that and there are some fine facilities in Denver."

Cordell nodded. "I'll make arrangements right away then."

"ARE YOU LEAVING?" Pepper Winchester asked in surprise.

Her daughter Virginia turned from packing clothing into her suitcase, her expression sour. "There is no reason to stay here under the circumstances."

"The circumstances being that your mother isn't dying quickly enough?"

"Mother, don't start," Virginia said. "You don't want or need me here. You have Enid. She is more like a daughter to you than I am."

Pepper couldn't hold back the laugh. "Enid?"

"Fine. If not Enid then definitely Brand and the others."

"Oh, Virginia, must you always come back to this?" Behind her, Pepper heard Brand and Worth come up the hall. They were carrying their overnight bags. Apparently they were all leaving.

What surprised her was how hollow that made her feel. She didn't want them to go. She realized how incongruous that was since she still believed one of them was an accomplice to murder.

"I'll let you say goodbye to your brothers," Pepper said and, cane tapping, went down the hall where she found Enid eavesdropping. She stopped next to the elderly housekeeper, who didn't seem the least bit upset about being caught.

Even though she knew what would be said about her and how much it would hurt, Pepper stayed there by Enid to listen.

"Why *did* she get us back here?" Virginia demanded

in her shrill voice. "She really can't believe that one of us had something to do with Trace's death."

"I don't know," Brand said and sighed. "Maybe she needs us."

Worth swore. "A little late, don't you think?"

"He's right, Mother never needed anyone but Trace," Virginia said, close to tears.

"I think you're smart to leave," Brand said, always the sensible one. "Being here just seems to bring back all those old resentments."

Pepper could almost hear her daughter bristle.

"Don't pretend I'm the only one who can't forgive Mother."

"Virginia, I really don't want to get into this," Brand said. "I have one son recovering from gunshot wounds and another in a coma. I'm much more concerned about the future than I am the past."

"At least you have children," Virginia spat.

In the silence that followed Pepper could hear what none of them could bring themselves to say. Pepper knew they were all thinking about the child Virginia had given birth to and lost.

"Virginia," Brand said, clearly trying to be diplomatic. "You didn't have anything to do with Trace's—"

"Is that what you think? That I had something to do with killing him?" Virginia let out a laugh.

"You knew the woman who confessed to killing him."

"So did you. So did Worth and Angus, not to mention Enid and Alfred. Who said it had to be one of us?"

"She's right," Worth spoke up. "Alfred might be dead, but Enid doesn't appear to be going anywhere and any fool can see that something is going on between Enid and Mother. If I had to guess I'd say blackmail. I wouldn't put it past Enid for an instant."

Beside Pepper, Enid let out a snort and whispered, "I never liked that boy."

"I'm sure it will all sort itself out," Brand said. "Who says the woman didn't lie about one of us being involved?"

"Oh, that is so like you, Brand," Virginia snapped. "You always just put your head into the sand and pretend everything is fine. Sort itself out. In other words, you're not going to do a damned thing, are you?"

"What would you like me to do? I can't change Mother and I can't change the past. What is it you want me to do, Virginia? Just tell me and I'll do it."

Virginia was crying again.

Pepper heard Worth and Brand start down the hall. She and Enid hurriedly took the servants' stairs to the kitchen.

"Mother?" Brand called when they reached the front entry.

Pepper came out of the kitchen to tell her sons goodbye. Virginia joined them, sans suitcase. Apparently she'd changed her mind about leaving.

"Are you coming back for the wedding at Christmas?" Pepper asked them after she'd given her sons both awkward hugs.

Worth merely nodded, expressing what Pepper knew

to be true of him. He would come back if the others did. It was as if he didn't have a mind of his own and never had. She sighed inwardly.

"Are you sure it's a good idea to have the wedding here?" Virginia asked. "I know McCall's the sheriff and her fiancé is some kind of law enforcement, but they aren't bulletproof and Winchester Ranch doesn't seem to be the safest place."

Pepper ignored her as she looked to Brand. The others would do whatever he did. Until that moment, she hadn't realized just how much this meant to her to have them all here. Sentiment aside, there was still a murderer among them. If it was on her last dying breath, she would know which one it was.

"I'll be here," Brand said as if he had a bad feeling he'd better come home for Christmas this year.

RAINE HAD JUST PICKED UP her VW bug at the garage when Cordell drove up in his brother's pickup. It was one of those Montana summer days, not a cloud in the brilliant blue sky, the sun bright and warm, the breeze scented with freshly mown grass.

She watched him from the shade of the building as he climbed out, still taken aback that this gorgeous man loved *her*.

Raine realized for the first time she wasn't worried about the future. For sixteen years, she'd lived with the knowledge that there were people out there who would kill her if they knew who she really was. She hadn't been able to forget for even a minute that she was Emily Frank, the victim of child abductors.

But as Cordell Winchester came toward her, she realized she was Raine Chandler, a woman who could finally dream of a happily ever after.

"Hi, beautiful," Cordell said now as he took her in his arms and kissed her. He held her tight and she could tell he didn't like even a temporary separation. But he had to take care of his brother and she had to discuss with Marias selling her half of their investigative business in California.

Last night, lying out on a blanket under the Montana midnight sky, Cordell had asked her to marry him. She'd told him it was too soon. He'd argued that some things you just knew for certain and this was something he just knew and more time together wouldn't change his mind.

So she'd made him a deal. They would get married when Cyrus was able to be the best man at the wedding. Cordell's eyes had filled with tears. He'd started to ask but what if Cyrus never—

Raine had stopped him. "That's the deal," she'd said. In the meantime, they would take care of business and see each other as often as they could.

"Promise me I'll see you in Colorado soon," Cordell said now as the kiss ended.

She gazed into his dark eyes, felt her heart fill to overflowing with love for this man, and whispered back, "I promise."

* * * * *

SHOTGUN
SHERIFF

BY

DELORES FOSSEN

All the characters in this book have no existence outside the imagination of the author, and have no relation whatsoever to anyone bearing the same name or names. They are not even distantly inspired by any individual known or unknown to the author, and all the incidents are pure invention.

First published in Great Britain 2011
by Mills & Boon, an imprint of Harlequin (UK) Limited,
Eton House, 18-24 Paradise Road, Richmond, Surrey TW9 1SR

© Delores Fossen 2010

ISBN: 978 0 263 88536 1

46-0711

Harlequin (UK) policy is to use papers that are natural, renewable and recyclable products and made from wood grown in sustainable forests. The logging and manufacturing processes conform to the legal environmental regulations of the country of origin.

Printed and bound in Spain
by Blackprint CPI, Barcelona

Imagine a family tree that includes Texas cowboys, Choctaw and Cherokee Indians, a Louisiana pirate and a Scottish rebel who battled side by side with William Wallace. With ancestors like that, it's easy to understand why Texas author and former air force captain **Delores Fossen** feels as if she was genetically predisposed to writing romances. Along the way to fulfilling her DNA destiny, Delores married an air force top gun who just happens to be of Viking descent. With all those romantic bases covered, she doesn't have to look too far for inspiration.

Chapter One

Comanche Creek, Texas

Something was wrong.

Sheriff Reed Hardin eased his Smith and Wesson from his leather shoulder holster and stepped out of his mud-scabbed pickup truck. The heels of his rawhide boots sank in the rain-softened dirt. He lifted his head. Listened.

It was what he *didn't* hear that bothered him.

Yeah, something was definitely wrong.

There should have been squawks from the blue jays or the cardinals. Maybe even a hawk in search of its breakfast. Instead there was only the unnerving quiet of the Texas Hill Country woods sardined with thick mesquites, hackberries and thorny underbrush that bulged thick and green with spring growth. Whatever had scared off the birds could be lurking in there. Reed was hoping for a coyote or some other four-legged predator because the alternative put a knot in his gut.

After all, just hours earlier a woman had been murdered a few yards from here.

With his gun ready and aimed, Reed made his way

up the steep back path toward the cabin. He'd chosen the route so he could look around for any evidence he might have missed when he'd combed the grounds not long after the body had been discovered. He needed to see if anything was out of place, anything that would help him make sense of this murder. So far, nothing.

Except for his certainty that something was wrong. And he soon spotted proof of it.

There were footprints leading down and then back up the narrow trail. Too many of them. There should have been only his and his deputy's, Kirby Spears, since Reed had given firm orders that all others use the county road just a stone's throw from the front of the cabin. He hadn't wanted this scene contaminated and there were signs posted ordering No Trespassers.

He stooped down and had a better look at the prints. "What the hell?" Reed grumbled.

The prints were small and narrow and with a distinctive narrow cut at the back that had knifed right into the gray-clay-and-limestone dirt mix.

Who the heck would be out here in high heels?

He thought of the dead woman, Marcie James, who'd been found shot to death in the cabin about fourteen hours earlier. Marcie hadn't been wearing heels. Neither had her alleged killer. And Reed should know because the alleged killer was none other than his own deputy, Shane Tolbert.

Cursing the fact that Shane was now locked up in a jail he used to police with Reed and Kirby, Reed elbowed aside a pungent dew-coated cedar branch and hurried up the hill. It didn't take him long to see more evidence of his something-was-wrong theory. There were no signs of his deputy or the patrol car.

However, there was a blonde lurking behind a sprawling oak tree.

Correction. An *armed* blonde. A stranger, at that.

She was tall, at least five-ten, and dressed in a long-sleeved white shirt that she'd tucked into the waist of belted dark jeans. Her hair was gathered into a sleek ponytail, not a strand out of place. And yep, there were feminine heels on her fashionable black boots. But her attire wasn't what Reed focused on. It was that lethal-looking Sig-Sauer Blackwater pistol gripped in her latex-gloved right hand. She had it aimed at the cabin.

Reed aimed his Smith and Wesson at her.

Maybe she heard him or sensed he was there because her gaze whipped in his direction. She shifted her position a fraction, no doubt preparing to turn her weapon on him, but she stopped when her attention landed on the badge Reed had clipped to his belt. Then, she did something that surprised the heck out of him.

She put her left index finger to her mouth in a *shhh* gesture.

Reed glanced around, trying to make sense of why she was there and why in Sam Hill she'd just shushed him as if she'd had a right to do it. He didn't see anyone other than the blonde, but she kept her weapon trained on the cabin.

He walked closer to her, keeping his steps light, just in case there was indeed some threat other than this woman. If so, then someone had breached a crime scene because the cabin was literally roped off with yellow crime-scene tape. And with the town's gossip mill in full swing, there probably wasn't anyone within fifty miles of Comanche Creek who hadn't heard about the latest murder.

Emphasis on the word *latest*.

Everyone knew to keep away or they'd have to deal with him. He wasn't a badass—most days, anyway—but people usually did as he said when he spelled things out for them. And he always spelled things out.

"I'm Sheriff Reed Hardin," he grumbled when he got closer.

"Livvy Hutton."

Like her face, her name wasn't familiar to him. Who the devil was she?

She tipped her head towards the cabin. "I think someone's inside."

Well, there sure as hell shouldn't be. "Where's my deputy?"

"Running an errand for me."

That didn't improve Reed's mood. He was about to question why his deputy would be running an errand for an armed woman in fancy boots, but she shifted her position again. Even though she kept her attention nailed to the cabin, he could now see the front of her white shirt.

The sun's rays danced off the distinctive star badge pinned to it.

"You're a Texas Ranger?" he asked.

He hadn't intended for that to sound like a challenge, but it did. Reed couldn't help it. He already had one Ranger to deal with, Lieutenant Wyatt Colter, who'd been in Comanche Creek for days, since the start of all this mess that'd turned his town upside-down. Now, he apparently had another one of Texas's finest. That was two too many for a crime scene he planned to finish processing himself. He had a plan for this investigation, and that plan didn't include Rangers.

"Yes. Sergeant Olivia Hutton," she clarified. "CSI for the Ranger task force."

She spared him a glance from ice-blue eyes. Not a friendly glance either. That brief look conveyed a lot of displeasure.

And skepticism.

Reed had seen that look before. He was a small-town Texas sheriff, and to some people that automatically made him small-minded, stupid and incapable of handling a capital murder investigation. That attitude was one of the reasons for the so-called task force that included not only Texas Rangers but a forensic anthropologist and apparently this blonde crime-scene analyst.

As he'd done with Lieutenant Colter, the other Ranger, Reed would set a few ground rules with Sergeant Hutton. Later, that was. For now, he needed to figure out if anyone was inside the cabin. That was at the top of his mental list.

Reed didn't see anyone near either of the two back curtainless windows. Nor had the crime-scene tape been tampered with. It was still in place. Of course, someone could have ducked beneath it and gotten inside—after they'd figured out a way to get past the locked windows and doors. Other than the owner and probably some members of the owner's family, Reed and his deputy were the only ones with keys.

"Did you actually see anyone in the cabin?" he asked in a whisper.

She turned her head, probably so she could whisper as well, but the move put them even closer. Practically mouth to cheek. Not good. Because with all that closeness, he caught her scent. Her perfume was high-end, but that was definitely chocolate on her breath.

"I heard something," she explained. "Your deputy and I were taking castings of some footprints we found over there." She tipped her head to a cluster of trees on the east side of the cabin. "I wanted to get them done right away because it's supposed to rain again this afternoon."

Yeah, it was, and if they'd been lucky enough to find footprints after the morning and late-night drizzle, then they wouldn't be there long.

"After Deputy Spears left to send the castings to your office," she continued, "I turned to go back inside. That's when I thought I heard someone moving around in there."

Reed took in every word of her account. *Every word.* But he also heard the accent. Definitely not a Texas drawl. He was thinking East Coast and would find out more about that later. For now, he might have an intruder on his hands. An intruder who was possibly inside with a cabin full of potential evidence that could clear Shane's name. Or maybe it was the cabin's owner, Jonah Becker, though Reed had warned the rancher to stay far away from the place.

With his gun still aimed, Reed stepped out a few inches from the cover of the tree. "This is Sheriff Hardin," he called out. "If anyone's in there, get the hell out here now."

Beside him, Livvy huffed. "You think that's wise, to stand out in the open like that?"

He took the time to toss her a scowl. "Maybe it'd be a dumb idea in Boston, but here in Comanche Creek, if there's an intruder, it's likely to be someone who knows to do as I say."

He hoped.

"Not Boston," she snarled. "New York."

He gave her a flat look to let her know that didn't make things better. A Texas Ranger should damn well be born and raised in Texas. And she shouldn't wear high-heeled boots.

Or perfume that reminded him she was a woman.

Reed knew that was petty, but with four murders on his hands, he wasn't exactly in a generous mood. He extended that non-generous mood to anyone who might be inside that cabin.

"Get out here!" he shouted. And by God, it better happen now.

Nothing. Well, nothing except Livvy's spurting breath and angry mumbles.

"Just because the person doesn't answer you, it doesn't mean the place is empty," she pointed out.

Yeah. And that meant he might have a huge problem. He didn't want the crime scene compromised, and he didn't want to shoot anyone. *Yet.*

"How long were Deputy Spears and you out there casting footprints?" he asked.

"A half hour. And before that we were looking around in the woods."

That explained how her footprints had gotten on the trail. The castings and the woods search also would have given someone plenty of time to get inside. "I'm guessing Deputy Spears unlocked the cabin for you?"

The sergeant shook her head. "It wasn't necessary. Someone had broken the lock on a side window, apparently crawled in and then opened the front door from the inside."

Reed cursed. "And you didn't see that person when you went in?"

Another head shake that sent her ponytail swishing. "The place was empty when I first arrived. I checked every inch," she added, cutting off his next question: *Was she sure about that?*

So, he had possibly two intruders. Great. Dealing with intruders wasn't on his to-do list today.

Now, he cursed himself. He should have camped out here, but he hadn't exactly had the manpower to do that with just him and two deputies, including the one behind bars. He'd had to process Shane's arrest and interrogate him. He had been careful. He'd done everything by the book so no one could accuse him of tampering with anything that would ultimately clear Shane's name. Kirby Spears had guarded the place until around midnight, but then Reed and he had had to respond to an armed robbery at the convenience store near the interstate.

Lately, life in Comanche Creek had been far from peaceful and friendly—even though that was what it said on the welcome sign at the edge of the city limits. Before the spring, it'd been nearly a decade since there'd been a murder. Now, there'd been four.

Four!

And because some of those bodies had been dumped on Native American burial ground, the whole town felt as if it were sitting on a powder keg. With the previous murder investigations and the latest one, Reed was operating on a one-hour nap, too much coffee and a shorter fuse than usual.

He glanced around. "How'd you get up here?" he asked the sergeant. "Because I didn't see a vehicle."

"I parked at the bottom of the hill just off the county road. I wanted to get a good look at the exterior of the crime scene before I went inside." She glanced around as well. "How'd you get up here?" she asked him.

"I parked on the back side of the hill." And for the same reason. Of course, that didn't mean they were going to see eye-to-eye on anything else. Reed was betting this would get ugly fast.

"Reed?" someone called out, the sound coming from the cabin.

Reed cursed some more because he recognized that voice. He lowered his gun, huffed and strolled toward the front door. It swung open just as Reed stepped onto the porch, and he came face-to-face with his boss, Mayor Woody Sadler. His friend. His mentor. As close to a father as Reed had ever had since his own dad had died when Reed was seven years old.

But Woody shouldn't have been within a mile of the place.

Surrogate fatherhood would earn Woody a little more respect than Reed would give others, but even Woody wasn't going to escape a good chewing-out. And maybe even more.

"What are you doing here?" Livvy demanded, taking the words right out of Reed's mouth. Unlike Reed, she didn't lower her gun. She pointed the Blackwater right at Woody.

Woody eased off his white Stetson, and the rattler tail attached to the band gave a familiar hollow jangle. He nodded a friendly greeting.

He didn't get anything friendly in return.

"This is Woody Sadler. The mayor of Comanche

Creek," Reed said, making introductions. "And this is Sergeant Livvy Hutton. A Texas Ranger from New York."

Woody's tired gray eyes widened. Then narrowed, making the corners of his eyes wrinkle even more than they already were. Obviously he wasn't able to hold back a petty reaction either. "New York?"

"Spare me the jokes. I was born in a small town near Dallas. Raised in upstate New York." As if she'd declared war on it, Livvy shoved her gun back into her shoulder holster and barreled up the steps. "And regardless of where I'm from, this is my crime scene, and you were trespassing," she declared to Woody and then fired a glance at Reed to declare it to him as well.

"I didn't touch anything," Woody insisted.

Livvy obviously didn't take his word for it. She bolted past Woody, grabbed her equipment bag from the porch and went inside.

"I swear," Woody added to Reed. "I didn't touch a thing."

Reed studied Woody's body language. The stiff shoulders. The sweat popping out above his top lip. Both surefire signs that the man was uncomfortable about something. "You're certain about that?"

"I'm damn certain." The body language changed. No more nerves, just a defensive stare that made Reed feel like a kid again. Still, that didn't stop Reed from doing his job.

"Then why didn't you answer when I called out?" Reed asked. "And why'd you break the lock on the window and go in there?"

"I didn't hear you calling out, that's why, and I didn't break any lock. The door was wide open when I got here about fifteen minutes ago." There was another shift in body language. Woody shook his head and wearily ran his hand through his thinning salt-and-pepper hair. "I just had to see for myself. I figured there'd be something obvious. Something that'd prove that Shane didn't do this."

Reed blew out a long breath. "I know. I want to prove Shane's innocence, too, but this isn't the way to go about doing it. If there's proof and the New York Ranger finds it, she could say you planted it there."

Woody went still. Then, he cursed. "I wouldn't do that."

"I believe you. But Sergeant Olivia Hutton doesn't know you from Adam."

Woody's gaze met his. "She's gunning for Shane?"

Probably. For Shane and anyone who thought he was innocent. But Reed kept that to himself. "Best to let me handle this," he insisted. "I'll talk to you when I'm back in town. Oh, and see about hiring me a temporary deputy or two."

Woody bobbed his head, slid back on his Stetson and ambled off the porch and down the hill, where he'd likely parked. Reed waited until he was sure the mayor was on his way before he took another deep breath and went inside.

He only made it two steps.

Livvy threw open the door. "Where's the mayor?" she demanded.

"Gone." Reed hitched his thumb toward the downside of the hill. "Why?"

Her hands went on her hips, and those ice-blue eyes turned fiery hot. "Because he stole some evidence, that's why, and I intend to arrest him."

Chapter Two

Livvy was in full stride across the yard when the sheriff caught up with her, latched on to her arm, whirled her around and brought her to an abrupt halt.

"I'm arresting him," she repeated and tried to throw off his grip.

She would probably have had better luck wrestling a longhorn to the ground. Despite Sheriff Reed Hardin's lanky build, the man was strong. And angry. That anger was stamped on his tanned face and in his crisp green eyes.

"I don't care if Woody Sadler is your friend." She tried again to get away from the sheriff's clamped hand. "He can't waltz in here and steal evidence that might be pertinent to a murder investigation."

"Just hold on." He pulled out his cell phone from his well-worn Wranglers, scrolled through some numbers and hit the call button. "Woody," he said when the mayor apparently answered, "you need to get back up here to the cabin right now. We might have a problem."

"Might?" Livvy snarled when Sheriff Hardin ended the call. "Oh, we *definitely* have a problem. Tampering with a crime scene is a third-degree felony."

The sheriff dismissed that with a headshake. "Woody's the mayor, along with being a law-abiding citizen. He didn't tamper with anything. You said yourself that someone had broken the lock, and Woody didn't do that."

"Well, he obviously isn't so law-abiding because he walked past crime-scene tape and entered without permission or reason."

"He had reason," Reed mumbled. "He's worried about Shane. And sometimes worried people do dumb things." He looked down at the chokehold he had on her arm, mumbled something indistinguishable, and his grip melted away. "What exactly is missing?"

"A cell phone." Livvy tried to go after the trespassing mayor again, but Reed stepped in front of her. Worse, her forward momentum sent her slamming right against his chest. Specifically, her breasts against his chest. The man was certainly solid. There were lots of corded muscles in his chest and abs.

Both of them cursed this time.

And Livvy shook her head. She shouldn't be noticing anything that intimate about a man whom she would likely end up at odds with. She shouldn't be noticing his looks, either. Those eyes. The desperado stubble on his strong square jaw and the tousled coffee-brown hair that made him look as if he'd just crawled out of bed.

Or off a poster for a Texas cowboy-sheriff.

It was crystal-clear that he didn't want her anywhere near the crime scene or his town. Tough. Livvy had been given a job to do, and she *never* walked away from the job.

Sherriff Hardin would soon learn that about her.

By God, she hadn't fought her way into the Ranger

organization to be stonewalled by some local yokels who believed one of their own could do no wrong.

"What cell phone?" Reed asked.

Because the adrenaline and anger had caused her breath and mind to race, it took her a moment to answer. First, she glanced at the road and saw the mayor inching his way back up toward them. "One I found in the fireplace when I was going through the front room. You no doubt missed it in the initial search because the ashes were covering it completely. The only reason I found it is because I ran a metal detector over the place to search for any spent shell casings. Then, I photographed it, bagged it and put it on the table. It's missing."

His jaw muscles stirred. "It's Marcie's phone?"

"I don't know. I showed it to Deputy Spears, and he said he didn't think it was Shane's. That means it could be Marcie's."

"Or the killer's."

She was certain her jaw muscles stirred, too. "Need I remind you that you found Deputy Shane Tolbert standing over Marcie's body, and he had a gun in his hand? Marcie was his estranged lover. I hate to state the obvious, but all the initial evidence indicates that Shane *is* the killer."

Livvy instantly regretted spouting that verdict. It wasn't her job to get a conviction or jump to conclusions. She was there to gather evidence and find the truth, and she didn't want anything, including her anger, to get in the way.

"Shane said he didn't kill her," Reed explained. His voice was calm enough, but not his eyes. Everything else about him was unruffled except for those intense green eyes. They were warrior eyes. "He said Marcie called him and asked him to meet her at the cabin. The moment he stepped inside, someone hit him over the head, and he fell on the floor. When he came to, Marcie was dead and someone had put a gun in his hand."

Yes, she'd already heard the summary of Shane's statement from Deputy Kirby Spears. Livvy intended to study the interrogation carefully, especially since Reed had been the one to question the suspect.

Talk about a conflict of interest.

Still, in a small town like Comanche Creek, Reed probably hadn't had an alternative, especially since the on-scene Ranger, Lieutenant Colter, had been called back to the office. If Reed hadn't questioned Shane, then it would have been left to his junior deputy, Kirby, who was greener than the Hill Country's spring foliage.

The mayor finally made his way toward them and stopped a few feet away. "What's wrong?"

"Where's the cell phone that I'd bagged and tagged?" Livvy asked, not waiting for Reed to respond.

Woody Sadler first looked at Reed. Then, her. "I have no idea. I didn't take it."

"Then you won't mind proving that to me. Show me your pockets."

Woody hesitated, until Reed gave him a nod. It wasn't exactly a cooperative nod, either, and the accompanying grumble had a get-this-over-with tone to it.

The mayor pulled out a wallet from the back pocket of his jeans and a handkerchief and keys from the front ones. No cell phone, but that didn't mean he hadn't taken it. The man had had at least ten minutes to discard it along the way up or down the hill to his vehicle.

"Taking the cell won't help your friend's cause," she pointed out. "I already phoned in the number, and it'll be traced."

Woody lifted his shoulder. "Good. Because maybe what you learn about that phone will get Shane out of jail. He didn't kill Marcie."

Reed stared at her. "Can the mayor go now, or do you intend to strip-search him?"

Livvy ignored that swipe and glanced down at Woody's snakeskin boots. "You wear about a size eleven." She turned her attention to Reed. "And so do you. That looks to be about the size of the footprints that I took casts of over in the brush."

"So?" Woody challenged.

"So, the location of those prints means that someone could have waited there for Marcie to arrive. They could be the footprints of the killer. Or the killer's accomplice if he had one. Sheriff Hardin would have had reason to be out here, but what about you? Before this morning, were you here at the cabin in the past forty-eight hours?"

"No." The mayor's answer was quick and confident.

Livvy didn't intend to take his word for it.

"You can go now," Reed told the mayor.

Woody slid his hat back on, tossed her a glare and delivered his parting shot from over his shoulder as he walked away. "You might do to remember that Reed is the law in Comanche Creek."

Livvy could have reminded him that she was there on orders from the governor, but instead she took out her binoculars from her field bag and watched Woody's exit. If he stopped to pick up a discarded cell phone, she would arrest him on the spot.

"He didn't take that phone," Reed insisted.

"Then who did?"

"The real killer. He could have done it while Kirby and you were casting the footprints."

"The real killer," she repeated. "And exactly who would that be?"

"Someone that Marcie got involved with in the past two years when she was missing and presumed dead."

Livvy couldn't discount that. After all, Marcie had faked her own death so she wouldn't have to testify against a powerful local rancher who'd been accused of bribing officials in order to purchase land that the Comanche community considered their own. The rancher, Jonah Becker, who also owned this cabin, could have silenced Marcie when she returned from the grave.

Or maybe the killer was someone who'd been furious that Marcie hadn't gone through with her testimony two years ago. There were several people who could have wanted the woman dead, but Shane was the one who'd been found standing over her body.

"See? He didn't take the cell phone," Reed grumbled when the mayor didn't stop along the path to retrieve anything he might have discarded. The mayor got into a shiny fire-engine-red gas-guzzler of a truck and sped away, the massive tires kicking up a spray of mud and gravel.

"He could be planning to come back for it later," Livvy commented. But probably not. He would have known that she would search the area.

"Instead of focusing on Woody Sadler," Reed continued, "how about taking a look at the evidence inside the cabin? Because naming Shane as the primary suspect just doesn't add up."

Ah, she'd wondered how long it would take to get to this subject. "How do you figure that?"

"For one thing, I swabbed Shane's hands, and there was no gunshot residue. Plus, this case might be bigger than just Shane and Marcie. You might not have heard, but a few days ago there were some other bodies that turned up at the Comanche burial grounds."

"I heard," she said. "I also heard their eyes were sealed with red paint and ochre clay. In other words, a Native American ritual. There's nothing Native American or ritualistic about this murder."

Still, that didn't mean the deaths weren't connected. It just meant she didn't see an immediate link. The only thing that was glaring right now was Deputy Shane Tolbert's involvement in this and his sheriff's need to defend him.

Livvy started the walk down the hill to look for that missing phone. Thankfully, it was silver and should stand out among the foliage. And then she remembered the note in her pocket with the cell number on it. She took out her own phone and punched in the numbers to call the cell so it would ring.

She heard nothing.

Just in case it was buried beneath debris or something, she continued down the hill, listening for it.

Reed followed her, of course.

Livvy would have preferred to do this search alone because the sheriff was turning out to be more than a nuisance. He was a distraction. Livvy blamed that on his too-good looks and her stupid fantasies about cowboys. She'd obviously watched too many Westerns growing up, and she reminded herself that in almost all cases the fantasy was much hotter than the reality.

She glanced at Reed again and mentally added *maybe not in this case.*

In those great-fitting jeans and equally great-fitting blue shirt, he certainly looked as if he could compete with a fantasy or two.

When she felt her cheeks flush, Livvy quickly got her mind on something else—the job. It was obvious that the missing cell wasn't ringing so she ended the call and put her own cell back in her pocket. Instead of listening for the phone, she'd just have to hope that the mayor had turned it off but still tossed it in a place where she could spot it.

"The mayor's not guilty," Reed tried again. "And neither is Shane."

She made a sound of disagreement. "Maybe there was no GSR on his hands because Shane wore gloves when he shot her," she pointed out. Though Livvy was certain Reed had already considered that.

"There were no gloves found at the scene."

She had an answer for that as well. "He could have discarded them and then hit himself over the head to make it look as if he'd been set up."

"Then he would have had to change his clothes, too, because there was no GSR on his shirt, jeans, belt, watch, badge, holster or boots."

"You tested all those items for gunshot residue?"

"Yeah, I did," he snapped. "This might be a small town, Sergeant Hutton, but we're not idiots. Shane and I have both taken workshops on crime-scene processing, and we keep GSR test kits in the office."

It sounded as if Sheriff Hardin had been thorough, but she would reserve judgment on whether he'd learned enough in those workshops.

"But Shane was holding the murder weapon, right?" Livvy clarified.

"Appears to have been, but it wasn't his gun. He says he has no idea who it belongs to. The bullet taken from Marcie's body is on the way to the lab for comparison, and we're still searching the databases to try to figure out the owner of the gun."

Good. She'd call soon and press for those results and the plaster castings of the footprints. Because the sooner she finished this crime scene, the sooner she could get out of here and head back to Austin. She didn't mind small towns, had even grown up in one, but this small town—and its sheriff—could soon get to her.

Livvy continued to visually comb the right side of the path, and when they got to the bottom, they started back up while she examined the opposite side. There was no sign of a silver phone.

Mercy.

She didn't want to explain to her boss how she'd let possible crucial evidence disappear from a crime scene that she was working. She had to find that phone or else pray the cell records could be accessed.

"What about the blood spatter in the cabin?" Reed asked, grabbing her attention again.

"I'm not finished processing the scene yet." In fact, she'd barely started though she had already spent nearly an hour inside. She had hours more, maybe days, of work ahead of her. Those footprint castings had taken priority because they could have been erased with just a light rain. "But in my cursory check, I didn't see any spatter, only the blood pool on the floor. Since Marcie was shot at point-blank range, that doesn't surprise me. Why? Did you find blood spatter?"

"No. But if Shane's account is true about someone clubbing him over the back of the head, then there might be some. He already had a head injury, and it had been aggravated with what looked like a second blow. But the wood's dark-colored, and I didn't want to spray the place with Luminol since I read it can sometimes alter small droplets. Judging from the wound on Shane's head, we'd be looking for a very small amount because the gash was only about an inch across."

She glanced at him and hoped she didn't look too surprised. Most non-CSI-trained authorities would have hosed down the place with Luminol, the chemical to detect the presence of biological fluids, and would have indeed compromised the pattern by causing the blood to run. That in turn, could compromise critical evidence.

"What?" he asked.

Livvy walked ahead of him, up the steps and onto the porch and went inside the cabin. "Nothing."

"Something," Reed corrected, following her. He shut the door and turned on the overhead lights. "You'd dismissed me as just a small-town sheriff."

"No." She shrugged. "Okay, maybe. Sorry."

"Don't be. I dismissed you, too."

Since her back was to him, she smiled. For a moment. "Still do?"

"Not because of your skill. You seem to know what

you're doing. But I'm concerned you won't do every-thing possible to clear Shane's name."

"And I'm concerned you'll do anything to clear it."

He made a sound of agreement that rumbled deep in his throat. "I can live with a stalemate if I know you'll be objective."

The man certainly did know how to make her feel guilty. And defensive. "The evidence is objective, and my interpretation of it will be, too. Don't worry. I'll check for that blood spatter in just a minute."

Riled now about the nerve he'd hit, she grabbed a folder from her equipment bag. "First though, I'd like to know if it wasn't Woody Sadler, then who might have compromised the crime scene and stolen the phone." She slapped the folder on the dining table and opened it. Inside were short bios of persons of any possible interest in this case.

Reed's bio was there on top, and Livvy had already studied it.

He was thirty-two, had never been married and had been the sheriff of Comanche Creek for eight years. Before that, he'd been a deputy. His father, also sheriff, had been killed in the line of duty when Reed was seven. Reed's mother had fallen apart after her husband's murder and had spent the rest of her short life in and out of mental institutions before committing suicide. And the man who'd raised Reed after that was none other than the mayor, Woody Sadler.

She could be objective about the evidence, but she seriously doubted that Reed could ever be impartial about the man who'd raised him.

Livvy moved Reed's bio aside. The mayor's. And

Shane's. "Who would be bold or stupid enough to walk into this cabin and take a phone with me and your deputy only yards away?"

Reed thumbed through the pages, extracted one and handed it to her. "Jonah Becker. He's the rancher Marcie was supposed to testify against. He probably wouldn't have done this himself, but he could have hired someone if he thought that phone would link him in any way to Marcie."

Yes. Jonah Becker was a possibility. Reed added the bio for Jonah's son. And Jerry Collier, the man who ran the Comanche Creek Land Office. Then Billy Whitley, a city official. The final bio that Reed included was for Shane's father, Ben Tolbert. He was another strong possibility since he might want to protect his son.

"I'll question all of them," Reed promised.

"And I'll be there when you do," Livvy added. She heard the irritation in his under-the-breath grumble, but she ignored him, took the handheld UV lamp from her bag and put on a pair of monochromatic glasses.

"Shane said he was here when he was hit." Reed pointed to the area in front of the fireplace. It was only about three feet from where Marcie's body had been discovered.

Livvy walked closer, her heels echoing on the hardwood floor. The sound caused Reed to eye her boots, and again she saw some questions about her choice of footwear.

"They're more comfortable than they look," she mumbled.

"They'd have to be," he mumbled back.

Though comfort wasn't exactly the reason she was

wearing them. She'd just returned from a trip to visit her father, and one of her suitcases—the one that contained her favorite work boots—had been lost. There'd been no time to replace them because she had been home less than an hour when she'd gotten the call to get to Comanche Creek ASAP.

"I do own real boots," Livvy commented and wondered why she felt the need to defend herself.

With Reed's attention nailed to her, she lifted the lamp and immediately spotted the spatter on the dark wood. Without the light, it wasn't even detectable. There wasn't much, less than a dozen tiny drops, but it was consistent with a high-velocity impact.

"Shane's about my height," Reed continued. And he stood in the position that would have been the most likely spot to have produced that pattern.

It lined up.

Well, the droplets did anyway. She still had some doubts about Shane's story.

Livvy took her camera, slipped on a monochromatic lens and photographed the spatter. "Your deputy could have hit himself in the head. Not hard enough for him to lose consciousness. Just enough to give us the cast-off pattern we see here. Then, he could have hidden whatever he used to club himself."

Reed stared at her. "Or he could be telling the truth. If he is, that means we have a killer walking around scot-free."

Yes, and Livvy wasn't immune to the impact of that. It scratched away at old wounds, and even though she'd only been a Ranger for eighteen months, that was more than enough time for her to have learned that her baggage and old wounds couldn't be part of her job. She couldn't go back twenty years and right an old wrong.

Though she kept trying.

Livvy met Reed's gaze. It wasn't hard to do since he was still staring holes in her. "You really believe your deputy is incapable of killing his ex-lover?"

She expected an immediate answer. A *damn right* or some other manly affirmation. But Reed paused. Or rather he hesitated. His hands went to his hips, and he tipped his eyes to the ceiling.

"What?" Livvy insisted.

Reed shook his head, and for a moment she didn't think he would answer. "Shane and Marcie had a stormy relationship. I won't deny that. And since you'll find this out anyway, I had to suspend him once for excessive force when he was making an arrest during a domestic dispute. Still…I can't believe he'd commit a premeditated murder and set himself up."

Yes, that was a big question mark in her mind. If Shane had enough forensic training to set up someone, then why hadn't he chosen anyone but himself? That meant she was either dealing with an innocent man or someone who was very clever, and therefore very dangerous.

Because she was in such deep thought, Livvy jumped when a sound shot through the room. But it wasn't a threat. It was Reed's cell phone.

"Kirby," he said when he answered it.

That got her attention. Kirby Spears was the young deputy who'd assisted her on the scene and had carried the footprint castings back to the sheriff's office so a Ranger courier could pick them up and take them to the crime lab in Austin.

While she took a sample of one of the spatter droplets, Livvy listened to the conversation. Or rather that was what she tried to do. Hard to figure out what was going on with Reed's monosyllabic responses. However, his jaw muscles stirred again, and she thought she detected some frustration in those already intense eyes.

She bagged the blood-spatter sample, labeled it and put it in her equipment bag.

"Anything wrong?" Livvy asked the moment Reed ended the call.

"Maybe. While he was in town and running the investigating, Lieutenant Wyatt Colter made notes about the shoe sizes of the folks who live around here. He left the info at the station."

That didn't surprise Livvy. Lieutenant Colter was a thorough man. "And?"

"Kirby compared the size of the castings, and it looks as if three people could be a match. Of course, the prints could also have also been made by someone Marcie met during her two years on the run. The person might not even be from Comanche Creek."

Livvy couldn't help it. She huffed. "Other than you, who are two possible matches?"

"Jerry Collier, the head of the land office. He was also Marcie's former boss."

She had his bio, and it was one of the ones that Reed had picked from the file as a person who might be prone to breaking into the cabin. Later, she'd look into his possible motive for stealing a phone. "And the other potential match?"

Reed's jaw muscles did more than stir. They went iron-hard. "The mayor, Woody Sadler."

"Of course."

She groaned because she shouldn't have allowed Reed to stop her from arresting him. Or at least thoroughly searching him. Mayor Woody Sadler could have hidden that phone somewhere on his body and literally walked away with crucial evidence. Lost evidence that would get her butt in very hot water with her boss.

"I'll talk to him," Reed said.

"No. *I'll* talk to him." And this time she didn't intend to treat him like a mayor but a murder suspect.

In Reed's eyes, she saw the argument they were about to have. Livvy was ready to launch into the inevitable disagreement when she heard another sound. Not a cell phone this time.

Something crashed hard and loud against the cabin door.

Chapter Three

Reed drew his Smith and Wesson. Beside him, Livvy tossed the UV lamp and her glasses onto the sofa so she could do the same. Reed had already had his fill of unexpected guests today, and this sure as hell better not be somebody else trying to "help" Shane.

"Anyone out there?" Reed called out.

Nothing.

Since it was possible their visitor was Marcie's killer who'd returned to the scene of the crime, Reed approached the door with caution, and he kept away from the windows so he wouldn't be ambushed. He tried to put himself between Livvy and the door. It was an automatic response, one he would have done for anyone. However, she apparently didn't appreciate it because she maneuvered herself to his side again.

Reed reached for the doorknob, but stopped.

"Smoke?" he said under his breath. A moment later, he confirmed that was exactly what it was. If there was a fire out there, he didn't want to open the door and have the flames burst at them.

There was another crashing sound. This time it came

from the rear of the cabin. Livvy turned and aimed her gun in that direction. Reed kept his attention on the front of the place.

Hell.

What was happening? Was someone trying to break in?

Or worse. Was someone trying to kill them?

In case it was the *or worse,* Reed knew he couldn't wait any longer. He peered out from the side of the window.

And saw something he didn't want to see.

"Fire!" he relayed to Livvy.

She raced to the back door of the cabin. "There's a fire here, too."

A dozen scenarios went through his mind, none of them good. He grabbed his phone and pressed the emergency number for the fire department.

"See anyone out there?" Reed asked, just as soon as he requested assistance.

"No. Do you?"

"No one," Reed confirmed. "Just smoke." And lots of it. In fact, there was already so much black billowy smoke that Reed couldn't be sure there was indeed a fire to go along with it. Still, he couldn't risk staying put. "We have to get out of here now."

Livvy took that as gospel because she hurried to the table, grabbed the files and the other evidence she'd gathered and shoved all of it and her other supplies into her equipment bag. She hoisted the bag over her shoulder, freeing her hand so she could use her gun. Unfortunately, it was necessary because Reed might need her as backup.

"Watch the doors," he insisted.

Not that anyone was likely to come through them
with the smoke and possible fires, but he couldn't take
that chance. They were literally under siege right now
and anything was possible. The smoke was already
pouring through the windows and doors, and it wouldn't
be long before the cabin was completely engulfed.

The cabin wasn't big by anyone's standards. There
was a basic living, eating and cooking area in the main
room. One bedroom and one tiny bath were on the other
side of the cabin. There was no window in the bathroom
so he went to the lone one in the bedroom. He looked
out, trying to stay out of any potential kill zone for a
gunman, and he saw there was no sign of fire here.
Thank God. Plus, it was only a few yards from a cluster
of trees Livvy and he could use for cover.

"We can get out this way," Reed shouted. The smoke
was thicker now. Too thick. And it cut his breath. It must
have done the same for Livvy because he heard her
cough.

He unlocked the window, shoved it up and pushed
out the screen. The fresh air helped him catch his breath,
but he knew the outside of the cabin could be just as
dangerous as the inside.

"Anyone out there?" Livvy asked.

"I don't see anyone, but be ready just in case."

The person who'd thrown the accelerant or whatever
might have used it as a ruse to draw them out. It was
entirely possible that someone would try to kill them the
moment they climbed out. Still, there was no choice
here. Even though he'd already called the fire department, it would take them twenty minutes or more to
respond to this remote area.

If they stayed put, Livvy and he could be dead by then.

"I'll go first," he instructed. He took her equipment bag and hooked it over his shoulder. That would free her up to run faster. "Cover me while I get to those trees."

She nodded. Coughed. She was pale, Reed noticed, but she wasn't panicking. Good. Because they both needed a clear head for this.

Reed didn't waste any more time. With his gun as aimed and ready as it could be, he hoisted himself over the sill and climbed out. He started running the second his feet touched the ground.

"Now," he told Livvy. He dropped the equipment bag and took cover behind the trees. Aimed. And tried to spot a potential gunman who might be on the verge of ambushing them.

Livvy snaked her body through the window and raced toward him. Despite the short distance, she was breathing hard by the time she reached him. She turned, putting her back to his. Good move, because this way they could cover most of the potential angles for an attack.

But Reed still didn't see anyone.

He blamed that on the smoke. It was a thick cloud around the cabin now. There were fires, both on the front porch and the back, and scattered around the fires were chunks of what appeared to be broken glass. The flames weren't high yet, but it wouldn't take them long to eat their way through the all-wood structure. And any potential evidence inside would be destroyed right along with it. If this arsonist was out to help Shane, then he was sadly mistaken.

Of course, the other possibility was that the real killer had done this.

It would be the perfect way to erase any traces of himself. Well, almost any traces. There was some potential evidence in Livvy's equipment bag. Maybe the person responsible wouldn't try to come after it.

But he rethought that.

A showdown would bring this fire-setting bozo out into the open, and Reed would be able to deal with him.

"Will the fire department make it in time to save the cabin?" Livvy asked between short bursts of air.

"No." And as proof of that, the flames shots up, engulfing the front door and swooshing their way to the cedar-shake roof. The place would soon be nothing but cinders and ash.

Reed was about to tell her that they'd have to stay put and watch the place burn since there was no outside hose to even attempt to put a dent in the flames. But he felt Livvy tense. It wasn't hard to feel because her back was right against his.

"What's wrong?" Reed whispered.

"I think I see someone."

Reed shifted and followed her gaze. She was looking in the direction of the county road, which was just down the hill from the cabin. Specifically, she was focused on the path that Woody had taken earlier. He didn't see anyone on the path or road, so he tried to pick through the woods and the underbrush to see what had alerted Livvy.

Still nothing.

"Look by my SUV," she instructed.

The vehicle was white and barely visible from his angle so Reed repositioned himself and looked down the slope. At first, nothing.

Then, something.

There was a flash of movement at the rear of her vehicle, but with just a glimpse he couldn't tell if it was animal or human.

"There's evidence in the SUV," she said. Her breathing was more level now, but that statement was loaded with fear and tension. "I'd photographed the cabin and exterior with a highly sensitive digital camera. Both it and the photo memory card are inside in a climate controlled case, along with some possible hair and fibers that I gathered from the sofa with a tape swatch."

Oh, hell. All those items could be critical to this investigation.

"The SUV's locked," she added.

For all the good that'd do. After all, the person out there had been gutsy enough to throw Molotov cocktails at the cabin with both Reed and a Texas Ranger inside, and he could have broken the lock on the SUV or bashed in a window.

Livvy grabbed her equipment bag from the ground and repositioned her gun. Reed knew what she had in mind, and he couldn't stop her from going to her vehicle to check on the evidence. But what he could do was assist.

"Stay close to the treeline," he instructed.

He stepped to her side so that she would be semi-sheltered from the open path. Another automatic response. But this time, Livvy didn't object. However, what she did do was move a lot faster than he'd anticipated.

Reed kept up with her while he tried to keep an eye on their surroundings and her SUV. None of the doors or windows appeared to be open, but he wouldn't be surprised if it'd been burglarized. Obviously, someone didn't want them to process that evidence.

He saw more movement near the SUV. A shadow, maybe. Or maybe someone lurking just on the other side near the rear bumper. Behind them, the fire continued to crackle and burn, and there was a crash when the roof of the cabin gave way and plummeted to the ground. Sparks and ashes scattered everywhere, some of them making their way to Livvy and him.

Livvy didn't stop. She didn't look back. But when Reed saw more movement, he latched on to her arm and pulled her behind an oak. This was definitely a situation where it would do no good to try to sneak up on the perp because the perp obviously was better positioned. Despite the cover of the trees, Livvy and he were in a vulnerable situation.

"This is Sheriff Hardin," he called out. "Get your hands in the air so I can see them."

He hadn't expected the person to blindly obey. And he didn't. Reed caught a glimpse of someone wearing a dark blue baseball cap.

Reed shifted his gun. Took aim—just as there was a crashing sound, followed by a flash of light. Someone had broken the SUV window and thrown another Molotov cocktail into the vehicle.

"He set the SUV on fire," Livvy said, bolting out from cover.

Reed pulled her right back. "He might have a gun." Except there was no *might* in this. The guy was probably armed and dangerous, and he couldn't have Livvy running right into an ambush.

"But the evidence…" she protested.

Yeah. That was a huge loss. Like Livvy, his instincts were to race down there and try to save what he could, but to do that might be suicide.

"He could want you dead," Reed warned.

That stopped Livvy from struggling. "Because of the evidence I gathered from the cabin?"

Reed nodded and waited for the rest of that to sink in. It didn't take long.

"Shane couldn't have done this," she concluded.

"No." Reed kept watch on the vehicle and the area in case the attacker doubled back toward them or tried to escape.

"But someone who wanted to exonerate him could have," Livvy added.

Reed nodded again. "That means the fire starter must have thought you saw or found something in the cabin that would be crucial evidence."

That also meant Livvy was in danger.

Reed cursed. This was turning into a tangled mess, and he already had too much to do without adding protecting Livvy to the list.

In the distance Reed heard the siren from the fire department. Soon, they'd be there. He glanced at the cabin. Then at Livvy's SUV. There wouldn't be much to save, but if he could catch the person responsible he might get enough answers to make up for the evidence they'd lost.

More movement. Reed spotted the baseball cap again. The guy was crouched down, and the cap created a shadow that hid his face. He couldn't even tell if it was a man or a woman. But whoever it was, the person was getting away.

"Stay put," Reed told Livvy.

Now it was her turn to catch onto his arm. "Remember that part about him having a gun."

Reed remembered, but he had to try to find out who was behind this.

"Back me up," he told her. That was to get her to stay put, but the other reason was he didn't want this cap-wearing guy to sneak up on him. Reed wouldn't be able to hear footsteps or much else with the roar of the fire and the approaching siren.

Keeping low as well, Reed stepped out from the meager cover of the oak. He kept his gun ready and aimed, and he started to run.

So did the other guy.

Using the smoke as cover, the culprit darted through the woods on the other side of the SUV and raced through the maze of trees. If Reed didn't catch up with him soon, it'd be too late. He ran down the hill, cursing the uneven clay-mix dirt that was slick in spots. Somehow, he made it to the bottom without falling and breaking his neck.

Reed didn't waste any time trying to save the SUV. The inside was already engulfed in flames. Instead, he sprinted past it, but Reed only made it a few steps before there was another sound.

Behind him, the SUV exploded.

He dodged the fiery debris falling all around him and sprinted after the person who'd just come close to killing them.

Chapter Four

Livvy dove to the ground and used the tree to shelter herself from the burning SUV parts that spewed through the air. She waited, listening, but it was impossible to hear anything, especially Reed. Beyond the black smoke cloud on the far side of what was left of her vehicle, she saw him sprint into the woods.

Since Reed might need backup, she got up, grabbed the equipment bag and went after him. Livvy kept to the trees that lined the path and then gave the flaming SUV a wide berth in case there was a secondary explosion. She'd barely cleared the debris when the fire engine screamed to a stop on the two-lane road.

"Sergeant Hutton," she said, identifying herself to the men who barreled from the engine. "Sheriff Hardin and I are in pursuit of a suspect."

Livvy hurried after Reed but was barely a minute into her trek when she saw Reed making his way back toward her. Not walking. Running.

"What's wrong?" she asked.

Reed drew in a hard breath. "I couldn't find him, and I was afraid he would double back and come after you."

Because the adrenaline was pumping through her and her heart was pounding in her ears, it took Livvy a moment to realize what he'd said. "I'm a Texas Ranger," she reminded him. "If he'd doubled back, I could have taken care of myself."

Reed tossed her a glance and started toward the fire department crew. "I didn't want him to shoot you and then steal the evidence bag," he clarified.

Oh. So, maybe it wasn't a me-Tarzan response after all. And once again, Livvy felt as if she'd been trumped when she was the one in charge.

By God, this was her case and her crime scene.

She followed Reed back to the chaos. The fire department already had their hose going, but there was nothing left to save. Worse, with everyone racing around the SUV and the cabin, it would be impossible to try to determine which footprints had been left by the perpetrator.

Reed stopped in front of a fifty-something Hispanic man, and they had a brief conversation that Livvy couldn't hear. A minute later, Reed rejoined her.

"Come on," he said. "We'll use my truck to take that evidence to my office."

Livvy looked around and realized there was nothing she could do here, so she followed Reed past the cabin to a back trail. It wasn't exactly a relaxing stroll because both Reed and she hurried and kept their weapons ready. With good reason, too. Someone had just destroyed crucial evidence, and that same someone might come after them. The woods were thick and ripe territory for an ambush.

Reed unlocked his black F-150 and they climbed in

and sped away. He immediately got on the phone to his deputy, and while Reed filled in Deputy Spears, Livvy knew she had to contact her boss, Lieutenant Wyatt Colter.

She grabbed her cell, took a deep breath and made the call. Since there was no way to soften it, she just spilled it and told him all about the burned cabin, her SUV and the destroyed evidence.

On the other end of the line, Lieutnenant Colter cursed. "You didn't have the evidence secured?"

"I did, in the locked SUV, but the perp set it on fire." She was thankful that she'd already stashed her personal items at the Bluebonnet Inn where she'd be staying so at least she would have a change of clothes and her toiletries. Of course, she would have gladly exchanged those items, along with every penny in her bank account, if she could get back that evidence.

More cursing from the lieutenant, and she heard him relay the information to someone else who was obviously in the room with him. Great. Now, everyone at the regional office would know about this debacle.

"Things are crazy here," Lieutenant Colter explained. "I'm tracking down those illegally sold Native American artifacts, and I'm at a critical point in negotiations. But I'll be out there by early afternoon."

"No!" Livvy couldn't get that out fast enough. "There's no need, and there's nothing you can do. I have everything under control."

The lieutenant's long hesitation let her know he wasn't buying that. "I'll talk with the captain and get back to you."

"I don't need reinforcements," she added, but Livvy

was talking to herself because Lieutenant Colter had already hung up on her.

"Problem?" Reed asked the moment she ended the call.

"No," she lied.

He made a sound to indicate he knew it was a lie.

Since it was a whopper, Livvy tried to hurry past the subject. "After I get this evidence logged in and started, I'd like to question Shane about the murder."

Reed didn't answer right away. He had her wait several moments, making Livvy wish she'd made it sound more like an order and not a request.

"Shane will cooperate," Reed finally said. He paused again. "And while you're talking to him, I'll call your lieutenant and let him know this wasn't your fault."

"Don't." She stared at him as he drove onto the highway that led to town. "I don't need your help." Though she probably did. Still, Livvy wouldn't allow Reed to defend her when she was capable of doing it herself. "I'll call him in an hour or two and explain there's no need for him to be here."

And somehow, she would have to make him understand.

"This case seems personal to you," Reed commented. "Why? Did you know Marcie?"

"No." But he was right. This was personal. Murders always were. "My mother was murdered when I was six, and she was about the same age as Marcie. This brings back…memories."

And she had no idea why she'd just admitted that. Sheez. The chaos had caused her to go all chatty.

"Was the killer caught?" Reed asked.

Livvy groaned softly. She hadn't meant for this to turn into a conversation. "No. He escaped to Mexico and has never been found."

"That explains why you're wrapped so tight."

She blinked. Frowned. "Excuse me?"

"You think if you solve Marcie's murder, then in a small way, you'll get justice for your mom."

She was sure her mouth dropped open when she scowled at him. "What—did you take Psych 101 classes along with those forensic workshops?"

He shook his head. "Personal experience. My dad was shot and killed when I was a kid. Every case turns out to be about him." Reed lifted his shoulder. "Can't help it. It's just an old wound that can't be healed."

Yes.

Livvy totally understood that.

"That's why I jumped to defend Woody back there," Reed continued. "He raised me. He became the dad who was taken away from me." But then he paused. "That doesn't mean I can't be objective. I can be."

She wanted to grumble a *hmmmp* to let him know she had her doubts about that objectivity, but her doubts weren't as strong as they had been an hour earlier. Livvy blamed that on their escape from death together. That created a special camaraderie. So did their tragic pasts. For that matter so did this bizarre attraction she felt for him. All in all, it led to a union that she didn't want or need.

"Oh, man," Reed groaned.

Livvy looked ahead at the two-story white limestone building with a triple-arch front and reinforced glass doors. It was the sheriff's office, among other things.

Livvy had learned from Deputy Spears that it also housed the jail and several municipal offices.

Right next to the sheriff's building was an identical structure for the mayor's office and courthouse. However, it wasn't the weathered facades of the buildings that had likely caused Reed's groan. As he brought the truck to a stop, he had his attention fastened to the two men and a Native American woman standing on the steps. Another attractive woman with long red hair was sitting in a car nearby.

"Trouble?" Livvy asked.

"Maybe. Not from the redhead. She's Jessie Becker, but her father's the one on the right. He's probably here to stir up some trouble."

Jonah was the owner of the cabin. And, as far as Livvy was concerned, he was a prime murder suspect. Even if he hadn't been the one to actually kill Marcie, he might have information about it.

Though she'd scoured Jonah's bio, this was Livvy's first look at the man, and he certainly lived up to his reputation of being intimating and hard-nosed. Jonah might have been wearing a traditional good-guy white cowboy hat, but the stare he gave her was all steel and ice.

"You let somebody burn down my cabin," Jonah accused the moment Reed and she stepped from the truck. "The fire chief just called. Said it was a total loss."

"We didn't exactly *let* it happen," Reed snarled. He stopped. Met Jonah eye-to-eye. "There was a phone stolen from the cabin before the place was set on fire. Know anything about that?"

Jonah's mouth tightened. "Now, you're accusing me of thievery from a place I own?"

"I'm asking, not accusing," Reed clarified, though from his tone, it could have been either. "But I want an answer."

The demand caused a standoff with the two men staring at each other. "I didn't take anything from the cabin," Jonah finally said, "because I haven't been out there. Last I heard, you'd roped off the place and said for everybody to stay away. So, I stayed away," he added with a touch of smugness.

If Reed believed him, he didn't acknowledge it.

"I'm Billy Whitley," the other man greeted Livvy, extending his hand to her. He tipped his head to the Native American woman beside him. "And this is my wife, Charla."

Livvy shifted her equipment bag and shook hands with both of them. "Sergeant Hutton."

Unlike Jonah, Billy wasn't wearing a cowboy hat, and the khaki-wearing man sported a smile that seemed surprisingly genuine. "Welcome to Comanche Creek, Sergeant Hutton."

"Yes, welcome," Charla repeated, though it wasn't as warm a greeting as her husband's had been. And she didn't just look at Livvy—the woman's intense coffee-brown eyes stared.

Livvy didn't offer her first name, as Billy had done to her. Yes, it was silly, but she wanted to hang on to every thread of authority she had left. After what'd just happened, that wasn't much, but somehow she had to establish that she was the one in charge here. That wasn't easy to do with Reed storming past Jonah and Billy.

And her.

That left her trailing along after him.

"I'm the county clerk here," Billy continued. "Charla is an administrative assistant for the mayor." All three followed into the building, too. "I handle the records and such, and if I can help you in any way, just let me know."

That *such* might become important to Livvy since Billy would be in charge of deeds, and the land that Jonah had bought might play into what was happening now. Of course, Livvy had a dozen other things to do before digging into what might have been an illegal land deal.

Jonah caught up with them and fell in step to her left. Since the entry hall was massive, at least fifteen feet wide, it wasn't hard for the four to walk side by side, especially with Reed ahead of them. "I'm not even gonna get an apology for my cabin?" Jonah complained.

"I'm sorry," Livvy mumbled, and she was sincere. Losing the cabin and the evidence inside was a hard blow to the case.

Reed turned into a room about midway down the hall, and he walked past a perky-looking auburn-haired receptionist who stood and then almost immediately sat back down to take an incoming call.

They walked by a room where Deputy Spears was on the phone as well, but he called out to her, "The castings are on the way to the lab. The courier just picked them up."

"Thanks," Livvy managed but didn't stop.

She continued to follow the fast-walking Reed into his office. Like the man, it was a bit of a surprise. His desk was neat, organized, and the slim computer monitor and equipment made it look more modern than Livvy had thought it would be. There was a huge calendar on the wall, and it was filled with appointments at precise times, measured not in hours but in quarter hours.

"You can put the equipment bag there," Reed instructed, pointing to a table pushed against one of the walls. There was also an evidence locker nearby. Good. She wanted to secure the few items she had left.

Reed snatched up the phone. "I need to call some of the other sheriffs in the area and have them send over deputies to scour the woods for anything the arsonist might have left behind. After that, I'll take you up to the jail so you can talk to Shane."

Reed proceeded to make that call, but he also shot a what-are-you-still-doing-here? glare at Billy, Charla and Jonah, who were hovering in the narrow doorway and watching Livvy's every move. Livvy didn't think it was her imagination that all three were extremely interested in what she had in the equipment bag. Still, Billy tipped two fingers to his forehead in a mock salute and Charla and he left.

Jonah didn't.

"So, did you come to town to arrest me for Marcie's murder?" Jonah asked her.

Livvy spared him a glance and plopped her bag onto the table. "Why, are you confessing to it?"

"Careful," Jonah warned, and his tone was so chilling that it prompted Livvy to look at him.

"I'm always careful. And thorough," she threatened back. She tried not to let her suspicions of this man grow. After all, they had a suspect in jail, but she wondered if Shane had acted alone.

Or if he'd acted at all.

It wouldn't be a pleasant task to challenge Shane's guilt or innocence because if she proved Shane hadn't murdered Marcie, then she would have to prove that someone else had. That was certain to rile a lot of people.

She remembered the uncomfortable stare that Charla Whitley had given her. And the way the mayor had reminded her of Reed's authority. She wasn't winning any Miss Congeniality contests—and probably wouldn't.

"Good day, Mr. Becker," Livvy said, dismissing Jonah, and she took out the bag with the sample from the blood spatter. If this was indeed Shane's blood, and if future analysis of the pattern indicated that it was real castoff from blunt force, then that would put some doubt in her mind.

Since Reed was still on the phone, Livvy secured her bag in the evidence locker, and with the blood sample clutched in her hand, she walked to the doorway. Jonah was still there, but she merely stepped around him and went to Deputy Spears's office. She shut the door so they'd have some privacy.

"I need this analyzed ASAP," she instructed. "It's possible that it's Shane's blood."

Kirby Spears nodded. "I can run it over to the coroner. He does a lot of this type of work for us, and we have Shane's DNA on file in the computer so we can compare the sample." He took the bag and put his initials on the chain of custody form.

Again, Livvy was surprised with the efficiency. "What about the murder weapon and the bullet?"

"The bullet's still being analyzed at the Ranger crime lab, and there's no match to the gun. We have the serial number, but so far, there's no info in the database about it."

Livvy made a mental note to call the crime lab, but first she wanted to visit Shane. Without Reed. Even though Reed had said he would be the one to take her, she didn't need or want his help during this particular interrogation. She knew how to question a suspect.

"Where's the jail?" she asked the deputy.

"Up the stairs, to the right."

Livvy thanked him and walked back into the hall. She halfway expected Jonah to be waiting there, but saw thankfully he had left. Since Reed was still on the phone, she made her way up the stairs to where she found a guard sitting at a desk. He wore a uniform from a civilian security agency, and he obviously knew who she was because he stood.

"Shane's this way," he commented and led her down the short hall flanked on each side with cells. All were empty except for the last one. There, she found the deputy lying on the military-style cot.

Livvy's first thought was that he didn't look like a killer. With his dark hair and piercing blue eyes, he looked more like a grad student. A troubled one, though.

"Sergeant Hutton," he said, slowly getting to his feet.

"Word travels fast," she mumbled.

The corner of his mouth lifted into a half smile that didn't quite make it to his eyes. "There aren't many secrets in Comanche Creek. Well, except for the secret of who murdered Marcie. I loved her." He shook his head. "I wouldn't have killed her."

"The evidence says differently."

He walked closer and curved his fingers around the

thick metal bars. "But since I didn't do it, there must be evidence to prove that. Promise me that you'll dig for the truth. Don't let anyone, including Jonah, bully you."

She shrugged. "Why would Jonah want to bully me?"

"Because you're a woman. An outsider, at that. He won't respect your authority. For that matter, most won't, and that includes the mayor."

Well, Livvy would have to change their minds.

"What do you know about a cell phone that I found in the ashes of the fireplace?" she asked.

There was a flash of surprise in his eyes. Then, another headshake. "I don't know. Is it Marcie's?"

"Maybe. Any reason the mayor would steal the phone to try to help you out?"

"Woody? Not a chance. He might not care for outsiders like you, but he wouldn't break the law. Why? You think he had something to do with the fire at the cabin?"

Livvy jumped right on that. "How'd you know about it?"

"The guard. His best friend runs the fire department."

"Cozy," Livvy mumbled. But she didn't add more because she heard the footsteps. She glanced up the hall and saw Reed making his way toward them.

"You could have waited," Reed mumbled.

Livvy squared her shoulders. "There was no reason. I'm trying to organize my case, and questioning Deputy Tolbert is a critical part of that."

Reed gave her a disapproving glance—she was getting used to those—before he looked at Shane. "We found blood spatter on the mantel in the cabin." It definitely wasn't the voice of a lawman, but it wasn't exactly friendly, either.

Shane blew out his breath as if relieved. "I've been going over and over what happened, and I'm pretty sure the person who clubbed me was a man. Probably close to my height because I didn't get a sense of anyone looming behind me before I was hit. I think you're also looking for someone who might be left-handed because the blow came from my left."

"Did you notice any particular smell or sound?" Livvy asked at the same moment Reed asked, "Did you remember what he used to hit you?"

Reed and she looked at each other.

Frowned.

"No smell or sound," Shane answered. "And I saw the object out of the corner of my eye. I think it might have been a baseball bat."

Livvy was about to ask if the bat had possibly been in or around the cabin, but her phone rang. One glance at the caller ID, and she knew it was a call she had to take—her boss, Lieutnenant Colter. She stepped away from the cell and walked back toward the desk area. Behind her, she heard Reed continue to talk to Shane.

"Livvy," Lieutenant Colter greeted her. "I wanted to let you know that I won't be able to get to Comanche Creek after all. There's too much going on here. And with a suspect already arrested—"

"Don't worry. I can handle things."

His pause was long and unnerving. "I talked with the captain, and we've agreed to give you three days to process the scene and the evidence. By then, we can send in another Ranger. One with more experience."

Oh, that last bit stung.

"Three days," Livvy said under her breath. Not much time, but enough. She would use those three days to prove herself and determine if the evidence did indeed conclude that the deputy had murdered his former girl-friend. "Thank you for this opportunity."

"Don't thank me yet. Livvy, there's one condition about you staying there."

Everything inside her went still. "What?"

"You're not in charge of this case. Sheriff Reed Hardin is. And while you're there in Comanche Creek, you'll be taking your orders from him."

Chapter Five

Reed made his way across the back parking lot of the sheriff's building. With the sun close to setting, the sky was a dark iron-gray, and the drizzle was picking up speed. He hadn't even bothered to grab an umbrella from the basket next to his desk, but then he hadn't thought Livvy would creep along at a snail's pace either.

"This isn't necessary," Livvy complained again. She was a good ten feet behind him, and she had her equipment bag slung over her shoulder. "I can walk to the Bluebonnet Inn on my own."

Reed ignored her complaint and opened his truck door so she could climb inside. "The inn's a mile away, and in case you hadn't noticed, it's raining." And because her expression indicated she was still opposed to a lift, he added, "The sooner you get settled into your room, the sooner you can go over the recording of my initial interview with Shane."

Since Livvy had the envelope with the disk tucked under her arm, Reed knew she was anxious to get to it. But then, she was also anxious to be away from him, and a ride, even a short one, would only remind her that she'd essentially been demoted as lead on this case.

And he was in charge.

Reed didn't know who was more ticked off about that—Livvy or him. Even though he'd wanted to handle this investigation himself, he certainly hadn't asked to play boss to a Texas Ranger who already thought he was lower than hoof grit.

When Livvy stopped and stared at him, Reed huffed, blinked away the raindrops spattering on his eyelashes and got into his truck, leaving the passenger's-side door open. The rain had caused wisps of her hair to cling to her face and neck. No more sleek ponytail. The rain had also done something to her white shirt.

Something that Reed wished he hadn't noticed.

The fabric had become somewhat transparent and now clung to her bra and breasts. And the rest of her.

You're her temporary boss, he reminded himself.

But the reminder did zero good. Nada. Zip. His male brain and body were very attentive to Livvy's ample curves and that barely-there white lace bra she was wearing.

As if she'd realized where his attention was, her gaze dropped down to her chest. "Oh!" leaped from her mouth. And she slapped the large manila envelope over the now-transparent shirt. She also got in the truck. Fast. And slammed the door.

"You could have said something," she mumbled, strapping on her seat belt as if it were the enemy.

"I could have," he admitted, "but let's just say I was dumbfounded and leave it at that."

He drove away with her still staring at him, and her mouth was slightly open, too.

Reed didn't want to defend himself, especially since gawking at her had been a dumb thing to do, but her continuing stare prompted him to say something. "Hey, just because I wear this badge doesn't mean I'm not a red-blooded male."

"Great." And that was all she said for several moments. "This won't be a problem."

"This?" Yeah, it was stupid to ask, but Reed couldn't stop himself.

"My breasts. Your male red blood."

Well, that put him in his place and meant the attraction was one-sided. His side, specifically. Good. That would make these next three days easier.

Parts of his body disagreed.

Reed stopped in front of the Bluebonnet Inn, a two-story Victorian guesthouse that sported a crisp white facade with double wraparound porches and a ton of windows. Livvy got out ahead of him and seemed surprised when he got out as well and followed her up the steps.

"I just want to check on a few things," he explained.

"Such as?"

"Security."

That stopped her hand in mid-reach for the cut-glass doorknob. She studied his eyes, and then her forehead bunched up. "You think the person who burned the cabin might come after me?"

"It's a possibility." Reed glanced at her equipment bag. "He might be after that."

"There's no evidence in it. The blood's being

analyzed, and I left the photos of the spatter pattern at your office in the secure locker." Then she quickly added, "But the arsonist doesn't know that."

Reed nodded and opened the door. He didn't want to feel uneasy about Livvy's ability to protect herself. After all, as she'd already informed him, she was a Texas Ranger, trained with a firearm. And he was reasonably sure his feelings had nothing to do with her being a woman and more to do with the fact there was someone obviously hell-bent on destroying any and everything that might have been left at the crime scene.

Someone he likely called a friend or a neighbor. Not exactly a comforting feeling.

"Reed," the landlady greeted him when he stepped inside. Like most of the townsfolk, he'd known Betty Alice Sadler all his life. She was Woody's sister and the owner of the Bluebonnet Inn and she had a smile that could compete with the sun.

"Betty Alice," Reed greeted her back. He tipped his head to Livvy. "You've met Sergeant Hutton?"

The woman aimed one of her winning smiles at Livvy. "For a second or two when she dropped her things off this morning. In and out, she was, before we hardly had time to say a word." The smile faded, however, when she glanced at the bulky-looking suitcase and garment bag in the corner. "One of those McAllister boys was supposed to help me out around here today, but he didn't show up."

Reed knew what Betty Alice didn't explain. The woman had a bad back, and all the guestrooms were upstairs. No elevator, either. Taking up the bags herself would have been next to impossible.

"I'll carry them up," Reed volunteered. "Has anyone dropped by today? Maybe someone who could have slipped into the rooms?"

Betty Alice pressed her left palm against her chest. "Lord have mercy, I don't think so. But you know I'm not always at this desk. When I'm in the kitchen or watching my soaps, it's hard to hear if somebody comes in."

Yes, he did know, and that meant he needed to do some further checking. "I'm sure everything's fine. It's just we had some more problems out by Jonah Becker's cabin, and I want to take some precautions."

Betty Alice's hand slipped from her chest, and her chin came up a fraction. "Nobody around here would try to set fire to my place. Now, Jonah's cabin—well, that's a different story. Most folks know he's got money and things to burn so that cabin was no real loss to him. Still, I'm real sorry about the sergeant's car."

"How did you know about my car?" Livvy asked.

"My second cousin's a fireman, and he was at home when he got the call to respond. His wife heard what was going on and phoned me. I hope your car was insured."

"It was," Livvy assured her. And she walked toward her bags.

Reed walked toward them, too. "Let me guess—you put Sergeant Hutton in the pink room?" Reed asked Betty Alice.

The woman's smile returned. "I did. You know it's where I put all my single female guests. That room's my pride and joy. I hope you like it, Sergeant."

"I'm sure I will," Livvy answered, and in the same breath added, "I can carry the things myself."

He would have bet his paycheck that was what she was going to say, but Reed took the suitcase and garment bag anyway, and since Livvy had the equipment and the envelope, she couldn't exactly snatch the items away from him.

"You'll set the security alarm tonight?" Reed said to Betty Alice. "And lock all the windows and doors?"

"Of course. I'll keep my gun next to my bed, too. Since all that mess with Marcie, I'm being careful, just like you told me."

"Good. But I want you to be extra careful tonight, understand?"

Betty Alice bobbed her head and nibbled on her bottom lip that'd been dabbed liberally with dark red lipstick. Reed hated to worry the woman, but he wanted Livvy and her to be safe.

"I really can carry my own bags," Livvy repeated as they made their way up the stairs.

Reed stopped at the top of the stairs in front of the pink room and set down the bags. Yes, it was dangerous, but he turned and met Livvy eye-to-eye. Since she was only about four inches shorter than he was, that made things easier because he wanted lots of eye contact while he cleared the air.

"Three days is a long time for us to be at odds. Yeah, I know you can carry bags. I know you can protect yourself, but I'm an old-fashioned kind of guy. A cowboy. And it's not in my genes to stand back when I can do something to help. Now, if that insults you, I'm sorry. And I'm sorry in advance because I'm about to go in your room and make sure it's safe. Just consider that part of my supervisory duties, okay?"

The staring match started. Continued. Reed had been right about the eye contact. And the other close contact. After all, Livvy was still wearing that transparent blouse, and she smelled like the smoky bacon cheese-burger and chocolate malt the café had delivered not long before Reed and she had called it a night and left the office. Normally, Reed wouldn't have considered a burger and malt to be tempting scents, but they were working tonight.

"Okay," she said, her voice all silk and breath.

Or maybe the silk part was his imagination.

Nope. When she cleared her throat and repeated it, Reed realized this close contact was having an effect on her as well.

Both of them stepped back at the same time.

"I want to go back out to the cabin in the morning." She cleared her throat again. "Will you be able to arrange a vehicle for me?"

Reed mentally cleared his own throat and mind. "I can take you. Two of the nearby sheriffs sent deputies out to scour the woods. Don't worry, they all have forensic training. They won't contaminate the scene, and they might be able to find and secure any evidence before the rain washes it all away."

That was a Texas-size *might* though since it'd been drizzling most of the afternoon.

She turned toward the door. Stopped. Turned back. "I'm sorry."

Puzzled, Reed shook his head. "For what?"

"For being so…unfriendly. I'm just disappointed, that's all."

He didn't know which one of them looked more uncomfortable with that admission. "I understand. I didn't ask Lieutenant Colter to be in charge."

"I know. He doesn't trust me."

Reed shrugged. "Or maybe he just wanted you to have some help on a very tough investigation."

She made a sound to indicate she didn't agree with that and opened the door. He supposed the room had some charm with its lacy bedspread and delicate—aka prissy—Victorian furniture, but it was hard to see the charm when the entire room looked as if it'd been doused in Pepto-Bismol.

"It *really* is pink, isn't it?" Livvy mumbled.

"Yeah. You could ask for a different room, but trust me, you don't want to do that because then you'd have to listen to Betty Alice explain every décor decision that went into the final result."

"This'll be fine. After all, it's where she puts all her single female guests."

And that was one of the primary reasons Reed had wanted to accompany her to the room. Everyone in town would know Livvy was staying there. It wouldn't help to put her in a different room either because secrets had a very short shelf life in Comanche Creek.

Reed set down the bags and went to the adjoining bathroom to make sure it was empty. It was. No one was lurking behind the frilly shower curtain ready to start another fire. No threatening messages had been scrawled on the oval beveled mirror.

Maybe, just maybe, the threat had ended with the destruction of the SUV and cabin.

Reed was in such deep thought with this suite ex-amination that it took him a moment to realize Livvy was standing in the bathroom door, and she was staring at him. "You're really concerned that I can't take care of myself. But I can. My specialty might be CSI, but my marksmanship skills are very good."

He didn't doubt her. Didn't doubt her shooting ability, either. But after the past few days, he wasn't sure any skill was good enough to stop what was happening.

"I have a spare bedroom at my place just on the edge of town," he offered. "And it's not pink," he added because he thought they both could use a little levity.

The corner of her mouth lifted. Not quite a smile though. And her eyes came to his. "Thanks but no thanks. I'll have a hard enough time getting people to respect me without them thinking that I'm sleeping with the boss."

He nodded. Paused. Reed walked past her and back into the bedroom. "They're likely to think that anyway."

Reed waited for her to look shocked. Or to protest it. But she didn't. "I take it you don't have a fiancée or long-time girlfriend?" she asked.

"No." And he left it at that.

Of course, Livvy would soon hear all about the breakup with Elena Carson four years ago when his high-school flame had decided to move to London to take a PR job. Heck, she'd even hear about the attorney from San Antonio that Reed had dated for a couple of months. The one who'd pressed him to marry her because her biological clock was ticking. And yeah, Livvy would even hear about the cocktail waitress who'd worn an eye-popping dress to the city hall Christmas party. No one would say he was a player, but he wouldn't be labeled a saint.

"What about Charla Whitley?" Livvy asked. "Did you date her?"

Reed was sure he was the one who looked a little shocked now. "No. What made you think that?"

"She was giving me the evil eye, and I thought it was maybe because of you. Probably had more to do with the fact that her husband could be a suspect, and she doesn't want me here investigating things."

Probably. But then, just about everyone in town was a suspect. Livvy could expect a lot of evil eyes in the next few days.

"What about you?" Reed asked, knowing it was a question that should be left unasked. "No fiancé or long-time boyfriend?"

She shook her head. "I don't have a lot of time for serious relationships."

"Ever?" And, of course, he should just hit himself so he'd stop prying, but for some stupid reason, a reason that had generated below his belt, he wanted to know more about Livvy Hutton.

"I dated someone in college, and it got serious. Well, on his part. You probably know it's hard to keep up with a personal life when the badge is there. And my badge is always there," she added, tapping the silver star on her chest while eyeing the one clipped to his belt.

He couldn't stop himself. "Must make for interesting sex if you never take off your badge."

There was another flash of surprise in her eyes. Then, she laughed. It was smoky and thick, the laugh of a woman who knew how to enjoy herself when the time was right. But she clamped off the laugh as quickly as she had the smile.

"You should go," she murmured. There it was

again. The sound of her voice trickled through him. Warm and silky.

Reed looked at her face. At her mouth. And knew Livvy was right. He should go. Betty Alice was probably already on the phone to her garden club, telling them that the sheriff had been in the lady Ranger's room for a whole ten minutes.

A lot could happen in ten minutes.

His imagination was a little too good at filling in the possibilities. Sex against the door. On the floor. Location wasn't important. It was the sex that he wanted.

But he wouldn't get it.

Reed forced himself to repeat that several times until it finally sank in.

"I'll pick you up at 7:00 a.m.," he told her. "And after a bite or two of breakfast at the café, we can drive out to the cabin."

"Can we get the breakfast to go?" she asked. "I'm anxious to return to the crime scene, and we can eat on the way."

Reed nodded. "Takeout, it is. I'll even see if the cook can figure out a way to add some chocolate to whatever's on the breakfast menu."

Livvy blinked. "How did you know I like chocolate?"

"Your breath, this morning. I smelled it. Milky Way?"

"Snickers," she confessed.

He didn't know why, but that confession seemed just as intimate as the sex thoughts he'd been having about her. He obviously needed to remember that he was a badass Texas sheriff. A surly one at that. Certainly not a man who cared to make a mental note to buy Livvy a Snickers bar or two.

"I'll see you in the morning." Reed headed out the door. However, he did wait in the hall until Livvy had closed it and he heard her engage the lock. She also moved something—a chair, from the sound of it—in front of the door.

Good.

Livvy was at least a little scared, and though that likely meant she wouldn't get much sleep, her vigilance might keep her safe. Now, Reed had to make sure that that safety extended to other things.

As soon as the borrowed deputies got to his office, he would send one of them out to patrol Main Street. Specifically, the Bluebonnet Inn. And he'd make copies of anything Livvy had left in the storage locker. That way, if the arsonist struck again, they wouldn't lose what little evidence they had left.

While Reed was making his mental list, he also added that he needed to call about the bullet, the missing cell phone, the gun and the DNA sample that Livvy had sent to the coroner.

It'd be another night short on sleep.

Reed went down the stairs, said goodnight to Betty Alice and watched as the woman double-locked the door and set the security alarm. Since the inn was also Betty Alice's home, it meant she, too, would be staying there, and Reed hoped everything would stay safe and secure. No more fires.

Because the drizzle had turned to a hard rain, he hurried down the steps toward his truck. But something had him stopping. He glanced around and spotted the black car parked just up the street in front of the newspaper office. That office had been closed for several hours, and there should have been no one parked there.

Reed tried to pick through the rain and the darkness and see if anyone was inside.

There was.

But because the windows were heavily tinted, he couldn't see the person. Nor the license plate. However, Reed could see the sticker that indicated it was a rental car. Definitely not a common sight in Comanche Creek.

He eased his hand over the butt of his Smith and Wesson and started toward the car. Maybe this had nothing to do with anything. Or maybe the fact it was a rental meant this was someone not local. Maybe someone Marcie had met while she was in hiding.

Either way, Reed braced himself for the worst.

The farther he made it down the sidewalk, the less he could see. That was because the only streetlights in this area were the two that flanked the front of the Blue-bonnet Inn. The person had chosen the darkest spot to park.

And wait.

Reed was about fifteen feet away from the vehicle when he saw the movement inside. Someone gripped onto the wheel. A moment later, the engine roared to life. Reed kept moving toward it, but the sudden lurching motion of the car had him stopping in his tracks.

It happened in a split second. There was more movement from the driver, and the car barreled forward.

Right at Reed.

Drawing his gun, he dove to the side. And not a moment too soon. He landed on the wet grass of the vacant lot, his shoulder ramming into a chunk of limestone.

The car careened right into the spot where seconds earlier he'd been standing.

Reed cursed and came up on one knee. Ready to fire. Or to dive out of the way if the car came at him again.

But it didn't.

The driver gunned the engine, and before he sped away, Reed caught just a glimpse of the person inside.

Hell.

Chapter Six

"Where the heck is he?" Livvy heard Reed demand.

He'd been making such demands from everyone he'd called, and this wasn't his first call. Reed had been on the phone the entire time since he'd picked her up at the Bluebonnet Inn ten minutes earlier. And while Livvy ate her scrambled-egg breakfast taco that Reed had brought her from the diner, she tried to make sense of what was going on.

"Leave him another message," Reed added, his voice as tense as the muscles of his face. "Tell him to call me the minute he gets back." And with that, Reed slapped his phone shut and shoved it into his pocket.

Livvy waited for an explanation of what had gotten him into such a foul mood, but he didn't say a word. She wondered if it was personal, and if so, she wanted to stay far away from it. There was already too much personal stuff going on between Reed and her, including that little chat they'd had about chocolate, badges and relationships.

She'd dreamed about him.

Not a tame dream either, but one that involved kissing and sex.

Hot, sweaty sex.

She would have preferred to dream about catching a killer or processing evidence, but instead she'd gotten too-vivid images of what it would be like to be taken by a man who almost certainly knew how to take.

Livvy felt herself blush. And decided she needed a change of thoughts. "Is there a problem?" she asked Reed.

Still no immediate answer, which confirmed there was indeed something wrong. "When I was leaving the Bluebonnet last night, I saw a rental car parked just up the street. When I went to check it out, the driver gunned the engine and nearly plowed right into me."

Oh, mercy. "Any reason you didn't tell me this sooner?"

More hesitation. "I wanted to check into a few things first."

Which, of course, explained nothing. Well, nothing other than why during the night there'd been a deputy positioned in a cruiser on the street directly in front of the inn. When Livvy had noticed him, she'd gotten upset with Reed because she'd assumed once again that he thought she couldn't take care of herself. But the rental-car incident was what had prompted him to add some extra security to the inn.

Reed had wanted someone in place in case the guy returned.

With her appetite gone now, Livvy wrapped up the rest of the breakfast taco and shoved it back into the bag. "Were you hurt?" she asked, starting with the most obvious question.

"No." That answer was certainly fast enough, though

she did notice the scrape on the back of his right hand. It was red and raw.

Livvy moved on to the next questions. "Any idea who the driver was, and why he'd want to do something like this?"

The possible theories started to fire through her head, but the one at the forefront was that the person who'd done this had also destroyed the cabin and her SUV. And this person wanted all the evidence destroyed and the investigation halted so the real killer wouldn't be caught. Or maybe the person thought the real killer was already behind bars and wanted him free.

Shane's father, maybe.

Or the other suspects.

Jerry Collier, Billy Whitley, Charla, Jonah Becker or Woody.

Reed stopped his truck just off the road that led to the burned-out cabin. Just yards away there was a police cruiser from another county. The vehicle no doubt belonged to the backups that Reed had called in. But it wasn't the activity that had her staring at him. Suddenly, the calls and his surly mood made sense.

"You saw the driver," she accused.

He scrubbed his hand over his face. "I saw his hat. A white Stetson with a rattler's tail on the band." Reed got out and slammed the door.

It didn't take her long to remember where she'd seen one matching that description. "Woody Sadler's hat," she clarified, getting out as well. Since Reed had already started to storm up the hill, she had to grab her equipment bag and hurry to keep up with him.

"A hat like his," Reed corrected.

"Or his," Livvy corrected back. She thought of the calls Reed had made in the truck. "And you haven't been able to speak to Woody to ask where he was last night."

The glance he gave her was hard and cold, but he didn't deny it. "Woody's secretary said he'd decided to take a last-minute fishing trip. His cell phone doesn't have service at the lake." He stopped so abruptly that Livvy nearly lost her balance trying to do the same. He aimed his index finger at her. "But let's get one thing straight. Woody wouldn't have tried to run me down."

Livvy wanted to argue with that, but it was true. It wouldn't make sense. Now, if Woody had come after her, that would have been more believable.

"Okay." Livvy nodded. "Then that means someone wanted you to think it was Woody. Who would have access to a hat like that?"

"Anyone in Texas," he grumbled.

Of course. It was dumb of her to ask. "But you're sure it was a man behind the wheel of the car?"

"Pretty sure. The person had the hat angled so that I couldn't see his face. And I got just a glimpse."

She glanced at the scrape on his hand again. Reed had gotten lucky, because even if this had been a stunt to scare them, it could have gone terribly wrong and he could have been killed. The thought made her a little sick to her stomach.

Okay, not sick sick.

Troubled sick.

She didn't like to think of anything bad happening to him, even though they were, for all practical purposes, still on opposite sides of a very tall fence.

"What?" he asked, glancing down at his hand and then at her.

"Nothing." And so that it would stay that way, she started up the hill again.

Reed snagged her by the arm and stopped her in her tracks. *"Something,"* he corrected.

She thought of her dream, felt the blush return. Livvy tried to shrug, and she quickly tried to get her mind off those raunchy images. "I know you're the boss, but from now on, please don't keep anything from me that might relate to the case."

And to make sure this didn't continue, she pulled away from his grip and started toward the uniformed deputy standing near the burned-out swatch of her SUV. Someone had already gathered up the debris. Nearby, just several feet inside the start of the thick brush and trees, she spotted a uniformed officer.

Livvy also spotted the soggy, muddy ground that was caking onto her boots. That mud wasn't good for her footwear or the crime scene. It had certainly washed away any tracks, and it'd sent a stream of ashes down the hill from the cabin. The black soot slivered through the crushed limestone, creating an eerie effect.

Reed said something to the uniformed officer and then looked at her. He motioned for Livvy to follow. Despite the mud weights now on her soles, she did. Not easily though. Reed began to plow through the woods like a man on a mission.

"They found something," he relayed to her without even looking back to make sure she was there.

That got Livvy moving faster, and she followed him

through the maze of wet branches, underbrush and wildflowers. "What?"

But Reed didn't answer. He made his way to some yellow crime-scene tape that had been tied to a scrawny mesquite oak. "They didn't collect it," he explained. "They figured you'd want to do that."

Livvy walked around the tree and examined what had caused Reed to react the way he had. It didn't take her long to see the swatch of fabric clinging to a low-hanging branch. It was fairly large, at least two inches long and an inch wide. She immediately set down her equipment bag and took out the supplies she needed to photograph and tag it. Thank goodness she had a backup camera because her primary one was destroyed in the fire.

"It looks as if it came from the cuff of a shirt," Reed pointed out.

Possibly. It was thick, maybe double-layered, and there was enough cloth for her to see that it was multi-colored with thin stripes of dark gold and burgundy on a navy blue background. It wouldn't have been her first choice of clothing to wear to commit a crime because the pattern really stood out.

Livvy snapped pictures of the swatch from different angles. "Did you see the perp's clothing when he was by my SUV and then running into the woods?"

"Just the baseball cap. But it's possible he had on a jacket, and that's why I didn't see the shirt."

Yes, or maybe this didn't belong to the suspect. Still, Livvy continued to hope because something like this could literally solve the case.

"You think it has DNA on it?" Reed asked.

"It might. If not on the fabric itself, then maybe the

tree branch snagged some skin." It looked as if the fabric had been ripped off while someone was running past the branch.

Reed got closer, practically arm to arm with her, and took his own photograph using his cell phone. "I'm sending this to Kirby at the office." He pressed some buttons on his phone to do that. "I'll have him ask around and see if anyone recognizes the fabric."

Good idea. She wished she'd thought of it first, and then Livvy scolded herself for even going there. Reed and she were on the same side, and maybe if she repeated it enough, she would soon believe it. She certainly wasn't having trouble remembering everything else about him.

Livvy finished the photographing, bagged the fabric and then snipped the tip of the branch so she could bag it as well. While she did that, Reed walked deeper into the woods.

"See anything else?" she asked.

"No." He stopped, propped his hands on his hips and looked around. "But if I were going to commit a crime and then make a fast escape, this is the route I'd go. If he'd gone east, that would have put him on the road. There's a creek to the west, and this time of year it's swollen because of the spring rains. With the fire and us behind him, this was the only way out."

Picking up the equipment bag, she went closer. "So, you're thinking the person was local?"

He nodded. And remained in deep thought for several long moments. "Jonah doesn't exactly encourage people to go traipsing onto his land, so there aren't paths through here." Reed pointed to the even thicker brush and trees ahead. "And once the arsonist made it to that point, I wouldn't have been able to see him. If that fabric belongs to him and if he ran in a fairly straight line, he would have ended up there."

Reed pointed to a trio of oaks standing so close together they were practically touching. Around them were thick clumps of cedars.

"The deputies searched that area?" Livvy asked.

Reed glanced around at the tracks on the muddy ground. "Yeah. But I'd like to have another look."

So would she, so Livvy followed him. She checked for breakage on the branches and shrubs, but when she didn't see any, she went farther to her right because the perp could have wavered from a straight-line run, especially once he was aware that Reed was in pursuit.

Since any point could be the escape route, she took some pictures, the flash of the camera slicing through the morning light. She was aware of the sound of Reed's footsteps, but Livvy continued to photograph the scene while moving right.

"Stop!" Reed shouted. But he didn't just shout.

He grabbed on to her shoulder and jerked her back so that she landed hard against his chest. Suddenly she was touching him everywhere and was in his arms.

"What are you doing?" she managed to ask. She looked up at him, but Reed's attention wasn't on her. It was on the ground.

"Trap." He pointed to a clump of soggy decaying leaves.

Livvy didn't understand at first, but she followed Reed's pointing finger and spotted the bit of black metal poking out from the clump.

Reed reached down, picked up a rock and tossed it at the device. It snapped shut, the claw-like sides closing in as they were meant to capture whatever—or whoever—was unfortunate enough to step on it. If she'd walked just another few inches, that trap would have clamped on to her foot.

"The perp probably wouldn't have had time to set that," Livvy managed to say. Not easily. Her heart was pounding and her breath had gone so thin that she could barely speak.

"Not unless he put it here before he started the fires."

Yes, and if he'd done that, then this crime had been premeditated. Worse, if there was one trap, there might be others.

"I need an evidence bag," Reed told her, moving toward the trap. "The trap might have fingerprints on it."

Livvy handed him a large collection bag and watched as he carefully retrieved the trap. "I'll have the deputies go through the area with a metal detector. After we're sure it's safe, we'll come back and keep looking."

She wasn't about to argue with that. First the fires. Then, Reed's encounter with the rental car. Now, this. It didn't take any CSI training to know that someone didn't want them to investigate this case.

Reed's cell phone rang, and he handed her the bagged trap so that he could take the call. Livvy labeled the item and eased it into her evidence bag so that she wouldn't smear any prints or DNA that might be on it.

"Billy said what?" Reed asked. And judging from his suddenly sharp tone, he wasn't pleased about something.

Since she couldn't actually hear what the caller was

saying, she watched Reed's expression and it went from bad to worse.

"What's wrong?" she asked the moment he ended the call.

Reed turned and started back toward his truck. "Kirby faxed the picture of the fabric to all the town agencies, and Billy Whitley said he'd seen that pattern before, and that it'd come from a shirt."

Billy Whitley. The county clerk she'd met in front of the sheriff's office the day before. The one who might also have ties to Marcie and her murder. "And did Billy happen to know who owns that shirt?"

"Yeah, he did." That was all Reed said until they made it back into the clearing. "Come on. We need to question a suspect."

Chapter Seven

Reed pulled to a stop at the end of the tree-lined private road that led to Jonah Becker's sprawling ranch house. He couldn't drive any farther because someone had closed and locked the wrought-iron cattle gates. Since he'd called about fifteen minutes earlier to let Jonah know he was on the way to have a *chat,* Reed figured the surly rancher had shut the gates on purpose.

It wouldn't keep Reed out.

Livvy and he could simply use the narrow footpath to the side of the gates. But it would mean a quarter-mile walk to question Jonah about how the devil a piece of his shirt had gotten torn on a tree branch mere yards from a double crime scene.

Though he figured it was futile, Reed called the ranch again and this time got the housekeeper. When he asked her to open the gate, she mumbled something about her boss saying it was to stay shut for the day. She further mumbled there was trouble with some of the calves getting out.

Right.

Jonah just wanted to make this as hard as possible.

Even though Reed hadn't specifically mentioned the shirt fabric they'd found, Jonah no doubt suspected something was up, and that *something* wasn't going to work in his favor. Of course, the real question was— had Jonah really committed a felony by burning Livvy's SUV and destroying evidence at a crime scene? And if the answer to that was yes, then Reed also had to consider him a candidate for Marcie's murder.

Livvy and he got out of the truck and started the trek along the deeply curved road. Thankfully, the road was paved so once they made it through the turnstile pedestrian gate, they didn't have to continue to use the muddy ground or pastures that fanned out for miles on each side of the ranch.

"It's a big place," Livvy commented, while shifting her equipment bag that had to weigh at least twenty-five pounds, especially now that it had the trap inside.

Reed figured it would result in a glare, but he reached out and took the bag from her. He waited for the argument about her being able to do it herself, but she simply mumbled "Thanks."

"Thanks?" he repeated.

Her mouth quivered a little. A smile threatened. "This doesn't mean anything. Well, other than you're stronger than I am."

But the smile that finally bent her mouth told him it might be more than that. The slight change of heart was reasonable. They were spending nearly every waking moment together, and they were both focused on the case. That created camaraderie. A friendship, almost. It definitely created a bond because they were on the same side.

Reed frowned. And wondered why he felt the need to justify his attraction to a good-looking woman. True, he hadn't planned on an attraction that might result in a relationship, but he was coming to terms with the notion that not having something in his plans didn't mean it wasn't going to happen anyway.

"Hold up a minute," Livvy said. She picked up a stick and used it to scrape some of the mud from those city heels on her boots.

"Those boots aren't very practical out here," Reed commented.

"No. My good pair was lost with some luggage when I was visiting my dad. I ordered another pair last night off the Internet, and I'm hoping they'll get here today."

So, this wasn't normal for her. What was, exactly? And what did she wear when she wasn't in her usual Ranger "uniform" of jeans and a white shirt? While Reed was thinking about that, he realized she'd stopped scraping mud and was staring at him.

"We, uh, both started off with some misconceptions about each other," she admitted.

"You're still from New York," he teased. But Reed immediately regretted his attempt at humor. He saw the darkness creep into her eyes and realized he'd hit a nerve. "Sorry."

"No. It's okay." She looked down and started to scrape at the mud again.

Since she wobbled and seemed on the verge of losing her balance, Reed caught on to her arm. He immediately felt her muscles tense. And her eyes met his again. Not a stare this time. Just a brief glance. But a lot of things passed between them with that glance.

Both of them cursed.

It'd been stupid to touch her, and Reed upped the ante on that stupidity by moving in closer still, lowering his head and putting his mouth on hers. Reed expected profanity. Maybe even a slap. He certainly deserved it, and a slap might just knock some sense into him.

But Livvy didn't curse or slap him.

She made a sound of pleasure, deep within her chest. It was brief and soft, barely there, but she might as well have shouted that the kiss was good for her, too. It was certainly *good* for Reed. Her mouth was like silk and, in that kiss, he took in her breath and taste.

That taste went straight through him.

And for just a moment he had a too-vivid image of what it would be like to kiss her harder and deeper. To push her against the nearby oak and do things he'd wanted to do since the first time he'd laid eyes on her.

Now, Livvy cursed and jerked away from him. "I know what you're thinking," she grumbled.

Hell. He hoped not. "What?"

"You're thinking that was unprofessional."

"Uh, no. Actually, I was thinking you taste even better than I thought you would, and my expectations were pretty damn high."

The smile threatened again, but it was quickly followed by a full-fledged scowl that she seemed to be aiming at herself. Livvy grabbed the equipment bag from him and started marching toward the ranch house.

"I have to do a good job here," she said when Reed fell in step alongside her. "I have to prove I can handle a complex crime scene on my own."

Reed understood the pressure, though he had never

experienced it firsthand. "It's been the opposite for me," he admitted. "My father was the sheriff so folks around here just accepted that I was the best man for the job."

"Lucky you." But she didn't say it as a snippy insult. More like envy.

"Well, maybe that luck will rub off on you." Which sounded sexual. His body was still begging for him to kiss her again. That would be a bad idea, especially since they were now close to the ranch house.

Livvy must have realized that as well because she looked ahead at the massive estate that peeked through the trees. "Jonah will probably try to convince us that the fabric's been there for a long time."

"Probably. But it hadn't been there long because it showed no signs of wear or of being exposed to the elements."

Jonah would try to refute that as well, but the man was still going to have a hard time explaining how he tore his shirt in that part of the woods, just yards from a murder scene.

As they got closer, Reed saw Jonah. He was waiting for them on the front porch.

And he wasn't alone.

Jonah's daughter, Jessie, had just served her father and his guest some iced tea. She tipped her head toward them in greeting.

"Don't work yourself up into a state," Jessie told her father, and she gently touched his arm. Her gaze came back to Reed, and she seemed to issue him a be-nice warning before she disappeared into the house.

Seated in a white wicker chair next to Jonah was a sandy-haired man Reed knew all too well: Jerry Collier.

"He's the head of the Comanche Creek Land Office," Livvy pointed out.

Reed nodded. "Jerry was also Marcie's former boss. And on various occasions, he acts as Jonah's attorney."

"Jonah lawyered up," she grumbled.

Apparently. And that was probably wise on Jonah's part. The man's temper often got in the way of his reason, and he must have guessed something incriminating had turned up.

"Reed," Jerry snapped, getting to his feet. Everything about him was nervous and defensive. That doubled when he turned his narrowed dust-gray eyes on Livvy. "Sergeant Hutton. I'm guessing you're responsible for this visit because Reed knows Jonah didn't have anything to do with what went on in his cabin."

"Is that true?" Livvy asked the rancher.

Jonah stayed seated and didn't seem nearly as ruffled as Jerry. "I understand you found a piece of cloth."

Reed groaned and didn't even bother to ask who'd told the man, but he'd ask Kirby about it later. His deputy apparently hadn't kept quiet as Reed had ordered.

Livvy set the equipment bag on the porch steps and took out the bagged swatch of fabric. She held it up for the men to see. "Does this belong to you?"

"Don't answer that," Jerry insisted. He wagged his finger at Reed. "First you accuse Woody of wrongdoing, and now Jonah? Am I next?"

"That's entirely possible," Reed calmly answered. "The investigation's not over. Who knows what I'll be able to dig up about you."

"And everybody else in town?" Jerry tossed back.

"No. Just the folks with motive to kill Marcie. Like you, for instance. I can't imagine you were happy when she showed up, ready to testify against you. And you couldn't have been pleased about it, either," Reed added, tipping his head toward Jonah.

Jerry aimed his comments at Livvy. "Marcie could testify all she wanted, but that doesn't mean Jonah and I did anything wrong."

"You're talking to the wrong person," Jonah told his lawyer. A faint smile bent the corner of Jonah's mouth. "Reed's in charge of this investigation, aren't you? The Rangers don't have a lot of faith in Sergeant Hutton."

Reed didn't have to look at Livvy to know that brought on a glare.

"Oh, they trust her," Reed corrected before Livvy could get into a battle of words with Jonah and Jerry. "The only reason I'm in charge is because the Rangers believe I know folks around here well enough that I can help Livvy get to the truth. And one way or another, we will get to the truth," Reed warned.

Jerry motioned toward the road. "You're looking for truth in the wrong place. Neither one of us had anything to do with Marcie's death."

Reed stepped closer, making sure he got way too close to Jerry. He knew Jerry wouldn't like that. For lack of a better word, the man was anal. Everything in its place. Everything *normal*. It wouldn't be normal for Reed to get in his face.

"Jerry, if I thought for one minute you were innocent in all of this, I wouldn't be talking to you. I believe you're just one step above being a snake-oil salesman. *One step,*" Reed emphasized, showing him a very narrow space between his thumb and index finger. "And I think you'd kill Marcie in a New York minute and then come here and pretend that you need to defend your old friend Jonah."

That caused the veins to bulge on Jerry's forehead, and he opened his mouth, no doubt to return verbal fire.

"Jerry, why don't you head back to your office?" Jonah ordered. "Just use the code I gave you to open the gate."

"I'd rather stay here," Jerry insisted, glaring at Reed.

Jonah angled his eyes in Jerry's direction. "And I'd rather you didn't. Go ahead. Head on out."

But Jerry didn't. Not right away. It took Jerry turning to Jonah, probably to plead his case as to why he should stay, but Jonah's eyes held no promise of compromise.

"Leave now," Jonah growled.

That sent Jerry cursing and storming off the porch and toward his silver-gray Mercedes. He gave Reed and Livvy one last glare before he got in, slammed the door and sped off.

Jonah calmly picked up his glass of iced tea and had a sip. He looked at Reed over the top of his glass that was beaded with moisture. "That fabric you found—it came from a shirt I used to own."

"Used to own?" Livvy questioned.

Jonah lazily set the glass aside as if he had all the time in the world. "I did some spring cleaning about two weeks ago and sent a bunch of old clothes to the charity rummage sale the church put on. That shirt was just one of the things I donated."

Well, there *had* been a rummage sale two weeks ago, but Reed had never known Jonah to be a charitable man.

"You donated it," Livvy repeated. "That's convenient."

"It's the truth." Jonah didn't smile, but there was a smug look on his face. He took a folded piece of paper from his pocket and handed it to Reed. "That's a copy of the things I donated."

Reed glanced over the dozen or so items, all clothing, and there were indeed three shirts listed on the tax receipt form.

Livvy leaned over and looked at it as well. "I don't suppose the church group would know who bought the shirt."

"No need," Jonah said before Reed could answer. "I already know because I saw him wearing it in town just a couple of days ago. I guess some people don't have any trouble with hand-me-downs."

Reed waited. And waited. But it was obvious Jonah was going to make him ask. "Who bought the shirt?"

"Shane's father, Ben Tolbert."

If Jonah had said any other name, Reed would have questioned it, but Ben probably did buy his clothing at rummage sales. Better yet, Ben had a powerful motive for burning down that cabin and Livvy's SUV.

Shane.

Ben wasn't a model citizen, but no one in Comanche Creek could doubt that he loved his son. Add to that, Ben did have a record and had been arrested several times. Nothing as serious as this, though.

"I already called Ben," Jonah continued, "and he didn't answer his phone. When you get a chance to talk to him, tell him I'm none too happy with him burning down my place and that I'm filing charges. I want his butt in a jail cell next to his murdering son."

Reed figured it was a good thing that Jonah's own

son, Trace, wasn't around to hear his dad call Shane a killer. Trace and Shane had been friends since child-hood, and Reed knew for a fact that Trace believed Shane to be innocent and had even tried to pay for a big-time lawyer to be brought in if the case went to trial.

"If I find out you're lying about Ben having the shirt, then you'll be the one in a jail cell next to Shane," Reed warned.

"And I'll be the one right there to make sure you're fired," Jonah warned back. "I won't be railroaded into taking the blame for something your own deputy and his loony father have done."

Since Reed knew there was no benefit to continuing this discussion, he turned and motioned for Livvy to follow him. "I need to talk to Ben before I go any further with this," Reed told her when they were a few yards away from the porch. He could practically feel Jonah staring holes in his back.

"If Ben doesn't corroborate Jonah's story about the shirt, will you be able to get a search warrant?" Livvy asked.

"Yeah. But it wouldn't do any good. If Jonah set those fires, then trust me, that shirt is long gone."

"True. He doesn't seem like the kind of man to keep incriminating evidence lying around." Livvy shrugged. "Which makes me wonder why he would have worn such a recognizable shirt to commit a crime."

Reed could think of a reason—to throw suspicion off himself by drawing attention to himself. A sort of reverse psychology. Still, that didn't mean Jonah hadn't hired someone to wear that shirt and destroy the evidence.

"I'll talk to Shane," Reed assured her. "He might know something about all of this."

"And he'd be willing to incriminate his father?"

"He has in the past. Three years ago when Ben got drunk and trashed some cars in the parking lot of the Longhorn Bar, Shane arrested him."

"Yes, but this is different. This is a felony. His father could go to jail for years."

Reed couldn't argue with that. But if Shane couldn't or wouldn't verify the shirt issue, then there were other ways to get at the truth, even if it meant questioning everyone in town.

"Look," Livvy said. She pointed to a storage barn in the pasture to their right.

Reed immediately saw what had captured her attention. There were several traps hanging on hooks. Traps that looked identical to the one someone had set near the cabin.

"You think they'll have serial numbers or something on them to link them to the other one?" she asked.

"Possibly. But even if they do and if they match the one we found, Jonah could say he set the trap because he owned the property and was having trouble with coyotes or something."

She shook her head. "But I have the feeling the trap was set for us. For me," Livvy softly added. "Someone in Comanche Creek doesn't want us to learn the truth about what happened to Marcie."

Reed had a bad feeling that she was right.

He thought about her alone at night in the inn and considered repeating his offer for her to stay at his place. She'd refuse, of course. Probably because she knew that would lead to a different kind of trouble. But even at the risk of Livvy landing in his bed, he wanted to do more to make sure she stayed safe while working on this case.

Reed mentally stopped.

Cursed.

"What's wrong?" Livvy asked, firing glances all around as if she expected them to be ambushed.

Reed wasn't sure this would sound any better aloud than it did in his head. "I'm thinking about staying at the inn. Just until this case is wrapped up."

She stopped, turned and stared at him. "And the profanity wasn't because of the element of danger. You know that being under the same roof with me isn't a good idea."

He tried to shrug. "Depends on what you consider a good idea."

Her stare turned flat. "Having a one-night stand with you wouldn't be a good idea. Or even a two-night stand, for that matter. Besides, you wouldn't even make the offer to stay at the inn if I were a man."

"True," he readily admitted. "But if you were a man, I wouldn't be torn between wanting you and protecting you."

She huffed and started to walk again. She was trying to dismiss all of this. But Reed figured the time for dismissing was long gone.

"My advice?" she said, her voice all breathy and hot. "We forget that kiss ever happened."

"Right." And he hoped his dry tone conveyed his skepticism. He'd have an easier time forgetting that he was neck-deep in a murder investigation. "We'll head back to the jail and talk to Shane about his father."

And once they'd done that, he'd think about his possible upcoming stay at the inn.

The cattle gates were wide open when they approached them. Jerry had no doubt left in a huff, especially since Jonah had essentially told him to get lost. That was something else Reed needed to give some thought. If Jonah hadn't wanted Jerry there in the first place, then what had the man been doing at Jonah's ranch? Reed trusted Jerry even less than he did Jonah, and he hoped Jerry hadn't made the visit because he had something to plot with Jonah.

Or something to hide.

They passed through the gate just as his phone rang. From the caller ID, he could see that it was Kirby.

"Don't tell me something else has gone wrong," Reed answered.

"No. Well, not that I know of anyway. I still haven't been able to reach Ben Tolbert like you asked. But I did just get a call from the crime lab about the gun Shane was holding when he was found standing over Marcie's body."

Reed took a deep breath and put the call on speaker so Livvy could hear this as well.

"That gun was the murder weapon," Kirby confirmed.

Hell. Reed glanced at Livvy. No I-told-you-so look on her face. Instead, her forehead was creased as if she were deep in thought.

"They also IDed the gun owner. A dealer in San Antonio who said he sold the piece over a week ago to a man named Adam Smith."

Reed shook his head. "Let me guess—Adam Smith doesn't exist."

"You're right. The documents he provided for proof of identity are all fake."

So, either Shane had faked them, or this was looking more and more like a complex, premeditated murder of a person who could have been a potential witness against both Jonah and Jerry for their involvement in that shady land deal.

Yeah. Reed really needed to do some more digging on both men.

"Kirby, could you please have the lab courier the murder weapon back to Reed's office?" Livvy asked. "I want to take a look at that gun."

"It's already on the way. Your boss figured you'd want to examine it so he sent it with the courier about an hour ago. Should be here any minute."

"Thank you."

Reed hung up and opened the door so that he could toss in Livvy's equipment bag. He heard the sound.

The too-familiar rattle.

And he reacted just as much from fear as he did instinct. He pushed Livvy to the side.

It wasn't a second too soon.

Because the diamondback rattler that was coiled on the seat sprang right at them.

Chapter Eight

Everything was a blur. One minute Livvy was getting ready to step inside the truck, and the next, she was on the ground.

She heard the rattling sound, and it turned her blood to ice. Livvy rolled to her side and scrambled to get away.

The rattler shot out of the truck again, aiming for a second attempt to strike them, and she shouted for Reed to move. He did. And in the same motion, he drew his gun.

And fired.

The shot blasted through the countryside, and he followed it up with a second one. That didn't stop the snake. Livvy watched in horror as the rattler made a third strike. Its fangs stabbed right into Reed's leather shoulder holster. He threw it off, fired a fourth shot, and this time the bullet hit its intended target.

Still, the snake didn't stop moving. It continued to coil and rattle before it slithered away.

"Did it bite you?" Livvy managed to ask. Her heart felt as if it were literally in her throat.

Reed shook his head and looked at her. "Are you okay?"

She took a moment to assess her situation. "I'm fine, but what about you?" Livvy got to her feet and checked out his arm and shoulder.

"I wasn't hurt." He checked her out as well, and when his gaze landed on her now-muddy jeans and shirt, he cursed. "This wasn't an accident. That snake didn't open my truck door and crawl in."

No. And that meant someone had put it there. "Who would do this?"

"The same person who's been trying to make our lives hell for the past two days." He paused to curse again. "The snake probably wouldn't have killed us even with multiple bites, and the town doc keeps a supply of antivenom. But it would have made us very sick and put us out of commission for God knows how long."

"And it scared us. Scared *me*," she corrected. Livvy flicked the loose bits of mud off her clothes. "But it won't scare me enough to stop this investigation."

"No, it won't," Reed readily agreed. He checked his watch, eyed the truck and then eyed her. "You think you can get inside?"

She could. Livvy had no doubts about that, but she couldn't quite control her body's response to nearly being the victim of a snake attack.

"You believe Ben Tolbert is capable of this?" Livvy took a deep breath and got inside.

Reed did the same, and he started the engine. "He's capable all right. Rattlesnakes aren't exactly hard to find around here, and some people trap and sell them.

There's a trapper about twenty miles from here who runs a rattlesnake roundup. I'll call him and see if anyone's recently purchased a diamondback from him."

It would be a necessary call, just to cover all bases, but Livvy doubted the culprit would go that route where he could be easily identified. "What about Jerry Collier? He left the ranch house in plenty of time to plant the snake."

Reed nodded. "And he was riled enough to do it."

Yes, he was. "But that would indicate premeditation."

"Maybe. Or maybe he spotted the snake as he was driving out and did it on the spur of the moment."

She tried to imagine the suit-wearing, nervous head of the Comanche Creek Land Office doing something like picking up a live rattler on a muddy road, but it didn't seem logical. Well, not logical in her downtown office in Austin, but out here, anything seemed plausible.

"Don't worry—I'll question Jerry," Reed continued, his voice as tight as the grip he now had on the steering wheel. "Ben, too. And I'll have the outside of the truck dusted for prints. We might get lucky."

"I'm sorry," he added a moment later.

Since his tone had just as much anger as apology, she looked at him. Yes, he was riled. Maybe it was simply because of the leftover adrenaline from the attack, but Livvy got the impression that he was angry because of her, because she'd been placed in danger.

And because there was now *something* between them. Something more than the job.

She was about to remind him that the kiss and attraction really couldn't play into this, but he grabbed his phone from his pocket, scrolled down through the recent calls he'd made and pressed the call button.

"I want to speak to Jerry," Reed demanded of who-ever answered. There was at least a five-second pause. "Then take a message. He needs to call me immediately, or else I'll arrest his sorry ass."

Reed ended that call and made another. This time, he put it on speaker, and she heard the call go straight to Ben Tolbert's voice mail. Reed issued another threat-ening order very similar to the one he'd left for Jerry. But he didn't stop there. Reed continued to call around: to the mayor, then someone on the city board, and he asked both men to help him locate Jerry Collier and Ben Tolbert. He was still making calls when he pulled to a stop in the parking lot of his office.

Livvy knew it wasn't a good time to be close to Reed, not with so much emotion still zinging around and between them, so she grabbed her equipment bag, got out of the truck and, with Reed right behind her, she hurried inside.

Eileen, the receptionist, gave her a warm smile and a hello. Livvy tried to return the greeting but wasn't pleased to hear the tremble in her voice. Her hands were shaking, too, and since she didn't want to risk a meltdown in front of anyone, she mumbled something that she hoped would sound composed and raced into Reed's office.

Livvy hurried to the desk that he'd set up for her to work, and she took out the trap and fabric swatch so she could start the paperwork to send them to the lab in Austin.

It also gave her hands and her mind something to do.

She wasn't a coward and knew full well that danger was part of the job, but she wasn't immune to the effects of coming so close to Reed and her being hurt.

She heard the door shut and glanced over her shoulder at Reed. He stood there as if trying to collect himself, a response she totally understood.

"Here are the trap and the fabric," she said. Her voice was still shaky, and Livvy cleared her throat hoping it would help. "When the courier gets here with the murder weapon, I'll have him go ahead and take the items to the crime lab for testing."

Livvy picked up a note. A message left for her by Kirby. She read it out loud: "'The lab checked on the number I gave them for the missing phone. It was one of those prepaid cells, and the person who bought it must have paid cash because there's no record of purchase. That means we can't trace the buyer, and we won't be able to find out about any calls he might have made.'"

Reed didn't respond to that latest dose of disappointing news. Instead, he reached behind him, locked the door and pushed himself away. But he did more than just walk toward her. When he reached her, he latched on to her arm and hauled her against him. Reed pulled her into a tight embrace.

"I'll try very hard not to let something like that happen again," he said.

Confused, Livvy looked up at him. "You mean the snake or the kiss?"

He smiled, but it was short-lived and there was no humor in it. "The snake."

Yes, but both were dangerous in their own way, and Reed and she knew that. Still, Livvy didn't move away, even when he slid his arm around her waist and pulled her closer. Not even when her breasts pressed against his chest. Not even when she felt his warm breath push through the wisps of her hair.

Livvy could have sworn the air changed between them. The nerves and adrenaline were still there, but she felt another emotion creep into the already volatile mix.

Attraction.

Yes, it was there, too, and all the talk and head-shaking in the world wouldn't make it go away. She opened her mouth to say, well, she had no idea what to say. But despite the hot attraction, she knew she had to say or do something to stop the escalation of all these crazy emotions.

But she didn't stop it.

Instead, she did the opposite. She came up on her tiptoes…

And she kissed him.

Not a peck, either, like the other one at the ranch, though it started that way. Reed took things from there. He made sure this one was hard, French.

And memorable.

Livvy didn't do anything to stop this either, despite the intense argument going on between her head and the rest of her body. No. She made things better—and worse—by slinging her arm around his neck and moving even closer.

That taste.

It was amazing. And the man moved over her mouth as if he owned her. She did her own share of kiss-deepening as well, and they didn't break the intimate contact until they both realized they needed to catch their breaths.

Reed looked stunned and confused when he drew

back. Livvy knew how he felt. They were both in a lot of trouble, and she didn't think they'd be getting out of this trouble any time soon.

"The evidence," she said as a reminder to both herself and Reed.

"Yeah." Still, he didn't pull away. He pressed his forehead against hers and groaned. "I would promise not to do that again, but you and I both know it's a promise I can't keep."

"We can't just land in bed, either." Though that suddenly seemed like a great idea. Sheez. Her body really wasn't being very professional.

Now, he smiled and looked down at her. "The bed is optional. Sex with you? Not so optional." He pressed harder against her. So hard that she could feel the proof of their attraction. "I want you bad, Livvy, and all the logic and the danger in the world won't wish that away."

That seemed to be a challenge, as if he expected her to dispute what he was saying. She couldn't.

The sound of his ringing cell phone shot through the room, and that sent them flying apart. Good. They weren't totally stupid.

Just yet, anyway.

"Kirby?" he answered after glancing at the caller ID screen.

Livvy welcomed the reprieve. Well, part of her did anyway. But she knew it was just that: a reprieve. Somehow, she would have to force herself away from Reed. Maybe she could move her side of the investigation to the inn, just so they wouldn't be elbow to elbow. That might minimize the temptation of the mouth-to-mouth contact.

But then she looked at him.

All six feet plus of him. With that rumpled dark hair and bedroom eyes, he wasn't the sort of man that a woman could *minimize*.

"As soon as he steps foot in his office, let me know. Thanks, Kirby." He closed his phone and shoved it into his pocket. He tipped his head to the fabric and trap. "I'll have Eileen arrange to have that taken to the crime lab, but it might not happen before we get to question Jerry. He's on his way back to his office."

"Good. We can ask him about the rattlesnake." Livvy put the evidence into the locker so it would be safe until the courier arrived.

"We can ask him more than that. Kirby just learned the results from the footprint castings that you took. And they're a perfect match to Jerry Collier."

Livvy sank down into the chair just a few inches from her worktable. "Is there any valid reason why his footprints would be there?"

"None that I know of. Plus, he has one of the strongest motives for wanting Marcie dead. If she had managed to stay alive long enough to testify against him, Jerry would have ended up in jail. Without her testimony, the state doesn't have a strong enough case."

That was a huge motive indeed, and Livvy was about to use her laptop to request a full background check on Jerry, but there was a knock at the door. Reed crossed the room, unlocked the door, and when he opened it, Kirby was standing there. The young deputy looked puzzled and maybe even suspicious as to why the door had been locked.

Great.

If Kirby sensed the attraction between Reed and her, God knew how little time it would take to get around town. She was betting everyone would know by lunchtime.

Livvy took the bagged and tagged gun from Kirby and initialed the chain of custody form. He also handed her the report file from the lab. While Kirby and Reed discussed whether or not they should issue an APB for Ben Tolbert, Livvy put on her gloves and got to work examining the gun.

It was a Ruger .22 Rimfire pistol. Common and inexpensive. A person could buy it for under three hundred dollars at any gun store in the state. Just about anyone who wanted a gun badly enough could afford it.

Including all of their suspects.

The Ruger had already been processed, and even though it was indeed the murder weapon, according to the report, it contained no DNA. Just fingerprints that had been dusted and photographed. The photographs had then been fed into AFIS, the Automated Fingerprint Identification System. The result?

They were Shane's prints.

The fact there was no DNA was odd, especially since the lab had run a touch test, which should have been able to detect even a minute amount of biological material.

Yet, nothing.

Since Shane had supposedly shot Marcie at close range, there should have been some blood spatter or maybe even sweat from Shane's hand. First-time killers normally weren't so calm and cool that they didn't leave a piece of themselves behind at the crime scene.

She set the gun aside, and went through the report file. There were several photos of the fingerprints on the weapon, and the tech who'd taken them had been thorough. Livvy could see the placement of every print, including the one on the trigger, which had a much lighter point of pressure than the others.

Also odd.

It should have been about the same, or maybe even heavier. Killers didn't usually have such a light touch when it came to pulling a trigger.

She picked up the gun again and took a magnifying glass from her case so she could look at the actual pattern. Even though some of the fingerprint powder and the prints themselves had been smeared during transport and processing, she could still see where the shooter had gripped the gun. That created a vivid image in her mind.

Shane pointing the gun at Marcie.

Then firing.

Livvy replayed the scene again. And again. Each time, she made tiny mental changes to see if she could recreate the end result: Marcie's murder with Shane pulling the trigger.

"Something about this doesn't look right," she mumbled. She glanced over her shoulder to see if Reed had heard her, but his attention wasn't on her. It was on the phone call that he'd just answered.

"Good, because we want to talk to you, too," Reed snarled. But his expression morphed into concern. "We'll be right there."

"What happened?" Livvy asked when he slapped the phone shut.

"That was Jerry Collier, and he's back in his office. He says someone is out to kill you, and he knows who that person is."

Chapter Nine

"If you'd rather stay at the office and finish examining the gun, I can do this alone," Reed offered, though he knew what Livvy's answer would be.

"No, thanks." Her response was crisp and fast, like the speed at which she exited the building. "I'd like to learn the identity of the person who wants me dead."

So would Reed, but he wasn't certain they would be getting that information from Jerry. Still, he wasn't about to pass up the opportunity to question the man about the dangerous attempts that had been orchestrated to prevent Livvy and him from doing their jobs.

They went into the parking lot, and he spotted one of the loaner deputies who was examining his truck for prints and other evidence. Reed didn't want to interrupt that or destroy any potential evidence by using the vehicle. The other deputies were apparently still at the crime scene or else on patrol because his official vehicle was nowhere in sight. That left the one cruiser, which Reed hated to tie up in case Kirby had to respond to an emergency.

The Comanche Creek Land Office was just up the

street about a quarter of a mile away, but it wouldn't be a comfortable stroll. It was already turning into a scorcher day with the heat and humidity. Plus, there was the potential danger, which mostly seemed to be aimed at Livvy. Maybe it wasn't wise to have her out in the open.

"It'd be safer if I have someone drive us," Reed suggested.

She looked at him as if he'd sprouted a third eye. "I won't let this scare me. We're both peace officers, and if we can't walk down the street in broad daylight without being afraid, then that sends a message to the perp that I don't want to send."

And with that, she started walking again. "Besides, I need a few minutes to clear my head," Livvy added. "I don't want to go storming into Jerry's office like this."

Reed was on the same page with her. First, the footprints that were a match to Jerry, and then his bombshell comment about knowing who wanted to kill Livvy. Up to this point, Reed had hoped and believed that the incidents were meant to scare her off. Not kill her. But by God, if that was someone's intention, then there'd be hell to pay.

He didn't curse himself or groan at that thought. Somewhere along the way, he'd crossed the line with Livvy, and cursing and groaning weren't going to make him backtrack even if that was the sensible thing to do.

"You said there was no gunshot residue anywhere on Shane?" she asked, pulling him out of a fit of temper that was building because of Jerry.

"None. Why?"

She lifted her shoulder. "I've just been trying to get the picture straight in my mind."

Yeah. He'd done that as well, and this was one picture that hadn't fit right from the start. Well, unless Shane truly was a cold-blooded killer who'd set all of this up.

"You make a fine-looking couple," someone called out.

Reed glanced across the street and spotted Billy Whitley, the county clerk, and his wife, Charla, who were just going into the diner, probably for an early lunch.

"Careful," Billy teased. "People will say you're in love."

Reed stopped to set him straight, but Charla got in on the conversation.

Charla nudged her elbow into Billy's ribs. "I know you got better sense than that, Reed," Charla countered. "That woman's trying to tear this town apart."

"Actually, I'm just trying to do my job," Livvy fired back.

That earned Livvy a *hmmmp* from Charla, and the woman threw open the door of the diner and stormed inside. Billy gave an apologetic wave and followed her.

Reed didn't know which was worse—Billy's innuendo or Charla's obvious dislike of Livvy. "Sorry," he mumbled to Livvy once they started walking again.

"No need to apologize. Will this cause trouble for you?" she asked but didn't wait for his answer. "Would it be better if we did separate investigations?"

Reed didn't even have to think about this. "It wouldn't help. You're a woman and I'm a man. We're both single. If people don't see us together, they'll just say we're staying apart so we don't raise suspicions about a secret relationship."

And that was really all he wanted to say about that, especially since the gossip was really going to heat up because Reed planned to spend a lot more time with her at work and at the inn.

Reed would break that news to Livvy later.

"We were discussing the gun," he prompted.

"Yes." She wiped the perspiration from her forehead and repeated it. "I think there's a problem with the pressure points. The print isn't that strong on the trigger."

Despite the heat, Reed slowed a bit so he could give that some thought. Now, he got that picture in his mind. "The person who hit Shane over the head could have used gloves when he shot Marcie. Then, he could have pressed Shane's prints onto the weapon."

Hell. Why hadn't he thought of that sooner? Probably because this case had come at him nonstop. It was almost as if someone wanted to make sure that his focus was disrupted. Maybe that was the real reason for all the diversions, like that snake.

"I need to do some further testing," Livvy added. Her forehead creased. "It could mean that Shane just has a light touch when it comes to his trigger finger. I'd like to compare this weapon to his service pistol, just to see how the grip pattern lines up."

That would give her information if Shane hadn't recently cleaned his gun. For the first time in Reed's law-enforcement career, he was hoping his deputy had been lax about that particular standard procedure. "You can do that as soon as we finish with Jerry because I have his gun locked up in the safe in my office."

Ahead of them on the steps to the county offices were three men and a woman, all Native Americans, and all carrying signs of protest.

"Sheriff Hardin," the woman called out, and her tone wasn't friendly, either. Not that Reed expected it to be, since she was carrying a big poster that demanded justice for her people.

"Ellie," Reed greeted her. He caught onto Livvy's arm and tried to maneuver her around the protesters, but the trim Comanche woman, Ellie Penateka, stepped in front of them.

Reed had known Ellie all his life, and though she was passionate about her beliefs, she could also toe the line of the law.

"When will you do your job and arrest Jonah Becker and his cronies?" Ellie demanded.

"When I have some evidence that warrants an arrest." Reed wasn't unsympathetic to her demand. After all, Jonah probably had participated in a dirty deal to get land that belonged to the Native American community. Jerry might have helped him, too, but he couldn't arrest anyone without probable cause.

Since it was obvious that Ellie didn't intend to move, Reed met her eye-to-eye. "If and when I get proof, any proof, that Jonah's done something wrong, I'll arrest him. You have my word on that."

Ellie stared at him and then turned her dark eyes on Livvy. "Help us," she said, her voice still laced with anger. "This land deal has to be undone."

Livvy opened her mouth, looking as if she were about to say she was there to solve a murder, not get involved with community issues, but she must have rethought that because she nodded. "If I find anything, the sheriff will be the first to know."

That seemed to soothe Ellie enough to get her to move to the side, and Livvy and Reed continued up the steps to the county offices.

"How long has the protest been going on?" Livvy asked under her breath.

"On and off since the land deal over two years ago." And what Reed had said to Ellie hadn't been lip service. He would arrest Jonah if he could, and that arrest might go a long way to soothing the split that was happening in Comanche Creek.

He opened the door to the office building, and the cool air-conditioning spilled over him. Inside, there were some curious folks who eyed Livvy and him and then did some behind-the-hand whispers. Reed doled out some warning scowls and made his way down the hall. Jerry's office door was wide open, and he was seated at his desk, apparently waiting for them.

They stepped inside, and Reed shut the door. Not that they would have much privacy since the glass insert in the door allowed anyone and everyone to see in.

Livvy and he took the seats across from Jerry's desk. "Start talking," Reed insisted.

But Jerry didn't. Instead, he pulled out a manila file and slid it toward them. Reed opened it and saw that it was case notes from a murder that had happened over twenty years ago. The name on the file was Sandra Hutton.

Livvy's mother.

He aimed a raised eyebrow at Jerry and passed the file to Livvy. "What does this have to do with anything?" Reed asked.

"Sandra Hutton's killer has been hiding out in Mexico," Jerry explained with a tinge of smugness. "Maybe he's decided to return to Texas and create some havoc with Sandra's daughter. He could be the person who set fire to that cabin."

Livvy's reaction was slight. Just a small change in her breathing pattern. She moistened her lips, closed the file and tossed it back on Jerry's desk. "How did you get this information?" she asked.

"I requested it from the county sheriff's office. I told them it could be relevant to the investigation into the land deal that's got the Comanches so riled up."

In other words, Jerry had pulled strings so he could pry into Livvy's past.

"My mother's killer has no part in this," Livvy insisted.

"You're sure?" Jerry challenged.

"Positive."

Reed only hoped she was, but he'd do some checking when he got back to his office. For now though, he wanted answers and not a possible smokescreen.

"Were you at the cabin around the time Marcie was killed?" he asked Jerry.

There was no quick denial. Jerry studied Reed's expression and then nodded. "Why?"

"Because we found your tracks there." Reed studied Jerry as well, and the man certainly didn't seem particularly rattled by all of this. Of course, maybe that's because Jerry always seemed on edge about something. Like a pressure cooker ready to start spewing steam.

"I was at the cabin the morning of the murder." But then, Jerry hesitated. He had a pen in his hand, and he began rolling it between his fingers. "I got a call, telling me Marcie would be there, and I wanted to talk to her, to ask if she intended to go through with her testimony against Jonah Becker."

"And you," Livvy supplied. "Because if she'd testified against Jonah, you also would have been implicated."

Jerry bobbed his head, and rolled the pen faster. "At the time I put it together, I didn't know the land deal could be construed as illegal. I'm still not convinced it is. But I understand why the Native American community is upset. That's why they're protesting outside. I also understand they want someone to blame, but I wanted to make sure Marcie was going to get me a fair shake when she was on the witness stand."

"And did Marcie agree?" Reed asked.

"I didn't see her. She wasn't at the cabin when I got there so I left. That following morning, I heard about her murder. I swear, I had nothing to do with her death."

Reed wasn't sure he believed that. "So who called you to tell you about Marcie being at the cabin?"

This hesitation was a lot longer than the first, and the pen just started to fly over his fingers.

"Billy Whitley," Jerry finally said.

"Billy," Reed repeated, not that surprised but riled that he hadn't been given this information sooner. "How did he know Marcie was going to the cabin?"

Jerry picked up his phone. "I don't know, but you can ask him yourself." He pressed some numbers. "Billy, could you come over here a minute? Reed and the lady Ranger want to know why I was at the cabin that morning." He hung up. "He'll be here in a couple of minutes."

Reed wasn't going to wait for Billy to continue this

interrogation. "When Billy called to tell you about Marcie being at the cabin, you didn't ask him how he'd come by that information? Because Marcie hadn't exactly announced her whereabouts."

Jerry shook his head, tossed the pen on his desk and grabbed a Texas Longhorns mug near where the pen had landed. He gulped down enough coffee to choke himself. "I didn't ask. I was just thankful to finally have a chance to talk to her."

"And you're positive she wasn't there when you arrived?" Livvy asked.

"No sign of her. I didn't go in, but I looked in the windows. No one was in that cabin."

Livvy made a sound of disagreement. "She could have been hiding. I can't imagine that Marcie would have been happy to see her former boss, especially when she was scared to death of you."

Jerry couldn't and didn't deny that. It was common knowledge around town that Marcie had been afraid of him, so maybe she had indeed been wary enough to hide when she saw him skulking around the place.

"Did you happen to notice Shane while you were there?" Reed wanted to know.

"No." His answer was fast and prompted him to drink yet more coffee. "I told you, there was no one at that cabin."

Still, it was possible that both Shane and Marcie had come later. Jerry could be telling the truth.

Or not.

Reed wasn't ready to buy the man's story when Jerry had so much to lose from this situation.

There was a knock at the door, one sharp rap on the

glass insert, before it opened and Billy strolled in. "You wanted to see me," he said, aiming the not-too-friendly comment at Jerry. Charla was there, too, but she stood back in the doorway and didn't come in. "Charla and I were in the middle of eating lunch."

"I told them you were the one who called me about Marcie being at the cabin," Jerry volunteered.

"And we want to know how you came by that information," Reed added.

"I see." Billy pulled in a long weary breath and sat on the edge of Jerry's desk. "If you don't mind, I'd rather not divulge that information."

Reed stopped his mouth from dropping open, but that comment was a shocker. "I do mind." He got to his feet. "And if you don't tell me, I'll arrest you on the spot for obstruction of justice."

The usually friendly Billy suddenly didn't seem so friendly, and he tossed a glare at Jerry, probably because he wasn't pleased that the man had given Reed what Billy would have thought was private information.

Charla obviously ignored Billy's glare. "Ben Tolbert told Billy that Marcie was going to be at the cabin," the woman confessed.

Livvy and Reed exchanged glances, and he was certain neither was able to keep the surprise out of their eyes. "How did Ben know?"

Billy wearily shook his head and sighed. "He said he found out from Jeff Marquez."

Reed was very familiar with the name. Jeff Marquez was the EMT who'd helped Marcie fake her own death. "He's in county jail on obstruction of justice charges, and he won't be getting out anytime soon."

Billy nodded. "But he told Ben before he was arrested. Why, I don't know. Maybe Ben bribed him."

Ben didn't have the money for that, but Jonah sure did. Which brought them back full circle without eliminating any of the suspects. Jerry, Billy, Ben and Jonah all had the means, motives and opportunities to kill Marcie, but Reed was having a hard time believing that Ben would have allowed his son to take the blame for something he'd done.

That meant, he could focus more on the two men in the room, and the one rancher friend they had in common: Jonah. He wouldn't take Ben off his suspect list, but he did mentally move him to the bottom.

"I've done nothing illegal," Billy reiterated. "Neither has Jerry. And you're barking up the wrong tree, Reed. You already have the killer in custody."

"Maybe," Livvy mumbled. She got to her feet and stood next to Reed. Reed followed.

"Maybe?" Jerry challenged, and Reed didn't think it was his imagination that the man suddenly seemed very uncomfortable. Also, that wasn't a benign glance he aimed at Billy. And then Charla.

"Maybe," Livvy repeated, keeping a poker face. She walked out past Charla and into the hall.

Since there were lots of people milling around, too many, Reed didn't want to say anything that would be overheard and reported to Charla and the men. He waited until they were outside and away from the protestors.

"Smart move," he said under his breath, "to let them think you might have some evidence to prove Shane's innocence. And maybe their guilt."

"Well, I wanted to say something to shake them up a bit."

Mission accomplished. Now, they would have to wait to see who would react, and how, to the possibility that the charges against Shane weren't a done deal.

"I'm sorry Jerry brought up your mother," Reed told her.

"Not your fault. And this has nothing to do with her. That was an attempt to muddy the waters on his part. Makes you wonder just how deep he is into this. After all, other than Jonah, Jerry has the strongest motive because Marcie could have sent him to jail for years."

"Yeah, and he doesn't have Jonah's big bankroll to fight a long legal battle."

Livvy stayed quiet a moment. "So, of all our suspects who would be most likely to kill a woman and set up her former lover to take the blame?"

"Jerry," Reed said without hesitation. Still, that didn't mean Jonah or someone else hadn't put him up to it or even assisted. "While you're reexamining the gun, I want to talk to Shane again. Maybe he remembers something that'll help us unravel all of this."

He heard Livvy respond, but he didn't actually grasp what she said. That was because Reed saw something that got his complete attention.

The black rental car parked just up the street less than a block from his office.

"That's the vehicle that nearly ran me down," he told Livvy.

She put her hand over the butt of her service pistol. Reed did the same and tried to walk ahead of her so he could place himself between the car and her. Of course, Livvy wouldn't have any part of that. She fell in step beside him, and they made their way to the car.

"Can you see if anyone's inside?" she asked.

"No. The windows are too dark." And with the sunlight spewing in that direction, there was also a glare.

With each step they took, Reed's heart rate kicked up. It certainly couldn't be Billy, Charla or Jerry in that car since he'd just left them in Jerry's office, but it could be someone who'd been hired to intimidate Livvy and him.

Reed and Livvy were only a few yards away when the engine roared to life.

Livvy stopped and drew her weapon. Reed was about to push her out of harm's way, but it was already too late. The driver slammed on the accelerator, the tires squealing against the hot asphalt.

Reed cursed as the car sped past them. He cursed again when he got a glimpse of the driver.

This time it was Shane's father, Ben Tolbert.

Chapter Ten

Livvy stepped from the claw-footed tub and wrapped the thick terry-cloth towel around her. The hot bath had helped soothe some of her tight back and shoulder muscles, but it hadn't soothed her mind.

She dried off, slipped on her cotton nightgown and smeared her hand over the steam-coated mirror. A troubled face stared back at her, and she tried to assure herself that neither her career nor her personal life were in deep trouble.

But they were.

The Ranger captain had hit the roof when he learned about the destroyed crime scene, and it didn't help matters that she hadn't been able to confirm the arrest of their main suspect.

In fact, she'd done the opposite.

She'd created doubt with her questions about the murder weapon, and those doubts were fueling animosity between the Native American community and the rest of the town. According to the inn's owner, Betty Alice, there were whispers that Livvy was trying to clear Shane because of her personal involvement with Reed.

Maybe the new lab tests she'd ordered on the gun would help. Well, they might help clear Shane anyway, so they could concentrate on other suspects. But that wouldn't clear the rumors about Reed and her.

Worse, those rumors were partly true.

Other than that kiss, Reed and she hadn't acted on this crazy attraction, but that was no guarantee it wouldn't happen in the future.

And that was a sobering thought.

Despite all the problems a relationship with Reed would cause, she still wanted him. Bad. She wanted more than kisses. Livvy wanted sex.

No.

Sex wouldn't have been as unnerving as the fact that Livvy wanted Reed to make love to her. Something long, slow and very, very hot. And not a one-time shot, either. She was thinking of starting an affair with a lawman who could put some serious dents not just in her heart but in her professional reputation.

Cursing herself, Livvy brushed her teeth and reached for the door.

She heard it then.

A soft bump.

The sound had come from the bedroom.

Livvy turned to reach for her gun, only to realize she'd left it holstered on the nightstand. She hadn't wanted the gun in the steamy bathroom with all the moisture and humidity. Thankfully, she remembered she did have her cell phone with her though, because she had been concerned that she might not be able to hear it ring while the bathwater was running.

Of course, she'd locked the door to the room, and it

was entirely possible that Betty Alice had come up to bring her some towels or something. Still, with everything that'd happened, Livvy wished she had her gun.

She walked closer to the bathroom door, listening. And it didn't take long before she heard a second thump. Then, footsteps.

Someone was definitely in her room.

"Betty Alice?" she called out.

Nothing. The heavy footsteps stopped just outside the bathroom door.

Livvy grabbed her phone from the vanity, flipped it open but then hesitated. Calling Reed wasn't at the top of her list of things she wanted to do, but she might not have a choice.

"Who's out there?" she tried again.

No answer.

So, she waited, debating what she should do. She wasn't defenseless since she'd had some martial arts and hand-to-hand combat training, but she didn't want to go hand-to-hand with someone who was armed.

Like Marcie's killer.

The doorknob moved, and her heart dropped to her knees. This wasn't Betty Alice or even someone with friendly intentions, or the person would already have answered her.

There was another rattle of the doorknob, and then someone bashed against the door. That caused her heart to bash against her ribs. Oh, God. The door held, but Livvy knew she had no choice. She called Reed.

"This is Livvy. There's an intruder outside my door."

She didn't stay on the line. Livvy tossed the phone back onto the vanity so she could free her hands for a fight.

The person rammed against the door again, and she heard some mumbled profanity. She was almost positive it was a man's voice.

Another bash, and this time the wood cracked. It wouldn't hold up much longer, and she had to do something to improve her chances of survival if this turned into a full-fledged assault.

Livvy grabbed the scissors from her makeup bag and slapped off the lights. Since the lights were still on in her room, she hoped the intruder's eyes wouldn't have time to adjust to the darkness if he managed to get through that door.

Or rather *when* he got through.

The next bash sent the door flying open right at her, and Livvy jumped to the edge of the tub so she wouldn't get hit. Her heart was pounding. Her breathing was way too fast. And she had no hopes of being concealed in the dark room since her white nightgown would no doubt act as a beacon.

The man came at her.

Because the room was dark, Livvy couldn't see his face, but she caught his scent, a mixture of sweat and whiskey. He reached for her, but she swung the scissors at him and connected with his arm. She heard the sound of tearing fabric, and prayed she'd cut skin as well. He cursed in a raspy growling voice.

A voice she didn't recognize.

In the back of her mind, she was trying to identify this intruder. No. He was an assailant now, not merely an intruder, and with the profanity still hissing from his throat, he latched on to her hair and dragged her away from the tub. His grip was strong, and was obviously being fed with booze and adrenaline. Still, Livvy didn't just stand there and let him assault her.

Using the scissors again, she slashed at his midsection and followed it with a kick aimed at his shin. She missed. But he released the grip he had on her.

"Livvy?" someone shouted.

Reed.

She'd never been more thankful to hear someone call out her name. Better yet, he was nearby, and she could hear him barreling up the stairs. Her attacker must have heard Reed as well because he turned and raced out of the bathroom.

Livvy went after him.

Only the lamp was on, but she had no trouble seeing the man's back as he dove through the open window that led to the second-floor balcony.

"Livvy!" Reed shouted again.

He banged on the door, which was obviously still locked because the intruder hadn't entered that way. He'd apparently entered the same way he exited through the window. A window she was certain she'd locked as well because the balcony had steps that led down in the garden. She had known full well it was a weak security point.

Livvy hurried across the room to unlock the door, threw it open and faced a very concerned-looking Reed. "Are you okay?" There were beads of sweat on his face, and his breath was gusting.

Livvy didn't trust her voice. There'd be too much fear and emotion in it. Instead she pointed to the window where the evening breeze was billowing the pink curtains.

She dropped the scissors on the nightstand and grabbed her gun so she could go in pursuit, but Reed beat her to it.

He bolted through the window and started running.

REED RACED across the balcony, following the sounds of footsteps.

Unfortunately, whoever had broken into Livvy's room had a good head start, and Reed caught just a glimpse of the shadowy figure when he leaped off the bottom step and raced through the English-style country gardens that were thick with plants and shrubs.

There were too many places to hide.

And worse, too many ways to escape.

Reed barreled down the steps, but he no longer had a visual on the guy. Heck, he couldn't even hear footsteps on the grounds. Since finding him would be a crap shoot, Reed ran straight ahead because where the gardens ended there was a thick cluster of mature oaks. Beyond that was a greenbelt and then another street lined with businesses that would already be closed for the night. If the intruder was local, then he knew all he had to do was duck into one of the many alleys or other recesses.

And that was probably what had happened.

Because once Reed tore his way through the greenbelt and onto the street, he saw no one.

He stopped, listened and tried to hear any sound over the heartbeat that was pulsing in his ears.

Nothing.

Well, nothing except for his racing imagination. Maybe the escape had been a ruse. Maybe the guy was doubling back so he could have another go at Livvy. That put a knot in Reed's gut, and he whirled around and raced toward the inn.

A dozen scenarios went through his head. None were good. But he forced himself to remember that Livvy could take care of herself. Most of the time.

Tonight had obviously been the exception.

It might take a lifetime or two for Reed to forget the look of sheer terror he'd seen on her face when she'd unlocked the door to let him in.

He took out his cell phone and called his office so he could request backup. "Get any and all officers to Wade Street and the area back of the Bluebonnet Inn," he told the dispatcher. "We're looking for an unidentified male. About six feet tall. Dressed in black. Find him!" he ordered.

Reed didn't have to make it all the way back to the inn before he spotted Livvy. Dressed in her gown and bathrobe—and armed—she was making her way down the balcony stairs.

"Did you catch him?" she called out.

"No." And even from the twenty feet or so of distance between them, he saw her expression. The fear had been quickly replaced by anger.

Reed understood that emotion because he was well beyond the anger stage. He wanted to get the guy responsible for putting Livvy through this.

"Are you hurt?" he asked. He closed the distance between them and glanced around to make sure they weren't about to be ambushed.

"I'm fine," Livvy insisted.

But they both knew that was a lie. He caught onto

her arm to lead her back up the steps because he didn't want her out in the open.

"Betty Alice called a couple of minutes ago," Livvy explained. Her voice sounded calm enough. It was a cop's tone. Clinical, detached. She would have pulled it off, too, if he hadn't been touching her. Reed could feel her trembling. "She heard the noise and wanted to know what was going on. I told her to stay put and make sure all the windows and doors were locked."

"Good." He didn't want anyone in the path of his guy. Because it was entirely possible they weren't just dealing with an intruder but a killer.

Marcie's killer.

Reed led her back into her room, and closed the gaping window that had been used as the escape route. Because he didn't want anyone seeing their silhouettes, he turned off the lights as well.

"He broke through the bathroom door," Livvy explained. Her voice was soft now, practically a mumble, and she cleared her throat. "It was dark, and I couldn't see his face."

"But you're sure it was a man?"

"Positive. He smelled of sweat and liquor. And he had a strong grip." She rubbed her wrist. Even though she was a peace officer, that didn't make her bulletproof or spare her the emotion that came with an attack. Soon, very soon, the adrenaline would cause her to crash. "I'd left my gun in here so I couldn't get to it."

The fear in her voice was hard for Reed to hear, but he wouldn't be doing either of them any favors if he gave in to it. He had to have more answers if they hoped to catch this guy.

"Did he have a weapon?" Reed asked.

She hesitated a moment and then shook her head. "If he did, he didn't use it. He just grabbed me."

Now, that was odd. A killer, especially the one who'd shot Marcie, would likely have a gun. Or he could have grabbed Livvy's own weapon before going after her in the bathroom. But he hadn't.

Why?

Maybe this wasn't about harming Livvy but rather about scaring her. *Again.* If so, this SOB was persistent.

"I might have cut him with those scissors," Livvy added, tipping her head to where they lay on the night-stand. "I need to bag them."

"Later," Reed insisted. The scissors could wait.

She was shaking harder now, and Reed looped his arm around her and eased her down onto the bed so they were sitting on the edge. It wouldn't be long, maybe a few minutes, before he got an update from the deputies. If they got lucky, they might already have the attacker in custody. But just in case, Reed wanted to hear more.

"What about the possibility of transfer of DNA from him to you?" he asked.

"No," she answered immediately. "I wasn't able to scratch him, and other than his hand on my wrist, there was no physical contact."

Reed was thankful for that. Livvy hadn't been hurt. But the DNA proof would have been a good thing to have. Still, if she'd managed to cut him, that would give them the sample they needed.

"The door was locked," she continued, "but I guess he broke in through the window." Her voice cracked. The trembling got even worse.

And Reed gave up his fight to stay detached and im-personal. He pulled her even closer against him, until she was deep into his arms, and he brushed what he hoped was a comforting kiss on her forehead.

It didn't stay at the comfort level.

Livvy looked up at him, and even though the only il-lumination was coming from the outside security lights filtering through the curtains, he could clearly see her face. Yes, the fatigue and fear were there. But there was also an instant recognition that he was there, too, touching her.

Maybe it was just the adrenaline reaction, but Reed forgot all about that possibility when he lowered his head and kissed her.

There it was. That jolt. It slammed through him. So did her taste. After just one brief touch of their mouths, Reed knew he wanted more.

He slid his hand around the back of her neck so he could angle her head and deepen the kiss.

Yeah, it was stupid.

French-kissing his temporary partner and subordi-nate was a dumb-as-dirt kind of thing to do, but he also knew he had no plans to stop. He could justify that this was somehow easing Livvy's fear, but that was BS. This wasn't about fear. It was about this white-hot at-traction that had flared between them since they first met.

Livvy didn't exactly cool things down, either. She latched on to him, bunching up his shirt in her fist, and she kissed him as if he were the cure to the trauma she'd just experienced.

And maybe he was.

Maybe they both needed this to make it through the next few minutes.

Her gown was thin. Reed quickly realized that when her chest landed against his. No bra. He could feel her breasts warm and soft against him. He felt even more of them when Livvy wound herself around him, leaning closer and closer until it was hard to tell where she started and he began.

Reed made it even closer.

He hauled her into his lap. Again, it was a bad idea. Really bad. But his body was having a hard time remembering why it was so bad because Livvy landed not just on his lap but with her legs straddling his hips.

The kisses continued. It was a fierce battle, and they got even more intense. So did the body contact. Specifically, her sex against his. And that was when Reed knew. This might have started as a kiss of comfort, but this was now down-and-dirty foreplay.

He made it even dirtier.

Reed slid his hand up her thigh, pushing up the flimsy gown along the way. She was all silk and heat, and the heat got hotter when he reached the juncture of her thighs. He paused a moment, to give Livvy a chance to stop things, but she only shoved her hips toward his hand.

And he touched her.

There was a lot more silk and heat here, and even though she was wearing panties, it wasn't much of a barrier. Part of him—okay, all of him—wanted to slide his fingers and another part of him into that slick heat. Only his brain was holding him back, and it just wasn't making a very good argument to convince the rest of him.

"This will have to be quick," she mumbled and took those wild kisses to his neck.

Quick sounded very appealing. Heck, any kind of sex with Livvy did. He wanted her. Worse, he wanted her now.

And that was why he had to stop.

She slid her hand over his erection and reached for the zipper on his jeans. However, Reed snagged her wrists. That didn't stop the other touching and, fighting him, she ground herself against his erection until he was seeing stars.

And having a boatload of doubts about stopping.

"Livvy," he managed to get out.

She finally stopped. Stared at him. Blinked. "You don't want to do this."

"Oh, I want it, and that's the understatement of the century. But you know what I'm going to say."

"The timing sucks." Her weary sigh shoved her breasts against his chest again.

He nodded and used every bit of willpower to ease her off his lap and back onto the bed. It didn't exactly end things. She landed with her legs slightly apart, and he got a glimpse of those barrier panties.

Oh, yeah. Definitely thin and lacy.

Reed had to clench his hands into fists to stop himself from going after her again.

"I'm sorry," she mumbled, shoving down her gown and scrambling away from him.

Hell. Now, she was embarrassed, and that was the last thing he wanted her to feel.

Even though it was a risk, Reed latched on to her shoulders and forced eye contact. "We will have sex," he promised. "It doesn't matter if it'll complicate the devil out of things, we'll land in bed. I'd just prefer if it happened when you weren't minutes off surviving an attack. I want to take my time with you. I want to be inside you not because you're scared but because you really want me inside you."

Her stare held, and for the briefest of moments, the corners of her mouth lifted into a smile. "I'm pretty sure the want was real. *Is* real," she corrected.

But Livvy waved him off, sighed again and scooped her hair away from her face. "I didn't think you'd be the sensible one."

He shrugged. "I don't feel too sensible. Actually, I'm damn uncomfortable right now."

They shared a smile, and because Reed thought they both could use it, he leaned over and kissed her. Not a foreplay kiss. But not a peck, either. He hoped it would serve as a reminder that this really wasn't over.

"Tonight's shot," he told her, pulling back. "We'll have reports to do. Maybe a suspect to interrogate. But tomorrow, why don't you plan on spending the night at my house?"

Her right eyebrow came up. "That'll get the gossips going."

"Yeah." It would. And it wouldn't be pretty. "I figure having you in my bed will be worth the gossip."

Livvy's eyebrow lifted higher. "You're sure about that?"

He was, but gossip was only part of it, and the look in her eyes indicated she understood that.

"I'm a Texas Ranger," she stated. "You're married to that badge, and this town. You don't have time to have an affair with me. Besides, judging from the way women around here look at you, you're the number-one catch. Husband and daddy material."

Reed couldn't disagree with any of it. He didn't consider himself a stud, but being single, male and employed did put him in big demand in a small town like Comanche Creek.

"What?" she questioned. "Did I hit a nerve?"

"No. I want marriage and kids someday," he admitted. Or at least he had at one time. Lately, however, those things seemed like a pipe dream. "What about you?"

But she didn't get a chance to answer. There was a knock at the door. "It's me, Kirby."

The sound of his deputy's voice sent them scurrying off the bed. "Did you find him?" Reed immediately asked.

"Not yet. But there's someone who wants to see you. He says it's important."

Livvy grabbed her clothes from the back of a chair and hurried into the bathroom. "I need to dress, but I won't be long," she assured him. Since the bathroom door was off its hinges, she got into the tub and pulled the shower curtain around her so she'd have some privacy. "And talk loud so I can hear what you're saying."

Reed unlocked the bedroom door, eased it open, and came face-to-face with someone he certainly hadn't expected to see.

Ben Tolbert.

Reed drew his weapon, surprising Kirby almost as much as he did their visitor.

Shane's father stared at the gun, then him. Actually, it was more of a glare with intense blue eyes that were a genetic copy of his son's. The dark brown hair was a match, too, though Ben's was threaded with gray.

"Did you come back to finish the job?" Reed asked.

"I don't know what you mean." He tipped his head to Reed's gun. "And is that necessary?"

"It is." Reed leaned in so he could get right in Ben's face. "Now, you're going to tell me why you've been harassing Sergeant Hutton."

"I haven't been," Ben insisted.

Reed had to hand it to him. It certainly didn't look as if Ben had just committed a B and E and then escaped on foot. However, Reed couldn't rule out that it was exactly what had happened.

"You want me to believe it's a coincidence that you're here tonight, less than thirty minutes after Sergeant Hutton was attacked?" Reed tried to keep the anger from his voice. He failed.

"Call it what you will. I didn't attack anyone, including that Texas Ranger. I'm just here to set the record straight."

Good. But Reed figured there would be a lot of lies mixed in with Ben's attempt to explain anything. First though, Reed looked at Kirby. "I'll handle this situation. Go ahead and help out the others by securing the place. I want the whole area checked for prints or any other evidence."

Kirby issued a "Will do," and headed down the stairs.

Reed heard the shower curtain rattle, and Ben's gaze flew right to Livvy. His snarl deepened. "So, there you are. I understand you're hell-bent on keeping my boy behind bars."

Livvy walked across the room and stood next to

Reed. "Actually, I'm hell-bent on examining the evidence. Too bad I keep getting interrupted." She paused just a heartbeat. "Did you try to kill me tonight?"

"I already answered that. No. Got no reason to go after you. *Yet.*"

That did it. Reed was already operating on a short fuse. He grabbed Ben with his left hand and slammed him against the doorjamb. "Threatening a peace officer's a crime, Ben. One I won't take lightly."

It took a moment for Ben to get his teeth unclenched. "I've done nothing wrong."

"What about burning down the cabin?" Reed challenged.

"I didn't do that." No hesitation. None. But Reed wasn't ready to believe him. Ben had one of the best motives for wanting Livvy out of town.

"In the woods near the cabin, we found a piece of a shirt that belongs to you," Livvy challenged.

"Yeah. I heard about that. Jonah said I bought it from a charity sale. Well, you know what? Jonah was lying, probably to save his own rich butt. But I'll be damned if I'll take the blame for something that man's done."

"So you're saying you're innocent?" Livvy clarified.

"Damn right I am."

Ben began a tirade of why he was being railroaded, but Reed was no longer paying attention to him. That was because he had spotted something.

Something that could blow this case wide open.

Reed latched on to Ben and got him moving toward the stairs. "Ben Tolbert, you're under arrest."

Chapter Eleven

Livvy gulped down more coffee and hoped the caffeine would help clear the fog in her head. The adrenaline from the attack had long since come and gone, leaving her with a bone-deep fatigue that was worse because she'd gotten only an hour or so of real sleep. That probably had something to do with the lumpy sofa in the sheriff's office break room that she'd used as a bed.

But it had more to do with Ben Tolbert's arrest.

God, was he really the one who'd attacked her? If so, Reed and she would soon know. The tiny rip on the sleeve of Ben's shirt had prompted his arrest.

A rip that she was thankful Reed had noticed.

She'd been too shaken from the attack to notice much of anything. So much for all her training. She'd reacted like a rookie, and it didn't really matter that she was one. She expected more of herself.

Livvy checked her watch again. It was 9:00 a.m. The start of the normal workday for most people, but Reed and she had been working this case most of the night. With luck, they would soon know if the small cut on Ben's shirt had been made with her nail scissors. Well, they'd know if the Ranger lab could match the fibers. Reed had had one of the deputies hand-deliver both Ben's shirt and the scissors, and any minute now, they should know if it was a match.

"I'm not releasing Ben Tolbert until I'm sure he's innocent," she heard Reed bark. He was no doubt still talking to Jerry Collier, the head of the land office and also Ben's newly hired attorney.

"Then schedule an arraignment," Jerry insisted. "I don't want you holding him without making it official."

"I'm doing us all a favor. It'll only create a mountain of paperwork if I officially arrest Ben."

"But you can release him until you get back that evidence." And Jerry continued to argue his client's case.

Livvy, however, shut out the conversation when her phone rang. It was the crime lab, but the number on the caller ID wasn't for trace and fibers, it was from the firearms section.

"Sergeant Hutton," she answered.

"It's me. Sam McElroy." This was someone she knew well. A firearms expert who'd been examining the weapon that had killed Marcie. But Livvy hadn't just sent him that particular gun. She had also couriered Sam the primary firearm that Shane used in the line of duty.

"You found something?" Livvy asked.

"I did. Your instincts were right. Someone tampered with the Rimfire pistol used to kill Marcie James."

Livvy let out the breath she'd been holding. She'd tried to stay objective, but because her feelings for Reed had softened to the point of melting, she'd automatically found herself rooting for his deputy. And, yes, that was a blow to her professionalism, but in the end, it was the truth that mattered anyway.

"The fingerprints were planted on the murder weapon," she said, stating a conclusion she'd already reached.

"Yes," Sam verified. "I compared the two firearms, and the grip pattern on the Rimfire is way off. There weren't enough pressure points to indicate Deputy Tolbert fired the gun, even though it was in his hand."

"Probably placed there by the real killer while the deputy was unconscious."

Shane had been set up, just as he said.

But by whom?

Had his father been the one to kill Marcie? Maybe. But why would he set up his son to take the fall? Still, he certainly wasn't the only suspect. Ben's attorney, Jerry, was on the short list. So was the mayor. Billy Whitley. And Jonah Becker.

"There's more," Sam continued. "I checked the lab, and one of the results was ready. I thought you'd like to know."

She listened as Sam explained the results of the sample she'd submitted after examining the cabin crime scene.

Livvy thanked Sam, ended the call and got up from the desk so she could give Reed the news, but the moment she saw his face, she knew he had news of his own.

"I'm getting my client out of jail," Jerry insisted. *"Now."* And with that, he stormed off.

Reed scrubbed his hand over his jaw, drank some coffee and then looked at her. "I just got a call from the lab. The fibers on your scissors didn't match Ben's shirt."

Her heart dropped to her stomach. "But what about the rip on the fabric?"

Reed lifted his shoulder. "It wasn't caused by the scissors."

Livvy forced herself to take a step back. "Ben could have changed his shirt after he attacked me."

"Yeah. He could have." But there was skepticism in Reed's voice.

Livvy shared that skepticism. Why would Ben have chosen to replace the shirt worn during the attack with one that was torn in such a way that it would only cast more suspicion on him?

"I have to let him go," Reed said. "As soon as Jerry and he sign the papers, he'll be out. But I'll keep an eye on him. And I'll take some measures to make sure you're safe."

She remembered his invitation when they'd kissed in her room. "You want me to stay at your place?"

"Yes." More skepticism. "I know what you're thinking. It'll set tongues wagging, but I'd planned on spending more time with you anyway whether that was at work or the inn. This just makes it easier for me to keep you safe because I'm not going to let Ben or anyone else have a go at you."

Livvy wanted to object. She wanted to remind him that she could take care of herself. But she wasn't stupid. And she didn't want to die.

"I have news, too." It seemed a really good time to change the subject. "The fingerprint pattern on the murder weapon doesn't match the one on Shane's service pistol."

She saw the fatigue drain from Reed's face. "You mean he's innocent."

She nodded. "That's what the evidence indicates."

So why was she so reluctant to declare that Shane wasn't a killer?

All the pieces fit for him to have been set up. It was also obvious that someone else was out there, someone who wanted to stop them from learning the truth. Shane certainly hadn't been responsible for those attacks because he had been behind bars when they occurred. But Livvy couldn't totally dismiss the possibility that perhaps Shane was the mastermind who'd set all of this in motion.

Still, there were others with more powerful motives than love gone wrong.

"The firearms expert who called me about the gun also had the results from one of the lab tests," she continued. "The blood spatter we found in the cabin was consistent with the head injury that Shane described. And it was his blood."

Now there was relief in his eyes. Reed looked as if he were about to shout in victory, but his mood changed again.

Did he have doubts as well?

"Thank you," he said.

He reached out and almost idly ran his fingers through the ends of her ponytail. It was the gesture of a man comfortable with touching her. A gesture that shocked Livvy but not nearly as much as her own reaction did. She moved in to the touch, letting his thumb brush against her cheek.

It was intimate.

And wrong.

As usual, the timing was awful. They were both exhausted. Both had a dozen things to do that were important and related to the job. But it was as if those deeply seeded primal urges just weren't going to leave them alone.

"You know, I'll be leaving as soon as we've wrapped up this case," Livvy said. Not that she needed to remind him or herself of that.

"I know." And he seemed genuinely disappointed. "But Austin's not that far from here. Less than an hour away."

Far enough, she silently added.

If she stopped this now…but then she halted that particular thought because it was useless.

She couldn't stop this now.

It was only a matter of time before they landed in bed, and her hope was that this heat between them would be so intense that it would quickly burn itself out and Reed and she could get back to normal.

Reed drew in a hard breath, pulled back his hand and turned. "I need to do the paperwork for Shane's release." Then, he paused. "You're sure he's innocent?"

"No," she admitted. "But the evidence doesn't point to him being guilty."

Reed nodded and walked away, leaving Livvy to wonder if she'd just given a killer a get-out-of-jail-free card.

The phone on Reed's desk rang, and Livvy glanced out into the reception area to see if Eileen was there to answer it. She wasn't, so Livvy took the call.

"It's me, Ben Tolbert," the caller said.

Livvy tried to keep the strain out of her voice. "Are you already out of jail?"

"Yeah, as of thirty seconds ago."

Her heart suddenly felt very heavy. "Where are you?"

"I'm going nowhere near you. Where's Reed?"

"Busy. I'm surprised you didn't see him because he was headed to the jail." She'd let Shane be the one to tell his father that he'd been cleared of the murder charges.

"I musta missed him. I didn't exactly hang around the place after I told my boy I'd be gettin' him out of that cell soon enough."

Sooner than Ben thought. "I don't expect Reed back for ten or fifteen minutes, but I can take a message."

Silence. Several long seconds of it. "Tell him I've been doing some digging."

Livvy had to get her teeth apart so she could speak. "We don't want you to interfere in this case."

"Well, somebody has to. You got the wrong man in jail, and I intend to do everything I can to prove it. So, consider this a tip. I heard from a reliable source that Billy Whitley faked historical documents that allowed Jonah Becker to buy that land—the land that's causing all the ruckus with the Comanches."

Billy Whitley, another suspect. "Why would Billy have done that?"

"Money, what else? Jonah paid him to do it. Jonah's too smart to make a payment that could be traced back to him, but there will be a trail all right. You're just gonna have to hunt hard and find it."

Maybe. If this was a legit lead. "Who's your reliable source?"

"Can't tell you that."

"Then why should I believe you?" Livvy pressed. "You might be saying all of this to take suspicion off yourself."

"No reason for that. I haven't done anything wrong."

The attack came racing back at her. The man's scent.

The rasp of his breathing. How he'd come at her. She'd been lucky not to have been hurt. Or worse.

"I think Billy's the one who set up my boy," Ben continued, and that accusation immediately grabbed her attention.

"Why do you think that?"

"Because if Billy did fake those documents, then he's as much of a suspect as Jonah."

"And your lawyer," Livvy pointed out. "Jerry has motive, too."

"A lot of people have motive," Ben admitted, "but I'm betting Billy or his wife is responsible for this."

Yes, Charla could have been in on it. "Again, do you have proof?"

There was another hesitation, longer than the first. "What's the fax number there?" he asked.

Surprised by his request, Livvy looked at the machine and read the fax number that she located on the top of it. "Why do you need it?"

"Because I'm about to send you something. Consider it a gift."

Livvy didn't really want any gift from a suspected killer, but it didn't take long before the machine began to spit out a faxed copy.

"The first page is a copy of the way the deed was filed decades ago," Ben explained. "Look at line eight. When you get the second page, you'll see how it was changed. It no longer says 'the Comanche people.' It lists ownership as none other than Billy and Charla Whitley."

Livvy didn't say a word until both documents had finished printing, and her attention went to line eight on the pages.

There had indeed been a change.

"How did you get these?" she demanded.

"I can't tell you that."

"You stole them," Livvy accused. Then, she cursed under her breath. "And if you did, that means we can't use them as evidence. We wouldn't be able to prove that you're not the one who did the tampering."

His silence let her know that Ben was considering that. "What if I swear on my son's life that those papers are real?"

"That won't stand up in court." But it did in some small way convince her that Ben might be telling the truth, about this anyway. Livvy decided to put him to the test. "Shane will be out of jail soon. It appears someone planted his prints on the murder weapon."

"Are you sure?" Ben snapped.

"Sure enough for Reed to be processing his release as we speak."

Ben paused. "Is this some kind of trick? It is, isn't it? You're just telling me what I want to hear. You want to hang my boy."

"I want to hang the person responsible for Marcie's murder," Livvy clarified. "And if that had turned out to be Shane, he'd still be in jail. That's true for any future evidence we might find. But for now, the evidence isn't enough for us to hold your son."

Ben mumbled something. "Guess that means you're still gunning for him."

Livvy huffed. "Only if Shane's guilty of something. Is he?"

"I knew it." Ben cursed again. "I knew you'd still go after my boy."

Livvy didn't even bother to repeat that she wasn't on some vendetta to convict Shane of anything. But Ben might have a vendetta of his own.

"Did you tamper with these documents to implicate Billy so you could get your son cleared of murder charges?" Livvy asked.

"No. The documents are real, and Billy changed them so Jonah could buy that land."

His answer was so fast and assured that it surprised Livvy. Ben could have taken the easy way out. Heck, he could have hung up the phone and raced to the jail to see Shane.

But he hadn't.

Instead, Ben had stuck to his story about Billy's involvement.

Livvy looked at the documents again. They certainly seemed real, and that meant she had to call Reed.

They needed a search warrant ASAP.

"My advice?" Ben said. "Be careful, Sergeant Hutton. Because once everyone in town knows what Billy and Jonah did, somebody's gonna get hurt. Bad."

Livvy didn't question the threat because she knew Ben was right. The town was already on the verge of an explosion, and this certainly wouldn't help.

"One more thing," Ben added. "Everything we've said here, somebody's probably overheard. Somebody who's probably running to tell Billy to destroy anything that might put these murders on him. He'll be desperate. Real desperate. If I was you, I'd get over there right now."

Livvy didn't argue or disagree. She dropped the phone back onto its cradle and hurried to find Reed.

Chapter Twelve

Reed replayed everything Livvy had told him about her conversation with Ben. In fact, Reed had spent a good deal of the day replaying it and trying to figure out what the devil was going on.

He wasn't any closer to the answer than he had been when the day started.

Thankfully, Woody had come back from his fishing trip. Well, he had after Reed had sent his deputy out to tell the man what had been going on in town. Woody had returned immediately, just in time to give Reed permission to search Billy's office in the city building.

Reed had personally gone through every inch of Billy's office. Nothing was out of order, nor were there any signs of tampered documents. It'd helped that Billy hadn't been there during the search, but he would find out about it. That was a given, even though Reed had sworn Billy's secretary to secrecy.

Besides, there was a bigger secret that Reed had to unravel.

Shane was out of jail now. Cleared because of

planted evidence that Livvy had discovered. So, that meant there was a killer out there who had to be caught.

Reed just wasn't sure this was the way to go about doing it.

Beside him on the seat of his truck, Livvy was napping. Thank God. She was the only person in town who in the past twenty-four hours had had less sleep than him. Of course, she hadn't wanted the nap. In fact, she'd fought it like crazy, but in the end, the boring stakeout of Billy's house had been too much for the fatigue, and she was now asleep with her head dropped onto his shoulder.

Reed didn't mind the close contact with her rhythmic breath brushing against his neck. He didn't even mind that her left breast was squished against his arm. The touching was a surefire way of remembering that she was a woman, and that in turn was a surefire way of keeping him awake.

Shifting a little so that his arm wouldn't go numb, Reed checked their surroundings again. It was dark now, still hotter than hell, and no one had come or gone from the Whitley house in the entire three hours that Livvy and he had been keeping watch. The area wasn't exactly brimming with activity since it was located just outside the city limits and a good half mile from any neighbors.

Reed had called Billy earlier, before he'd even gone to the man's office to search. Billy had been home then. Sick with a sudden case of the stomach flu, he'd said, and he had a doctor's appointment in San Antonio and wouldn't be home until later in the evening. Then, he'd hung up and hadn't answered the phone when Reed tried to call him again. That'd sent Livvy and Reed out to Billy's place because they didn't want the man to try to destroy any evidence.

But where were Billy and Charla now? Still at the doctor's office or perhaps pretending to be there?

And had someone already tipped him off about Ben somehow finding the doctored land record? Or the office search? Maybe. But if Billy did know, the last thing Reed expected the man to do was go on the run.

Well, unless Billy really was a killer.

Reed checked his cell phone again. Nope. He hadn't missed a call. Not that he thought he had since the phone was set to a loud ring. That meant Kirby hadn't succeeded in getting the search warrant yet. Reed hadn't needed one for a municipal office because Woody had given him permission to search. But he'd need one for a private residence.

He'd get it, too.

There was no way a judge would turn it down with the evidence of the doctored documents, but Comanche Creek wasn't exactly flooded with judges, and Kirby had gotten stuck driving all the way over to Bandana, a good hour away, just to find Judge Calder, who was visiting relatives.

Reed had considered just going in and looking around Billy and Charla's place. But that wouldn't be smart if Livvy and he managed to find something in-criminating. If Billy was the killer, Reed didn't want anything like an unlawful search to stand in the way of the man's arrest and conviction. Of course, Reed had considered that this could be an exigent circumstance, where a peace officer could conduct a search without a warrant if there was a likelihood that evidence might be destroyed, but again, he didn't want that challenged. He wanted to follow the letter of the law on this one.

Livvy stirred, her breath shivering as if she were in the throes of a bad dream. But Reed rethought that theory when her eyes sprang open and her gaze snapped to his.

Even though the only illumination came from the hunter's moon and the yellow security light mounted at the end of the drive, he could clearly see her expression. No nightmare. But no doubt disturbing.

This dream was perhaps of the sexual variety.

Or maybe that was wishful thinking on his part. His thoughts were certainly straying toward that variety when it came to Livvy.

"You shouldn't have let me fall asleep," she mumbled and eased her breast away from his arm.

Maybe it was his surly mood, or even his own fatigue, but Reed put his hand around the back of her neck, hauled her to him and kissed her.

He got proof of the direction of her thoughts when she didn't resist. She kissed him right back.

And more.

Livvy caught onto his shoulders and adjusted their positions so that he got more of that breast contact. Both of them. He'd been hot before, but that kicked up the heat even more.

The kiss continued. Deepened. So did the body contact. They were both damp with sweat, and with the moisture from the kiss, everything suddenly felt right for sex.

It wasn't, of course.

And because they were literally sitting in his truck in front of a suspected killer's house, Reed remembered that this was not a safe time to engage in an oral rodeo with a woman he wanted more than his next breath.

He pulled back. Man, his body protested. But before his body could come up with a convincing argument as to why this could continue, Reed moved Livvy back onto the seat so that they were no longer touching.

"I feel like I'm back in high school," she complained.

Not Reed. In high school his willpower had sucked, and he wouldn't have let something like common sense or danger get in the way of having sex.

And if he wasn't careful, he wouldn't let those things get in the way now.

His phone rang, slicing through the uncomfortable silence that followed Livvy's confession. Reed wasn't pleased with the interruption, but he was damn happy about getting this call.

"Kirby," Reed answered. "Tell me you have a search warrant."

"I got it. The judge didn't put any limits on it, either. You can go through the house, grounds and any out-buildings or vehicles. You still waiting at Billy's house?"

"Yeah. Bring the warrant to us."

"Will do. I'll be there in about forty-five minutes."

Reed hung up, knowing he wouldn't wait that long. The warrant had been issued and that was enough. "Let's go," he instructed.

Livvy immediately grabbed her equipment bag, got out and joined him as they walked toward the front of the house. "You plan to bash down the door?" she asked.

"No need." Reed lifted the fake rock to the left side of the porch and extracted a key.

"That's not very safe," she commented.

No, but until recently most people around Comanche Creek hadn't had cause to be concerned about safety.

Reed unlocked the door and stepped inside. "Anyone home?" he called out just to be sure that Billy or his wife weren't hiding out. But he got no answer.

He was thankful that the house wasn't huge and also that he had been there often enough to know the layout. "Billy's office is this way," he said, leading Livvy down the hall that was off the living room. "His wife, Charla, is somewhat of a neat freak so if he brought the land documents home, they'd be in here."

They went into the office, turned on the lights and immediately got to work. The room wasn't large, but it was jammed with furniture, including a desk that held a stack of papers, folders and an open laptop. Reed went there first, and Livvy headed to a filing cabinet.

"What are some possible file names that would be red flags?" she asked.

"Anything that deals with Native American land. Or something called the Reston Act. That's the name of the old law that gave the Comanches the land."

Livvy took out some latex gloves from her bag, put them on and tossed him a pair. She then pulled open the drawer. "So, if that law is on the books, why wasn't the land deal challenged when it happened two years ago?"

"It was, by the activist Native American group. But then Billy produced this document that supposedly superseded the Reston Act. It seemed legit, and there were other documents on file to back it up. Basically, those documents claimed that the land had only been leased to the Comanches and that ownership reverted to the original owner, who was Jonah's great-great-grand-father."

"Convenient," Livvy mumbled.

"Maybe." Reed put on the gloves and thumbed through the papers and files. "Or maybe someone doctored that, too. The activist group didn't have the funds to fight a long legal battle, so they turned to Marcie. They wanted her to testify that at Jonah's urging, Jerry Collier orchestrated the illegal land deal."

"And we know what happened to Marcie." Livvy paused, and he heard her rifling through the files. "Other than Billy, who else could have faked the documents?"

Reed figured she wouldn't like the answer. He certainly didn't. "Anyone with access to the land office."

Woody, Billy, Jerry and, yes, even Jonah. Basically, anyone with enough motive and determination could have figured out a way to get into those files since security was practically nonexistent.

That had changed. Since the murders, Reed had insisted the city council install a better security system, one with surveillance cameras. But this crime—the altered documents—had happened long before the murders.

"I might have something," Livvy said.

But when he looked at her, she no longer had her attention on the files. She was studying something in the bookcase behind the cabinet. "There are two books here, one on Comanche burial rituals and another on local Native American artifacts."

That grabbed his attention, especially the one about rituals. Reed pulled it from the shelf, went straight to the index and saw the references for the red paint and ochre clay used in burials. It was critical because two dead bodies found the previous week had been prepared with red paint and clay.

"Hell," Reed mumbled. He continued to thumb through the book and noticed the pages with the clay references had been dog-eared.

Of course, Billy's wife was Native American. Maybe the books were hers. But Reed suspected if they had been, they wouldn't be in Billy's office. "It's circumstantial, but we can still use it to build a case. If Billy's guilty," he added.

"I think we might have something more than just circumstantial," Livvy corrected.

Reed looked up from the book. Livvy was photographing the trash can. She took several pictures and then carefully pushed aside some wadded-up paper and pulled out a latex glove, one very similar to the pair she was wearing.

"Any reason Billy would need this in his office?" she asked.

"None that I can think of." Especially none that involved anything legal.

Livvy eased the glove right side out and examined it. "We might be able to get DNA from the inside," she explained.

She placed the glove back on top of the paper wads, took the spray bottle of Luminol from her bag. She put just a fine mist on a small area that would cover the back of the hand.

It lit up.

An eerie blue glow.

Indicating there was blood.

Reed cursed again. "Is there enough for a DNA match to Marcie's blood?"

"All it takes is a tiny amount." She leaned in closer. "There's a smudge. It could be gunshot residue. Let's go ahead and bag this, and I'll bring the entire trash can in case the other glove is down in there."

Reed took one of the evidence bags to encase the glove while Livvy clicked off more photographs. The trash can and the glove would be sent to the lab that would have the final word on any biological or trace evidence, but it wasn't looking good for Billy.

Was Billy really a killer?

Reed had to admit it was possible. He'd known Billy all his life and had never seen any indication that the man was violent. Still, he'd also seen desperate people do desperate things, and Billy might have been desperate to cover his tracks and therefore kill Marcie.

"Once Kirby gets here with the warrant, I'll have him lock down the place so we can have time to go through everything else," Reed explained.

It also might be a good idea for them to drive the glove and trash can to the lab themselves. If they could get a quick match to Marcie on the blood, then Reed would arrest Billy.

"Are you okay?" Livvy asked.

Reed realized then that he was staring at the bagged glove with what had to be an expression of gloom and doom on his face. "I was just hoping the killer was someone else. Someone I didn't know."

"I understand." She touched his arm with her fingertips. A gesture no doubt meant to soothe him.

And it might have worked, too, if there hadn't been a sound. A slight rustling from outside the house.

"Probably the wind," Livvy said under her breath.

"Probably." But Reed set the bagged glove aside in case he had to reach for his gun. "It's not Kirby. We would have heard the cruiser drive up." Besides, it was too soon for the deputy to have arrived.

There was another sound. One that Reed couldn't quite distinguish, but it had come from the same direction as the first.

"I'll have a look," he insisted, and drew his weapon.

Livvy put down the trash can and did the same. "You think Billy's out there?" she whispered.

Someone certainly was—Reed was positive of that when he heard the next sound.

Footsteps, just outside the window.

He turned, aiming his gun.

Just as the lights went out and plunged them into total darkness.

Reed saw the shadow outside the window and reached for Livvy to get her out of the way. But he was a split second too late.

The bullet tore through the glass and came right at them.

Chapter Thirteen

Livvy heard the shot, but she wasn't able to see who had fired at them. That was because Reed shoved her to the floor. She landed, hard, and the impact with the rustic wood planks nearly knocked the breath out of her.

Thankfully, Reed didn't have any trouble reacting.

He rolled to the side, came up on one knee, and using the desk as cover, he took aim. She couldn't see him clearly, but she heard the result. His shot blasted through what was left of the glass on the far right window.

"Who's out there?" she whispered, getting herself into position so she could fire as well.

"I can't tell."

Well, it was obviously someone who wanted them dead.

That hadn't been a warning shot. It'd come much too close to hitting them. And worse, it wasn't over. Reed and she were literally pinned down in a room with three large windows, any one of which could be an attack point. But it wasn't the only way a gunman could get to them.

There was a door behind them.

Livvy rolled onto her back so she could kick it shut.

At least this way the culprit wouldn't be able to sneak up on them. And that led her to the big question.

Who exactly was the culprit?

"Billy Whitley," Livvy mumbled under her breath. Livvy scrambled to the side of the desk as well.

Another shot came through the window. Not from Reed this time. But from their attacker. Reed immediately returned fire, but Livvy held back and tried to peer over the desk and into the night. She hoped to get a glimpse of the shooter's location, but the only thing she saw was the darkness.

The next shot tore through the oak desk and sent a spray of splinters right at them. Reed shoved her back to the floor, and she caught onto his arm to make sure he came down as well.

More shots.

One right behind the other.

Livvy counted six, each one of the bullets slamming into the desk and the wall behind them. A picture fell and smashed on the floor next to her feet. The crash blended with the sounds of the attack. The chaos. And with her own heartbeat that was pounding in her ears.

Then, the shooting stopped.

Livvy waited, listening, hoping the attack was over but knowing it probably wasn't.

"He's reloading," she mumbled.

"Yeah." Reed glanced over at her. "How much ammunition do you have on you?"

"A full magazine in the gun and a backup clip. You?"

"Just what I have here. The rest is in the truck."

The truck parked outside where the shooter was.

Livvy didn't need to do the math. She knew. Reed

and she wouldn't be able to go bullet-to-bullet with this guy because he probably had brought lots of backup ammunition with him. However, that was only one of their problems.

There was Kirby to consider.

The deputy would arrive soon, maybe in twenty minutes or less. The shooter might gun him down if Reed and she didn't warn him.

"I have to call Kirby," Livvy let him know.

Reed kept his attention nailed to the windows and passed her his phone. "Request backup, too, but don't have them storming in here. Tell him to keep everyone at a distance until they hear from me. But I do want lights and sirens. I want this SOB to know he's not going to escape."

Livvy agreed and made the call. She'd barely got out the warning when the shots started again. Obviously, the gunman had reloaded, and he began to empty that fresh ammunition into the room. He was literally tearing it apart, and that included the desk. It wouldn't be long before the shots destroyed the very piece of furniture they were using as cover.

"Kirby's calling backup," she relayed to Reed and tossed the phone back to him.

"The shots are getting closer."

Because of the noise, it took a moment for that to sink in. Livvy's gaze whipped in the direction of the windows again, and she listened.

God, Reed was right. The shots were getting closer, and that meant the shooter was closing in on them. If he made it all the way to the windows, he'd have a much better chance of killing them.

"He knows we don't have enough ammunition to hold him back," Reed explained. "We have to get out of this room."

Livvy didn't have any doubts about that. But what she did doubt was they'd be able to escape without being shot. The gunman might already be at the windows.

Of course, Reed and she could fire right back.

And they would. Until they were out of bullets. After that, well, they'd still fight. Livvy had no intentions of letting this goon get away, and Reed no doubt felt the same.

With the shots still knifing all around them, Livvy crawled to the door and reached for the knob.

"Be careful," Reed warned. "He might not be alone out there."

Mercy. She should have already thought of that. If this was Billy firing those shots, then he could be working with his wife. Charla could be in the house. Not that there had been any signs of that, but it was something Livvy had to prepare herself to face.

She aimed her gun and used her left hand to open the door. Just a fraction. She peered out into the hall. Thankfully, her eyes had adjusted to the darkness so even though the lights were off, she didn't see anyone lurking outside the doorway.

"It's clear," she relayed to Reed.

That got him moving. With his back to her and his attention still on the windows, he made his way to her and fired a glance into the hall.

"I'll go first, and you come out right behind me," Reed explained over the thick, loud blasts. "Stay low, as close to the floor as possible. You cover the right side of the hall. I'll cover the left."

Livvy's heart sank lower because the shots were even closer now.

Reed came up a little and fired a bullet in the direction of those shots. He didn't even aim, because it was meant to get the guy to back off. It might buy them a second or two of time, but that was all they needed.

Livvy didn't bother with the equipment bag. It was too big and bulky to take with them. She only hoped that it would still be there at the end of this attack. Just in case it wasn't, she snatched the bagged glove and shoved it into the waist of her jeans.

"Now!" Reed ordered.

Livvy didn't waste any more time. She scrambled to the side so Reed could get by her. He practically dove into the hall but as he'd instructed, he stayed on the floor. Livvy did the same, and she landed out in the darkness with her back to his.

She had the easy end of the hall to cover. Only one room that was directly at the end. Probably a bedroom. And the door was closed. However, that didn't mean the shooter wouldn't go through one of the room's windows to get to them and try to stop their escape.

"I don't see anyone," she reported.

"Neither do I."

Livvy didn't exactly breathe easier because that side contained all the main living areas. There were multiple points of entry, and if the gunman was indeed Billy, he would know the way to get in that would cause the biggest threat to Reed and her.

"This way," Reed instructed.

He remained crouched, with his gun aimed and ready, and he began to inch his way toward the front of the house where they'd entered. Livvy did the same while keeping watch on the bedroom. She didn't want anyone blasting through that door.

Then, again, the shots stopped.

Reed and she froze, and Livvy tried to steady her heartbeat so she could listen. But the only thing she heard was their breathing.

"Let's move," Reed insisted.

Yes, because they were still in the line of sight of the office windows, and Livvy couldn't risk reaching up to close the door. The last thing they wanted was for the shooter to have a visual on them.

Reed began to move again, and Livvy followed. She kept watch on both the office and the bedroom door, but there were no sounds coming from either.

Mercy.

Where was the shooter?

She doubted he'd just give up. No. He was looking for a place to launch another attack.

Reed stopped again when they got to the end of the hall, and she glanced at him as he peered out into the living room. It was just a quick look, and then he whipped his attention to the other side, to the kitchen. He didn't say anything, didn't make a sound, but Livvy figured he didn't see anyone or else he would have taken aim.

She heard it then. The knob on the kitchen door rattled. Reed and she both shifted in that direction, but she continued to watch the bedroom and now the office.

Another rattle. Someone was obviously trying to get

in, but the door was apparently locked because the third try wasn't just a rattle. Someone gave it a frantic, violent shake.

Livvy had just enough time to wonder why Billy hadn't just used his key to gain entry when she heard another sound.

A siren.

Kirby or one of the backup deputies had finally arrived. Or would soon. Reed and she wouldn't have to hold out much longer.

But that brought a new concern. A new *fear*.

The gunman might get away.

That couldn't happen. Reed and she couldn't continue to go through this. They had to catch the killer and get him off the streets. If not, this wouldn't stop.

Reed obviously had the same concern because he moved out of the hall so he'd be in a better position if the gunman did indeed come through the kitchen door. The siren might scare him off.

Or not.

The *or not* was confirmed when someone kicked at the door. Hard. And then it sounded as if someone was ramming against it.

Livvy considered shooting at the door. Reed likely did, too, but this might not be the gunman. It could be Charla who was trying to get away from her now deranged husband. Or maybe it was someone from backup responding.

"This is Sheriff Hardin," Reed called out. "Who's out there?"

Nothing. And the attempts to get inside stopped.

Livvy couldn't hear if the person moved away

because the sirens drowned out any sound the person might have made.

Reed cursed and scurried to the snack bar area that divided the living room from the kitchen. He kept his aim and focus on the door while Livvy tried to keep watch all around them.

"Call Kirby." Reed tossed her his phone again. "Make sure he's locking down the area."

But it might be too late. The killer could already be on the move and escaping.

"Smoke," she heard Reed say.

She lifted her head, pulled in a long breath, and cursed. Yes, it was smoke, and she figured it was too much to hope that it was coming from some innocent source.

Livvy pressed Redial, and Kirby answered on the first ring. She relayed Reed's message and told the deputy to await further orders. She'd barely managed to say that before there was another shot.

This one, however, hadn't been fired into the house. It'd come from outside but in the direction of the driveway.

Reed and she waited for several long seconds. Breaths held. With her pulse and adrenaline pounding out of control. Livvy didn't take her eyes off the bedroom just up the hall, and she was primed and wired for an attack when the cell phone rang.

The unexpected sound caused her to gasp, and she glanced down at the lit screen. It was Kirby.

"There's a fire on the back porch," Kirby shouted. "You need to get out of there."

Maybe Reed heard the deputy because he motioned for her to move toward the front door.

"Do you see the shooter?" Livvy asked Kirby.

"I think so. He's on the west end of the house."

By the driveway, just as she'd expected. "Is he trying to get in?"

"No. He's just sitting there, leaning against the wall."

Sitting? Or maybe crouching and waiting? "Can you see who it is?"

"No," Kirby quickly answered. "I'm using my hunting binoculars. They have night vision, and I'm getting a pretty close look, but he has a hat covering his face."

So if it was Billy, he could be trying to conceal his identity. "How bad is the fire?" The smoke was starting to billow into the living room.

"Not bad right now, but I wouldn't stay in there much longer. Uh, Sergeant Hutton?" Kirby continued. "I think the guy's been shot. He's got his hand clutched to his chest, and his gun is on the ground beside him."

Shot? It was possible. Reed and she had fired several times, and any one of the bullets could have hit the gunman.

"The shooter might be wounded," she told Reed. "He's by the driveway."

Reed didn't say anything for several seconds. "Tell Kirby to cover us. We're going out there."

Livvy told Kirby their plan while they were on the move toward the front door. Reed opened it.

Nothing.

Certainly there was no gunman waiting just outside.

Reed went first, and Livvy followed him. As they'd done inside, they moved back to back so they could cover all sides. At the end of the road, she saw Kirby standing next to a cruiser. Covering them. She hoped they wouldn't need it.

The night was sticky and hot, and the smoke was already tainting the air. Livvy heard the high, piercing buzzing of mosquitoes that immediately zoomed in on them.

Reed batted the mosquitoes away and hurried to the back of the house. He paused only a few seconds to check the area where the last shot had been fired.

Then, Reed took aim.

And fired.

Livvy tried to scramble to get into position so she could assist, but Reed latched on to her arm and held her at bay. "I fired a warning shot," he told her. "The guy didn't move an inch."

Which could mean the gunman was perhaps too injured to react. Or this could be a trick to lure them out into the open so he could kill them.

"Cover me," Reed insisted.

He stood, braced his wrist for a better aim and started toward the shooter.

Livvy eased out so she could fire if necessary. She saw the shooter then. Dressed in what appeared to be jeans, a dark shirt and a baseball cap that covered his face. His back was against the exterior of the house. His handgun on the ground beside him.

The guy certainly wasn't moving.

Reed inched closer. So did Livvy. And thanks to the moonlight she saw the man did indeed have his left hand resting on his chest.

She also saw the blood.

Ahead of her, Reed stooped and put his fingers

against the man's neck. Livvy waited and didn't lower her guard just in case this was a ploy.

"He's dead," Reed relayed.

"Dead," Livvy repeated under her breath.

She walked closer and stared down at the body. Though she was more than happy that this guy wasn't still taking shots at them, it sickened her a little to realize that she might have been the one to kill him.

Reed reached down with his left hand and eased the cap away from the man's face.

Livvy's stomach roiled.

It was Billy Whitley.

"We have to move the body," she heard Reed say, and he reached for Billy's feet. "The fire's spreading fast."

Livvy took hold of Billy as well and glanced at the flames that were eating their way through the back of the house. Reed was right—they didn't have much time. The fire had swelled to the wood-shake roof, and there were already tiny embers falling down around them.

They had dragged the body a few yards when she saw something fall out of the pocket of Billy's jeans.

A piece of paper.

Since she was still wearing a latex glove, she reached for it, but reaching was all she managed to do. The cabin seemed to groan, the sound echoing through the smoke-filled night. Livvy looked up to see what had caused the sound.

It was the heavy wood-shake roof.

And a massive chunk gave way.

Falling.

Right toward them.

She let go of the body. Reed did the same. And they both dove to the side as the flaming wood came crashing down.

Chapter Fourteen

"What was the cause of death?" Reed asked the coroner. He had his office phone sandwiched between his ear and shoulder so he could use his hands to type the incident report on his computer.

"The obvious," Dr. McGrath answered. "Gunshot wound to the chest. The single shot hit him in the heart, and he was probably dead before the bullet even stopped moving."

Yeah. It was obvious, but Reed needed it officially confirmed. All the *i*'s had to be dotted and the *t*'s crossed. Behind him at the corner desk, Livvy was doing a report as well. He glanced at her and saw the same stark emotion in her eyes that was no doubt in his.

The adrenaline rush had long since ended for both of them. They were somewhere between the stages of shock and exhaustion, and the exhaustion was slowly but surely winning out. That was why Reed had tried to convince Livvy to go back to the inn and get some rest. He would have had better luck trying to talk a longhorn into wearing a party dress.

Still, he'd keep trying.

"The gunshot was self-inflicted?" Reed asked the coroner.

"That's my official opinion. The angle is right. So is the stippling pattern. Billy also had gunshot residue on his right hand." Dr. McGrath cursed. "How the hell did it come to this, Reed? I've known Billy for years."

"We all have." Thankfully, the fatigue allowed him to suppress the gut emotion and keep it out of his voice. "If Marcie had testified against him, Billy would have gone to jail for a long time."

That was the motive, and it was a powerful one. Everything fit. All the pieces had come together. Billy had killed Marcie, set up Shane and then tried stop Livvy and him from learning the truth.

"I need your report when it's finished," Reed told Dr. McGrath and ended the call.

Two lights were blinking on his phone, indicating he had other calls. Probably from Woody or someone else in town. Maybe even Billy's widow, Charla. The woman had called five times in the past four hours, but Reed didn't want to go another round with her trying to convince him that her husband had been set up. If Billy was innocent, then it would come through in the evidence.

"What are you reading?" Reed asked, looking over at Livvy again.

"A fax from the county sheriff's office. I asked them why they'd given Jerry the file on my mother."

"And?" Because this was something Reed wanted to know as well.

"Apparently, Jerry asked a clerk, who also happens to be his cousin, to get the file for him. Jerry thought I would jump on this lead and wouldn't focus on Jonah, his client."

Damn. Talk about a slimy move. "I hope the clerk was fired."

"He was."

That was a start, but Reed would have a long talk with Jerry about dredging up old wounds just so he could try to help out his client.

Reed ignored the blinking lights on the phone, stood and went to Livvy. Reed caught onto her arm and lifted her from the chair. She wobbled a little, and he noticed her hand was still trembling.

"It's past midnight," he reminded her. "You need some rest."

She opened her mouth, probably to argue with him, but Reed opened his, too. He started to tell her that he could carry her out of there, caveman style. But he re-thought that and simply said, "Please."

Livvy blinked. Closed her mouth. That *please* apparently took away any fight left in her, and she sagged against him as they made their way out the door.

The receptionist had gone home hours earlier, and the front office was staffed with loaner deputies, some of whom he barely knew. But Shane was there, and even though he probably needed some rest, too, Reed preferred to have his own men in the thick of things.

"We'll be back in a couple of hours," Reed told Shane. But Reed hoped he could extend that couple of hours until morning. Maybe he'd need a few more *please*s to get Livvy to shut her eyes and try to recover from yet another attempt to kill her.

"I'm waiting on a call about that glove we found in Billy's trash," Livvy said as they walked out. "And that piece of paper that dropped from Billy's pocket. It was too burned for me to read, but I'm hoping the lab will be able to tell us what it says."

"Don't worry," Reed assured her. "They'll call one of us on our cells when the tests are back." Even though it was a short walk, he helped her into his truck so he could drive her to the inn.

She wearily shook her head. "That glove is critical. My equipment bag was destroyed in the fire."

Reed didn't respond to that except with a heavy sigh that he just couldn't bite back. Fires, rattlesnakes and bullets. All of which had been used to get to Livvy. Billy had certainly been persistent.

And maybe he hadn't acted alone.

That thought had been circling around in Reed's mind since he'd seen Billy's body propped against the house. Of course, there was no proof of an accomplice, but once they'd gotten some rest he'd look into it.

Reed stopped his truck in front of the inn, and Livvy didn't protest when he helped her out and went inside. Her silence bothered him almost as much as the trembling. He grabbed the spare room key from the reception desk and led her up the stairs.

"You okay?" he asked her.

A soft burst of air left her mouth. Almost a laugh. But it wasn't from humor. "I'm fine," she lied. Her eyes met his as he unlocked her door. "You?"

"I'm fine," he lied right back.

She stopped in the doorway and stared at him. "Your friend tried to kill you tonight."

Hearing those words aloud packed a punch. "He tried to kill you, too."

"Yes, but I didn't know him the way you did. He certainly wasn't my friend." She touched his arm. Rubbed gently. "I'm worried about you, Reed."

Now, it was his turn to nearly laugh. "You're worried about me? No need. I'm worried about you."

Livvy broke the stare, turned and went into the room. But she didn't turn on the light. "No need," she repeated. "True, I'd never really had my life on the line until I came to Comanche Creek, but this baptism by fire will give me a lot of experience to deal with future cases."

That sounded, well, like something a peace officer would say. But he knew for a fact that this particular peace officer wasn't made of stone. He reached for her, but she moved away from him and waved him off.

"Not a good idea," she insisted. "If you touch me, we'll end up kissing. And then we'll have aftermath sex. It won't be real. We'll be doing it to make ourselves forget just how close we came to dying tonight."

Now, that sounded too damn logical. And she was right. If he touched her, they would kiss, and they would have sex. But Reed was afraid she was wrong about the "not being real" part. He figured Livvy was afraid of that, too.

"I'll take a nap," she continued. "Then, I'll pack." Thanks to moonlight filtering through the gauzy curtains, he could see her dodge his gaze. "Because once the lab confirms that Marcie's blood was on that glove we found in Billy's trash can, the case will be over. I'll need to head back to my office. And Comanche Creek can start returning to normal."

That did it. All this calm logic was pissing him off. So did her packing remark. Yeah, it was stupid, but Reed figured if he didn't do this, then he would regret it for the rest of his life.

He slid his hand around the back of her neck, hauled her to him and kissed her.

Reed expected her to put up at least some token resistance, but she didn't. Livvy latched on to him and returned the kiss as if this would be the one and only time it would ever happen.

Her taste slammed into him. Not the fatigue and the fear. This was all heat and silk. All woman. And the kiss quickly turned French and desperate.

She hoisted herself up, wrapping her legs around his waist, while they continued to wage war on each other's mouths. Reed stumbled, hoping they'd land on the bed, but instead his back slammed into the wall. He'd have bruises.

He didn't care.

Nothing mattered right now but taking Livvy.

She took those frantic kisses to his neck and caused him to lose his breath for a moment or two. Turnabout was fair play so he delivered some neck kisses to her as well and was rewarded with a long, feminine moan of pleasure. So Reed took his time with that particular part of her body.

Or at least that was what he tried to do.

Livvy obviously had other ideas about how fast this was all moving. Her hands were as frantic as her mouth, and she began to fight with the buttons on his shirt. She didn't even bother with the shoulder holster, and speed became even more of a necessity.

Reed tried to slow things down a bit because he wanted to add at least a little foreplay to this, but foreplay didn't stand a chance when Livvy got his shirt unbuttoned. She unhooked her legs from his waist and slid down so she could drop some tongue kisses on his chest. And his stomach.

All right, that did it.

To hell with foreplay because she was playing dirty in the best way possible. Every part of his body was on fire, and sex with Livvy was going to happen *now*.

LIVVY COULDN'T THINK. Didn't want to think. But she did want to feel, and Reed was certainly making sure that was happening. For the first time in years, every part of her felt alive.

And needed.

Reed was making sure of that as well.

Livvy had him pressed against the wall, literally, and they were both grappling at each other's shirts. Even though Livvy had his open, she still lost the particular battle when Reed threw open her shirt, shoved down her bra and took her left nipple into his mouth.

Everything went blurry and fiery hot.

She had to stop kissing him. Because she couldn't catch her breath. She could only stand there while Reed took her to the only place she wanted to go.

Well, almost.

The breast kisses sent her body flying, but soon, very soon, they weren't nearly enough. She needed more, and she knew just how to get it.

Livvy went after his belt and somehow managed to get it undone. He didn't stop those mindless kisses, making her task even harder, but she finally got the belt unlooped from his jeans, and she shoved down his zipper. She would have gotten her hand inside his boxers, too, if he hadn't pushed the two of them toward the bed. Not gently either.

But she didn't want gentleness anyway.

This was how she'd known it would be with Reed. Intense. Frantic. Hot. Memorable. So memorable that she knew he was a man she'd never forget.

In the back of her mind she thought of the broken heart that was just down the road for her. Their relationship couldn't be permanent. This would have to be it. But even one time with Reed would be worth a lifetime with anyone else.

A thought that scared her.

And got her even hotter.

Because even in the heat of the moment, Livvy knew this wasn't ordinary.

Another push from Reed, and they landed on the bed, with him on top of her. The kisses took on a new urgency. And a new location. With her shirt still wide open, he used that clever mouth on her stomach and circled her navel with his tongue.

He went lower.

And lower.

Kissing her through her jeans and making her very aware yet again of just how good this was going to be.

She felt him kick off his boots and tried to do the same. It didn't work, and Livvy cursed the difficulty of clothing removal when both of them were dressed in way too much and were way too ready for sex.

Livvy changed their positions, flipping Reed on his back so she could reach down and drag off the boots. Reed helped himself to her zipper and peeled off her jeans.

Her panties, too.

With her thighs and sex now bare, she became all too

aware that he was still wearing jeans, a barrier she didn't want between them.

Reed obviously felt the same because he turned them again until he was on top. Both grabbed his jeans, pulling and tearing at the denim. Livvy considered trying to use a little finesse but gave up when the jeans and boxers came off and she had a mostly naked Reed between her legs.

"Condom?" he ground out. "I don't have one with me."

"I'm on the pill," she answered, though she didn't try to explain she was taking them to regulate her periods. For once she praised that particular problem because without it, there would have been no birth control pills. And no sex tonight with Reed.

Livvy wasn't sure either of them would have survived that. This suddenly felt as necessary as the blood rushing through her body.

They both still had on their shoulder holsters and weapons, and the gun metal clanged against the metal when Reed grabbed on to her hair, pulled back her head and kissed her. No ordinary kiss. His tongue met hers at the exact second he entered her.

He tried to be gentle.

Livvy could tell.

But gentleness didn't stand a chance tonight. She dug her heels into the soft mattress and lifted her hips, causing him to slide hard and deep into her. She stilled just a moment. So did Reed.

And in the moon-washed room, their eyes met.

Livvy wanted the fast and furious pace to continue. She didn't want to think about the intimacy of this now. But Reed forced her to do just that. The stare lingered, piercing through her. Until she could take no more. She grabbed on to his hips and drew him into a rhythm that would satiate her body.

Too soon.

She couldn't hang on to the moment. Instead, Livvy gave in to that rhythm as well. She moved, meeting him thrust for thrust, knowing that each one was taking them closer and closer to the brink.

Livvy heard herself say something, though she hadn't intended to speak. But she did. In that moment when she could take no more of the heat, no more of those rhythmic strokes deep inside her…

She said Reed's name, repeating it with each breath she took.

And then she surrendered.

Chapter Fifteen

Reed forced his eyes open. His body was still exhausted, but humming, and already nudging him for a second round with Livvy. It wouldn't happen.

Well, not anytime soon.

She needed to sleep, and what he wanted to do with her involved the opposite of sleeping.

Reed checked the blood-red dial on the clock next to the bed. Four o'clock. Livvy and he had been asleep for nearly three hours, more than just the catnap stage. He should get up and make some calls to find out what was going on at the station.

Livvy's bare left leg was slung over him, and he eased it aside. She reached for him, groping blindly, and Reed brushed a kiss on her hand before moving it aside as well. Even though he kept everything light and soft, Livvy still woke up.

"I fell asleep," she grumbled and started to climb out of bed as well.

"And you need to keep on sleeping."

"So do you, but you're up."

He couldn't argue with that. Heck, he couldn't argue

with his body, which was begging him to climb back into bed with her. She was a sight, all right. Naked, except for her rumpled white shirt and bra that was unhooked in the front. That gave him a nice peek-a-boo view of her breasts.

And the rest of her.

Later, after he'd cleared up some things at work, he would see if he could coax her into taking a shower with him. Reed was already fantasizing about having those long athletic legs wrapped around him.

He had to do something to stave off an erection, so he pulled on his boxers and jeans. He, too, still wore his shirt, and it was a wrinkled mess. He also had a bruise on the side of his chest where his gun and holster had gouged him during sex. Livvy and he hadn't gotten around to removing their weapons until they'd finished with each other.

"I need to call the lab," she explained. She peeled off her shirt and bra, leaving herself naked.

There wasn't enough devotion to duty in the world that would make Reed pass up this opportunity. He caught her arm, pulled her to him and kissed her.

She melted against him.

She smelled like sex. Looked like sex. And that was sex melt. A hot body slide against his that let him know it wouldn't take much coaxing to get her back in bed.

Reed pulled away, looked down at her. "Give me just a minute to check in at work. *Just a minute,*" he emphasized.

Smiling, she kissed him again. "Tempting. Very tempting," Livvy added, skimming her fingers along his bare chest. "But we both need to take care of a few things. Then, before I leave, maybe we can spend some time together."

Before I leave.

Yeah. Reed had known that was coming. Still, work could wait at least another half hour, so he leaned in to convince her of that. Their mouths had barely met when the ringing sound had them jumping apart. It was his cell, and when he checked the ID screen, he knew it was a call he had to take.

"Shane," Reed answered.

But before Shane could respond, Livvy's cell phone rang as well.

"We have a problem," Shane explained. "Charla Whitley's out front, and she's got a gun pointed at her head. She says she'll kill herself if we try to come any closer. I've cleared the area, but I haven't had any luck talking her into surrendering."

Hell. Charla was obviously distraught, and with good reason, since only hours earlier she'd lost her husband. "Has she made any specific demands?" Reed wanted to know.

"She's insisted on speaking to you—and to Sergeant Hutton. I wouldn't advise that, by the way. Personally, I think Charla wants to kill both of you because she blames you for Billy's death."

Of course she did. Charla certainly wouldn't want to blame her own husband, even though the guilt might solely be on Billy's shoulders.

"I'll be there in a few minutes," Reed informed him. "I'll drive around back so Charla can't get off an easy shot at me, but if she moves, let me know."

"Will do, Reed. Right now, she's hiding in the shrubs on the west side of the building. Be careful."

Oh, he intended to do that. After he talked Livvy into staying put so she could get some more rest. However, he quickly realized that would be a losing battle because Livvy was dressing as she talked on the phone. Since he couldn't make heads nor tails of her conversation, he finished putting on his clothes as well.

"Charla's at the station," Reed explained the moment she ended her call. "She's demanding to speak to us."

Livvy blew out a long breath and shook her head. "So, we'll *speak* to her." She collected her boots from the floor. "That was the lab. The blood on the glove was a match to Marcie James. Billy's DNA was on it as well, and in the right place this time. The DNA inside the finger portions of the glove was his."

So, there it was, the proof that connected Billy to Marcie's murder. "What about the charred piece of paper that fell out of his pocket?"

Livvy sat down on the bed and pulled on her boots. "It was a suicide note. Handwritten. Billy confessed to all the murders and the attempts to kill us. The lab tech pulled up Billy's signature from his driver's license, and the handwriting seems to be a match."

Seems. Reed wanted more. After the fiasco with Shane, he wanted layers and layers of proof. "I'll send them more samples of Billy's handwriting so they can do a more thorough analysis. What about fingerprints on the paper? Did they find any?"

"Just Billy's." She hooked her bra, ending his peep show, and grabbed a fresh white shirt from the closet.

That could mean that Billy had indeed written it—

voluntarily. But maybe it meant he was coerced and the coercer had worn gloves or perhaps not even touched the paper.

But he didn't want to borrow trouble. Everything pointed to Billy, and for now, Reed would go with that.

Livvy and he strapped on their holsters, and as they hurried down the stairs, she gathered her hair back into a ponytail. They obviously woke Betty Alice because the woman threw open the door to her apartment and peered out at them.

"Is there more trouble?" she asked.

"Could be." Reed tried not to look overly alarmed about the situation with Charla. And he also tried not to look as if he'd just had sex with Livvy. It wouldn't matter, of course. The gossips would soon speculate about both, especially since his truck had been parked in front of the inn for several hours.

Betty Alice clutched the front of her pink terry-cloth robe, hugging it even tighter. "Anything I can do?"

"Just stay put. And you go ahead and lock your door."

Her eyes widened, and she gave an alarmed nod, but she shut the door, and Reed heard her double-lock it.

Livvy and he headed out, locking the front door securely behind them. They hadn't even made it down the steps when his phone rang again. From the caller ID, he could see it was Shane.

"Reed, you said you wanted to know if the situation changed," Shane said, his words rushed and laced with concern. "Well, it changed. Charla disappeared."

Reed's stomach knotted. "What do you mean she disappeared?"

"She'd been hiding in the bushes like I said, and I had one of the deputies on the top floor using night goggles to keep an eye on her. She started running, and the deputy didn't want to shoot her in the back."

Reed could understand that, especially since Charla hadn't actually threatened anyone but herself.

"I'm in pursuit of her," Shane added. "And we're both on foot."

"What direction is Charla running?" Reed asked.

Shane didn't hesitate. "She's headed your way."

WHEN REED drew his gun, Livvy did the same.

She hadn't heard all of Reed's conversation, but the last part had come through in Reed's suddenly tense expression.

What direction is Charla running?

"She's on her way here?" Livvy clarified.

"Yeah. And according to Shane, she's armed and possibly gunning for us."

Great. Here, Livvy had thought they'd dealt with the last of the attempts to kill them, but she had perhaps been wrong.

"Go after Charla," Reed instructed Shane. "But don't fire unless it's absolutely necessary. We don't know her intentions, and she could mean us no harm." Though Reed didn't sound as if he believed that.

Reed ended the call, and changed the phone's setting so that it would vibrate and not ring. He put away his phone, but he didn't hurry to his truck, probably because it was parked out in the open and not far up the street from the police station. Charla could possibly be on the very sidewalk next to the truck and ready to take aim if either Reed or Livvy stepped toward the vehicle.

"We need to take cover," Reed insisted, tipping his head to the four-foot-high limestone wall that stretched across the entire front and side yards of the inn.

Reed took the left side of the gate, and Livvy took the right. Both crouched low so they wouldn't be easy targets.

And they waited.

Because of the late hour, there were no people out and about. Thank goodness. There was little noise as well. The only sounds came from the soft hum of the streetlights and the muggy night breeze stirring the shrubs and live oak trees. What Livvy didn't hear were any footsteps, but that didn't mean Charla wasn't nearby.

The woman was apparently distraught and ready to do something stupid to avenge her husband's suicide. That meant Reed and she had to be prepared for anything, and that included defending themselves if Charla couldn't be stopped some other way. Livvy didn't want it to come down to that. There had already been enough deaths and shootings in Comanche Creek without adding a recent widow to the list.

Livvy heard a soft creaking noise and lifted her head a fraction so she could try to determine where the sound had originated.

"Behind us," Reed whispered. He turned in the direction of the inn. "Keep watch on the front."

Livvy did, and she tried to keep her breathing quiet enough so it wouldn't give away their positions. It would be safer for everyone if they could get the jump on Charla and disarm her before she had a chance to use her gun.

There was another sound. Maybe the leaves rustling in the wind. But Livvy got the sickening feeling in the pit of her stomach that it was much more than that.

Maybe even footsteps.

The sound was definitely coming from behind them, where there was no fence, only the lush gardens that Betty Alice kept groomed to perfection. Did that mean Charla had changed course so she could ambush them? If so, maybe the woman wasn't quite as distraught as everyone thought she was.

She could possibly even be her husband's accomplice.

That wasn't a crazy theory, since Billy had no doubt profited from the sale of the land that Jonah had ended up buying. Maybe Charla hadn't gotten personally involved and had no idea it would lead to her husband's death.

"My phone," Reed whispered, reaching into his pocket. It'd apparently vibrated to indicate he had a call.

Reed glanced down at the back-lit caller ID screen and put the phone to his mouth. "Shane?" His voice was barely audible, and she was too far away to make out a single word of what Shane was saying.

She continued to wait. The seconds ticked off in Livvy's head, and she held her breath for what seemed to be an eternity. She cursed the fatigue and the fog in her head. She needed to think clearly, but the lack of sleep and the adrenaline were catching up with her.

Reed finally eased the phone shut and slid it back into his pocket. His expression said it all—he was not a happy man. "Charla got into her car and drove off. Kirby and another deputy are in pursuit. Shane's staying at the station in case she heads back there."

"Shane's alone?" she asked.

Reed nodded.

Livvy glanced up both ends of the street. There were no signs of an approaching vehicle. Well, no headlights anyway, but if the car was dark-colored, Charla might have turned off her lights so she could get close to them without being detected.

"You think she'll come this way?" Livvy asked.

"No." But then he lifted his shoulder. "Not unless she doubles back."

Which she could do. *Easily.* After all, Main Street wasn't the only way to get to the inn. She could park on one of the back streets and make her way through the inn's garden.

Of course, that was only one of many places Charla could end up. She might have other people she wanted to confront—including Jonah Becker.

"You should get to the station so Shane will have some backup," Livvy reminded him. "But I'm concerned about leaving Betty Alice here alone. If Charla does double back, she might come here and try to get in."

His gaze met hers, and there was plenty enough light for her to see the argument he was having with himself. Livvy decided to go on the offensive.

"I'm not a civilian, Reed. I'm trained to do exactly this sort of thing."

Reed scowled. "If I leave, then you don't have backup."

"True. But I can go inside. Stand guard. And I can call you if something goes wrong."

He continued to stare and scowl at her. A dozen things passed between them. An argument. Some emotion. Also the reminder that they weren't just partners on a case. Sex had changed things.

But it couldn't stay that way.

Both of them were married to their badges, and they couldn't let sex—even the best sex ever—get in the way of what had to be done.

Livvy tried to give him one last reassuring glance before she checked the street and surrounding area.

No sign of Charla.

"Go to the station," she insisted.

"No." He matched her insistent tone. "We both go, and we'll take Betty Alice with us."

Livvy huffed to show her disapproval at the veto of her plan, but she had to admit it was, well, reasonable. Or at least it would be if they could get Betty Alice safely out. Livvy didn't like the idea of a civilian being brought out into the open when a shooter might be in the area.

"The inn doesn't have a garage," she commented, looking at the house. "Maybe you should pull the truck to the back, and we can get Betty Alice out through the kitchen."

Reed nodded. "Call her and let her know the plan. Then we'll get in the truck together. I don't want to leave you out here waiting."

Livvy took out her phone, and for a moment she thought the sound she heard was from her hand brushing against the pocket of her jeans.

It wasn't.

The sound was footsteps. Frantic ones. And they had definitely come from behind.

Both Reed and she spun in that direction. They had their guns aimed and ready. But neither of them fired.

Livvy tried to pick through the murky shadows in the shrub-dotted yard to see who or what was out there. She didn't see anyone, but that didn't mean they weren't there.

She tightened her grip on her pistol. Waited. And prayed.

The next sound wasn't a footstep. More like a rustling. And she was able to determine that it had come from a cluster of mountain laurels on the west side of the yard.

She aimed her gun in that direction.

Just as the shot blasted through the silence.

Livvy didn't even have time to react. But she certainly felt it.

The bullet slammed right into her.

Chapter Sixteen

Everything happened fast, but to Reed, it felt as if he were suddenly moving in slow motion.

He saw the bullet slam into Livvy's left shoulder. He saw the shock on her face.

The blood on her shirt.

Cursing, he scrambled to her and pulled her down onto the ground so she wouldn't be hit again. It wasn't a moment too soon because another shot came flying their way.

"Livvy?" he managed to say, though he couldn't ask how badly she was hurt. That was because his breath and his heart were jammed in his throat.

She had to be okay.

"I'm fine," she ground out.

But it was another lie. The blood was already spreading across her sleeve, and she dropped her gun.

Though the shots continued to come at them, Reed didn't return fire. He ripped off the sleeve of his shirt and used it to apply pressure to the wound.

The bullet had gone into the fleshy part of her

shoulder. Or at least that was what he hoped. Still, that was only a few inches from her heart.

He'd come damn close to losing her.

The rage raced through him, and he took Livvy's hand, placing it against her wound so he could return fire and stop the shooter from moving any closer. He hoped he could blast this SOB for what he'd done.

Or rather what *she* had done.

Charla.

She must have doubled back after all.

Reed sent a couple of shots the shooter's way and took out his phone. He didn't bother with dispatch. He called Shane.

"I need an ambulance. Livvy's been shot. Approach the inn with caution because we're under attack." That was all he had time to say because he didn't want to lose focus on either Livvy or the gunman.

"I'm okay," Livvy insisted. Wincing, she picked up her gun, and holding it precariously, she also tried to keep some pressure on her bleeding shoulder.

"You're not okay," Reed countered. He maneuvered himself in front of her with his back to her so he could keep an eye on the shooter. "But you will be. Shane will be here soon to provide backup, and he's getting an ambulance out here."

She shook her head. "It won't be safe for the medics. We need to take care of this before they get here."

Livvy was right. It was standard procedure to secure the scene before bringing in medical personnel, but Reed wasn't sure he could take the risk of Livvy bleeding to death. Somehow, he had to get her to the hospital, even if he had to drive her there himself.

He glanced back at the truck.

It was a good twenty feet away, and they'd be right in the line of fire if they stood. That meant Reed had to draw this moron out because he couldn't waste any more time with the attack.

The shots were all coming from the side of the house near some shrubs. It was a dark murky space, most likely why the shooter had chosen it. But it wasn't the only shadowy place. He, too, could use the shrubs and get closer so he could launch his own assault.

Reed looked over his shoulder at Livvy. "Can you shoot if necessary?"

She winced again and forced out a rough breath. But she nodded. "I can shoot."

"Then I'm going out there." He wanted to take a moment to tell her to be safe. To hang in there. Hell, he even wanted to wait until Shane had arrived, but all of that would eat up precious seconds.

Time they didn't have.

Crouched down, Reed inched forward and kept his gun ready in case the shooter came running out of those shrubs and across the lawn. But there was no movement. And the only sound was from the shots that were coming about ten seconds apart.

He went even closer to the shooter, but then stopped when he heard the footsteps. They weren't coming from in front of him, but rather from behind.

"Shane?" Reed said softly.

No answer.

And the shots stopped.

Hell. He turned so he could cover both sides in case the shooter was making his move to get closer. As Livvy leaned against the wall for support, she lifted her gun and aimed it as well.

They waited there, eating up precious moments while Livvy continued to lose blood.

"Shane?" Reed tried again.

"No," someone answered.

Definitely not Shane. It was a woman's voice, and a quick glance at Livvy let him know that she was as stunned as he was.

"It's me, Charla," the woman said.

Since her voice was coming from the area by the gate, an area that was much too close to Livvy, Reed hurried back in that direction.

Just as Charla dove through the gate opening.

Reed caught just a glimpse of her gun, and his gut clenched. No! He couldn't let Charla shoot Livvy again. This time, the bullet might be fatal.

Charla landed chest-first on the ground, her gun trapped beneath her. Livvy moved, adjusting her position so she could aim her gun at the woman.

Reed did more than that. He launched himself toward Charla and threw his body on hers so she couldn't be able to maneuver her weapon out into the open.

There wasn't time to negotiate Charla's surrender, so Reed grabbed her right wrist and wrenched the gun from her hand. He tossed it toward Livvy and then shoved his forearm against the back of Charla's neck to keep her pinned to the ground.

"Call Shane," Reed instructed Livvy. "Tell him to get that ambulance here now."

With her breath racing and her chest pumping for breath, Livvy took out her phone. Beneath him, Charla didn't struggle, but she did lift her head and look around. Her eyes were wild, and Reed could feel her pulse racing out of control.

"Who was shooting at you?" Charla asked.

The question caused both Livvy and Reed to freeze.

"You," Reed reminded her.

Charla frantically shook her head. "No. It wasn't me. I didn't fire my gun. I heard the shots and took cover on the other side of the fence."

Reed was about to call her a liar, but he didn't manage to get the word out of his mouth. That was because the next sound turned his blood to ice.

Someone fired another bullet at them.

LIVVY DROPPED back to the ground.

Her wounded shoulder smashed against the limestone fence, and the pain shot through her. She gasped, causing Reed's gaze to whip in her direction.

"I'm okay," she lied again.

The pain was excruciating, and the front of her shirt was wet with her own blood. She needed a doctor, but a doctor wasn't going to do any of them any good if the shooter managed to continue.

And obviously, the shooter wasn't Charla.

Mercy, what was going on?

Livvy had been so sure those shots had come from the grieving widow, but obviously she'd been wrong. Someone else was out there, and this person wanted them dead.

But who?

There was another shot. Another. Then another. Each of the thick blasts slammed through the air and landed

God knew where. Livvy prayed that none of them were landing inside the inn, and while she was at it, she also prayed that Betty Alice would stay put and not come racing out in fear.

Livvy waited. Listening. But the shots didn't continue. That was both good and bad. She certainly didn't want Reed to be wounded, or worse, but the lack of shots could mean the gunman was on the move.

Maybe coming straight toward them.

She heard the sirens from the ambulance and saw the red lights knifing through the darkness. But the lights didn't come closer, and the sirens stopped, probably because Shane had told them to stay back. Livvy hadn't managed to call him as Reed had ordered. And that was a good thing. If she had, if she'd told them that Reed had the shooter subdued, the medics would have driven straight into what could be a death trap.

Reed jerked his phone from his pocket, and since the screen was already lit, it meant he had a call.

"Shane," Reed answered. "Where are you?"

Because Reed had his hands full with the call, keeping watch and with Charla, Livvy hoisted herself back up to a sitting position so she could return fire if necessary. Maybe, just maybe, her body would cooperate. The pain was making it hard to focus, and Livvy was afraid she wouldn't be able to hear anything over her heartbeat pounding in her ears.

"We don't know who the gunman is," Reed told Shane. "But it's not Charla. She's with us." He paused, apparently listening to Shane. "Okay. But Livvy and Charla are staying put. Call Livvy if there's a change in plans."

With that, Reed shut his phone and shoved it back

into his pocket. "Shane's going to try to sneak up on the gunman," he whispered. "And I need to help him."

Livvy understood. Reed couldn't help if he had to hang on to Charla. Though it took several deep breaths and a lot of willpower to force herself to move, Livvy reached out with her left hand and began to pull Charla in her direction. Reed moved to the side, and together they maneuvered the woman in place just to the side of Livvy.

Charla didn't resist.

She went willingly and pressed her body against the fence. She also covered her face with her hands. Livvy didn't think the woman was faking her fear, so that probably meant Charla had no idea who their attacker was.

"I'm going straight ahead," Reed mouthed. But he didn't move. He paused just a moment to meet her gaze, and then he started to crawl forward again.

"Don't get hurt," Livvy mumbled under her breath, but she was sure he didn't hear her.

She instantly regretted that she hadn't said more, something with more emotion and volume. But that would have been a stupid thing to do. Reed didn't need emotion from her now. He needed her to keep Charla subdued and safe, and for that to happen, she had to stay alert and conscious.

The next shot put her right back on high alert. The bullet slammed into the limestone just inches from Charla's head. Charla yelped and dropped on her stomach to the ground, and Livvy sank lower. She couldn't go belly-down as Charla had done, she needed to be able to help Reed, but she did slide slightly lower.

Another bullet.

This one hit just inches from the last one. God, she hoped the shooter hadn't managed to pinpoint them somehow. But there was some good in this because the shots didn't seem to be aimed at Reed.

She heard Reed move forward, making his way across the lawn. Livvy couldn't see him, but she knew he would use the shrubs for cover. Maybe that would be enough, but bullets could easily go through plants and leaves. She choked back the rest of that realization because the physical pain was one thing, but she couldn't bear the thought of Reed being hurt.

Beside her, Charla began to sob. Livvy was about to try to stop her when her phone rang. Unlike Reed, she hadn't put hers on vibrate, so the ringing sound was loud.

There was a shot fired.

Then another.

The third one bashed into the limestone and sent a spray of stone chips flying through the air. Livvy tried to shield her eyes, and she snatched up her phone so it wouldn't ring again.

"It's me, Shane," the caller said.

Livvy released the breath she'd been holding. It wasn't Reed calling to tell her that he'd taken one of those bullets.

"Where's Reed?"

"I'm not sure. Somewhere between the fence and the west side of the inn." She tried to pick through the darkness and shadows, but she couldn't see him either. "Where are you?"

"The back porch of the inn. I'm going to try to sneak up the stairs to the upper porch."

It was a good idea. That way, he might be able to spot the shooter. If the shooter didn't spot Shane first, that was. The outside stairs weren't exactly concealed, and the shooter might have an unobstructed view of both the stairs and the upper porch.

"Be careful," Livvy warned. "But hurry. Whoever's doing this isn't giving up."

She got instant proof of that. The shooter fired again, and this time the bullet didn't go into the fence. It went into the wooden gate just on the other side of Charla. The woman screamed, covered her head with her hands and tried to scramble behind Livvy.

"Were you hit again?" Shane immediately asked.

"No." Livvy pressed the phone between her right shoulder and ear so she could focus on keeping aim. No easy feat. The pain was worse now, and it seemed to be throbbing through every inch of her body.

"Just hang in there," Shane told her. "We'll get the medics in ASAP."

He'd obviously heard the pain come through in her voice. Livvy hoped the shooter didn't sense that as well because she was in no shape to win a gunfight.

"I've got to hang up now," Shane continued. "I'm at the stairs, and— Wait…"

That *wait* got Livvy's complete attention. "What's wrong?"

"I see the shooter. He's wearing dark clothes, and he's behind the oak tree."

Not the mountain laurels as Reed had thought. She quickly tried to remember the landscape, and if her memory was right, Reed could soon be crawling right past the gunman.

Or right at him.

Shane cursed, and the call ended.

Livvy mumbled some profanity as well. She considered phoning Reed but figured it was too late for that.

"Reed?" she shouted. "Watch out!"

But her warning was drowned out by the gunfire that blasted through the air. Not from the direction where the shooter had originally been.

The shots came from directly in front of them.

Chapter Seventeen

Reed heard Livvy's warning, but it was too late for him to do anything but duck his head and hope the bullets missed him.

And her.

God knew how much pain Livvy was in right now, and she certainly wasn't in any shape to be in the middle of this mess.

"Stay down!" Reed called out to Livvy, Charla and Shane.

He hoped they all listened and had the capability to keep out of the line of fire. Shane certainly wasn't in the best of positions. Or at least he hadn't been when Reed had last spotted his deputy at the base of the stairs. Then Shane had disappeared, and Reed hoped like hell that he'd taken cover.

Since there was no safe way for him to go forward and because he was worried about Livvy, Reed turned and began to make his way back to her. It was obvious the gunman was on the move, and Reed didn't want him to manage to sneak up on Livvy.

Moving as fast as he could while trying to keep his

ear attuned to the directions of the shots, Reed maneuvered his way through the damp grass and the shrubs.
He spotted Livvy. She was crouched over Charla, protecting her, but Reed knew Livvy needed someone to
protect her.

God, there was even more blood on her shirt.

He scrambled to her, keeping low because of the
barrage of bullets, and he clamped his hand over her
wound again. It wasn't gushing blood, but even a trickle
could cause her to bleed out.

"We can't wait for the ambulance," he whispered. "I
need to get you out of here."

She didn't argue. Well, not verbally anyway. He saw
the argument in the depths of her eyes, but he also saw
that the blood loss had weakened her.

"I'm going to stay in front of you," he instructed
Livvy. "Do you think you can crawl through the gate
and onto the sidewalk?"

"Yes." Now, she shook her head. "But I won't leave
you here to fend for yourself."

He nearly laughed. *Nearly.* So, there was some fight
left in her after all. "I have Shane for backup. I'll cover
you while you get to the sidewalk. Get as far away from
the inn as you can, and I'll have the medics meet you."

Charla moved when Livvy did, but Reed latched on
to the woman. "You're staying here." Though he
doubted Charla was truly involved in the shooting, he
didn't want Livvy to have to worry about watching her
back.

Livvy had barely made it to the gate when Reed
heard the sound. Not more gunfire, but movement. It
wasn't just footsteps either. There seemed to be some

kind of altercation going on, and whatever it was, it was happening in front of them.

Shane.

Hell, his deputy had likely come face-to-face with the gunman.

Reed motioned for Livvy to keep moving, but she didn't. She stopped and aimed her gun in the direction of those sounds. Someone cursed. It was definitely Shane, and then there was a loud thump. Reed had been around enough fights to know that someone had just connected with a punch.

The silence returned.

But it didn't last.

It was mere seconds before the footsteps started. This wasn't a quiet skulking motion. Someone was running straight toward them.

Reed couldn't call out Shane's name because it would give away Livvy's and his positions. Besides, whoever this was, it wasn't Shane. His deputy was well-trained and would have identified himself to avoid being shot.

The gunman darted out from one of the eight-foot-high mountain laurels.

Reed fired.

And missed.

But he'd gotten a glimpse of the person. Shane was right about the dark clothes, and it was definitely a man.

Reed got a sickening feeling. He hoped it wasn't Woody out there.

The shots started again, and the man rushed out, coming closer. Each shot and each movement was wasting time, and Reed was fed up. He needed to get Livvy out of there.

He motioned for Livvy to stay down. Whether she would or not was anyone's guess. Reed picked up a chunk of the limestone that'd broken off in the attack, and tossed it to the center of the yard. When the stone landed on the ground, the gunman left cover.

Reed fired again.

This time, he didn't miss.

The shooter howled in pain and clamped his hands onto his left thigh.

"Fire a couple of shots into the ground but in that direction and then get to the medics," he told Livvy, pointing to the area on the west side of the inn but still far enough away from where he would be heading. He needed a diversion in case their attacker could still manage to shoot.

Reed hurried, racing toward the gunman who'd done his level best to kill them. And this wasn't over. He had no idea just how badly Livvy, and maybe even Shane, were hurt. There had to be a good reason his deputy wasn't responding.

When he was closer, Reed saw that the shooter was wearing a black baseball cap that was tilted down to cover the upper portion of his face. Reed didn't stop or take the time to figure out who this was; he dove at the guy.

The shooter lifted his gun.

Aimed.

But he didn't get off another shot before Reed plowed right into him.

Both of them went to the ground, hard, and the guy's gun rammed into Reed's rib cage. It nearly knocked the breath right out of him, but Reed fought to pull air into his lungs while he fought to hang on to his gun.

But he wasn't successful.

The man swiped at Reed's arm, and it was just enough to send his weapon flying.

Still, Reed wasn't about to give up. He used every bit of his anger and adrenaline so he could slam his fist into the man's face.

It worked.

The guy's head flopped back. He wasn't unconscious, but the movement caused his baseball cap to fall off. And Reed got a close look at the gunman's face.

He cursed.

Because it was a face he knew all too well.

The shock stunned Reed for a moment. Just a moment. But that was apparently all the time the man needed to get his weapon back into place.

The gun slammed hard against the side of Reed's head.

LIVVY COULD no longer feel the pain. That was good. Because one way or another she was going to make her way to Reed, and dealing with the pain was one less obstacle that could get in her way.

Charla was still sobbing and cowering against the fence. It was a risk to leave her there alone, but it was an even bigger risk to let Reed take on the gunman without backup. Yes, Shane was out there somewhere, but he didn't seem to be responding. She hoped he hadn't been shot, or killed.

Livvy forced herself to stand, and since there were no more bullets flying, she didn't exactly crouch. Her goal was to make it to Reed as quickly as possible.

Still, that wasn't nearly fast enough.

She felt as if she were walking through sludge, and

it didn't help that she had to keep her shooting hand clamped to her shoulder. That meant her gun was out of position if she had to fire, but she would deal with that if and when it came down to it. She couldn't let the blood flow go unchecked, or else this rescue mission would fail, and she would be in just as much serious trouble as Reed and Shane.

She trudged through the grass and shrubs, and she heard the sounds of a struggle.

Reed and the gunman, no doubt.

At least they weren't shooting at each other, and even though she dreaded the idea of Reed having to fist-fight his way out of a situation, he'd apparently cornered the shooter, and maybe that meant this was on its way to being over.

Just ahead of her, Livvy heard a different sound. Much softer and closer than the battle going on at the other side of the yard. This was a moan, and it sounded as if someone was in pain. The person was lying on the ground just ahead of her. She unclamped her arm so she could aim and moved closer.

It was Shane.

He moaned again and touched his head. "Someone knocked me out," he whispered.

Livvy didn't take the time to examine him further. The deputy was alive and could fend for himself for a little while so she could get to Reed.

She silently cursed. The sex had indeed changed everything. Or maybe the sex was just the icing on this particular cake. Livvy had to admit that the reason the sex had happened in the first place was because she'd fallen hard and fast for the hot cowboy cop.

Worse, she was in love with him.

She hadn't realized that until she'd seen him rush away after the gunman. And he'd done that to save her. That's the kind of man he was. A man worth loving. Too bad that wouldn't solve all their problems. Still, that was a matter for a different time and place. Right now, she needed to focus all her energy on helping Reed.

Oh, and she needed to stay conscious.

She didn't think she'd lost too much blood, but the shock was starting to take over. Soon, very soon, she wouldn't be much help to Reed.

"I'll be back," she whispered to Shane and stepped around him.

Livvy didn't have to walk far before she saw Reed and the other man. They were fighting, and in the darkness she couldn't tell where Reed's body began and the other man's ended. She certainly couldn't risk firing a shot because she might hit Reed.

The man bashed his forearm into Reed's throat, and Reed staggered back. She saw the blood on his face. And on the front of his shirt.

Her heart dropped.

Livvy blinked back the dizziness and raced to get closer. They were there, right in front of her, less than a yard away, but she still didn't have a clean shot, and she didn't trust her aim anyway. The shooter would have to be out in the open before she could fire, and it didn't help that the man still had a weapon in his hand.

Reed's fist connected with the man's jaw, and that put a little distance between the two. Not enough for her to fire. But enough for her to catch a glimpse of the man's face.

It was Ben Tolbert.

God, had Ben knocked out his own son? And why was he doing this? Why was he trying to kill them?

"Stay back!" Reed shouted to her.

She didn't listen. Couldn't. Ben was armed and Reed wasn't. Plus, there was all that blood on Reed's shirt.

The milky-white moon cast an eerie light on Ben, and she saw him sneer at her. And lift his gun.

Ben aimed it right at her.

Her body didn't react as quickly as her mind did. Livvy recognized the danger. She realized she was about to be shot again, but she couldn't seem to get out of the way. Nor could she shoot. That was because her hand had gone numb. So had her legs, and she felt herself start to fall.

Reed shouted something. Something she couldn't understand. And she heard the shot the moment she hit the ground. The blast was thick and loud, and it echoed through her head.

"Reed," she managed to say. She prayed the bullet hadn't slammed into him.

Forcing herself to remain conscious, she turned her head and saw Reed lunge at Ben. This time, there was no real battle. A feral sound tore from Reed's throat, and he slammed his weight into Ben. In the same motion, Reed ripped the gun from Ben's hand. Both of them landed on the grass, not far from her. And she saw Reed put the gun to Ben's head.

"Move and you die," Reed warned. Every muscle in his face had corded and was strained with raw emotion.

Ben obviously believed him because he dropped his hands in surrender.

It was over. They were safe. Now, they just needed the medics.

Livvy tried to get up so she could go find them, but she only managed to lift her head a fraction before the darkness took over and closed in around her.

Chapter Eighteen

Reed paced, because he couldn't figure out what else to do with the powder keg of energy and emotion that was boiling inside him. Waiting had never been his strong suit, and it especially wasn't when he was waiting for the latest about Livvy's condition.

He heard the footsteps in the hall that led to the E.R. waiting room and whirled in that direction. It wasn't the doctor. It was Kirby, his deputy.

"Here are the things you asked me to get," Kirby said, handing Reed the plastic grocery bag. "I don't guess they've told you anything yet?"

"No. One of the nurses came out about ten minutes ago and said I'd know something soon." But *soon* needed to be *now* when it came to Livvy. "How's Shane?"

"He's got another bump on his head, but other than that, he's fine. The doc will be releasing him soon."

Good. That was one less thing to worry about, even though this wouldn't be the end of Shane's worries. After all, his father had just tried to murder Livvy and Reed. Ben Tolbert would likely to go to jail for the rest of his life.

"I called the station on the way over here, and Ben's talking, by the way," Kirby continued. "Jerry's trying to make him hush, but Ben confessed to setting the cabin on fire and trying to scare Livvy into leaving town. He didn't want any evidence that could link Shane to Marcie's murder."

Reed felt every muscle in his body tighten. He wanted to pulverize Ben for what he'd done. "But Livvy's the one who cleared Shane's name."

Kirby shrugged. "Ben evidently thought Livvy wasn't done with Shane. He figured she'd keep looking for anything and everything to put Shane back in jail."

Great. Because of Ben's warped loyalty to his son, Livvy might have to pay a huge price.

"What about Charla?" Reed asked.

"The medics took her to Austin, to the psych ward. After they've evaluated her, they'll give you a call."

Kirby had barely finished his sentence, when Reed heard more footsteps. This time, it was Dr. Eric Callahan, the man who'd forced Reed out of the E.R. so he could get to work on Livvy's gunshot wound.

"How is she?" Reed demanded, holding his breath.

"She lost quite a bit of blood so we gave her a transfusion. She's B-negative, and thanks to you, we have a small stockpile."

"You gave her Reed's blood?" Kirby asked.

Dr. Callahan nodded, but Reed interrupted any verbal response he might have given Kirby. Yes, Reed was a regular blood donor, and he was damn thankful the supply had been there for Livvy, but a transfusion was the last thing he wanted to discuss right now.

"How's Livvy?" Reed snapped.

"She's okay. The bullet went through and doesn't appear to have damaged anything permanently—"

"I want to see her." Reed didn't wait for permission. He pushed his way past the doctor and went to the room where they'd taken Livvy nearly an hour earlier.

Reed stormed into the room but came to a dead stop. There Livvy was, lying on the bed. Awake. Her shoulder sporting a fresh bandage. Heck, she even gave him a thin smile, but she looked pale and weak. That smile, however, faded in a flash when Livvy's gaze dropped to the front of his shirt.

Reed glanced down at what had snagged her attention and immediately shook his head. "It's not mine." The blood on the front of his shirt had gotten there during his fight with Ben.

Livvy gave a sigh of relief and eased her head back onto the pillow.

"You shouldn't be in here," the nurse on the other side of the room insisted.

"I'm not leaving," Reed insisted right back. "Not until I find out how you really are," he said to Livvy.

"I'll speak to the doctor about that," the nurse warned and headed out of the room.

Livvy motioned for him to come closer. "I'm fine, *really*. The doctor gave me some good pain meds so I'm not feeling much." Her eyes met his. "Well, not much pain anyway. Please tell me Ben Tolbert is behind bars."

Reed walked closer, the plastic grocery bag swishing against the leg of his jeans. "He is. Or soon will be. I had Ben sent to the county jail. He's receiving medical treatment for the gunshot wound to his leg, but after that, he'll be going to the prison hospital."

"Good." And a moment later she repeated it.

Livvy might have been medicated, but the painkillers didn't remove the emotion from her voice or face. She'd been through hell tonight, and Reed had taken that trip right along with her.

He sat down on the right side of the bed so he wouldn't accidentally bump into her injury and, because he thought they both could use it, he leaned over and kissed Livvy. Reed intended to keep it short and sweet. Just a peck of reassurance. But Livvy slid her hand around the back of his neck and drew him closer. Even after she broke the kiss, she held him there with his forehead pressed against hers.

"I thought I'd lost you," she whispered, taking the words right out of his mouth.

Reed settled for a "Yeah," but it wasn't a casual response. His voice had as much emotion as hers, and he eased back just a little so he could meet her eye to eye. "I'm sorry I let this happen to you."

She pushed her fingers over his lips. "You didn't 'let' this happen. You did everything to save me."

He glanced down at the bandage and hated the thought that she was alive in part because they'd gotten lucky. Reed didn't want luck playing into this.

"You can't stay," someone said from the doorway. It was the doctor.

"Give me five minutes," Reed bargained. He didn't pull away from Livvy, and he didn't look back at the doctor.

"Five minutes," he finally said, and Reed heard the doctor walking away.

"Not much time," Livvy volunteered.

"Don't worry. I'll be back after you've gotten some rest." But first, he had something important to do.

He took out the candy bars from the bag and put them on the stand next to her bed.

Her face lit up. "You brought me Snickers?" She smiled and kissed him again. "You know, I could love a man who brings me chocolate."

The realization of what she'd said caused her smile to freeze, and she got that deer-caught-in-the-headlights look.

"Don't take it back," Reed blurted out.

She blinked. "Wh-what?"

"Don't take that *love a man* part back, because that's what I want you to do."

"You want me to love you?" She sounded as if he'd just requested that she hand him the moon.

And in a way, he had.

"Yeah. I do," he assured her.

But Reed lifted his hand in a wait-a-second gesture so he could lay the groundwork for this. He took out a map from the bag and fanned it open. It took him a moment to find what he was looking for.

"This is Comanche Creek," he said, pointing to the spot. "And this is Austin." He pointed to the space in between. "I want to find a house or build one halfway between. That'd give us both a thirty-minute commute to work."

And because he wanted her to think about that for

several moments, and because he didn't want her to say no, he kissed her. He didn't keep it tame, either. But then, neither did Livvy. She might have been in the E.R., but it was crystal-clear that kissing was still on the agenda.

She pulled back, ran her tongue over his bottom lip and smiled. "You want us to live together. I'd like that."

"Like?" he questioned.

Her forehead bunched up. "All right, I'd *love* to do that. You really have love on the brain tonight." She winced. "Sorry, that didn't come out right. Blame it on the pain meds."

That had him hesitating. "How clearly are you thinking?"

"Why?" she asked.

"Because I'm about to tell you that I'm in love with you, and I want to make sure you understand."

Her mouth dropped open. "You're in love with me?"

"Yeah." And Reed held his breath again. He watched her face, staring at her and trying to interpret every little muscle flicker. Every blink. Every tremble of her mouth.

"You don't love me?" he finally said.

The breath swooshed out of her and she grabbed him again and planted a very hard kiss on his mouth. "I love you. I'm in love with you. And I want to live with you in a house with a thirty-minute commute."

She smiled. It was warm and gooey, and in all his life, Reed had never been happier to see warm and gooey.

"Good," he let her know. Another kiss. Before he moved on to the next part.

"Your five minutes are up," he heard the doctor say from the doorway.

"Then give me six," Reed snarled. He tried not to snarl though when he looked down at Livvy.

"Whatever you've got to say to her, it can wait," the doctor insisted.

"No. It can't." He looked into Livvy's eyes. "I don't want to just live with you."

She shook her head. "But you said—"

"I want to marry you, and then I want us to live together."

"You're proposing?" the doctor grumbled, and Reed heard the man walk away.

"Yes, I'm proposing," Reed verified to Livvy. "And now, I'm waiting for an answer."

An answer she didn't readily give. But she did make a show of tapping her chin as if in deep thought. "Let me see. I have a really hot sheriff that I love with all my heart. He buys me chocolate and jumps out in front of snakes and bullets for me. He's also great in bed. And he wants to marry me."

Reed smiled. "Does that mean you're saying yes?"

She pulled him closer. "Yes. With one condition."

Reed could have sworn his heart stopped. He didn't want conditions. He wanted Livvy, and he wanted all of her. "What condition?" he managed to asked.

There were tears in her eyes now, but she was also still smiling.

Reed thought those might be good signs. He was sure the lusty kiss she gave him was a good sign, too.

"The condition is—this has to be forever," Livvy whispered.

Well, that was a given. "It took me thirty-two years to find you, and I have no intentions of ever letting go."

And to prove that, Reed pulled Livvy closer and kissed her.

* * * * *

INTRIGUE...

2 FREE BOOKS
AND A SURPRISE GIFT

We would like to take this opportunity to thank you for reading this Mills & Boon® book by offering you the chance to take TWO more specially selected books from the Intrigue series absolutely FREE! We're also making this offer to introduce you to the benefits of the Mills & Boon® Book Club™—

- **FREE home delivery**
- **FREE gifts and competitions**
- **FREE monthly Newsletter**
- **Exclusive Mills & Boon Book Club offers**
- **Books available before they're in the shops**

Accepting these FREE books and gift places you under no obligation to buy, you may cancel at any time, even after receiving your free books. Simply complete your details below and return the entire page to the address below. You don't even need a stamp!

YES Please send me 2 free Intrigue books and a surprise gift. I understand that unless you hear from me, I will receive 5 superb new stories every month, including two 2-in-1 books priced at £5.30 each and a single book priced at £3.30, postage and packing free. I am under no obligation to purchase any books and may cancel my subscription at any time. The free books and gift will be mine to keep in any case.

Ms/Mrs/Miss/Mr _____ Initials _____
_____
Surname _____
Address _____
_____
_____ Postcode _____
E-mail _____

Send this whole page to: Mills & Boon Book Club, Free Book Offer, FREEPOST NAT 10298, Richmond, TW9 1BR